"Great," Angel said.
to be? The hell-
Frosty th

The quip sounded funny in his head, but coming out of his mouth it was all wrong, so thick and palpable with cold that the words seemed to have actual *weight* on the air.

From where Angel stood a few feet away from the hotel's industrial-sized water heater, he could see that the winter demon filled the corner across from the furnace. There wasn't anything pristine or pretty about it, either; instead it was kind of fuzzy and uneven, with a fur covering that was mottled white and gray like the folds of skin on a dirty polar bear . . . that had mutated to gargantuan size.

Everything moved in an unpleasant rolling motion as the creature hauled itself forward. Somewhere in that mass was a face but it, too, had that unsettling, constantly shifting thing going; first it seemed to be on the left side, then the right, then somewhere a little south of what might be the beast's head. The only reason Angel was convinced he was actually seeing a face at all was the two predatory, pinprick eyes, bloody red above the circular dark shadow of nose.

And, of course, the creature had a mouth.

Don't they always?

ANGEL™

the longest night

vol. 1

Angel™

City of
Not Forgotten
Redemption
Close to the Ground
Shakedown
Hollywood Noir
Avatar
Soul Trade
Bruja
The Summoned
Haunted
Image
Stranger to the Sun
Vengeance
Endangered Species
The Longest Night, vol. 1

Angel: The Casefiles, Volume 1—The Official Companion

Available from Simon Pulse

The Essential Angel Posterbook

Available from Pocket Books

ANGEL™

the longest night
vol. 1

An original anthology based on the television series created by Joss Whedon & David Greenwalt

SIMON PULSE

New York London Toronto Sydney Singapore

Historian's Note: These stories take place during the third season of *Angel*.

First Simon Pulse edition December 2002

SIMON PULSE
An imprint of Simon & Schuster
Children's Publishing Division
1230 Avenue of the Americas
New York, NY 10020

The text of this book was set in New Caledonia.

Printed in the United States of America
10 9 8 7 6 5 4 3 2 1

Library of Congress Control Number 2002110489
ISBN 0-7434-2756-4

Special thanks to Paul Ruditis for the idea

TIMELINE*

Sunset

*All times are P.S.T. approximate.

ANGEL™

the longest night
vol. 1

6 P.M.

THE HOUSE WHERE DEATH STOOD STILL

by Pierce Askegren

"That's him," she said, reaching across Wesley Wyndam-Pryce's desk with the photograph. It was a snapshot of a freckle-faced little boy with red hair and a beaming smile. He wore a playsuit with Tiger written across the front. "He was two then. That's my son, Timmy."

"Yes," Wesley replied. "I can see the resemblance."

So could Angel, when Wesley surrendered the picture to him. He glanced at it, then at the woman perched on the edge of the office guest chair. The resemblance was remarkable.

Rachel Gibson was attractive. Her hair was a rich auburn that Timmy's might become with age, and her eyes were the same gray as her son's. The expression she wore was quite different from his, however. In the snapshot, Timmy smiled eagerly for the unknown photographer. In Wesley's office, Rachel's look was one of terrible loss, a look that stirred unpleasant memories within Angel.

Angel had seen women look like that before. Angel had *caused* women to look like that before. Guilt, never very far away, ran cold fingers along his soul.

"How can we help?" he asked.

"Yes, Mrs. Gibson," Wesley said. "How *can* Angel Investigations be of service in this matter?" His annoyed glance at Angel was a pointed reminder of just who ran the agency these days, and when he spoke, it was with a precision born of testiness. If guilt were Angel's close companion, a vague impatience sometimes seemed to follow Wesley like an attendant.

"I want you to find him," she said to them both. "You're supposed to help the helpless, and I want you to help me."

"So you explained to Ms. Chase on the telephone," said Wesley. His tone softened as he spoke to her. "I would have preferred to meet with you earlier, but we've quite a heavy caseload just now. It's the holidays, you see. We're here to help, of course, but there may be others who—"

"What happened to him?" Angel interrupted. "To your son?"

"His father took him," she said. "Five years ago."

"Why?" Angel asked. As she turned to look at him, anguished, he continued. "We have to know."

"—are better suited to your needs," Wesley continued doggedly, but his tone was gentle. "A larger, more conventional agency may have resources we don't, and—"

Angel ignored him. "What happened?" he asked,

leaning closer to Rachel. "Divorce? Another woman?"

"No," she said. "No divorce. Luther and I love—*loved* one another very much, and he was the perfect father, really. I just came home one day and they were gone. Both of them."

"The majority of children who vanish each year are taken by a parent," Wesley murmured. "And, I'm sorry to say, the other parent often fails to see it coming. If Mr. Gibson had another life—"

She shook her head. "No. No, Mr. Wyndam-Pryce, he didn't have 'another life.' In fact, he was—he was dying."

Neither Angel nor Wesley said anything.

"Luther was dying," she continued, her voice thick with emotion. "And he was terrified of Timmy growing up without a father. He was a good man, but he had a fixation on that. His own father died before Luther was even born, and he grew up with only his mother. It scarred him terribly. He always said that it was the worst thing that could happen to a boy, to grow up without a father."

Angel could think of worse things, but he knew better than to mention them. Mrs. Gibson's pain was obviously still fresh and raw, not dulled by the passing years, and there was no need to make it greater. Instead, he limited himself to asking gently, "Worse than growing up without a mother? Without you?"

She made no reply, but her gray eyes became suddenly brighter. "And Luther wanted to see him grow up," she finally said.

"But you say he was dying?" Wesley asked her.

"Dead by now," Rachel Gibson said. Her voice sounded dead, too.

"There was no chance of a misdiagnosis?"

She shook her head again. "Brain cancer," she said. "Inoperable. When Luther took Timmy, he had six months left." She paused. "Except for the headaches and fatigue, he was still functional. Even with aggressive treatment, though, he had six months. Less than that before it would compromise him to the point of . . . nonfunctioning."

"But surely such things aren't absolutely certain," Wesley said. "He may have access to better doctors, other resources—"

Angel felt the first hint of a new kind of concern. He could think of many "other resources" that a desperate dying man might call upon, and none of them were pleasant.

"Luther had the best doctors and treatment the world had to offer," she replied. "We were both quite successful in our chosen careers, and Luther was a prominent attorney."

Wesley shifted in his chair. "But Mrs. Gibson . . . ," he started.

She interrupted with a correction. "*Dr.* Gibson."

"Oh." Wesley paused. As if a circuit had closed in his brain, comprehension lit his face. "Oh!" He looked again in Angel's direction. "*Dr.* Gibson is quite a famous surgeon," he said. He looked back at the visitor. "I hadn't realized you were *that* Rachel Gibson," he said. "I apologize."

"And that's why Cordelia insisted on our seeing you,"

Angel said. "Even this late in the day." Outside the hotel, only the final rays of the setting sun grayed the night sky.

Since coming to Los Angeles, Cordelia Chase had demonstrated new reserves of compassion, but pragmatism endured. Doctors made impressive amounts of money and could afford generous fees.

"I wasn't Luther's doctor," Rachel continued. "But I reviewed the diagnosis and charted his progress. Please believe me, there was no miracle of science that could save him. Luther died four years ago, at the very least. He's dead. He has to be dead. But he has our son."

Angel didn't like the sudden intensity in her gaze. He didn't much like the fact that she had spoken in the present tense, either.

"How can we help you?" he repeated.

"Find Timmy for me," she said.

"Five years is a long time," Wesley said. "If the authorities—"

"The authorities have done all they can, Mr. Wyndam-Pryce," Rachel Gibson said crisply. "And so have the best *conventional* private investigators money can buy. Or do you think I turned to you simply because of your handbills?"

"Well," Wesley said. "We've been getting an excellent response on those, actually . . ."

"I *know* the kinds of cases you people take," she continued.

Wesley raised one hand for attention. "All I'm saying

is that five years is a long time," he said. His voice was serious. "I'm afraid your son may not be out there to find."

"He is," Rachel Gibson said. "He calls me every year about this time. He calls me and he speaks to me." She paused. "And he says his father is with him."

Wesley's private office, just off the hotel's main reception area, was ordinarily cozy and warm. Now, suddenly, it seemed cold, even to Angel.

"I can look into it," he said.

Wesley shot him another glance, pointed and direct. "*We'll* work on it, Dr. Gibson," he said. "And if I think we can help, I'll assign an operative. Perhaps even Mr. Angel, here, if his schedule allows."

"You're in charge? But—the name of the agency—"

"Is just that. A name," Wesley concluded crisply. "Now, if you would be so good as to provide us with any additional information you have, we can begin."

Daddy came back in through the front door, which Timmy wasn't allowed to use, although he had spent some time studying it. Big and heavy and thick, it had a deadbolt and a knob almost as big as Timmy's head. It opened just long enough to admit Daddy and some fresh air, and then it slammed shut again.

Daddy's hands were full, his arms pinned to his sides by the weight of the bags he carried with hooked fingers. Timmy watched as he headed for the kitchen and pantry. Daddy was skinny like a twig and he stumbled once or twice. Despite that, he moved swiftly from the foyer to the front gallery, past the framed images that hung there.

Timmy had to lean out of the picture where he had waited in order to watch. He tried to be sneaky, but his father saw him anyway.

"Stay away from the door, Timmy," Daddy said over his shoulder. At the counter in the kitchen, he had set down his burdens. His words came in short gasps and his fair skin glistened with sweat. "I don't want you going anywhere."

"I won't, Daddy," Timmy said. The jig was up, so he stepped down and out of the picture, lowering himself from the low-hung frame's edge until his feet found the carpeted floor.

"Were you a good boy while I was gone?" Daddy's voice was stronger now and he didn't look sick anymore. Coming into the house did that for him, Timmy had noticed.

Timmy nodded. "I read, like you told me to. I was in the library."

Daddy glanced back at the picture Timmy had exited. It was a large image, so big that it hung low on the wall, and Daddy had told Timmy once that the picture was older than he was. From within the picture's frame crowded bookshelves beckoned, rendered in precise detail. The lower shelves held brightly colored spines that bore famous titles—*Robinson Crusoe, Robin Hood, King Arthur.* Two books lay open on the red oval rug that was Timmy's preferred reading station.

"Find anything you liked?" Daddy asked. He was

unpacking the bags now, one by one, and placing their contents in the paneled cabinets of the pantry. Timmy's eyes grew wide as he saw one package.

"Doodles!" he said. He loved the sugary pastries and the way each treat came in its own little package. It had been a very long time since Doodles had last graced his home, so long that he could barely remember. "Fruit Doodles! Can I have one?"

"No," Daddy said. "These are for later. You'd just spoil your appetite for dinner." He smiled but he looked sad, too. "And these have to last a while."

He put away another seven boxes of Doodles. Timmy watched them vanish into the cabinets' recesses, but he did not argue the point.

"Find any books you liked, Tiger?" Daddy asked again.

Timmy nodded again. He liked it when Daddy called him that. "*Pecos Bill,*" he said. "It's about a cowboy."

"That was one of my favorites when I was your age," Daddy said. He paused. "No, actually, when I was a bit older." He looked at Timmy. "You're sticking to your own shelves, aren't you, Tiger?"

Timmy had the run of the library when Daddy was busy, or on the rare occasions when he wasn't home, but there were rules he had to obey. He could not use the front door. He could not go to Daddy's basement workshop. And he could not read books from any shelves but his own.

"Yes, sir," Timmy said. He nodded. "You asked me to

read a page out loud and then you put the book there, remember?"

Daddy sighed and nodded. "You read better than I did when I was your age," he said. "I forget that sometimes. And I forgot about giving you the book, too. It all runs together."

Most of the sacks he had lugged inside were empty now, but not all. Brown paper crackled as Daddy opened a smaller bag and Timmy watched as he set a dozen plastic pill bottles on the countertop.

"Does your head hurt again?" Timmy asked.

Daddy had headaches a lot, especially after going outside.

"I feel better now," Daddy said. He opened one of the bottles and took out two yellow tablets. He gulped them without water. "These will help," he said, and then put the rest of the pill bottles in the high cabinet, where Timmy couldn't reach. Timmy knew that he kept things there that Timmy wasn't to touch. Seeing Daddy lock and unlock the hiding place reminded Timmy of something.

"You didn't lock the front door, Daddy," he said. "Should I do it?"

"No!" Daddy said. "Keep away from that door, do you hear me?" Moving with new energy, he loped the distance from the kitchen to the living room. By the time Timmy caught up with him, Daddy had slammed the deadbolt home. "You're never supposed to use that door!"

"I—I'm sorry," Timmy said. He knew that he had

done something wrong, but wasn't sure what. Now Daddy looked suddenly, terribly angry.

Or frightened, perhaps.

Daddy knelt down beside him and spoke gently now. "It's okay," he said. He ran his fingers through Timmy's hair, and Timmy could feel his hands tremble. "Everything's going to be okay, if you just keep away from the door." Then his skinny arms were around Timmy, hugging, and Timmy hugged his father back. "I won't," he said. "I promise." He hesitated a second, then asked, "Daddy?"

"Yes, son?"

"It's almost Christmas," Timmy said. He had something he needed to ask, but he knew that it wouldn't make his father happy.

Daddy's arms around him tensed, then relaxed. "I know, son," he said. "And I know what you want. We'll call your mother later."

Mother.

Timmy had almost forgotten her.

No, not forgotten her—forgotten *about* her. Mother was all smiles and laughter, kisses and hugs that were like the ones Daddy gave him, but *different.* Mother was gray eyes and red smiling lips. But Mother was also a very long time ago, and the memories had faded.

"Really?" he said tentatively. "Mother?"

Daddy nodded, and looked sad again. "I'm sorry it has to be like this, son. But you're happy here with me, aren't you?"

Timmy nodded, eager to please. "Sure, Daddy," he said. "We have lots of fun!"

"Good." Daddy reached into a pocket and then handed something to Timmy. It was a Fruit Doodle, still in its plastic wrapper. Raspberry, Timmy's favorite. He all but snatched it.

"Now, go back to your book. I have another errand to run, and when I come back, we'll have dinner," Daddy said. "And then later, maybe we'll call your mother."

"You're going out again?" That was a surprise.

"I have to. It's Long Night."

"Long Night?"

"Almost Christmas, I mean," Father said.

"And that means Santa Claus, right?" Timmy asked.

Daddy nodded.

Timmy took a deep breath, and then asked the question in a single rushing gasp. "Can we go *see* Santa Claus? He's going to be at the mall and I really want to—"

Daddy's face darkened with anger and his eyes seemed to light. His hand, so much bigger and stronger than Timmy's, reclaimed the Fruit Doodle.

"You weren't just reading, were you, Timmy?" he demanded.

Suddenly miserable, Timmy shook his head. "I watched TV," he said. "Just a little bit."

"You're not supposed to watch TV without me," Daddy said.

"I wanted to see a cartoon," Timmy said, still miserable and still filled with the knowledge that he had done something very wrong. His gaze never left the Fruit Doodle. "But the color channels were working. And they said Santa would be—"

His words stopped abruptly, as a new sound cut through them.

Someone was knocking at the front door.

Daddy stood, suddenly pale again. "You'd better go to your room, Timmy," he said, and handed Timmy the pastry. "Be a good boy and go to your room."

"But, Daddy—"

"Now," Daddy said. "I have to go back to the kitchen for a moment, and I don't want you here when I come back."

The knocking came again.

Timmy scrambled back into the library picture. He knew the house better than his father did. Going to his room this way meant that he didn't have to climb the long stairs or take the back hall. From inside the frame he stuck his head out for one last peek, just in time to see his father return and begin opening the door locks again. This time, however, Daddy did it more slowly, because he was using only one hand.

His other was busy holding a gun, and as Timmy watched, Daddy's thumb drew back the hammer.

The sun was far below the horizon by the time Angel could return to the hotel. Even in the tunnels that ran beneath the rambling structure, he could feel the dawn of the longest night. He could feel the darkness gather outside, and feel the shadows of his own vampiric nature stir in response. It was as if some heavy weight had been lifted from his shoulders, or as if some constant, annoying companion had fled. The darkness called to him, and it called more strongly as he climbed from the tunnels and made his way to the main lobby.

"Don't you look nice," Cordelia Chase said, as he opened the door. "Very stylish, in a lurid sort of way. Total Yule."

She spoke tartly. She almost always spoke tartly, even now, even after so much had changed. The familiar was a consistent reminder that, no matter how much she had matured, Cordelia was in some ways still very much the spoiled rich girl he had first met in Sunnydale.

Even if she wasn't rich anymore.

"Hello, Cordelia," he said.

She had set up shop at what had been the hotel's main desk, surrounding herself with open books and what seemed like dozens of manila folders. A laptop computer waited to one side, its pale glow drowned out by the lobby lamps. Above her hung the Angel Investigations' grudging and almost entirely secular concessions to the Christmas season—colored ornaments, electric candles, and a smiling blown-glass heavenly cherub that looked more like Cupid to Angel's eyes.

None of the decorations were crosses, of course. Even recalled images of them, scattered through Angel's memories of Christmases past, were enough to make him uncomfortable.

"Be careful!" she said to him. "I just cleaned those rugs!"

Angel stared at her blankly for a split second, but then comprehension dawned and he hastily stepped from the carpet and onto the polished marble floor. Just in time, too. The black leather duster he wore was spattered with green- and red-glowing gore, in lurid mockery of the season. A blob of the red had chosen that moment to tear free, and now it hit the marble floor and splashed.

The assignment had been very messy.

"I swear, I'm going to make you start changing your clothes before you come upstairs! Here!"

She threw him a roll of paper towels. He caught it easily and began dabbing at the latticed slime that decorated his long leather coat, realizing now what had prompted Cordelia's Yule comment. "Darn ichor," he muttered and felt a bit of relief as he realized that it was coming off cleanly. He had the grace and speed of something superhuman, but mussed clothes made him feel awkward and self-conscious.

"I take it things went well?" Cordelia asked.

"Pretty much what we expected. It was a demon in the old Chesney warehouse," Angel said. The report had come in earlier in the day, but he had waited to act on it until secure in the knowledge that he could hunt his quarry without risking the sunlight. "A Ch'sn'y demon, in fact. But the name part was probably a coincidence. You can bill the owners. They should be happy to pay."

"Coincidence. Hmph." Cordelia, trim and attractive, leaned back in the high chair behind the desk. Her expression was stern now, and she looked like the prettiest judge in the world. All that she needed to complete the effect were a robe and gavel. "Daddy used to say there was no such thing as a coincidence."

Angel shook his head. "Don't ever let a wizard hear you say that," he said. "Or Wesley." He glanced at the cluttered desktop. "What are you working on?"

"The Gibson case," Cordelia said. "*Rich* Dr. Gibson sent us the reports from her other searches for her son." She looked at him. "Oh, Angel—this is so sad."

She opened one of the folders, and spilled more pictures onto the desktop. Timmy Gibson smiled up at him again from scores of snapshots. He laughed, he cried, he ate ice cream and Fruit Doodles, and rode happily on the shoulders of a man who had to be his father.

Luther Gibson had been a tall man, lean, with laughter lighting his eyes. Angel wondered what, if anything, lit those eyes now.

"Timmy looks like he was a happy kid," was all he could think to say.

"*Was?*" Tartness gave way to something sharper as Cordelia glared at him.

"*Is,*" Angel hastily amended. But his thoughts were less optimistic. A little boy gone missing for five years, a possessive father who had to be dead but still called—those factors didn't suggest a happy ending. He had considered that point, even as he went about his business in the Ch'sn'y warehouse. The likely conclusion to Timmy's story was not a happy one.

"He planned this," she said, spitting the words. "He moved a huge amount of money into a sealed trust and locked it down, but good. Rachel's lawyers and accountants have been working on it for five years, and can't crack it. It's millions, Angel. *Millions.* Enough to live on for a very long time." She looked around the hotel lobby. "Actually, enough to live on just about forever."

"Cordelia," he said, with great reluctance. "About the Gibsons, about Timmy—"

"Thousands of children disappear every year, Angel," she said, interrupting. "We are here to help the helpless, and we are *not* going to turn our backs on this one."

"This isn't just an ordinary disappearance," Angel said. The unease he felt colored his tones, but he tried to choose his words carefully. "There've been other cases, when men tried to cheat death—"

"Wesley agrees that there's something funny," she continued, as if he hadn't spoken. "He's looking into Gibson's old neighborhood, where he grew up. People go back to their roots, he said. And the trust holds the deed on—"

"It's been five years, Cordy," Angel said patiently. "Five years is a long time."

Cordy raised her hand for silence like a prom queen holding court, a gesture that reminded him yet again of the old Cordelia. She had selected one sheet from the many before her and was inspecting it carefully. "Angel," she said, abruptly thoughtful. "What do you know about tungsten?"

"It's a metal," he said, baffled by her sudden change of subject and tone but used to such things by now. "Very tough. They use it in light bulbs and steel."

Cordy shook her head, making her auburn hair ripple

and flow beneath the electric candles. "That's not what I mean," she said. She spun in her chair and began typing on the portable computer. "Science was nowhere *near* my favorite subject, but I seem to remember something," she said. "Something about tungsten. There's got to be a Web page—"

"About the little boy, Cordy," Angel continued doggedly. "We have to expect the worst."

"He's alive," Cordelia said, as if that settled things. "He calls."

"Has he called this year?"

She shook her head. "Gunn's on alert, in case he does."

Angel sighed. "Death isn't the worst," he said patiently. "*I'm* not alive, Cordelia. Not really. But I talk to you every day."

She wasn't listening to him.

"His father was a lawyer," Cordelia said in a low voice. Words had formed on the screen and she was reading them. "A very *rich* lawyer. That means he was connected with bad people." She looked up at him. "The trust he set up is the Tungsten Trust. At first, I thought that was just because it was tough, too. But don't you see?" Her words came in a rush. "Do you know where they *get* tungsten, Angel?"

He looked at her blankly.

"The ore is wolframite," she said. "And another name for tungsten itself is—"

"Wolfram," Angel said softly.

A world away, in a room very much unlike this one,

Wesley Wyndam-Pryce had placed three books side by side, then displayed the results. Three images on the worn bindings, meaningless in themselves, had become a grim rebus when placed in a specific sequence. A wolf, a ram, and a hart—together they had spelled out "Wolfram & Hart." Angel had stared in shock and astonishment then, and now he felt those feelings anew.

The law firm of Wolfram & Hart had its claws—literally and figuratively—in every dimension, it seemed. They had managed to raise Darla from the dead and even had a scroll that mentioned Angel's coming.

"It can't be a coincidence," he said.

"There are no coincidences," Cordelia said, and displayed her perfect teeth in a smile that mocked, but only slightly. The smile faded as she continued. "They must have set up the trust. Wesley needs to know about this," she said.

"Where is he?" Angel asked. "Where was he going?"

"I told you—the old neighborhood," Cordelia said. She picked up the phone and punched numbers. "Gibson's family home is out on Aptora Drive, and the Tungsten Trust holds the deed. Dr. Gibson's people say that the place is sealed and alarmed, that no one lives there, but Wes wanted to make sure." She returned the phone to its cradle. "No answer. Either he's in a bad cell or he's in trouble."

Angel scarcely heard her. He had already stepped to the nearby weapons cabinet and opened it. Now he selected the tools of his trade, one after another. A dagger. A small ax. A dozen wooden stakes, honed to wicked points.

"Stakes?" Cordelia said, comprehension finally dawning. "Not the little boy?"

He looked at her and nodded. "That's what I'm thinking. The father, at least. Maybe both. That's what I'm afraid of," he said.

"I'll go with you," Cordelia said, reaching for her jacket.

Angel shook his head. "This could be bad, Cordy, and there's a lot going on," he said. "Keep trying Wes. Let me handle it myself."

Human emotions were strong, and sometimes endured even after death. A father who loved his son deeply enough, who was facing death and was terrified of it, might do terrible things—especially if he had access to the resources of Wolfram & Hart.

"Oh, yuck," Cordelia said softly.

"Four lives," Luther Gibson said. "Four days a year. Not such a terrible price, really."

"Even one life is too much," Wesley said tightly. He wanted to cross his legs, but could not. Instead, he sipped tea. It was Earl Grey, but stale and old. It was bitter but at least it was hot, and for a brief moment, he considered throwing it in Gibson's face. But his unwanted host moved with speed and grace that were remarkable for a man who was supposed to be dead, and Wesley was reasonably certain that the tactic would fail.

And if it did, there would be no second chance.

"Most of them were lives without value, Mr. Wyndam-Pryce," Gibson said. Despite his words, he looked infinitely sad. "And they bought something remarkably dear, really. A smile on a young boy's face." He paused. "My father never saw me smile. And I never saw him at all. That's the worst of it, I think."

They were opposite one another in the basement of Gibson's home. Wesley occupied an overstuffed easy chair, worn but comfortable, and Gibson had composed himself neatly on a matching couch. Between them was a low table with a tea service. Loops of heavy chain ran from shackles on Wesley's ankles to a ring set deep in the bare stone floor. The floor's slate flagging was scarred and stained with a murky brown that Wesley knew only too well.

It was the color of old, dried blood.

"I wish I could make you understand," Gibson said. He spoke with the studied, persuasive tones of a good lawyer. His right hand, resting on the couch arm, held his gun trained unswervingly at Wesley's chest. The weapon had not left his hand since he had opened the door to greet Wesley. "It's nothing personal, really."

"You'll forgive me if I take it personally," Wesley said. He hated this. He hated being helpless and being made the fool, but Gibson had taken him completely by surprise. Police reports and Dr. Gibson's files and neighborhood sources had all told him that the place was empty and shuttered. When Wesley had come calling, the ancestral manse's weathered exterior had seemed to confirm those reports.

Luther Gibson's presence there indicated differently, of course.

"Winos," Gibson said. "Shopping bag people. Hippies. Lives already empty. I can see that you're not like them, and I'm sorry that it's come to this. But you came to me, after all."

Wesley had taken stock of his surroundings carefully after being led down the stairs and chained in his chair, trying to be thorough while remaining discreet.

The geometry of the basement room was odd. The four walls, the ceiling, and the floor were all perfect squares of the same size. The space they bounded was a perfect cube. Except for couch, chair, and table, the chamber was nearly unfurnished. In one corner stood a rack of tools—shovels and picks, saws and axes—beside a break in the stone floor that let mounded earth show.

It wasn't hard to guess where the previous occupants of Wesley's chair had ended up.

"Four times a year," Gibson continued. "Equinoxes, vernal and autumnal. Both solstices, summer and winter." He paused. "Winter is the most important one. The longest night."

Wesley nodded and sipped some more tea. Sweat had formed on the back of his neck and now ran cold down his spine. "The Longest Night," he said, forcing himself to speak more calmly than he felt. "I have friends, you know. Friends who know where I am and who will come for me."

"And when they come for you," Gibson said, "they'll

find nothing but an empty house, shuttered and dusty. Except for four days a year."

If the basement room itself was nearly barren, the stone walls that bounded it were not. They were decorated with startlingly realistic pictures, images of lushly appointed rooms and hallways that reminded Wesley of what little he had seen of the upper floor. The one directly behind Gibson, for example, was of the main foyer. Between the framed images, complex glyphs and runes were painted and etched into the rock itself, from slate-flagged floor to timbered ceiling. Wesley took little note of the pictures, but the markings fascinated him. They hinted of a dozen extinct alphabets and visual vocabularies, but belonged specifically to none.

And they moved.

At first, Wesley had thought it an illusion, but now he was certain. Slowly but implacably, the complex and intertwining symbols were rewriting themselves. The patterns reminded Wesley vaguely of mathematical equations chalked on a blackboard. They gained in complexity as each moment passed.

"Four is a very important number in certain demonic pantheons," Wesley said. A guess wouldn't hurt. "Four is a sacred number to Dhoram-Gorath, for example."

"That might be his name," Gibson said, still agreeable. "I really don't know. My lawyers made all the arrangements."

"You're an attorney yourself," Wesley said. The trickle of sweat running down his back became colder.

"Criminal. I needed specialists in contract law," Gibson said. He sipped his own tea, and seemed to enjoy it no more than Wesley had his. "They made the arrangements, and told me what I had to do as my end of the deal. Four times a year, when the house synchronizes. That's when I secure the other supplies, too."

Synchronizes. Wesley considered the word, turning it over in his mind.

"Speaking of years, I must say that you're remarkably active for a man who was to have died of brain cancer nearly half a decade ago," he said bluntly. "I take it that's why you made the deal?"

"Not a cure," Gibson said. "A . . . a pause. For most of the year, Timmy and I are here together, and the world does not intrude. Neither does the disease. The house is as it used to be, when I was growing up here."

"Dhoram-Gorath it is," Wesley said. He was certain of that now. Dhoram-Gorath was a powerful time-binding demon of the Ch'sn'y pantheon.

"You can ask him yourself, in a bit," Gibson said. "Four days a year, I go out and get what I must, and that's when the cancer works on me." His eyes became brighter and more intense. "You can't imagine. It feels like rats are nesting in my brain, Mr. Wyndam-Pryce. You've saved me some of that this time, at least."

Wesley could think of only one law firm that might make such an arrangement. "I take it you're represented by Wolfram and Hart?" When there was no response, he continued. "I rather have to wonder if you're their client, or if the demon is."

Gibson said nothing.

Wesley shifted in his chair, making the chains that held him rub together and clink. Again, he considered the ballistic possibilities of hot tea. "I wonder if I might have a refill?" he asked, gesturing with his cup.

"Help yourself," Gibson said, but he kept the gun trained in Wesley's direction.

As Wesley leaned forward to the tea service, an electronic chirp sounded from his jacket pocket. His wireless phone had rung a dozen times since he had come here. He said, "I told you I have friends."

"Had," Gibson said, correcting him.

Wesley settled back in his chair. The newly filled teacup was warm in his hand. He gazed at Gibson and at the runes and the picture on the wall behind him. The arcane symbols were moving again, but so was something else, *inside* the framed image.

Beyond the picture's surface, a little boy with red hair and freckles trudged past his field of view.

Timmy was in the foyer when the big brass doorknob rattled. Daddy had told him to stay in his room tonight, upstairs on the top floor of his house, but the water in the kitchen tasted better than the water in the bathroom, so he had made his way there. He took the shortcut from his bedroom, through the library and the library picture and into the gallery, and was on his way to the kitchen. He was thirsty and wanted a drink of water.

First the doorknob rattled, then knuckles rapped

against wood for the second time that day. Timmy paused in his tracks again, considering the almost unprecedented sequence of events. He knew from reading and from television that you were supposed to answer a door when someone knocked.

But he wasn't allowed to use the front door.

The unknown someone knocked again, and Timmy heard a muffled voice through the wood. He wondered who it was.

Only Daddy was allowed to use the front door, but did *using* really meant going through the door. Could he *open* the door without breaking the rule? He decided that he could, if only just this once.

His hands were small and he had to stand on tiptoe to reach the bolt mechanism, but at last, the heavy panel of wood swung back and revealed a stranger standing on the doorstep. The stranger wore a long, black coat and a black shirt and black pants, so dark that he almost faded into the night behind him. Something about him was just a little bit scary, too.

"Hey, buddy," the stranger said. He smiled and made a little wave and knelt so that he could meet Timmy's gaze, all without entering. "Hey. You're Timmy Gibson, aren't you?"

Timmy nodded yes, but said nothing. He felt suddenly unsure of himself. He hadn't given any thought to what he would do after he opened the door.

The visitor peered at him. "And you're not—," he started to say, and then he smiled, showing big white teeth that were square and bright. "You're *not*. You're okay."

Timmy nodded, fascinated. This was the first new

person he had seen in as long as he could remember.

"Timmy, your mother sent me," the stranger said, after a moment.

Timmy wasn't sure what to say to that, either.

"I need to see your father," the stranger continued. "May I come into your house?" He said the words carefully, as if to make sure that Timmy would understand.

The words finally came. "I'm not allowed to let strangers in," Timmy said.

"Please," the stranger said. "I'm here to help."

Timmy shook his head. "It's almost Christmas," he said. "I have to be a good boy."

"You are a good boy, Timmy. Just let me in so that—"

Timmy decided not to listen to him anymore. He swung the door shut. It slammed with a reassuring *thump.* He put the lock back the way it had been, then headed for the kitchen and his water, secure in the knowledge that he had done the right thing.

Realization struck like lightning, a flash of awareness bright enough to illuminate all of the puzzle pieces and show Wesley how to put them in place. The cube-shaped room, the picture that was actually some sort of window, even the way the house went in and out of focus with the rest of the world—all those factors added up to only one thing.

The place was a tesseract.

Wesley's studies had focused more on history and the occult than on theoretical mathematics, but he remembered the term nonetheless. If a cube like this room was the three-dimensional equivalent of a two-dimensional square, then a tesseract was the four-dimensional version of a cube. Tesseracts were defined by lines that were straight in normal space, but which bent through a dimension that humans could not perceive directly. A tesseract was a cube with opposing faces that nonetheless met one another. The pictures on the walls weren't mere pictures, but windows into other sections of the tesseract's structure.

"They'll find nothing but an empty house, shuttered and dusty," Gibson had said. *"Except for four days a year."*

"Four is a sacred number to Dhoram-Gorath," Wesley's own words came back to him now, and Dhoram-Gorath was a powerful time-binder. Time and space were different aspects of the same thing, according to Einstein.

Wesley wished fleetingly that the agency's science authority, Fred, were here with him, but then gave silent thanks that she was not. Her expertise in mathematics and inter-dimensional physics would have come in handy. No doubt, she could have read the strange equations as easily as a child's primer, but he would not have wanted to see her in the danger that was surely coming.

The runes and symbols on the walls had coalesced now. They clustered in a complex knot in the center of one wall. They moved and they glowed and they lit the dingy basement with a brilliant light.

And as he watched, the knot of symbols emerged from the two dimensions of the room's walls into the three dimensions of the space those walls bounded. They became something real and physical, a glimmering tendril of incandescence, a glowing ribbon that reached outward. It groped as if searching.

"Scream if you like. It helps," Luther Gibson said, and set down his gun. "Timmy is up in his room and won't hear you."

Dhoram-Gorath's tentacle touched Gibson's shoulder.

Sleigh bells rang. Heavy boots clomped on the doorstep. Someone pounded yet again on the door, hard enough to shake it in its frame.

"Ho! Ho! Ho!" a deep voice called out. "Timmy? Timmy, are you there?"

Timmy raced down the staircase, his shortcuts forgotten. He half ran, half bounced down the carpet stairs, his heart pounding. With fingers made clumsy by excitement, he worked the big door's lock and knob again. Then he pulled the door open, for only the second time in his whole life. What he saw made him blink his eyes and rub them, then look again, in near disbelief.

Santa Claus was on his doorstep!

Santa was big and tall, and the only part of him that was fat was his big, round belly. He wore a red suit trimmed with white. His boots and belt and gloves were black leather, and he had a bag slung over his shoulder. A string of bells jingled in one glove-clad hand.

"Ho! Ho! Ho!" Santa said. "Hello, Timmy! I hear that you've been an extra-special good boy this year, haven't you?"

The whole world became a brighter place. Timmy was bouncing from one foot to the other, nearly hopping in his excitement.

"Santa!" he said. That was all that he could think to say. "Santa Claus!"

"That's right, Timmy," Santa said. His voice was booming and deep, just like Timmy had heard on the forbidden TV, and just like the voice that Daddy made when he read to Timmy about Santa. "Merry Christmas!"

The words made Timmy pause. "Hey," he said, suddenly puzzled. "It's not Christmas yet!"

"Ho! Ho! Ho!" Santa said again, with a little bit less energy this time. "It's the Christmas season, isn't it?"

Timmy nodded eagerly.

"One of my helpers told me a little boy here probably wouldn't get to see me, so I thought I would come by and visit in person!" Santa spoke like every sentence was a cheer. "You *have* been a good boy this year, haven't you, Timmy? Ho! Ho! Ho!"

A dozen remembered transgressions raced through Timmy's mind. Spilt milk, watching TV without permission, opening the front door, leaving his books on the floor, not finishing his vegetables. Surely none of them made him a bad boy. "Yes, sir, Mr. Santa Claus!" he said, nodding. "I've been very good!"

"Good," the strange visitor said. "Very good! Now,

why don't you invite ol' Santa inside, and we'll talk about what you want for Christmas?"

Timmy paused. "I'm not allowed to let strangers in," he said, for the second time that evening. This time, the words tore at him.

"Hey," Santa said softly. He smiled. "I'm not a stranger, kid. I'm Santa Claus, everyone's friend. And I sure could use some milk and cookies." Then he laughed again, "Ho! Ho! Ho!"

Timmy knew what to do then. "Come in, Santa," he said.

Santa's booted feet had barely crossed the threshold when Timmy heard the scream, distant and faint.

But familiar.

Gibson shrieked in agony at the shining tendril's touch. He continued screaming as the rippling tide of ideographs and glyphs flowed like quicksilver from the walls. They flowed like water into a sponge, or like ink into a blotter—penetrating, intermingling, *marking*. In an instant, his body was sheathed in an infinitely complex web of interlocking runes and glyphs, a pulsating sheath of cryptic symbology. The symbols themselves seemed to follow some otherworldly orthography, and the lines that made them met at angles that made Wesley's eyes hurt.

Then, where Gibson had stood, Dhoram-Gorath stood instead.

Even as he watched the transformation, Wesley worked to free himself. A dozen lock-picks rode in a pouch at his waistband, tools he had brought along when he expected to find the house sealed. Now, with fingers made nervous by circumstance, he found the little metal probes and inserted one into the massive lock of his leg-irons.

"No," Dhoram-Gorath said. He spoke the word with lips and tongue that might once have belonged to Luther Gibson, but he did not speak with the man's voice. It was a single gurgling syllable, barely comprehensible. A hand that had been Luther Gibson's rose and gestured in Wesley's general direction. Light flared from the tips of entirely too many fingers.

Wesley's lock-pick crumbled into rust and slipped through his now-trembling hands.

"Daddy?" Timmy asked, half to himself and half to Santa. The scream had been in a familiar voice. "That's my Daddy!"

"Take me to him, Timmy," Santa said, speaking with the voice of command. "Now."

"He's in the basement, but I'm not allowed—"

"Now, Timmy!" Santa said. "Where's the basement door?"

The basement door would be locked, Timmy knew. Instead of answering, he clambered into a gallery picture. He did not look to see if Santa followed.

Wesley threw himself to one side, drawing his chains taut as he stretched them. As he moved, he pawed desperately at his kit and found another lock-pick.

Before he could use it, however, more light flared from Dhoram-Gorath's far-too-many fingertips. The glaring radiance was of a color that Wesley had never seen before, even under the alien suns of another world. The strange fire licked out, retreated.

When it faded, the chains crumbled into rust and dust, freeing him. Wesley drew back his hands, confused. As his vision cleared he stared at them without comprehension. They shook with tremors. The skin on the backs of his hands was pale and mottled with liver spots. The knuckles were swollen with arthritis.

They were the hands of a very old man.

Timmy had spent nearly his whole life in the house, and he certainly knew all of its shortcuts. The normal route to the basement involved moving through the kitchen to the rear hallway, then to the utility room, then to a flight of stairs. Another hall ran the length of the basement, past the old coal bin and the furnace, and to Daddy's special workshop there. The normal route would take too long, even if the door were open.

He scrambled through the library picture and through the library, to the picture of the dining room that hung here.

"What—what is this?" Santa asked from behind him, baffled but following. "What are you doing?"

Timmy didn't answer, but kept going. Clambering through that picture and the next brought him to another. This one looked out over the special room Daddy had in the basement. Timmy had stumbled upon it early in his exploration of the house. Ordinarily, it held no interest to him; most days, Daddy's workshop was shadowed and dark. Now, however, as he approached it, the image within the frame glowed with strange colors and lights.

A hand found Timmy's shoulder. "Hold it, kid," Santa Claus said. "I'll take over from here."

More of Dhoram-Gorath's strange light flared. Wesley, rolling desperately, tried to avoid the pulsing glow, but his body would not move the way it should have. His joints hurt and his bones ached and his breath came in short gasps. The world went into soft focus as his vision blurred. He blinked to clear his eyes, but to no avail. The world was wrapped in fog and seen from a distance. Then the glow swept over him and the world seemed to move a little bit further away.

All he could focus on now was Dhoram-Gorath, in his chosen vessel of Luther Gibson. The demon's body was a glowing fractal network of curves and angles, none of which seemed quite right for the world in which Wesley lived. Only the eyes that glared from beneath his lettered brow remained those of Luther Gibson.

Again, Dhoram-Gorath gurgled, but the sounds he made were incomprehensible, not even remote approximations of human speech.

This time, Wesley was too weak even to try to dodge. He could only lay motionless as the eldritch luminescence found him. When the glow faded, he felt even older and weaker, and a hot line of pain stretched from his chest and down one arm.

He was dying, he knew. Dying of old age. Dhoram-Gorath was taking his years from him, and giving some of them to Gibson instead.

"Wesley!" a familiar voice shouted. "Hold on!"

For a brief moment, Wesley wondered if senility had come, and if he could trust what remained of his vision.

Behind Dhoram-Gorath, leaping from the picture that decorated one wall, a fighting-mad Santa Claus had erupted into the room.

With the instincts of a hunter, Angel took stock of the situation. There wasn't much to see. An old man who wore clothes Angel could recognize as Wesley's lay sprawled on the floor. He was clutching his chest. Another figure, man-size but not man-shape, and covered with glowing tattoos, loomed over the fallen one, with many-fingered hands raised to strike.

The problem wasn't vampires, then. That much was good news.

Angel leaped through the picture frame, driving himself through the air with muscles that were far stronger than those of any living human. The creature grunted as he slammed into its back. Immediately, Angel's left arm snaked around the demon's neck, and his right hand dug into Santa's bag of presents that still hung at his side.

"Dhoram-Gorath . . . ," the old man said, with a whispering gasp that was an aged echo of Wesley's voice. "Time . . . binder."

Cold fire radiated from Dhoram-Gorath's body as

Angel clung to him. Even through the thick layers of his Santa Claus costume, he could feel the demon's power touch him. It touched and it burned, and it stirred strange sensations within Angel's undead flesh.

His right hand had found the weapon it sought. Angel brought the stake up in an arc and then down, stabbing into what would have been the soft hollow between a man's neck and collarbone. The tip of the seasoned wood found its target, and dug in—

Then it crumbled into dust, the way wood crumbles beneath the passage of years. In a split-second, the stake was gone, as if it had never been.

Dhoram-Gorath reeled and bucked, trying to shake his attacker. Forgetting Wesley, the demon reached behind himself, clawing at Angel. His many fingertips glowed like suns.

Dodging one raking slash, then another, Angel groped again in his sack. This time, his strong right hand closed around the haft of the small battle-ax he had stowed there.

He never had a chance to use it. The barest tip of one demon finger found the curved blade and touched it, and then all Angel held was rust and dust.

"Santa!" Timmy Gibson wailed, from somewhere a world away.

The weapons he carried were useless, Angel realized. Rather than try for another, he pulled back hard with his left arm, attempting to strangle the thing. For a moment, the effort seemed to yield no results, but then something inside Dhoram-Gorath gave with a satisfying cracking sound. The demon howled in pain.

"That got your attention," Angel snarled. Fury surged through him, fury and bloodlust. His brow extended itself forward and down, and his teeth became a pair of ragged horizons as wrath lit his suddenly feral eyes. His free hand came up and clawed at Dhoram-Gorath's face. He scarcely noticed as the leather glove he wore decayed and then disintegrated.

"Santa!" Timmy cried again.

Wesley said something, too, barely audible to any senses less keen than a vampire's. "Years . . . ," the dying man said. "Took my years . . ."

Dhoram-Gorath reeled again, this time slamming into the hard stone nearest wall. The impact was hard enough to break Angel's grip. The vampire fell and rolled. Before he could rise, however, the demon's fingers of fire reached toward him.

Angel paused briefly in midlunge as the wave of radiance struck him. It hit like a physical force. Red tatters fell from his Santa Claus costume. Again, he felt unfamiliar sensations stir within him. This time, he realized what they were.

His body was trying to age.

"Won't work," he said as he lashed out at his assailant. "I'm done with that." He pounded on the demon, again and again.

Timmy shrieked, "Santa Claus! Don't hurt my Daddy!"

Daddy?

Angel paused in midblow, then realized he had no choice. He swung again.

The little boy rushed at the combatants and began flailing with balled fists. "Don't!"

"Don't . . . ," Wesley echoed. The croaked word was a grim echo of Timmy's, but he did not look to the child as he spoke, or to Angel. Instead, he stared, pleading, at the demon. "Don't . . . do it. Please."

"Years," Dhoram-Gorath slurred, his speech intelligible again, however barely. One hand reached for Timmy.

"Don't," Angel said. He understood now, too. With the realization came sick despair. "Please, stop."

"D-daddy?" Timmy asked. His voice was deeper now, no longer a child's lisp. He was taller, too, and the pajamas he wore split and fell away as he outgrew them. "Dad? I—I feel funny—"

"Don't do it," Angel said. "You'll kill him! You *are* killing him!"

Dhoram-Gorath paused then, drew back. The demon stared down at the young man who stood where a little boy had stood only seconds before. Already, the young man had become less young. With increasing speed, his hair thinned and faded, and wrinkles formed on his face and neck.

"Dad?" Timmy said, quavering.

"You—you'll kill him," Wesley gasped.

He was wrong.

With a scream far worse than the one that Luther Gibson had made earlier, Dhoram-Gorath drew back. His lips shaped a single, silent, "No!" The fire dancing on his fingertips retreated, and as it did, Timmy's age receded, too. In a moment, the rapidly aging man had become a very young boy once more.

Now, the demon's hands came up yet again—but this time, they pressed against Dhoram-Gorath's own brow. The pulsing curtain of runes and glyphs parted to reveal an agonized expression—but it was Luther Gibson's face once more.

"I'm sorry," he said. Tears spilled from his eyes. "I'm so sorry."

Then the curtain of luminous graffiti closed again, and the demon fell to the floor in a quaking heap.

The house began to shake. Ragged cracks opened in the stone floor and spread to mark the walls, as well.

"Go!" Wesley said. He rose, still trembling, but moving with new energy. "We—we'd best be leaving."

Even as he spoke, his youth and vitality were returning. Skin that had been pale and freckled by age was firm and ruddy now, and color had returned to his hair. The years that Dhoram-Gorath had stolen from him were returning, as the demon's host-body died.

The house shook some more. The worn stone floors of the basement workshop trembled as they split, and chunks fell from the ceiling. Timmy, frightened, began to move toward the picture again, but Angel intervened and scooped him up in strong arms.

"Not that route, kiddo," he said, over the boy's struggles and protests. "I have a hunch it's not going to work much longer."

"I have a suspicion that you're correct," Wesley said, very nearly his former self again. "Structures such as this have an alarming tendency to collapse when their hosts fall from grace. We'd best be going."

Timmy struggled against them both, desperate to go back to his father, only to learn what so many children had learned before him.

The small and the weak do not get to pick their paths, but must allow the big and strong to choose, instead.

There were many long miles between Luther Gibson's collapsing house on Aptora Drive and the secluded estate where Rachel Gibson lived. As Angel drove Wesley used the time to make some calls on his wireless. One was to Cordelia, to assure her that things had gone as well as could be expected. The other call was to Timmy Gibson's mother, to tell her that her son was on his way home.

Timmy, securely belted in the backseat of Angel's black convertible, listened but said nothing. He whimpered as the miles went by.

"Not a happy ending," Wesley said softly.

"I can think of someone who won't agree," Angel replied, but he said nothing more until they reached their goal.

"Timmy! Oh, God, Timmy!" Rachel Gibson said, her voice breaking.

"Mommy?" That was Timmy's voice, quavering and doubtful.

The words carried well on the night air and reached

Angel's ears easily. From a distance, he had watched Wesley lead the wayward son to the doorstep of the palatial home and now, he watched from that same distance as the dignified woman threw comportment to the winds and swept her son up in a desperate embrace. Hearing that could detect a human heartbeat let him listen to Wesley's mumbled explanations and Rachel Gibson's effusive thanks.

He listened from the curb because the house that Timmy would now call home was decorated for Christmas, with too many crosses in evidence for Angel's comfort. Besides, he did not want to explain to their client the costume he wore.

With Wesley, of course, he had no choice.

"So," the Englishman said, upon returning to the car. "Santa Claus. Ho ho ho."

Angel nodded, but said nothing.

"Jolly St. Nick," Wesley continued. His premature aging was reversed completely, and youth and fussiness alike had returned. "Isn't it odd? The cross is anathema to you, but a saint's vestments—"

"It was the only way," Angel finally said. The words came in a dead voice. He wasn't proud of how he'd fooled the little boy. "He wouldn't let me in otherwise. I had to fool him somehow. I bribed a charity Santa for the outfit. Good thing he had a pillow with him, too."

"Just so," Wesley said, climbing into the car. "Well, we'd best be getting back. It seems there's to be a party."

Angel glanced at him.

"When I called, Cordelia said that she and the others

are having a little get-together. A last-minute thing, in the spirit of the season," Wesley said. "Or seasons, I suppose. So many observances to be made. Even Mr. Gibson . . ."

Long miles went by in silence before Wesley spoke again.

"Why do you suppose he did it?" Wesley asked.

"He wanted to see his son grow up," Angel said. He spoke as if it were the most obvious truth in the entire world. "He wanted his son to grow up with his father."

"No. That's not what I mean," Wesley said. "Why did Gibson turn Dhoram-Gorath's power on himself? That's what saved us, you know."

"He did it to save Timmy," Angel said curtly, and wondered if Wesley could possibly understand, given what little he knew of Wesley's relationship with his own father.

A child like Timmy, with many years ahead of him, would be a source of temptation to a thing like Dhoram-Gorath, especially now that he'd had a sampling.

"He reached out some way and took back control," Wesley continued. "I was as good as dead, and you weren't enjoying much success, really."

"I haven't really enjoyed anything today," Angel said. "Anything at all."

He was thinking still of the elated little boy who had greeted him in the Gibson house on Aptora Drive, so gleefully excited that he couldn't stand in one place for even a moment. He was thinking about that same little boy, less than an hour later, sobbing and alone in the backseat of the black convertible as it raced along night-dark streets.

Timmy might remember this as the night he found his mother again, but he would also remember it as the night he had lost his father forever.

Wesley ignored the comment. "Why destroy himself, then?" he whispered. He spoke as much to himself as to Angel. "He wanted so badly to see his son grow up."

"And he did," Angel said, then nothing more.

7 P.M.

A JOYFUL NOISE

by Jeff Mariotte

The December night was cold, but it was cold by Los Angeles standards, which meant the mercury might head for the high forties or low fifties. Darren Meadows had been comfortable in the fuzzy red Santa Claus suit when the night had begun, but as he stood on his designated corner ringing his bell—and ringing and ringing and ringing—the suit's insides began to itch and he started to sweat, and after a while he felt the sweat running down his sides, down his ribs, and underneath the belly that made him such a natural for the Santa gig in the first place.

But a job was a job, so Darren determined to ignore the discomfort and do this one. It only lasted a couple more nights, and according to the weather report he'd heard, at considerable length and volume, delivered by the woman sitting behind him on the bus he'd taken to the employment agency that provided the Santas, the next few nights would be considerably cooler. He could last this one night, then get back to the residence hotel and take a shower, and then the last few nights of the job he wouldn't be such a sweaty Santa. The gig would make him enough money to pay his month's rent on the room, buy some groceries, and maybe even send a few bucks back to his kid in West Virginia.

"Thank you, sir," he said to an expensively dressed businessman type who'd tossed a quarter into his bucket as he hurried past. "Merry Christmas, ho ho ho."

But then again, he thought, *a bottle would be good on a cold winter's night. Or even a not-so-cold winter's night.* Maybe he'd just pick up a bottle of something—not too expensive, he didn't need the good stuff—for tonight, and then pay the rent and then figure out how much he could send back East.

A woman backed through the doors of the department store Darren had parked himself in front of, her arms laden with bags and packages. Her shoes alone must have cost five hundred bucks, and the burden she carried another thousand, but Darren could tell by the set of her mouth and the determined way her gaze bore right through him instead of seeing him that she wouldn't give a dime to help the—*what is it we're supposed to be helping*? he wondered. *Kids, I think. Or someone, anyway.* He hadn't paid a lot of attention to that part.

And he was right, Miss Half-a-Grand Pumps hustled right past him without a second glance. He rang the bell a little faster and a little louder, hoping to annoy her into at least acknowledging his presence, but she didn't. He slacked off as the staccato rap of her heels on the sidewalk dwindled away behind him.

Darren wondered what time it was. *A little after eight,* he guessed. He had pawned his watch months ago, and wasn't supposed to wear one in uniform anyway, because, as they explained at the agency, Santa wouldn't wear a watch. He didn't quite get that—how would the guy be able to schedule his Christmas Eve, hitting every single girl and boy, if he didn't have a watch? And a good one, not some cheapo drugstore watch like he'd owned. Santa would wear a Rolex.

If he was right—and he'd gotten pretty good at estimating the time since he'd hocked the watch—then he had less than two hours before the van came around to pick him up. He scratched at his ribs and gave the bell a couple of desultory rings. "Merry Christmas," he shouted at no one in particular, since the sidewalk was empty for the moment. "Ho ho ho!"

He heard a sound from behind him, the soft scuff of sneakers on the sidewalk, and did a kind of half-turn so he could glance back in that direction. But when he looked, there was no one there. Darren stopped ringing the bell, cupped his hand around it to silence the tone, and set it into the bucket that hung from a metal tripod. Maybe he'd been hearing things. He was still for a moment, listening. Cars rushed past on the cross street, "We Three Kings" echoed faintly from inside the department store, but his street was still quiet.

It remained quiet even when a powerful hand clamped over his mouth from behind him and a second arm snaked around his throat and dragged him into a nearby alley, the heels of his Santa boots scuffing lines across the sidewalk.

"Let me do this one," Georgie pleaded. "You did the last bunch of 'em, man."

Ash hesitated, the sacrificial blade poised over Santa's exposed throat. This one's whiskers had been phony, and Ash had tugged them to one side of his face, making them look like muttonchop whiskers gone berserk on that cheek. The elastic band stretched across the Santa's face, cutting directly between his nose and upper lip. Santa's eyes were wide with terror, his mouth working silently because Ash's grip on his throat was too tight to let sound come out. He looked over at R. C., who was tall and muscular, with the full complement of tentacles tattooed up his chest and neck and across his bald head. R. C. simply shrugged.

Neither of them liked Georgie too much. The kid was spoiled—his dad was the Grand High Wizard of the Order for the Imminent Ingestion of Earth, and he never let anyone forget it. He only had the beginnings of his tattoos—nothing that was even visible outside his coat yet, though Ash knew from meetings that he had the starter designs across his chest and back. He was a long way from being a full initiate, but if Ash didn't let the kid slice this Santa's throat, his voice would take on that plaintive tone, which turned rapidly into the really annoying whine. "My dad said I could do some of them," he'd say. "He'll be really mad if he finds out you wouldn't let me."

When the World Devourer came, Ash hoped that Georgie would be the first to go.

"Let him have one," R. C. said. "He's eager to take part."

"You sure you know how?" Ash asked him. The Santa tried to wriggle and kick, but Ash's hold was firm. The only thing he had to worry about was if he accidentally applied too much pressure. It wouldn't do for the Santa to die before the dagger could do its job.

"Yeah, I know how," Georgie said. "'Course I do. You think I never killed no one before?" He reached for the dagger, and Ash let him take it. He kept his grip on the Santa, though. Georgie wasn't physically strong; there was no way he'd be able to both hold the Santa and open his throat.

Georgie was right—he did know how to do it. Ash couldn't help being impressed with the skill the youngster showed when he plunged the dagger's crooked blade into the Santa and drew it cleanly across. After it was done and the Santa was still, Georgie even dipped the blade's tip into the Santa's blood and drew the proper design on the Santa's bell. Ash was surprised—maybe he'd underestimated the runt. *Kid shows some promise, after all.*

Right on schedule, a car pulled into the alley and Hugh got out, already dressed in a Santa suit. He barely glanced at the lumpy pile of red-and-white fur that they had shoved up against a Dumpster, and held out his hand. Georgie put the bell into it, and Hugh strolled out of the alley and back to the bucket, already ringing away.

"Merry Christmas!" he shouted. "Ho ho ho!"

That's seven, Ash thought. *Another thirteen to go.*

It was going to be a long night.

In the starry reaches high above the earth, a tear in the fabric of space began to widen.

"Are you really sure about this?" Angel asked. He was watching Fred weave red-and-green bunting between the balustrades on the stairway and having second thoughts. *Or tenth ones, more accurately.*

"Sure I'm sure," Cordelia said. She wore a long, clingy, deep red dress that shimmered like moonlight on the sea when she moved. Her rich brown hair was pinned up at the back, and a luminescence danced in her eyes. She had been looking forward to this night, Angel knew, and now it was here. "Angel, you can't change your mind now. Again. It's too late, there are already guests here. And I don't understand how you can possibly not like parties."

"It's really not hard," he said. "I just think about how much not-fun I've had at them over the centuries."

"But—gaiety and laughter and good cheer. People having fun together. It's great."

"People acting much sillier than they do in small

bunches, which is already pretty ridiculous to begin with much of the time. Sorry, Cordy. I understand they're sometimes a necessary evil, but—"

"Look who's talkin'," Gunn said.

"What?" Angel asked. "Me?"

"Not evil," Cordelia assured Gunn. "Just not exactly Mr. Sociable."

Angel looked at her for a moment until she added, "And definitely necessary." She brushed his arm with one hand and then went to the door to greet more guests.

"Cordy's right," Gunn told him. He was more dressed up than Angel had ever seen him, wearing a rented black tuxedo with a red-and-green pin-striped vest over his white shirt. The bow tie at his neck was red as well. It made Angel feel a little self-conscious about his own attire: black leather pants, gray shirt. *Not very holiday-themed.* "It's too late. Party's started, and you just got to make the best of it."

"I know," Angel said. "But it's the winter solstice, you know? Who knows what's going on out there in the city? There could be all kinds of bad guys at work."

"Cordelia had any visions?"

"No, I don't think so," Angel concurred.

"She did, you'd know about it. So just relax. You can't have fun, that's okay, just don't spoil hers."

Angel nodded. He knew Gunn was correct. Cordelia had thought of the Solstice Party several weeks ago, and wanted to hold it in the Hyperion Hotel's vast lobby. Angel had reluctantly agreed, then wavered, then finally agreed again. The party would be a good way, Cordelia argued, to introduce Fred to all their friends at once. She had met a few since returning with them from Pylea, but her emergence from her self-imposed isolation had been long and difficult. Now she was finally coming out of her shell, and Wesley and Gunn had joined Cordelia's mission to convince Angel that the party would be good for the young physicist.

"Plus," Cordy had added repeatedly, "it'll be fun."

That was where Angel drew the line. *There was a time when I believed that rampaging across Europe as Angelus was fun,* he thought. *Hanging out with Cordelia and Wesley and Gunn is fun. Opening the hotel up to dozens of people, some of whom might break into holiday caroling at any moment—that's more like mortal terror.* But the lobby smelled of fir from the enormous tree that was decorated and standing in a corner, and the place was filling up with the invited guests.

"Don't worry," he said at length. "I won't spoil her night."

"Not just her night," Gunn corrected him. "Big night for Fred, too." Angel saw his gaze go to where the young lady was coming down the stairs, her last-minute decorating finally complete. Her long brown locks were swept up in back, except for a few strands that framed her face. She wore a simple white peasant blouse with red embroidery at the neckline and sleeves, and an ankle-length skirt in a rich green velvet. Her smile was tentative at first, but then, as if sensing the impact she had on the gathered crowd—or at least, Angel thought, sensing the way Gunn looked at her—the hesitation disappeared and she beamed. Her last few steps were taken with a confidence Angel had rarely seen her display.

When she reached the bottom, Wesley was there, bowing deeply. "You look magnificent, Fred," he told her. He took her right hand and kissed it. "Happy Solstice."

Gunn looked away then, and the motion caught Angel's attention. "I know," he said. "It is a big night for Fred. I'm sure she'll pull it off, and everything will be fine."

"Better be," Gunn said. He flashed Angel a smile. "I'm gonna see if she needs a drink or somethin'."

The next Santa looked to be more of a problem.

He was in front of a popular music and video store. While much of L.A. emptied out at night, this part of Hollywood was just coming alive. Even tonight, so close to Christmas, when holiday parties were in full force across the city, people streamed in and out of the shop, picking up late presents or just treating themselves to the latest CDs and movies. The Santa was ringing his fool head off, and people chucked coins and a few bills into his pot with regularity.

Sitting in the car in the store's busy, narrow parking lot, Ash fretted.

"Do we really need this one?" Georgie asked from the back seat.

"We need all of them within the boundaries we've set," Ash reminded him. "By the fall of the hour, every bell needs to be ringing in just the right way." *Kid knows that,* Ash thought. *Or he did. He just doesn't seem to retain well. Wants everything to come the easy way, instead of being willing to put out some effort to make things happen.*

But summoning a World Devourer was no simple process. The timing had to be right, and it was; the Winter Solstice was a night of great power. The ritual had to be right, and they were working on that part. The bells had to be prepared in the correct fashion, with the proper symbols drawn in the blood of their most recent wielder. Then—and this part was trickiest of all, and most sensitive to error—they all had to be rung in precisely the right pattern. It had all been worked out mathematically—*or mathemagickally,* Ash thought. The ringing of the bells in the prescribed fashion would actually put into play a rigorously designed mathematical formula that would open a rift in space, through which the World Devourer would come.

Or so the Grand High Wizard had decreed. And he seemed to know his stuff. Ash glanced at R. C., who was sitting in the seat next to his, fully tattooed with the image of the World Devourer, as Ash himself was. On his chest was the World Devourer's midsection, with hundreds of eyes on stalks emanating from a bulbous cranium. Snaking out from his chest in every direction—up the acolyte's arms and down his legs, covering his neck to end on his shaved head, were the Devourer's many tentacles, bristling with suckers and barbed hooks. The scale, of course, could not be shown—Ash couldn't even imagine how big the World Devourer must be. But he knew it was out there, and hungry, and waiting to get in.

They had to take down this Santa.

"Great party, Angel."

Angel turned to see a tall, lean man with light brown hair and a huge smile, carrying a luminous blue drink in one hand. Pietro, one of Lorne's bartenders at Caritas, was serving tonight and he specialized in the unusual and obscure. "Thanks, Mars," Angel said in reply, speaking loudly to be heard over Springsteen's "Santa Claus Is Coming to Town," which boomed from the sound system Cordelia and Fred had rented for the evening. "What's new in the spa biz?"

"Oh, heavens," Mars said. "Botox, Botox, Botox. Everybody thinks those little critters can save their lives. If you ask me, the whole thing's just a little repulsive, don't you think? But I have to provide what the customers want. That's the name of the game, right?"

Mars owned the Palm Ridge Spa just outside of Los Angeles and—like everyone invited tonight—knew more than the average local about the hidden side of the city and her residents (and occasional visitors, like the Oden Tal females he had tried to hide from the Vigories who hunted them).

"Botox is botulism, right?" Angel asked.

"A purified form of the same bacteria," Mars explained. He sipped from his glowing blue beverage. "Paralysis and death on one hand, wrinkle-free skin on the other. I wonder what it'd do to your forehead when you're vamped out. Might be spectacular. Want to give it a whirl?"

"Thanks, but I'll pass."

"Suit yourself," Mars said. "Honestly, I don't blame you. What are a few deep furrows—ditches, really—between friends?"

"That's what I say too," Angel agreed.

"Well, I'll let you mingle," Mars said. "Besides, I hear Steve's coming, have you seen him yet?"

"Steve?"

"Guess not. Toodles." Mars drifted off into the crowd, leaving Angel, for the moment, mercifully alone.

"Y'all sure have a lot of interesting friends," Fred whispered. Wesley followed her gaze to see a trio of Mostark demons, statuesque and proud, with thick masses of hairlike tendrils that trailed from their heads down to the floor behind them, making their way between the guests.

"Well, in our line of work, you know, we meet quite a wide variety of people, and . . . well, not-people. Demons and the like."

"Those are some of the demons," Fred stated, pointing out the obvious.

"Mostarks," Wesley explained to her. He was happy just to be in Fred's presence. She was a sight to behold tonight; her pale skin gleamed like the finest Italian marble, and the evident pleasure she took in the tableaux that surrounded them was contagious. He had never before realized just how attractive she was. But then, she rarely came so far out of the shadows. "Quite noble, actually, in their way. They're warrior demons, but they do what they can to protect humanity from some of the more vicious varieties out there."

"That's a nice thing to do," Fred said.

"Very," Wesley concurred. "Not so different from what we do. But it's nice not to be alone in the doing of it."

"I used to love alone," Fred said. "In Pylea, alone was always better than not-alone. Here, I'm not so sure anymore. Here I think not-alone might be good."

Wesley drank in the smell of her, fresh with the slightest hint of peaches, as she crowded him to let the demons pass. "Not-alone is definitely good." He was about to say more when a familiar voice interrupted him.

"Wesley, there you are."

"Virginia?" *This is a surprise,* he thought. *I hadn't expected Virginia Bryce to be anywhere near this place . . . ever again. Certainly not tonight.* He glanced at Fred, who looked on with a questioning expression, then back at Virginia. She looked as beautiful as she ever had, which was considerably, Wesley believed. Her dress was floor-length and fitted, high-necked in front but cut away in the back, in an eggplant-colored material that reminded Wesley of a frosted glass Christmas ornament.

"Cordelia invited me," she said. "I wasn't sure it would be a good idea, but . . . well, I wanted to wish you happy holidays. And she said it would be okay. Is this your new . . . ?" She left the question unfinished, but Wesley understood it.

Fred, her cheeks crimsoning, seemed to as well.

"No," Wesley said quickly. "No, this is Fred, the newest member of our team. And a friend, of course. But not . . . well, you know."

Fred smiled radiantly and put her hand out. Virginia took it. "It's a pleasure to meet you, Fred," she said. "I'm Virginia Bryce. Wesley and I used to . . . go out."

"I've heard about you," Fred told her. "You're the one who thought he was Angel, right?"

"I'm the one who was led to believe that he was Angel, for a while, yes."

"That's what I meant." Fred was nothing if not gracious. "It's very nice to meet you too."

"I hope I didn't offend you," Virginia said. "About you and Wesley being a couple, you know. It's just that you're so pretty, and the way you two were walking so closely together, you know . . . anyway, a girl could do worse than Mr. Wyndam-Price."

"I'm sure she could," Fred answered brightly.

This whole conversation was making Wesley very uncomfortable. "I'm still, you know, standing here," he said. "Invisible, perhaps, but far from absent."

"I guess he means we shouldn't be talking about him as if he weren't here," Virginia stage-whispered to

Fred. "So we'll have to get together and talk about him sometime when he really isn't here."

"I'd like that," Fred agreed. "He says wonderful things about you."

"He does?" Virginia sounded genuinely surprised.

"Why wouldn't I?" Wesley asked, not really wanting to prolong the discussion but curious about her response.

"Well . . . it's just, you know. Sometimes when two people break up—and it was definitely my doing, I freely admit that—there's bad blood."

"I bear you no ill will, Virginia," Wesley said. "Not at all."

"I'm glad to hear that."

"I can vouch for that," Fred told her.

Wesley started to say something else but suddenly Gunn loomed behind Fred. "Excuse me," he said, his voice deep but quiet. "Can I see you for a minute, Fred? Got someone I want you to meet."

Fred looked at Wesley, as if for permission. He nodded, and she followed Gunn away, through the crowd.

"She's a lovely young lady," Virginia said.

"Indeed."

"You could do a lot worse."

"That's what you told her about me."

"Maybe it's true both ways."

Wesley hesitated a moment, then spoke. "I'm not sure I'm ready to take relationship advice from you, Virginia. Not that you might not be correct, but still."

"I understand, Wesley." Her lovely face looked sad,

though, as if he'd hurt her feelings. Not what he'd intended, to be sure. "Anyway, I mostly just came to see you and say happy holidays. I'm glad you seem to be doing well."

"Thank you," he said. "And likewise to you."

She leaned into him and they shared an awkward hug. "You look lovely," he whispered to her. "Thank you for coming tonight."

"Thank you," she replied, "for not throwing me out the door when I did."

"Can you help me catch my puppy, Santa?" Georgie asked the man. Ash watched from the corner of the building, away from Sunset. They'd picked Georgie to approach the Santa because he could do pathetic like nobody's business, as if he'd been born to the role. "I got him for my girlfriend for Christmas but he jumped out of the car when I got out."

"Where'd he go?" Santa asked, his forced jolliness forgotten for the moment.

Georgie pointed to the corner and Ash ducked back so Santa wouldn't see him. "I think he went around the building there. I figure if we team up we can, you know, kind of herd him and catch him."

"He's not, like, a pit bull or anything, is he?"

"No, no, he's a, you know, a terrier. A little white thing. I was gonna call him Snowball."

Nice improv, Ash thought. *How could Santa Claus refuse to help find a pup named Snowball?* He and R. C. waited for Georgie to bring Santa back, at which time they'd kill him and prepare the bell. Another car idled in the parking lot with the replacement Claus inside.

"Sure, for a minute, I guess," Santa reluctantly agreed. "I mean, I shouldn't let the pot out of my sight, but I guess I could go as far as the corner. If you can kind of drive him my way then I can grab him."

"That's great, I appreciate it," Georgie told him. "I mean, it wouldn't be a very merry Christmas if poor Snowball got flattened on the Sunset Strip, would it?"

Ash heard footsteps approaching the corner, and then Georgie's low whistle. "Here, Snowball! Here boy!" Georgie laughed softly. "Guess he don't know his name's Snowball yet, so that probably won't help, huh?"

"Probably not," Santa replied. "But I think it's tone of voice that matters more than the words, anyway."

"That's probably right." Georgie came around the corner. Ash and R. C. hugged the wall, waiting for Santa to appear. Ash felt his heart thudding in his chest in anticipation. *Like a kid on Christmas Eve,* he thought morbidly. A moment later, Santa did so, calling, "Snowball, where are you?"

Ash lunged at him, catching him by his full white beard—real, this time—and neck, and hauling him into the darkness behind the building. "Hey—," Santa started to protest, but R. C. clamped a hand over his mouth and shut him up. Ash drew the ceremonial dagger. Within minutes, a new Santa was at his post outside the store's busy front door, ringing his specially treated bell.

• • •

Miles and miles above the planet, the rift in space lengthened, and at one end of the opening the tip of a tentacle slipped through, wriggling and twitching like a worm coming into the light after years underground.

"I just met Steve," Melissa Burns said. "What a nice man."

"Steve who?" Angel asked.

Melissa was radiant in a jade green holiday gown, looking more poised and vibrant than Angel had ever seen her. For the first time he really understood what it was Dr. Meltzer had seen in her—okay, not to the point of wanting to stalk her, as the doctor had, or wanting to send individual body parts after her by themselves, as the doctor also had. But where before Angel had seen only a frightened young woman, there was now a powerful and self-confident beauty.

"Steve Paymer, silly," she explained with some amusement.

"David's brother? He's here?"

"Didn't you get to see the guest list?"

"I pretty much left that up to Cordelia," Angel said.

"Probably a good thing," Melissa told him. "Not that I'm not eternally grateful to you and everything, but I have to believe that Cordelia throws a better bash. You just don't seem like the 'get down, get funky' type, you know?"

Angel felt wounded, though he knew she was right. "I can get down," he attempted feebly.

"Anyway," she went on, as if trying to spare him any further humiliation, "life is great, thanks to you guys. I quit Pardell Paper Products and went into business for myself, and it's working out perfectly."

"That's terrific," Angel said. "Doing what?"

"You know those charts butchers have, showing all the different cuts of meat you get if you cut up a cow into all its different parts? I draw those."

Angel didn't quite know what to say to that. He tried to make sure he was smiling but his face felt frozen, unresponsive to his mental commands. Maybe Mars had Botoxed him without his knowledge.

"I'm kidding," Melissa assured him. "Don't look so stricken. I'm still in papers, providing specialty paper products for boutique stationers and the like. I'm my own boss and I actually have five employees. And I owe it all to you." She touched his arm and leaned toward him, lowering her voice. "And," she added, "I have a boyfriend. He's a doctor."

"That's . . . congratulations," Angel managed.

"Kidding again," Melissa said, and laughed brightly. "Actually, he's a police detective. We met when he was investigating the disappearance of Ronald Meltzer. A disappearance that's still officially unsolved, by the way. And staying that way."

"For the best," Angel said.

"That's what I think too. It's my only secret from him, though."

Angel was surprised to hear that. "Is he . . . here, then?"

Melissa shook her head vigorously. "No, he's on duty. This—you guys—you're all part of the same secret, you know? I don't think he'd really get you."

The image of Detective Kate Lockley flashed briefly through Angel's mind—Kate, who knew all about him and his kind, and couldn't let it go, and whose career had been ended by that knowledge. "You're probably right. A lot of people don't quite get us. You're doing the right thing."

"Thanks," Melissa said sincerely. "I mean that, Angel. For everything."

Angel didn't quite know what to say to that—small talk being not really his thing, and he felt like he'd already exhausted his supply of small talk for one party anyway. Besides, there was that whole element of naked emotion that made him just a bit uncomfortable. But before he had to reply, Cordelia was there with a hand on Melissa's arm.

"Melissa," she said cheerfully. "You've got to meet Fred!"

"Is he one of your new associates?"

"He's a she," Cordy said. Her gaze met Angel's. "But yes, exactly. And I'm sure Angel has a million people to schmooze. Party guy, you know."

As he watched them fade into the crowd, Angel thought, *I may have the name, but sometimes I think Cordelia's the real angel around here.* He turned away from the celebrants for a moment, rubbing his cheeks and wondering if his face would ache later from all the smiling he felt was expected of him tonight.

The job went faster than Ash had expected. The Santas fell one by one, interspersed with a few other charity workers in different costumes—some military-like, some looking like nurses or priests. It didn't much matter to Ash as long as they had a bell and were in approximately the right location. Each bell, at its loudest, had to be just audible from the next spot. Together, they'd weave a web of sound that reached into the heavens and opened the way for the World Devourer.

The last one in line was a woman in what looked like a military dress uniform, except that it carried no insignia from any force Ash had ever seen. It was all white, with a crisp, tailored jacket trimmed in gold, a braid around the shoulder, epaulets, and shiny buttons. White-on-white stripes decorated her pant legs, and her shoes were patent leather and highly polished. *This one's going to be tricky*, Ash thought. He knew they had some women standing by to take up her position, but none in a uniform even close to this one. Which would mean keeping hers clean enough to put on. Immaculate white clothes didn't necessarily go well with slit throats.

And there was plenty of traffic passing by her—mostly on the street, but some foot traffic as well. He didn't have a good feeling about this one as well.

"Maybe we should skip this one," he suggested.

"Can't," R. C. replied simply.

"Why not?"

"She's in exactly the right spot," R. C. explained. "We're at the point where we make a complete circle—where she is, the last one's bell will just be audible, and so will the one we started with. Another block and we'll lose it. But this one is right where we need her to be—if we skipped her we'd have to set up right next to her."

"I can do it," Georgie insisted from the back seat. "Let me do it."

"How are you gonna do it, Georgie?" Ash asked him.

Georgie leaned over the seats and pointed toward the corner. "See that alley back there?" he asked. It was halfway up the block, and dark inside. "Just get her up in there and do it."

"What about getting blood on her clothes?"

Georgie demonstrated with two hands around his own throat. "Strangle her first," he said. "Then get her uniform, then cut her to get the blood to treat the bell."

"Kid makes sense," R. C. said.

"Anyway," Georgie went on, "why do we have to always get the uniforms right? Couldn't we just replace her with someone else anyway?"

"Sure we could," Ash said. "And then in ten minutes when someone who passes by her five times a day passes by again, he'll wonder what's wrong."

"But he would anyway, right?"

"Most people see the uniform, not the individual, in a situation like that. They see the right uniform, they won't even look twice at the face. Even if they did they'd just think the organization replaced her for a while. But a different uniform in the same spot—that might raise alarms."

"Okay," Georgie said. "I gotcha. But I know I can do this."

"Kid did okay last time," R. C. pointed out.

Ash pulled the car into the dark alley and parked close to the wall. "Okay," he said. "Don't screw it up."

The tear in space widened as the chorus of bells from the planet below grew, each bell joining its partners in mathematical precision. Behind it, the Devourer waited. The Devourer didn't know impatience, or anticipation. The Devourer didn't think about the billions of souls on the world it would consume as anything but energy, any more than cows think about the inscets on the grass they eat or people do when they eat the cattle. The Devourer knew only hunger. And below, that which would satisfy its hunger, at least for a while. A planet teeming with life, with energy. It didn't question the motivations of those who invited it, or even recognize their sentience. There had been no communication between them. A rift appeared which would let the Devourer feast, anywhere in space, and the Devourer knew of it and was there. The system was foolproof, elegant in its simplicity, and it had always worked this way, since both universe and Devourer were young.

And it always would.

". . . anyway, I have this money I ought to invest—it's enough to keep the Teen Center running for years, decades maybe if I play my cards right. But I can't just keep it in the safe, you know? That seems dangerous, and it could be earning interest. The only trouble is I can't actually account for where it came from. It was more or less an anonymous donation."

David Nabbit, resplendent in a gold lamé top hat and tails, nodded seriously as Anne Steel spoke. "So these funds are liquid, I guess?"

"Any more liquid and they'd be running water," Cordelia interjected. "She's talking greenbacks, David."

"If you're talking about laundering cash, I'm not sure I'm the best one to talk to," David protested. "I don't exactly have a lot of experience in that arena."

"Don't think of it as laundering, then," Cordelia offered. "The money's plenty clean. The only people who might be looking for it are lawyers from Wolfram and Hart, and we all know what they're like."

"Like sharks circling a tour boat, hoping someone falls out," Anne said. "They're evil, like Angel told me."

"Of course they are," Cordelia said.

David fingered the brim of his sparkling hat. "I guess I could make some suggestions. You'll probably want to go offshore, but not the Caymans. Wolfram and Hart will be tapped in down there, and it's too obvious anyway. And Switzerland's out, of course . . ."

Cordelia touched both of them on the shoulder. She could listen to money talk all night, but there were other guests who needed to be checked on too. "My work here is done. I should have thought to get you two together ages ago."

Anne gave her a bright smile. "Thanks, Cordelia. I appreciate it."

"You'll be around later, won't you?" David asked eagerly. "Of course you will, it's your party."

"I'll be here," she told the billionaire. *If he wants to*

chat, or maybe fly me to Paris for a shopping spree, I'm always available.

She had barely made it five steps away before someone grabbed her arm, startling her out of a reverie in which she had unlimited use of David Nabbit's personal credit cards. "Cordelia, you seen Angel?"

It was Tom Cribb, a green-skinned demon who had always appeared to Cordelia as if his parentage included members of the reptile family. His long, darting tongue only reinforced that impression. He had fought beside Angel when they'd both been part of a demonic gladiatorial game, and since then he'd been working hard on turning over a new leaf and becoming accepted into L.A.'s community of peaceful demons who lived in harmony, instead of conflict, with the human world.

"Sure," she replied. "Tall, dark hair that kind of sticks up all over, broody. Hasn't finished his holiday shopping, last I heard. Why?"

"I mean in the last couple minutes." He didn't look like he was in a joking mood.

She scanned the hotel's lobby area quickly. "Maybe twenty minutes ago, I guess. He might have hidden out somewhere. Not exactly the kind of guy who puts a lampshade on his head and dances on the table, you know?"

"I gotta find him," Cribb insisted. "There's something goin' on out there." He inclined his head toward the doorway. "Something bad."

Not tonight, Cordy thought. *Any night but this one, yes. But this is party night.*

And it's also the Solstice, and it's not like Angel didn't warn us this could happen.

"Let's find him."

"Excuse me, ma'am, have you seen a little white puppy around here?"

Ash watched from the mouth of the alley as Georgie tried the puppy stunt again. It had worked once, and Ash figured that Georgie, not the sharpest tack in the box, was more comfortable going with the tried-and-true than improvising.

"Nope," the woman said crisply. "Been no dogs around here. I love dogs; I always say hi to them and pet them if I can. If there had been a puppy around here, I'd have seen it."

"But it just ran down this way," Georgie pressed. "I think it went into that alley back there. If you could just help me surround him, I think we can catch him. He's a Christmas present, you know. For my mom."

"You better look somewhere else, then," the woman answered. "He didn't come past me."

"I'm sure he did. Can you just come with me and check?"

"I can't leave my station, sorry."

"Just for a second. I'll go into the alley and flush him out toward you. You can still see everything going on down here."

She shrugged and turned toward the alley. Ash ducked back around the corner so she wouldn't spot him, and pressed himself up against the wall. He heard

Georgie's heavy footsteps and the lighter clicks of the woman's dress boots as they approached. When they stopped, though, Ash could just see the tip of her shadow, cast into the alley by a street lamp outside. She wasn't close enough to the mouth.

"I don't see any dog."

"He might be hiding. Let's just get closer and look."

But she held her ground. "I'll wait here where I can watch my station too. You see him, holler."

This isn't working, Ash thought. *Georgie's got to get her into the alley before he makes his move, or he'll be seen. And she's not coming anywhere near this alley with him.*

But this was the last one. They needed this one to get the rift open and the World Devourer through. If necessary, they'd just have to rush her, drag her in here, and hope it could all be done quickly and quietly enough to escape notice.

"Sorry you feel that way, lady," Georgie said, and Ash knew it was all about to go terribly wrong.

"What are you—get away from me!"

Ash and R. C. broke from their hiding places just in time to see Georgie lunge at the woman, without waiting for their assistance. And the military look of her clothing maybe wasn't just a costume after all, Ash thought, because she reacted to Georgie's advance by dropping into a fighting stance. When Georgie wouldn't back off, she released a snap kick that looked like it broke the young man's kneecap. He let out a shriek and hit the sidewalk. The woman followed up with two more quick kicks to his ribs, and he doubled up in pain.

Ash and R. C. ran toward her, but she spotted them before they were close, and took off running herself. She sprinted straight into the street, dodging a couple of passing cars, and screamed into the quiet night.

Angel was glad for any excuse to leave the party, and Tom Cribb's story was a good one. The demon had heard on the street that bodies were turning up all around the neighborhood with their throats slit. None of them had been identified yet, but it had only been a few minutes since they'd started being found. Chances were, it would be a police matter and not something along the lines that Angel usually concerned himself with. But it was the Solstice night, and a mass murderer loose on his own turf was troubling to Angel. He grabbed Wesley and Gunn and they went out into the streets to see what they could find.

And they hadn't gone two blocks when they saw a woman in a white uniform running toward them, screaming bloody murder at the top of her lungs, and two guys chasing her with what looked like knives in their hands.

"Angel!" Gunn shouted.

"I see 'em," Angel replied grimly, starting off.

"You take the men," Wesley called. "I'll see to the woman!"

Angel and Gunn dashed toward the woman, and past her, but as soon as they did, the two guys with the blades turned and ran off in the other direction. They had been well behind the woman to start with, so now they had a couple of blocks' head start on Angel and Gunn. *I could catch them,* he thought. *But maybe they're not the ones causing all the trouble tonight.* He let Gunn continue chasing the two of them and headed back to where Wesley was trying to calm the woman in white, and listening to her breathless tale.

"They . . . they just charged at me . . . out of nowhere," she said between panting. "I thought . . . they wanted my collection pail, maybe. But they came after me instead of going for it."

"Easy," Wesley said, his voice level and soothing. "They're gone now. Our friend will take care of them."

"I could have taken them," she said. She was catching her breath now, her words starting to come out faster. "If I'd known it was just two of them. But I didn't know how many were in the alley, or what they wanted with me."

"So you don't know who they were?" Angel asked her.

"No idea," she said. "There was a third one. I thought he was alone, a mugger or something. I took him down easy. But then when the others showed up, I thought running was a better idea."

"Yo, Angel!" Gunn shouted from down the block. Angel glanced back over his shoulder to see the dapper-looking young man hauling someone in their direction, one hand on the guy's collar. The man was disheveled, his face scraped and bloody.

"That the one you beat up?" Angel inquired.

"That's him," she confirmed. "I was working on the corner, ringing my bell for charity, right? This guy gave me some bogus story about wanting to go into the alley to look for his puppy. When I wouldn't go in with him, he jumped me."

Angel waited until Gunn reached them. The man he brought along, looking very much the worse for wear, had a defeated expression on his face. "I found this punk rolling around on the ground back there," Gunn explained. "He was callin' for those other two, but they didn't even give him a second glance."

"Looks like your friends deserted you," Angel said. "You want to tell us what this is all about, or do you want us to turn her loose on you again?"

The guy began to shudder. "No, keep her offa me, man! Keep her away, I'll tell you whatever!"

"Talk fast, then," Angel warned. "I've been smiling all night; I'm just about out of patience."

Gunn released the guy's collar and he put his hands up as if to ward off any blows that might be aimed his way. Angel looked past them, toward a distant corner several blocks away. If that had been the woman's station, she'd already been replaced. "Sure, no problem, man," the battered punk said. "I'll talk. Those guys shouldn't have blown me off, you know? I'm happy to talk. You know all those Santa Clauses you see on street corners . . ."

The circle of bells complete, the rift opened wider and wider. The World Devourer wriggled more tentacles through, dozens of them, and pressed at the sides of the crack in space, pushing it wide enough to force its massive body through. Its appetite was enormous now; it fairly salivated at the proximity of its next meal.

"She's not with you?" Angel asked, pointing down the street.

"No," the woman said. Her name was Rose, it turned out, and she was a veteran of the Gulf War and a black belt to boot. "No way I could have been replaced that fast."

"She's with us, then," the punk said. He had identified himself as Georgie, and described the basics of the operation.

"Is she the closest one, then?" Angel demanded. She was still several blocks away, and if Georgie was right, time was at a premium.

"No, I think there's a Santa right around the corner," Georgie said. "The one we started with. But it's not gonna help you now. It's too late. The bells are all in gear, and the rift is already open."

"We'll just see about that," Angel said. "I think we'll go have a chat with Santa."

The chasm that opened at the chime of bells was now almost indescribably vast. But the Devourer, the size of the many solar systems it had consumed, still had to squeeze its way through, masses of tentacles writhing before it like a thousand snakes. It could smell the planet now, practically hear the billions of hearts beating below, promising fuel and continued life. It pressed on.

• • •

"Hasn't Angel come back yet? And the others?" Fred's expression was one of concern—brow furrowed, lips pursed. "I was hoping they wouldn't have to miss much of the party."

"Wes and Gunn probably agree with you," Cordelia told her. *She doesn't know them well enough yet to understand how much Angel hates forced sociability,* she thought. "But Angel probably wouldn't mind not coming back until the last guest has gone home and all the dishes are done."

The Host tugged at the lapels of his bright red dinner jacket. "I think I'm with Fred on this one," he said. "I know Angel isn't a party machine, but I think he'd try to stay close to home tonight if he could. He knows how much this little soiree means to you, hostess with the mostest."

Cordelia shrugged. "Somehow I don't think Angel makes his decisions based on what he thinks I care about, Lorne. He's his own man."

"He is that," the green-faced demon agreed. "And part of being his own man is that he cares about you, little lady. Angel likes it when you're happy, and if it takes attending your party to do that, then he'd do what he could to make sure he was there."

"I think Lorne's right," Fred put in. "Angel wouldn't have been gone this long unless there was something important going on."

"Well, if Mr. Cribb is correct, mass murder," Lorne said. "Pretty important, by definition."

"I'm going outside," Fred said. "Just to see if they're coming or anything."

"I'll join you," Lorne offered. "I don't think going out alone is the best idea, you know, given the mass murder thing."

"That's a good idea," Cordelia said. "As much as I'd like to stay here, I think I'll tag along to make sure our guests don't catch any of the negative vibrations washing off the two of you." *Jeez,* she thought as the three of them made their way to the door. *How many ways can there be to spoil a party mood?*

Outside, the city was remarkably quiet. Only a few cars moved along its streets, and there was none of the usual dull background roar. Fred stood still, head cocked. "Listen," she said quietly.

"Kind of nice, isn't it?" Cordelia said.

"No, shh . . . do you hear the bells?"

Cordelia strained to listen more closely, and then she could make out a distant chiming, like many bells ringing in concert. *What about it, though?* she wondered. *Bells and the holidays kind of go together, don't they? Maybe it's reindeer.*

She noticed that Fred was paying rapt attention, but her lips were moving, almost as if she were speaking silently. Or counting.

"It's a mathematical formula," Fred announced.

"I've heard of word problems," Lorne said. "But bell problems? Fred, honey, have you been sipping from the eggnog on the right or the eggnog on the left? Because the right one is a little potent, if you know what I mean."

"It is, though," Fred insisted. "I think I understand what it's saying. And I don't think it's good."

Georgie may have been the son of the Grand High Wizard of whatever his dad's doomsday cult was called, but at least he had told the truth about the Santa Claus. He led them around the corner, and less than a block away, a charity Santa stood outside a movie theater ringing his bell and ho-ho-ho-ing into the night. He was kind of scrawny, for Santa Claus, Angel thought, and he didn't look all that jolly. He didn't even acknowledge the people who tossed money into his bucket, but seemed to be focusing on something else. All he did was laugh his laugh and ring his bell.

"It's the bells that do it," Georgie explained. "By now, they've opened the rift wide enough. The World Devourer is coming through. He'll eat this world whole, and in the next one those of us who brought him here will hold exalted stations."

"Hate to break it to you, dog," Gunn told him. "But this world gets eaten up, you get eaten too. All you'll be after that is waste matter, if you get my drift."

Angel ignored them and went straight to the Santa. A thin sheen of perspiration coated his face under the fake hair and beard, and his eyes were distant. "Hey, Santa," Angel said. "Stop ringing that bell a second."

Santa ignored him.

"I'm talking to you," Angel said, more forcefully.

Santa continued to ignore him.

"Put down the bell," Angel ordered.

"Can't."

People thought I was bad when I was Angelus, Angel thought. *And even then, I never did anything like this.*

He drew back his fist and, with everything he had, he slugged Santa Claus on the chin with a gigantic haymaker. Santa's head whipped back, his hat flew one way and his whiskers another, and he dropped to the ground, unconscious. His bell chimed as it rolled across the sidewalk, finally stopping up against Wesley's shoe.

"You know, I kind of enjoyed that," Angel said.

"Caroling time, cats and kittens," the Host shouted when they went back inside. "We're going to go outside and sing some old faithfuls. And we're going to sing them loud. Top of your voices loud, understand? I'm not concerned about pitch, as much as I hate to say that. I'm looking for volume."

Fred passed out pots and pans and spoons from the hotel's kitchen. "Noisemakers," she explained. "Everybody take something. This is going to be . . . well, it's going to be loud and disruptive."

"But . . . won't the neighbors complain?" Anne Steel asked.

"They might," Cordelia replied. "But they'll still be here to complain, which is better than the alternative, if Fred's right."

"I still wish Angel was here," Fred said as she passed out utensils.

"He's probably working on some other angle," Lorne assured her. "If you're right about this—"

"I am."

"—then I'm sure he's on it too."

"He'd better be, because this may not work."

When everybody was properly equipped, Lorne led them outside into the street in front of the hotel. People who didn't have pots or pans to bang on were positioned by cars, or light poles, or anything that would resonate and make a racket. "'Jingle Bells,'" Lorne called out. "Sing like your life depends on it."

The group started to sing. Lorne swept his hands into the air, urging them to sing louder, and louder still. The kitchenware came into play, and within minutes a horrible racket emanated from near the Hyperion Hotel—a cacophony that reached into the sky, that drowned out the faint chime of thirty bells, that broke the pattern Fred had identified in the bells' ringing. They sang for several minutes more, and while they had started because Lorne and Fred and Cordelia had seemed agitated and insisted on it, as the minutes passed and their voices and makeshift instruments blended, they began to sing for the sheer pleasure of it, with exuberance and enthusiasm, glad to be spending this holiday evening with friends and loved ones. Voices raised, spirits high, the congregated guests turned a thunderous din into a joyful noise.

In the deep reaches of space, the pattern of the bells was broken and the rift slammed shut. The World Devourer was most of the way through, but when the chasm healed itself, the Devourer could not move fast enough, and the closing gap cut the Beast in two. One section dropped back into the distant nether regions from which it came, while the other, lifeless now, fell into the sky and burst into spectacular flame as it passed into Earth's atmosphere.

"Man, what's that noise?" Gunn asked.

"It sounds as if it's coming from the hotel," Wesley replied. They had put the Santa's bell out of commission. Georgie insisted it was too late to make a difference, but they weren't willing to believe him. They were coming back toward the hotel, though, intending to start there and work around in the circle Georgie had described, taking out the rest of the phony bell ringers as they went. "It sounds like singing."

"In a way," Angel said. "Not in the Aretha Franklin sense, but maybe in the sense of drunken cats on a fence."

"It can't be," Georgie said, his face suddenly ashen. "It's not possible."

"What?" Gunn asked. Then he followed Georgie's gaze into the clear, starry night sky. The others did the same.

And, high above the earth, a light streaked across the velvet expanse, bright and pure, a tail flaming out behind it. They watched it for a moment, until its glow began to dim. "That's not the Star of Bethlehem," Angel said.

Gunn glanced at him. "No, you ain't that old. Are you?"

"I'm just guessing," Angel said.

"From the look on poor Georgie's face," Wesley speculated, "I'd say that's his World Devourer. Only it looks as if it's become a toasty morsel, now."

Gunn cocked a head toward the sound that issued from the hotel. "You know, that ain't soundin' half bad now."

Angel had to agree, almost in spite of himself. It would be nice to listen to some carols before he had to go out and join the throngs of last-minute shoppers. "I think you're right, Gunn. Let's go check it out." He smiled, glad to be here with two of his best friends, and glad that the world would still be here tomorrow and for all the tomorrows after that. "You know, maybe parties aren't that bad after all."

8 P.M.

I STILL BELIEVE

by Christopher Golden

Eyes wide and unblinking, Cordelia stared at Angel in abject horror. Then she sighed deeply, horror turning to frustration, and she stalked across the lobby of the former hotel where Angel Investigations based its operations to peer into the back room where Wesley kept his office. No activity back there—Wes had run out on an errand—nor up the stairs that led to Fred's room. Also no sign of Gunn.

For the moment, they were alone.

Thank God for small favors, she thought. Which was appropriate, because they never seemed to get any big ones.

Now she spun on Angel and shot him a withering glance before hurrying back across the lobby to where he stood gazing expectantly at her. He tried on that little boy smile of his that was meant to be disarmingly charming, with the mischievous sparkle in his Irish eyes. She had never had the heart to tell him that, champion for the benevolent powers of the universe or not, a smile like that on a vampire who had once been as vicious as they came was more unsettling than it was charming.

"Tell me you're kidding." Cordelia stared at him to make it clear that this was not a rhetorical statement, but a command.

"I could," Angel replied with a small shrug, "but that would be a lie."

"I . . . I don't believe you," she muttered, spinning on her heel to pace a few steps away, shaking her head as she tried to make sense of it. Then she frowned, hurried back, and punched him lightly on the arm. "What's the matter with you?"

His facial expression changed, apologetic now instead of disarming.

"Okay, just stop with the puppy dog look or I'll really have to hit you," she instructed. Her eyes rolled heavenward and she grumbled. "What were you thinking? I mean, it's four days away. Four. Days."

Angel scratched at the back of his head. "I know. But it isn't like we haven't been busy."

Cordelia was speechless a moment. Then she scanned the lobby again to make sure none of the others were around and she stepped in closer to him, having to look up to glare directly into his eyes.

"Christmas is four days away and you haven't gotten presents for any of us," she reminded him. "That's just . . . I don't even know what to say . . . it's just . . . I know you're not exactly Zen about the whole shopping experience, but if you wanted help you could have asked for it before now."

"That's not exactly true," Angel pointed out.

She narrowed her eyes. "What isn't?"

"Well, I already got *your* present."

Cordelia grinned, raising an eyebrow. "Really? So what'd you get me?"

It was Angel's turn to frown. "I can't tell you that. Christmas is only four days away. You can't wait four days?"

She hit him again.

"Hey!" he protested.

Cordelia wagged a finger at him. "Don't make me hurt you."

He shrugged. "I'm not telling you. But I do need your help. I've got your gift taken care of, and I've ordered something for Wesley that I have to pick up. But for Gunn and Fred . . . I thought maybe something leather for him, a long jacket. Maybe some perfume for Fred, something classy yet delicate, maybe floral, but then I figured—"

"Stop," she instructed, holding up a hand. "Just . . . just stop." Cordelia lowered her head and closed her eyes a moment, one hand going to her forehead.

"Cordy, are you all right?" Angel asked, grabbing her arm. "Is it a vision?"

Eyes still closed she shook her head. "Not a vision." Again she sighed as she finally looked up at him. "All right. Our motto at Angel Investigations *is* 'We Help the Helpless.' In this case, that'd be you. You cannot buy Gunn a long leather jacket because, number one," she raised a finger, "they're ridiculously expensive if you buy them off the rack and you don't have time to do it right, and number two," she raised a second finger, "he is not Shaft."

Angel seemed to be considering her words. "But, the perfume, that's okay?" he asked hopefully.

Once more she gazed up at the ceiling and the heavens beyond. "This is going to be a very long night." Then she strode to the counter that had once been the hotel's reception area, picked up her pocketbook and slung it over her shoulder.

Without waiting for Angel she marched toward the front door. "I may have a holiday party later, with that modeling agency? So we have to make this quick. Make up an excuse. Tell the others we're going out." She paused on the landing in front of the door and turned to give him one final stern glance. "And you owe me."

"I do," he agreed happily. "You're the . . . the Queen of shopping and all other . . . shoppers . . . must bow down before you."

Cordelia scowled. "Oh, give it a rest. I'll be in the car. And whatever you got me? It better be good."

She left him there to explain what errand was dragging the two of them away and went outside. There was a slight chill in the air now and she wished she had thought to grab a jacket. Cordelia knew a number of people who had grown up in climates where there were actually four seasons but she had lived in southern California her entire life. Christmastime wasn't about winter and wishes for snow in L.A.—that stuff was for old movies and TV specials. But as she strode down to the street in front of the hotel where Angel had left his car, amongst buildings with bright holiday lights and wreaths, she thought the cool breeze somehow appropriate.

Before she had even reached the car she heard him hurrying after her. Cordelia turned and waited for him at the convertible. When he reached the car he offered her a quick, grateful flash of a smile.

"Thanks again. I really appreciate it."

"So, what'd you get me?" she asked again.

Angel slipped behind the wheel and looked up at her. "Coming?"

Cordelia made a face but she climbed in beside him. Angel started the engine and pulled out and for several minutes he was busy navigating the streets of L.A. Cordelia was genuinely appalled that he had waited so late to do his Christmas shopping, but as she looked around at the multicolored lights of the city she had to confess to herself that she didn't really mind going out on this little jaunt with him. Once upon a time her family had been wealthy and she really had been the Queen of shopping. The mall had been her playground. But since her father had lost his money and she had come to L.A. to try to make it as an actress . . . well, there wasn't a lot of leisurely spending to be done on the salary Angel Investigations managed to pay her.

As he turned a corner, Angel gave her a sidelong glance. "You're too quiet. It's . . . sort of spooky."

"I'm cogitating on your predicament."

"Cogitating?"

"Yes," she replied, raising her chin defiantly. "Or don't you think I can cogitate?"

"Oh, no, absolutely. Feel free. So what's wrong with perfume for Fred?"

Cordelia stared at him. "You're not her boyfriend. Which pretty much guarantees you don't pay enough attention to buy her perfume. See, women are particular about scents. Unless you really understand what she likes, you have no business buying her anything she's supposed to splash or spray on her body."

They had found their way into some serious early evening traffic and now were gridlocked into a sandwich between a silver Lexus and a white van whose exhaust fumes made Cordelia wish Angel didn't drive a convertible. She wrinkled her nose and tried to breathe as little as possible, and through her mouth.

"So, what, a dress?" Angel asked, beginning to look worried now. "You can help me with that. Just tell me where to start. Hey, maybe I could get some nail polish to match the dress. Fred has nice hands, don't you think? Polish that sets off the dress would really bring out her hands."

The light changed ahead and they advanced all of three car lengths before being trapped once more. Cordelia leaned her head back on the seat and gazed up at the night sky.

"How can you call yourself an investigator when you're so completely not observant?" she asked.

"Look, here's an idea. What does Fred like? I mean, what does she like to do?"

Angel looked pensive a moment before he glanced at her. "She reads a lot. She writes. Does research. Sometimes on the computer but not all the time. She's pretty solitary, from all that cave time on Pylea."

Cordelia smiled. "Now you're thinking. Most of those things, the reading and researching and especially the writing, they're hard to do without a *surface* to do them on. And our girl's pretty solitary, but in her room, there isn't really a nice workspace for her, is there?"

The traffic had begun to move again and Angel edged in front of the noxious white van. The convertible just slipped through the light before it turned red again.

As he started to weave his way through traffic, Angel glanced at her again. "You want me to buy Fred a *desk* for Christmas? We have desks. I could bring one up to her if she wanted one. That doesn't make any sense."

"That depends on how you look at it. A solitary, quiet, brainy girl might really love a delicate, antique writing desk, something French I think."

Angel clicked on the left turn signal and as he rounded the corner he nodded slowly. "Y'know, that's really . . . an amazing idea. But don't you think that's a little expensive? You know the problem with antiques? Once upon a time they weren't. Antiques. They were new. And much, much less expensive."

Cordelia raised an eyebrow. "Uh-huh, and unless you have a time machine, Mr. Frugal, all those lovely old things are now antiques. Stop living in the past!"

"I'll just sidestep the irony of that statement from the woman who's suggesting the antique gift. Kind of surprises me, actually. I thought you'd relish the opportunity to shop for dresses. Still, it is the perfect gift for Fred."

Cordelia had been proud of herself for the idea. Now her mood faltered. "Wait, don't listen to me! A nice dress would be a perfectly good gift."

"No, no, the desk is perfect. I'll just have to find the right store."

"I'm my own worst enemy," Cordelia sighed. "Of course, it would have been torment anyway to walk around and drool over all the clothes I can't afford. And . . . messy. With the drool." She gave him her sweetest smile. "So . . . did you get *me* a dress?"

"It isn't Christmas yet."

Her eyes narrowed. "You didn't buy me perfume, did you?"

"No," Angel replied, eyes on the road. "I promise. Though I do like that vanilla-scented thing you wear sometimes. So, great idea for Fred. What about Gunn?"

Cordelia nodded slowly. "Yeah. He's difficult." Then she glanced around, realizing that she did not recognize the neighborhood they were in. It was lined with midlevel boutiques and an Epcot of world cuisine restaurants—she spotted Malaysian and Ethiopian and Brazilian on a single block—but she couldn't tell if the area was on the rise from trash to trendy, or had already crested the trendy peak and was in the midst of crashing back down. Neighborhoods in L.A. went through that cycle constantly.

"Where are we, anyway?" she asked.

"Remember I said I just had to pick up what I got for Wesley?" Angel pulled the convertible to a stop at the curb in front of a place called Cobwebs Antiquarian & Used Books. "Here we are."

"This is that place you're always talking about," Cordelia said as they stepped out of the car and started toward the shop. "Run by the Houdini guy."

Angel paused at the door. "His name's Elijah Carnegie. And don't mention Houdini. He hates the comparison."

"Why?" Cordelia sniffed. "Wasn't Houdini, like the greatest?"

"According to Elijah, Houdini was a poseur."

"So you got Wesley a book?" she asked. "That's original."

But Angel ignored the jibe, opening the door and stepping inside. A bell rang overhead as Cordelia followed him in. She wondered if Cobwebs was always open this late or if Angel's friend had kept the bookshop open just to accommodate a faithful customer who had a hard time shopping during the day.

Inside, Cordelia paused and glanced around appreciatively. Cobwebs was bigger inside than it looked from the street. The rear of the store was jammed tight with floor-to-ceiling shelves of used books. In the front the walls were lined with locked cabinets, with glass faces through which she could see hundreds of leather-bound volumes she assumed were "antiquarian," a word she doubted she had ever used in conversation. They were old and rare. Why fancy it up? On the other hand, she had heard Wesley use the word in casual conversation, so Angel had probably made the right choice for a gift.

Given all the old books Cordelia was surprised that the store did not have the musty odor that usually permeated such places. There was a strange, sort of unpleasant odor, but nothing that made her need to breathe through her mouth.

The store seemed empty. The checkout counter was on the wall to the right as they walked in, but no one stood behind it. Above the counter she noticed a trio of antique—or maybe antiquarian—theatrical posters advertising performances by Carnegie the Great. The garishly painted posters promised that the mysteries of the underworld would be revealed and that the audience would thrill to feats of mental and physical magick the likes of which had never been seen before. Upon one of the posters was the image of a man in a tuxedo and white gloves with a dove seated upon one shoulder. The magician was gesturing toward a lethal-looking guillotine.

"Elijah?" Angel called, his voice muffled as though the sound had been absorbed by the books.

Cordelia stood at the front counter and tapped her fingers impatiently. She had agreed to come along and help Angel, but that did not mean she wanted to hang out in some musty old bookstore waiting for one of his early twentieth-century running buddies to show up.

"Elijah?" Angel called again, and he began to walk deeper into the store.

"I'm here," came a strangled voice from the back.

Angel froze. Cordelia looked up anxiously. She did not like the sound of that voice. Her fears were substantiated a moment later when a white-haired, white-bearded old Santa Claus of a man stumbled out from a rear aisle. His beard was spattered with his own blood, from a cut on his forehead, and even in the gloomily lit store she could see the gravity in his eyes.

A long, muscular arm shot from the shadows of that aisle and snatched the back of the aged magician's shirt. Angel quickly glanced back at Cordelia; then he moved closer to his friend, and to whatever lurked in among the books.

"What's going on, Elijah?" Angel asked.

The old magician chuckled, despite the blood on his face and the malign intent of whatever it was that had hold of him. Cordelia liked him right away for that, and she silently urged Angel to save him.

"You wanted *The Book of Wu Ch'ang Kuei,*" Elijah reminded him. "I got it for you. Bought it from a dealer in Shanghai. But the dealer did not bother to mention that there were others who wanted it, and they weren't interested in paying."

Cordelia looked around for a weapon, anything solid she could use if it came to that. But this was a bookstore, and unless she wanted to hit someone with a hardcover copy of *War and Peace* or a cash register, she was out of luck. Her heart raced as she watched Angel crouch like a predator and begin to creep toward Elijah.

"Come out," Angel growled.

The sound of his voice alone was enough to tell her that his face had changed, and when he glanced at her again she saw that she was correct. His forehead was ridged and his entire face more feral, like an animal. In the dim light, his fangs gleamed and his eyes glowed yellow.

The wooden floor trembled under massive hooves as the thing came out from behind the shelf of books. The demon was humanoid, but towered at least two feet above Elijah, and its body was covered with brown hair that was like a horse's coat. It had the head of an ox, and it snorted dangerously as it glared at Angel, tugging the old magician even closer to itself with one huge hand that was clamped down on Elijah's shoulder.

"You are the one who desires *The Book of Wu Ch'ang Kuei*?" the demon asked, voice rumbling low in its chest, heavy with an accent Cordelia could not identify.

"Actually, it's a Christmas present for a friend. But, yes. I'm the one who *desired* it."

"It does not belong to you," the ox-headed demon noted, a warning in his tone.

Angel held up his palms in a placating gesture but his face was still that of the vampire. "Difference of opinion. I actually paid for the book in advance. So I'm going to have to insist that it does. And, did I mention Christmas present?"

The ox-headed demon snorted again, its fingers slipping around the aged magician's throat. "I am Niu T'ou, chief attendant of her highness Yen Lo, empress of Hell."

"And, hey, that's serious resume material," Cordelia noted. "Ever considered working in Hollywood?"

Niu T'ou ignored her. *"The Book of Wu Ch'ang Kuei* was stolen from her highness. I have been instructed to retrieve it, and to destroy whatever soul desired it."

Angel nodded toward Elijah. "I've already told you I'm the one who bought it, but I didn't steal it, and neither did Elijah there. So what do you want with him?"

"The book is in his possession but he will not tell me where it is," Niu T'ou sniffed, obviously distressed at the lack of cooperation.

"Well, why didn't you say so?" Angel said. He smiled and his face reverted to his human countenance, his eyes wide and guileless. "Look, you just pay me back what I paid for the book and you can take it. Elijah was just holding on to it for me."

The massive demon lowered its huge ox head and studied Angel with damp, stupid eyes. Cordelia did not know what her friend was playing at, but she had a feeling the manservant of the empress of Hell had not brought his Visa card.

"You taunt me," Niu T'ou said.

So maybe he's not as stupid as he looks, Cordelia thought.

"Actually you'll find I'm not much for the taunting," Angel replied. "Watch. A gesture of good faith." He focused on the old shopkeeper. "Elijah, is the book where you always keep your special orders?"

The magician nodded.

Angel moved to the counter, hoisted himself up, and slid across to drop behind it. He bent, reached underneath, and rifled around a moment. Then he stood up, brandishing a slim leather-bound volume. A rubber band held a store receipt tight against it.

"Here we go."

Niu T'ou's gaze locked onto the book like the eyes of a dog mesmerized by a ball in a game of fetch. The demon shoved Elijah to one side, and the old man crashed into a cart loaded with new purchases to be shelved, knocking it over in a tumble of books and limbs.

Angel leaped up onto the counter and walked along the top of it, casual, unconcerned. "So what do you say? Can we work something out?"

The demon's hooves scarred the wooden floor as it started across the shop toward Angel. "Yen Lo would not agree to pay for what is rightfully hers."

"Didn't think so," Angel sighed.

With a roar, the ox-headed demon charged toward the counter where Angel stood. The vampire's face changed, becoming hideous and feral again.

"Cordelia!" he snarled, and he flipped the book to her.

Her eyes went wide as she caught it, staring first at the book in her hands and then at the enormous, hirsute demon-beast that stopped short, caught off guard by Angel's action. The thing was fifteen feet away from her, no more. It faltered, hesitating.

Angel kicked it in the face.

Niu T'ou grunted deep in its chest as its head rocked back from the blow. As the demon turned to face him, its huge, powerful hands clenching, Angel shot his foot out again, his boot striking solidly beneath the demon's chin. Its jaws clacked together, and blood spattered the wood floor.

"That one looked like it hurt," Angel said.

The demon's eyes were clouded with rage as it lunged at him. Angel leaped up, reaching over his head to grab the top of a shelf behind the counter, and he dangled there as the huge, ox-headed demon brought its fists down and shattered the counter with a single blow. The cash register collapsed into the debris and popped open with a jangle of loose change.

Niu T'ou's hooves crunched bits of broken counter as it moved toward Angel. The demon cocked back its right arm and shot a sledgehammer blow toward Angel's midsection, but the vampire hauled himself up and out of the way, and Niu T'ou's fist tore a hole in the wall.

"Hey, handsome!" Cordelia shouted at the demon. "Remember this?"

It glanced up, fuming, and she raised the book and waved it in the air. Angel dropped, landed amid the debris, and fired a trio of rapid punches at the demon's midriff. Niu T'ou barely flinched. With a furious utterance like a loud bark it drove a piledriver fist into Angel's face.

The vampire crashed backward against the wall, hitting just beneath the hole Niu T'ou had made seconds before, and collapsed into the remains of the bookstore's checkout counter.

At the back of the shop, Elijah Carnegie regained his footing. His face and beard were still smeared with blood, and he shouted angrily at Angel, "Just give him the damned book!"

Angel scowled at him even as Niu T'ou grabbed him by his shirtfront and hauled him up off the ground. The demon cocked back its huge fist again.

"Maybe instead of criticizing, you could find me a weapon?" Angel growled at the aged magician.

Niu T'ou struck him in the face again but did not let go, and this time it was Angel who was spitting blood. The demon went to hit him once more and Angel brought both of his own hands up and jabbed, stiff-fingered, at Niu T'ou's throat. The ox-headed demon rasped in pain and dropped the vampire, staggering backward.

"I don't keep any weapons here," Elijah protested.

"Then, hello, maybe some magick!" Cordelia suggested. "Carnegie the Great! What's up with that?"

The old man paled and looked at her sorrowfully. "It's not that kind of magick, young lady."

But Cordelia wasn't listening to him anymore. The ox-headed demon had focused on her once again, and despite its bloody maw and the hand clamped over its throat where Angel had jabbed it, it started toward her. Panicked, Cordelia glanced around, trying to figure out where she could toss the book to keep the demon away. She took several steps backward, and then the thing roared and began to charge, hooves splitting the planks of the floor.

"Angel!" Cordelia shouted.

As if summoned, Angel rose up behind the demon. She could not at first see what he was up to, but then he raised the cash register over his head and lunged at Niu T'ou from behind, bringing the heavy metal register down on the demon's skull with a crack that echoed through the store.

Its eyes rolled up in its head, and it staggered two steps nearer to Cordelia before collapsing at her feet, its weight making the floor shake. She stared at it. She was tempted to poke it with her toe to be certain it was unconscious, but instead she stepped over it and walked to where Angel stood beside the ruins of the counter.

"You all right?" he asked, his face now human again.

"Oh, just peachy."

Elijah looked angry as he joined them. "Angel, why did you have to do it the hard way? You should just have given him the book."

Angel shrugged, a bit sheepish. "It's a Christmas present. I don't have time to figure out another gift."

The old man sighed. He lifted his hands, palms upward, and closed his eyes before whispering something beneath his breath. Cordelia felt an electric crackle inside the shop, like the static in the air before a thunderstorm, and with a shudder, as though reality convulsed around them, all the damage the fight had caused was repaired.

Cordelia stared at him. "Wait a second. I thought you said you couldn't do magick."

"Not the kind you mean. And it isn't that I can't. I simply don't," Elijah informed her. "A very long time ago I vowed to perform only positive magick."

"Yeah," Angel said, rubbing at his jaw where the demon had struck him. "And as much as I respect your pacifism, I wonder if maybe you could make an exception now and then."

The old magician gave him a grim stare. "Should you make exceptions as well, then? Drink human blood, take a human life, once in a while when it seems convenient?"

Angel's expression was grave. "Point taken."

"Okay, fine," Cordelia said, "but do you hire out? 'Cause sometimes my apartment gets to be just as much a shambles as this place was, and some Mr. Clean magick would come in pretty handy."

The shopkeeper smiled and stepped toward her with his hand out. "We haven't been properly introduced. Elijah Carnegie, at your service."

"Cordelia Chase," she replied as she shook his hand. "Very nice to meet you. Angel says nice things about you."

"And you, my dear," Elijah replied. "So I suggest we both presume he's telling the truth."

Cordelia smiled warmly. Now that the chaos had settled, she could not help but like the old man. "Angel says you've known one another a long time."

"Longer than long," Elijah replied, a mischievous glint in his eye as he glanced toward Angel. "I once sawed him in half onstage."

"You . . . I'm sorry?" Cordelia asked incredulously.

Angel smiled. "Long story," he said. "And we have other errands to do before the stores close. Elijah, we're square on this, right?" he asked, holding up the book.

"The shipping was more than I expected, but I quoted you what I quoted you, so I'll just have to overcharge you on something else later to make up for it," the old man said, his tone perfectly serious.

"All right, then," Angel replied. He glanced at Cordelia and then back at the shopkeeper. "Oh, listen, I want to get something else for another friend. Antique writing desk, maybe French. Something delicate. You know all the shops that deal in collectibles and antiques. Where would you go for something like that?"

A loud snort startled them all. Cordelia let out a tiny cry of alarm and spun, ready to flee from Niu T'ou, but the demon still lay unconscious on the floor, chest rising and falling. Its breathing deepened, and it began to snore.

"Are you going to be okay if we just leave him here?" Cordelia asked.

"I think so," Elijah said. "He doesn't want me. He wants the book. That's what Yen Lo sent him for. I'll tell him it was destroyed in the fight, but if he doesn't believe me, you should keep an eye out for him. He's not too bright, but he might be able to track you."

"I'll deal with him then," Angel said. "No time now. Shopping to do."

"Hang on," Elijah said. He went to the phone behind the newly restored counter and quickly dialed a number.

"Hello, David? It's Elijah Carnegie at Cobwebs. Yes, I just wanted to know what time you'll be closing. I have a customer I'm sending over to you."

A moment later he hung up and turned his attention to them again. "Traeger's Fine Antiques in Santa Monica, just up from the pier. He closes in half an hour. You'd better get going."

"I owe you," Angel told him.

"You always do," Elijah replied.

Cordelia and Angel stepped over the snoring demon, but at the door she paused and looked up at him. "So you've got Wesley and Fred covered—assuming this Traeger's has the kind of thing you're looking for—and we all know you've gotten me something spectacular, but what about Gunn? You went with the superoriginal arcane demon text for Wesley—don't tell me you want to get Gunn an antique battle-ax or something, because then I would have to hit *you* with the cash register."

Angel glanced at the ground, brows knitting together. "Gunn loves classic weaponry."

"Boring!" Cordelia exclaimed. "Don't be so predictable. It's like me buying my father a tie for his birthday five years running. Like he needed more ties?"

"You have a better idea?" Angel asked.

Cordelia shot him a withering glance. "That *is* why you asked me to come with you, isn't it? Because of me having better gift ideas than you?"

"True."

"Gunn loves movies. Lately he's been really getting into old movies, classic film noir stuff, a lot of Hitchcock.

I bought him a bunch of DVDs. Not just Hitchcock, but Humphrey Bogart movies too, and other film noir with some of the best leading ladies, like Lauren Bacall and Grace McCandless."

Angel stared at her. "But that's what *you* bought him. I can't do the same thing."

Cordelia shook her head and sighed, then turned to look at Elijah, who stood behind the counter watching them like a spectator at a tennis match.

"Elijah, do you know anyplace in L.A. that sells classic film posters? Not reprints, but the original lobby posters?" she asked.

The old man smiled. "That's easy. Tinseltown Galleries on South Sepulveda. They're on your way if you're going to Traeger's."

"You really are a magician," Cordelia told him. Then she turned to Angel. "See? It's all over but the pain of newly incurred credit card debt. Can we go now? Before something else tries to kill us?"

He gave her a quizzical look. "And I thought you'd enjoy the Christmas shopping."

Cordelia raised an eyebrow. "Don't push your luck."

They said their good-byes to Elijah and left the shop. The old magician turned the sign in the window around to CLOSED as soon as the door was shut behind them.

Traffic was mercifully light as they drove out to South Sepulveda. Cordelia noticed that Angel winced several times as he turned the wheel to maneuver the convertible, but he did not seem to have been hurt badly and soon enough the wincing stopped. They rode together in silence for a time. Despite the excitement at Cobwebs, or perhaps because of it, Cordelia was glad to have a few minutes to just breathe and enjoy the night air and the stars above.

She was also grateful that it was Angel behind the wheel. They'd known one another a long time now—though not by his standards—and it had reached the point where they didn't feel the need to talk, to entertain each other. With someone else, the silence in the car would have been awkward. With Angel, it was just not.

As they stopped at a red light, he glanced at her, a smirk on his face. "Well, that didn't go too badly."

Cordelia smiled. "Here's hoping your Christmas present to Wesley isn't going to get him killed by the minions of the empress of Hell. Kinda cocky of that Len Yo, or whatever her name is, though. I mean, 'empress of Hell,' who is she kidding with that? With all the demon dimensions out there, not to mention all the would-be monarchs and deities . . ." she rolled her eyes. "Give me a break. Anybody can be other-dimensional royalty. Look at me."

"Princess of Pylea," Angel noted, nodding sagely. "Maybe you should've brought that up. Niu T'ou might've given you diplomatic immunity to being thrashed."

"And started a war between this Wen Ho and Pylea? I don't think so."

Angel shrugged. "What's the use of being a monarch—even an abdicated one—if you can't pull rank once in a while?"

"You've got a point," she said.

They found Tinseltown Galleries without much difficulty. It was tucked into a strip mall between an upscale health and nutrition shop and a Spudnuts, where they served sinfully good doughnuts made from potato. An unlikely recipe for sugary goodness, but Cordelia considered them one of the most perilous temptations around. It was with great relief—and some small disappointment—that she realized Spudnuts was closed for the night.

Cordelia had expected the dark, musty sort of place that was common in L.A., the sort of store where they sold still photographs and posters and old scripts and things. Tinseltown Galleries was far more sophisticated than that: brightly lit, with framed posters on display all over the walls and others on stands and easels set up around the showroom floor. It really was a gallery, and though most of the posters were for classic films, there were others for more recent films that must have simply been rare or misprints. She saw one for *Revenge of the Jedi,* which she remembered Xander once telling her had been the title of *Return of the Jedi* before they realized that Jedi were too honorable to get revenge. She didn't even want to know how much they were charging for that one.

"Wow," Angel said.

Behind the counter, a slender blond woman with trendy little glasses smiled sweetly at him. She looked like a stripper disguised as a librarian, but Cordelia figured she was probably very good for business.

"Thank you," the woman said. "We get that a lot."

"I'll bet you do," Angel replied, gazing around at the walls.

Cordelia spotted posters for *Casablanca*, *Duck Soup*, *Blade Runner*, *North by Northwest*, and *Breakfast at Tiffany's.* Somehow she had a feeling that Angel was not going to be able to get out of this place without spending an awful lot of money.

"Angel—," she began.

But he was not listening. He wasn't even looking at the stripper-librarian behind the counter. His attention was on the posters, and he strolled through the gallery, smiling as he examined each of them. It struck her then that no matter how old any of these movies was, Angel was older. In the period where most of them had been made and released, he had been a tortured soul wandering the world, trying to make sense of his survival and the guilt that lay so heavy on his heart. It occurred to her that some of these movies probably meant a great deal to him.

He had paused beneath one particular poster. Cordelia walked over to him and studied it. *Breezy* had starred William Holden and Kay Lenz. Even though she was a student of cinema and had always wanted to be an actress, Cordelia had never heard of it.

"This was a good little movie," Angel muttered.

"You must be thinking of something else," the woman behind the counter said.

Angel turned to her. "I don't think so."

She smiled condescendingly and Cordelia wanted to slap her.

"*Breezy* was directed by Clint Eastwood. It hasn't seen the light of day since its original release. The rumor is that Eastwood bought up the rights because he wasn't happy with the film, and it's in a vault at his production company. So you see, you aren't nearly old enough to have seen it."

Angel glanced at Cordelia, amusement sparkling in his eyes. "Right. Of course. Must have been something else." Then he strode back to the woman, all business. "Listen, I'm hoping you can help me. I'm looking for a Christmas gift for a friend, but most of these are a little out of my range. He's a big Humphrey Bogart fan, likes the things from that era. Any suggestions?"

The woman put her sales smile back on. "Well, I'm afraid that anything with Bogart is going to be comparably priced with the things you've looked at on the walls. Are there other actors from that period your friend enjoys?"

"The classics," Angel said. "I'm guessing Cary Grant, Lauren Bacall—"

"Grace McCandless," Cordelia interrupted.

The woman nodded in understanding. "Oh, yes, perfect. Grace McCandless was in a lot of those film noir pictures. She never quite made the A-list, but nearly everyone who was anyone acted with her in something."

Cordelia smiled, revising her opinion of the woman. Anyone who called movies *pictures* couldn't be all that bad. "She was one of the most underrated actresses of her era," she told the woman.

"Absolutely elegant," the gallery attendant replied. "You know, I think I have the perfect thing." She came out from behind the counter and strode purposefully around the shop, examining the easels and displays with a studious frown. After a few minutes she shook her head and asked them to wait a moment while she went in the back. Barely another minute had passed before she returned with a tall, framed movie poster.

"Manhattan After Dark," the woman said, though the title was clearly legible. "Not hugely successful, but a nice poster, and it had James Cagney and Grace McCandless. Can't go wrong, even if he hasn't seen the movie. It's also about an eighth the price of any of the Bogart posters."

Cordelia gazed at the poster, a smile spreading across her face. "Well, if Gunn doesn't want it, I'll take it."

Angel glanced at her, then back to the woman. "I guess that's a yes." Then, as the gallery attendant brought the framed poster around behind the counter to wrap it up, he glanced at Cordelia. "If he doesn't like it, we'll talk."

"Deal."

There was a strange sort of smile on his face that Cordelia did not think she had ever seen before.

"Why are you looking at me like that?" she asked, uncomfortable. "Is there something on my face?"

"Like what?" Angel asked, turning away.

Soon enough they were back in the car and Angel drove west on South Sepulveda. It took only a few minutes to reach the Santa Monica pier, and several more to find Traeger's Antiques. To Cordelia it looked like a hundred other shops she had seen, but there was no denying the quality of the items behind the plate-glass windows. Some places calling themselves antique stores sold just about any piece of junk somebody else wanted to get rid of. There were three or four items in the front window of Traeger's that she would have liked to have for her own apartment, including a beautiful lamp that she prayed would be so ridiculously expensive that it would not even be within range so she would not be tempted to spend the money.

They were inside Traeger's for all of five minutes. Cordelia glanced around and immediately saw exactly the sort of thing she'd had in mind for Fred. She took a great deal of pleasure in Angel's purchase of the antique because she knew how much Fred would enjoy it, and because it wasn't her money.

The lamp was nearly eight hundred dollars. "It's a lamp," she said, when Mr. Traeger told her.

"Yes," the old man had agreed with a gentle smile. "A very valuable lamp."

Angel could have bought two antique writing tables for the price of that lamp, and still had plenty left over for Spudnuts. Cordelia had sighed and handed Traeger a business card so that he could deliver the writing table, and they had left.

Outside the shop he paused and looked at her. "Cordelia, I just wanted to say . . . thanks again for your help. I really couldn't have done this without your input."

"True," she agreed.

But he wasn't listening. A frown creased Angel's forehead and lifted his chin as though he had smelled something strange.

"Hang on," he said, then strode around behind the car.

Cordelia followed him, but Angel asked her to move over beside him while he opened the trunk. She wondered if he had something in there for her that he did not want her to see and she peeked from beside the trunk as he reached beneath the carefully packaged poster and the bag that held Wesley's book.

When he pulled a long sword from beneath the framed poster, her eyes widened.

"Angel, what—"

But then a long shadow blotted out some of the light from the streetlamp above—a shadow with the head of an ox.

"You have incurred the wrath of Yen Lo," a low voice rumbled.

Angel slammed the trunk and Cordelia stared over the car at Niu T'ou. The demon stood on the sidewalk, hunched over, ox-head hanging low as though he were about to charge. Apparently, whatever lies Elijah Carnegie had told him, Niu T'ou had not believed them.

"Yen Lo," Cordelia remembered. "That was it!"

"What are you, the library police?" Angel asked.

With a roar, the demon lunged at him. Angel spun out of the way and Niu T'ou collided with the back of the convertible, caving in the rear side panel with a crunch of metal. Angel shot an elbow at the back of the demon's head and Niu T'ou was driven down onto its belly on the trunk.

Angel swung the sword down, its keen blade gleaming under the streetlight, and hacked through the demon's neck with a splintering of bone. Niu T'ou's ox head fell off the back of the car, thunked off the bumper, and hit the pavement with a wet *thud.*

For a long moment, Angel stared down at it. At last he wiped the sword off on the demon's pelt, then opened the trunk again and returned the blade to its hiding place there.

"Sorry," Cordelia told the demon's corpse. "But he bought the book as a gift."

They got into the car and pulled away, leaving what remained of Niu T'ou for somebody else to explain. Her heart was beating rapidly as Angel drove back toward the office. No matter how many times she had dealt with the horrors the world had to offer, it still got her blood pumping.

Several minutes went by and then they were pulling into a parking lot. Cordelia glanced up in surprise, wondering how they could have gotten back so fast, thinking perhaps she had fallen asleep for a few minutes and been unaware of it.

But the apartment building that loomed up ahead of them was unfamiliar to her.

"Where are we?" she asked.

Angel's face was expressionless. "Just one last errand. I have to pick something up. Want to come in?"

She looked around. It wasn't the worst neighborhood, but it was quiet, and she thought it might be best not to sit in the convertible by herself.

"Why not?" she said as she climbed out.

The building was nicer on the inside than out. It had a doorman and a reception area where Angel had to go and speak to someone behind the counter before they would be allowed upstairs. It wasn't exactly ritzy, but the apartment building was certainly classy.

They rode the elevator to the seventh floor. When the doors opened Cordelia was impressed by the décor. There were attractive paintings and potted plants all along the corridor, and the woodwork was beautiful. She followed Angel down the hall to 18J, where he knocked.

It took several moments, but eventually a voice inside told them to wait just a minute.

"Angel?" the voice asked from within. A grandmotherly voice, the voice of an old woman.

Cordelia raised an eyebrow and glanced at him curiously, but Angel ignored her.

"It's me," he replied.

There came the sound of the lock being drawn back, and then the door opened. The old woman who stood just over the threshold was tall and had excellent, almost regal posture despite her age. The dress she wore was simple and attractive, and though her skin was wrinkled and her shoulder-length hair pure white, she seemed quite comfortable with herself. There was a sparkle in her eye as she gazed at Angel.

"This is your friend?" the old woman asked, glancing at Cordelia.

"Yes," Angel replied, also turning to her. "Cordelia Chase, I want to introduce you to an old friend."

The woman laughed throatily, her hand fluttering elegantly up to touch her hair. "A very old friend," she said. And then she put out her hand. "Pleased to meet you, Miss Chase. I'm Grace McCandless."

Cordelia felt herself go numb. She stared at the woman, speechless, and then her gaze shot toward Angel before returning to the well-lined face of one of the greatest actresses of a bygone age.

"But, how . . . I don't . . ." She turned to Angel again. "You know Grace McCandless!"

But it was the old woman who replied. "He was kind to me once, a very long time ago. I've never forgotten." For a moment her eyes went to Angel and lingered upon his face a moment, a wistful smile appearing upon her lips as she remembered events that must have happened many decades before Cordelia was even born.

Then Grace McCandless turned her attention back to Cordelia. "Angel tells me that you're an actress, Miss Chase, and that you've been growing discouraged of late. If you'd like, I'd be pleased if you'd come in and join me for a cup of tea, and we can chat for a little while."

Cordelia stared at her again and then, at last, she felt herself able to respond. "I'd love that, Ms. McCandless. You have no idea."

The elderly actress stepped back from the door, and Cordelia walked into her apartment. She paused once she was inside, though, and looked back at Angel. He had remained in the hallway.

"You had this planned all along? Before the thing with the poster?"

Angel only shrugged.

"You're not coming in?" Cordelia asked.

"I want to get back. Grace and I caught up earlier," he explained. "Take a taxi home when you're through. On me." Angel glanced past her at Grace. "You two have fun, okay?"

Then he smiled at Cordelia one final time.

"Merry Christmas."

9 P.M.

IT CAN HAPPEN TO YOU

by Scott and Denise Ciencin

The darkness was listening to him.

A crazy thought, Wesley knew, but he felt it strong and clear as he drifted down a lonely street near the hotel, a cool wind caressing him, the pale moon and twinkling stars above battling to penetrate the thick layer of smog that smothered Los Angeles. Head down, hands in his pockets, he shied away from yet another amber pool of light hammering at him from a well-meaning streetlamp and hugged the shadows near an unlit pawn shop window.

Something glittered between the rusted bars that protected the storefront, seducing Wesley's gaze, arresting his desire to take another step toward the hotel. Drawing closer to the display window, he saw a beguiling statuette rising majestically from the bric-a-brac. According to the little tag that drooped over the engraving on the figurine's base, obscuring any other details, it was an Academy Award from the 1930s.

Fitting, Wesley thought bitterly. Tarnished Hollywood gold, a symbol of dreams and victories that meant so much one day, and virtually nothing the next. Yes, indeed, the darkness *was* listening to him. It heard the gale-force winds of conflict blasting through his mind, it knew the decision he had to make and how little time he had to do so, and it was offering comfort the only way it knew how: by directing him to this site, proudly proclaiming the pointlessness of it all.

Why feel down, why fret? the darkness asked. *Especially when it all amounts to nothing in the end . . .*

A woman's scream shattered the night. Wesley spun in the direction of the cry and saw movement in a dark alley across the street. The piercing scream came again, but this time Wesley was in motion, flying in front of an oncoming car, ignoring the squeal of brakes and the angry honking, soaring up the sidewalk, darting into the darkness.

The shadows swallowed him whole and the screaming stopped. A single step forward and Wesley heard a crunch of glass beneath his shoe. He froze. Looking up, he dimly made out the remains of a shattered light moored near the roof of the building to his right.

Damn, he thought, staring ahead into the alley, the street at his back, picturing a pair of thieves—or something *worse*—crouched in the alley's darkness, about to make their move against the foolhardy do-gooder they had lured to the "rescue." Two beams of blinding light suddenly tore through the darkness, shredding the shadows, burning twin suns into Wesley's brain. A car's headlights. And beyond the glare, the dim forms of a big car and two figures registered despite the sea of stars stabbing at Wesley's field of vision.

Wesley turned to run—and froze at the sight of two college-age guys in bulky dark coats racing toward him from the street. They were as tall as Wesley and built like linebackers. What had he been cornered by? Demons? Vampires?

Angel Investigations had plenty of enemies . . .

Wesley looked for doors, low-hanging fire escape ladders, any possible means of escape, but there was no way out. He reached into the inner lining of his long wool coat, his fingers sliding past the chill wood of the stake he carried to the icy steel of his mystically charged dagger. The new pair stopped just as his fingers closed on the weapon's hilt, their features hard, their stares penetrating. The slightly bigger of the two, a red-haired guy with acne scars lining his cheeks, circled around Wesley and nodded to the car. "Nice ride."

Wesley almost choked on the acrid odor of sweat and grime as the man walked past him. He stepped back and cautiously glanced at the sleek red convertible whose lights drenched the alley, something out of the thirties, a vintage Rolls-Royce perhaps.

The other one, a dark-haired guy with swarthy skin, said, "Keys right in it. Be pretty tempting to take it out for a test drive, 'cept for one thing."

The redhead fixed his narrow gaze on Wesley. "What'd you do with the girl?"

Wesley let his hand drift away from the weapon.

"What did I . . . ?" he asked, momentarily confused. Then he understood. "No, I heard the screams just like you."

"Nice try," the redhead growled, edging closer to Wesley, his huge blunt hands balling into fists.

"Yeah, mess him up," his pal urged with a nasty little laugh. "Then he'll talk!"

Wesley didn't have time for this. The woman who had screamed may have been in true danger after all, and whatever made her scream was probably still in the alley with them. He had seen two figures near the car and there may have been more. "Listen, we may all be in trouble here. Now stand back or I'll be forced to take matters in hand. Trust me, that's something you *don't* want."

The college guys laughed so loud they almost drowned out the surprising sound of a high, wilting laugh, and the *click-clack* of high heels on concrete. Looking beyond the two flatheads who had accosted him, Wesley saw the silhouette of a woman sashaying toward them, easing out of the direct path of the car's headlights. Wesley gasped as the light washed over her form. She was young, beautiful—and dressed for a costume ball. Her shimmering blue-white gown was gossamer, almost *sheer*, and its plunging neckline left little to the imagination. The brilliant light caressed the short curly ringlets that were set in an old Hollywood-style bob wreathing her delicate heart-shaped face, and sparkled off the champagne glass she held in her bejeweled hand.

Wesley jumped as she threw her head back and shrieked bloody murder. The redhead and his bud spun, looking up and down the alley.

"There it is again," Red snarled.

His pal shoved Wesley toward the wall. "Where is she? In the trunk or something, you psycho?"

Wesley's heart hammered as he brushed off his coat and stared at the woman who was clearly in no danger of anything except getting a sore throat. What was going on here?

"She's . . . she's right there!" Wesley stammered, nodding at her.

The redhead stole a look in the direction of the woman, then whipped around and shook his head. "That's it. If you're not gonna share . . ."

Wesley's lips curled up in disgust as he stared into the hard eyes of the men before him. He thought they'd been acting out of chivalry and now saw that he couldn't have been more mistaken. Yet . . . why did they act as if the woman wasn't standing right there?

"You're dead," the redhead hissed as he attacked. Wesley ducked the man's clumsy swing and smiled as he heard the crunch of a fist connecting with brick. The dark-haired guy rushed him as his buddy howled in pain and Wesley leaped to one side, easily avoiding the brute, who slammed headlong into the wall with a grunt of surprise. Red was on him again, roaring like a mad beast. Wesley slid away from the wall, giving himself plenty of room to work as he brought the man down with a quick combination of jabs and uppercuts, then laid out his buddy with a swift high kick to the side of his skull. Then he turned to the woman, wondering where the other figure he had spied was hiding.

"Madam, would you care to explain yourself?" Wesley asked as politely as he could through gritted teeth. He was breathing hard; little white puffs of breath exploded into the air before him because of the suddenly freezing temperature. A moment ago, it had felt quite comfortable outside.

Then again, a moment ago, the woman had not been so close; she should have been freezing in her skimpy dress, yet she didn't seem at all affected by the cold. Had she somehow brought the chill with her? Wesley had seen stranger things. But if that were so, what did it mean?

"Would I care to explain myself? No, not especially," she said. "I prefer to let my actions speak for themselves, confusing as that may be for others. More fun, you see, for me."

The woman's smiling companion finally appeared, strolling up beside her, a glass in one hand, and a bottle in the other. His rugged good looks, complete with dimpled square jaw, slicked-back hair, double-breasted suit with wide lapels, checked tie, and swank vest made him look like he also might have stepped out of a red-carpet gala of the thirties. He crouched, setting his glass and the bottle on the ground.

"Sweetheart," the woman said, her gaze fixed on Wes. "It seems that this one isn't like the others. He can—"

"One moment." The man rose, then, holding his hands before him, he slapped them together with a violent *crack*. "Think you can cheat on me and get away with it?" he threatened in a brutish growl that was at odds with his dandy appearance and the wink he delivered to his companion. "I'll kill ya! That's right, kill ya I say!"

The woman just stared at him.

"You missed your cue, dear," he said, raising one eyebrow and frowning slightly. "You were supposed to moan with the slap, like I'd struck you."

She sighed. "P. J., perhaps you haven't noticed, but—"

"There are no *buts* when it comes to our sacred calling," P. J. said.

The woman sipped again, then set her drink down. One hand on her chest, the other on her forehead in an exaggerated gesture of distress, she rolled her eyes and screamed, "No, *no*! Please, someone—help me!"

"I take it that would be my cue to look around foolishly and fall into some bit of mischief you have planned," Wesley said, crossing his arms over his chest. He saw their chests rise and fall, but no breath left their bodies . . . apparently for good reason.

P. J. reeled. "Why . . . he can see us!"

"In my line of business, seeing dead people isn't all that uncommon," Wesley said. "Unfortunately."

The ghosts exchanged knowing smiles.

"Might as well make the most of it, then," P. J. said. "Oh, and look out for that—"

Wesley heard a slight shuffle behind him and a harsh

whistle of wind near his ear. He launched himself forward, taking only a glancing blow across the back of his shoulder from the two-by-four one of the college guys had aimed at his head. Caught off-balance, Wesley stumbled and *tripped* over the bottle P. J. had set down—just before sprawling into and through the ghosts!

Yet—how could the bottle be corporeal? Wouldn't the thugs have seen it, as they did the car? Could the ghosts change things from an immaterial to a material state at will? It seemed they could, and that was so much the worse for Wesley. He crashed into the classic car's grill and fell over the high wide fender as the college guys descended on him.

P. J. shook his head. "I suppose I really must do something."

He gestured—and the wall suddenly came to life, throbbing and twisting until it formed a huge claw that closed over the redhead's thick arms and hauled him off Wesley, lifting him several feet into the air. The redhead howled in terror as it tossed him a dozen feet, bouncing him off the lid of a garbage bin and sending him rolling to a properly undignified sprawl near the sidewalk.

"A bit strenuous, that, hard on the old ectoplasm, don't you know," P. J. said. "Kat, my dear, would you . . ."

She raised her hands. "Delighted."

The second guy gasped as round garbage can lids, bits of pipe, and shards of wood flew at him from every direction, as if he were a living magnet. He backed

Wesley from rocketing through the windshield onto the street ahead.

"Sorry, old chap," P. J. said, pointing at the light. "It was red and all."

Wes glanced at the rearview mirror and saw headlights coming up behind them and to their left. "Switch, switch, switch!"

Kat giggled as he passed right through her, sliding toward the driver's seat. "Whoa, and we barely knew each other!"

"None of that with me," P. J. said, vanishing as Wesley eased behind the wheel and reappearing next to the woman. "Now what was that all about?"

Wesley shook his head. "If I'm indeed the only one who can see you two, then it would appear to any onlookers that this was a driverless car zipping about!"

"Yes, that's always a good one!" P. J. said. "Been doing that for decades."

Kat smiled indulgently. "The classics never go out of style, not like *you*, sweetheart."

"I'm P. J., and this adorable but very naughty little minx is my eternal burden, Kat."

"Charmed," she said.

"She just couldn't grasp the business about till death do we part."

"Grasp it?" she snorted. "I grasped it until it was ready to choke."

"Not the only one," he muttered.

"A single lifetime simply wasn't nearly enough to properly torture a rake like you."

Wesley heard laughter from the car in the next lane. Three very cute women in a black Mustang were checking out the car—and its driver. A bubble-gum chewing brunette in a white stretch top set her chin on her hands as she caught Wesley's gaze and said, "Hey, handsome, great car!"

Raising his chin, Wesley ordered himself not to blush. "Um—thanks."

The bubble-gum chewer kept grinning. Wesley tried to think of something else to say, but nothing came to mind. Besides, he wasn't exactly at liberty to flirt. These mad spirits had to be corralled somehow before they caused any more mischief—and there was the decision weighing on him prompted by the letter in his breast pocket.

"She likes you," Kat said, tickling the side of Wesley's stubble-ridden face.

He swatted her hand away and rubbed his itchy face against his shoulder. "None of that, now."

"Life's short," P. J. said. "Believe me, I know. Don't let an opportunity go by!"

The brunette in the next car blew a bubble. "You listening to a book on tape? Is it something sexy? Your accent sure is and so's the car. I love convertibles. . . ."

Come on, he thought, glancing up at the light. *Change, change . . .*

"Why don't you come on over and we can let your top down?" a decidedly British-sounding voice called from beside Wesley.

Wesley nearly choked. It was P. J. imitating him! He knew from the unearthly screams and dramatic recitations heard by all in the alley that the ghosts could be heard by others—if they so desired—but not seen. Aghast, he whipped his head to the left and spat out, "Not me, wasn't me, I didn't say that."

The brunette was still smiling. "That's too bad."

The light changed and the Mustang sped off, leaving Wesley pale and confused. A car horn blared and he got back in gear, guiding the car down Hollywood Boulevard. They passed a handful of Hollywood landmarks and the ghosts seemed entranced by the brilliant facades of the Pig'n Whistle, the Guinness World of Records museum, and the Academy Awards theater. The glaring lights, screeching sounds, and dank, disgusting smells of Los Angeles didn't bother them one bit. But the jarringly brutal distractions made coming to *any* decision difficult, and tonight, Wesley had less than an hour to solve an impossible dilemma.

"All right now, we'll have to figure out what to do about the two of you," Wesley said, doing his best to sound in charge.

Kat's laugh filled the night. "The way you just let that one slip through your fingers? I think we need to think of something to do with *you*."

"I'm sensing a project coming on," P. J. said.

"Goody!"

Wesley yanked at the wheel, cutting across two lanes of traffic and jamming into a rare parking spot a few blocks down from Mann's Chinese Theatre. The theater looked packed, even at a distance; the street was choked with police cars, news crews, and spectators. Some event or another must have been going on . . . not that such frivolities concerned him right now. He sat fuming for several long seconds, then, "That's it. You two snatched me off the street—"

"It was an alley, dear boy," P. J. said. "God is in the details!"

"The point is, you two are not my problem. I have enough to deal with on my own without worrying about the pair of you."

"Want to talk about it, sweetie?" Kat asked, batting her eyes. "We're terrific listeners."

"Absolutely not." Wesley sniffed . . . and sniffed again. Kat swayed against Wesley, the heady scent of her perfume making his heart race and his thoughts suddenly scatter. It was strong and fresh, warm and flowery.

"Do you like that scent?" Kat asked, holding up a little blue bottle shaped like a tiny skyscraper. "It's Je Reviens, 1932. I love it. Jasmine, jonquil, ylang-ylang . . ."

"Don't forget narcissus," P. J. said brightly. "It wouldn't be like you otherwise."

"It's his favorite, too," she whispered, slipping the bottle into her odd little handbag. It was blue, rose, white, and green, with a silver-plated compact attached.

"Ah. Well . . ."

"Care to indulge yourself in the spirits?" she asked huskily, her gaze traveling the length, width, and height of Wesley's apparently impressive and clearly appreciated form.

Wesley didn't know if he should feel flattered—or appalled. *This ghost is getting fresh with me!*

Raising an eyebrow, she purred, "Seriously . . . when's the last time you had any?"

"Um, well, I—," he stammered.

P. J. burst into hysterical laughter, spilling his drink on the dash. "Dash it all, young squire, she's just offering you a sip of her bubbly!"

Wesley and the woman gasped in unison. She looked away, distressed, offended . . . and Wesley felt like a fool. Then she fell into her companion's arms, nearly collapsing with laughter. Wesley only then noticed the glass floated in midair beside the ghosts, gently easing its way around to sail lazily before Wesley's nose. It smelled richly intoxicating—just like the woman who had offered it to him.

"I . . . I . . . I don't drink," Wesley managed. That wasn't true, of course; Wesley simply didn't want to risk anything that might impair his abilities to deal with these mischievous spirits.

"It's just sparkling cider," P. J. said innocently. "Come on, dear boy, live a little!"

Wesley took a deep sniff of the drink and raised an eyebrow at the deep fruity scent of the fizzy concoction. He took the drink and brought it to his lips.

"I don't suppose the apples that went into this fell from any particularly famous tree," Wesley said suspiciously. "The tree of knowledge, perhaps?"

She sighed and rolled her eyes. "You'll be the death of us, I know it."

"No, no," P. J. chortled, "never trust a ghost, quite right, quite right . . ."

Wesley set down the glass. "I really must go."

Kat put her hand on his arm and gazed at him imploringly. "We'll be good, we *promise.* We're just lonely."

"That's right," P. J. put in. "And it's not like we'll be around all that long. All we're given is one hour every ten years. That's all the time we have to make some new acquaintances and live it up a little!"

"Huh," Wesley muttered.

"And you're the only one who can see us. That has to be for a reason."

Wesley again felt the weight of the letter from home in his pocket. He'd been uneasy ever since Cordelia found the buried notice that a registered letter from England was waiting for him at the post office, and the contents of the letter he had picked up during the post office's extended hours had caused him to take his time returning to the hotel, sparking a need to be alone and to consider the ramifications of what it said. Besides, he had known full well that Angel and Cordelia were going to be gone anyway, taking care of some last-minute shopping. But being on his own hadn't helped him work out what to do about the invitation he'd been given. Perhaps having something else to focus on for a little while might actually help.

"This really is quite a handsome car. Is it a Rolls?"

P. J. hopped out of the car and treated Wesley with a

theatrical flourish over the car's wheel-hugging fenders and sloping chrome grill. "A Duesenberg SJ. A very exclusive automobile, owned by people of great import, like William Randolph Hearst, Mae West, Clark Gable, and, naturally, the MacBrides!"

"That would be you two," Wesley said. "P. J. and Kat MacBride?"

"The very same," P. J. said. His grin faded for an instant. "Never heard of us, huh?"

"Oh, it's not that . . ."

Kat stroked his arm. "But it is."

He nodded gently. "Still, this car is amazing."

"That's *not* what the young ladies were admiring," Kat said, her fingers taking a friendly walk along the nape of Wesley's neck.

He cleared his throat. "So, spirits are usually bound to certain material objects. Is it safe to say this car was very important to you? Did you, by chance, cease to be in this very auto?"

"Oh, heaven's no!" Kat laughed. "Nothing like that. Why do you ask?"

"As I said, if I'm to help you move on to your reward, to free you from whatever binds you to this plane, I'll first need to learn what that is."

"We don't need help. We're perfectly happy as we are." Kat lounged seductively against the door while her husband stood with his hands in his pockets, looking out at the glittering lights of the theater down the block.

Kat followed his gaze and smiled. "Now *that* brings back memories," she said.

"You came here in life?" Wesley asked.

"We met at that theater. I was a candy girl and P. J. was the projectionist. He loved watching me . . . and I had fun distracting him. One time he forgot to change the reels because of my teasing and that got us both fired!"

"Sorry," Wesley said.

"Oh, no! That was the happiest day of our lives. P. J. said hang it all and proposed and just on a lark we went on our first audition together and landed the rolls that made us famous."

Wesley nodded. P. J. and Kat would had to have been successful in order to afford a car like this.

"I want to hear about you," Kat said, bouncing like a happy child as she positioned herself to face him directly. "You don't seem like you have a lot of fun. Don't you have any happy memories that keep you going?"

"Well . . ." he said, beginning to look around.

"No, tell me," Kat said, leaning forward, placing one hand on his knee, arresting his gaze with her own.

Looking into her dark green eyes, he found her impossible to resist. "I was happiest when I attended university; it was there, between assignments, that I developed the interests that brought me to the attention of the Watchers. Do you know what a Watcher is?"

She nodded.

"I was happy there. The world made *sense.* The answers to every question could be found in a book, or in a lecture by one of the professors, or so it seemed. It was similar later, after I graduated from university and I was being trained to be a Watcher. I recall one of my favorite assignments; ten of us were given different demons to research, but our objective was the same: Discover all we could about the demon, learn exactly when in the next few days it would rise, unearth the specific nature of the threat it posed, and come up with plans to help the Slayer stop it." He sighed, relaxing for the first time since Cordelia had given him the post office notice that she had found buried under an avalanche of catalogs and junk mail in his office. "Travers gave me such praise for my work."

"I sensed you had an agile mind," Kat said, caressing his knee. "Among other things."

Wesley cleared his throat. "My report of the Plargg demon earned me such praise from Travers and the others. And when I became a Watcher, I was so proud of myself. I had an entire career ahead of me as a protector of the innocent. Best of all, I was away from home, finally in a position to prove something to my—"

He gasped as Kat's hand . . . slipped. He looked around quickly, guilt and worry lighting his eyes—this was another man's wife, after all, deceased or no—and saw that P. J. was nowhere to be found.

The woman beside Wes did her best to look surprised. "Oh! The Kat's pajamas did it again."

"Please!" Wes exclaimed, leaping out of the car. "The two of you planned this! You were distracting me."

"Really?" asked the flamboyantly dressed spirit as she posed provocatively against the convertible. "It was working?"

"Oh, for heaven's sake," Wesley mumbled as he went

back and snatched her wrist. She giggled, allowing him to drag her toward the theater a few blocks down the street. Wesley was well aware that she could become insubstantial at a second's notice, or simply wink out of existence and end up somewhere else.

"Why do you think he went to the theater?" Kat asked, her voice high and brimming with overdone innocence.

"Because there are more people there than anywhere else, and people equals mischief, and mischief equals fun for you two. Never trust a ghost indeed!"

A great crowd was gathered at the famous forecourt where celebrities had been placing their handprints and more in cement since 1927. He passed impressions of John Wayne's fist, R2-D2's tread marks, and Harold Lloyd's wire-frame glasses, and placed his attention on the lovely young actress near the entrance who was addressing her adoring public as she readied herself to kneel and put her hands in cement.

"We were great friends of Sid, you know," Kat said swiftly. "Sid Grauman, the man who built the Chinese theater and the Egyptian. He came up with the idea for movie premieres. Did you know that?"

Wesley scanned the crowd, picking up immediately on the slight shimmer P. J. left as he dashed about the gatherers, pinching a bottom here, whispering a devilish word in an ear there.

"Oh, no, he's shimmering already," Kat said. "Where does the time go?"

At the podium, the actress beamed with joy. "And, of

course, I'd like to dedicate this to all the great actresses of the golden era of Hollywood," the actress said, "because they were my true inspiration."

Easing his way through the crowd, Wesley saw P. J. stop abruptly and focus all his attention on the actress accepting her great honor. She rattled off names like Garbo, Swanson, Turner, and Loy . . . but no MacBride. He surged through the mass of fans, his shimmering aftertrail a bright crimson as he darted right for the actress.

"Oh, no," Kat said with a giggle. "I do believe my knight is about to go and defend my honor!"

Wesley released his grip on Kat and struggled to catch up with the angry spirit, but he lacked the ghost's ability to simply pass *through* anyone or anything in his way. Shoving, sliding, and apologizing, Wesley caught up with P. J. just as the flush-faced ghost rose up behind the actress and flicked his wrists like a master conductor about to lead a symphony in an all-out attack on Wagner.

"Here's mud in your eye!" P. J. roared as he thrust his hands at the actress's bare back and sent her sprawling—ten-thousand-dollar designer silk gown and all—face first into the gray splatter of the soft wet concrete. It went everywhere, coating her soft golden tresses, her wide brown eyes, and her million-dollar smile. And when the fans, the police, and the paparazzi turned to look at the perpetrator, all they saw was Wesley.

Stinging bright camera flashes seared his retinas as explosive curses burst from the crowd. Then a wail rose up from the muck-encrusted actress and all attention reverted to her—at least for a second.

"Serves you right!" P. J. said, tromping past her, his pointy-toed Harvard Alumni Gold Bond leather shoes leaving no impression in the concrete.

And *that* bit of business ate up what little time Wesley had been granted to come up with a plan for avoiding jail time and tabloid notoriety for this little incident because everyone, even the actress, looked up at the sound of those callous words.

Yet . . . P. J. hadn't spoken with a British accent. . . .

Yanking his ID from his coat pocket, Wesley announced, "Everyone, there's no need to panic. I'm Wesley Wyndam-Pryce of Angel Investigations and I've been following a suspect with an unnatural fixation on this lovely and talented woman. She was in danger and I had no choice."

"Hey, I recognize him," one of the photographers said, scratching his stubbly beard. "He was with Virginia Bryce—"

Wesley saw P. J. reentering the crowd, angrily using his ectoplasm to shove a few people out of the way. "There he is now!" Wesley pointed right at the ghost, and confusion and chaos soon reigned as one fan looked to another, each thinking the other was responsible for the shoving, and therefore, the stalker.

"Thank you, thank you," the soaked actress sobbed. And others quickly followed, Wesley assuming the mantle of hero and . . . well . . . liking it.

And as P. J. stormed off, pushing and tripping and

goosing and grumbling, the madness engulfed the entire proceeding, allowing Wesley the chance to slip away and rendezvous with Kat, who drove up in the convertible. He leaped in alongside P. J. and the car screeched off into the night.

Wesley slid over, easing through the laughing Kat, who was also starting to shimmer, though not as much as her husband. P. J. looked pleased with himself, the incident at the theater apparently already forgotten. Kat snuggled him and cooed something about his heroism.

His heart thundering, his thoughts crackling like lightning, Wesley had to admit that he felt a guilty rush at the thought that he might be in the papers tomorrow as a hero rather than a rake. *But . . . that poor actress . . .*

"Hey, look what I picked up," P. J. said, whipping out a copy of the *Hollywood Reporter* that fluttered in the breeze. "I wonder what's shooting tonight . . ."

"None of that," Wesley said. He snatched the magazine from the ghost and jammed it curled-up into one of his coat's deeper inner pockets.

"But that's our bible!" P. J. protested.

Kat's eyes widened. "Our most holy of holies!"

"In a word?" Wesley whispered. "Tough."

Kat moaned with unearthly volume, clutching her head with both hands, and P. J. coughed and spat. The dramatic gestures were so far over the top that Wesley thought, *What a couple of hams. These two make Cordelia look ready for a David Mamet play. No wonder no one remembers them anymore.*

Wesley frowned, considering the plight of the humiliated actress he had left behind. Unlike the two college guys in the alley, she'd done *nothing* to deserve the treatment she'd received other than wound the vanity of his ghostly companions. Even worse, Wesley had managed to let himself feel proud of the way he'd extracted himself from the situation, when all he'd done was cover his backside. These spirits were dangerously seductive. Who knew what they might make a man do if he spent too much time with them?

He clutched the steering wheel with sweaty hands, knowing exactly what he must do.

"Splendid effort back there!" P. J. said. "You'd make quite the dashing hero!"

Wesley growled, "Put a sock in it."

"What's that you say?"

"Oh. Ah—my head. There are nights when I think I must have rocks in it. I'm looking for something fun to do with the two of you and the answer was staring me in the face."

P. J. brightened up, his shimmer a bright sky blue. "We like fun."

"We live for it," Kat added.

"Well, then, I was thinking," Wesley began, "how would you two like to visit an old Hollywood haunt?"

Both ghosts shimmered with joy. Soon they pulled up before the Yamashiro, where a valet took the convertible's keys. The pagoda sitting beside the vast restaurant had been brought over piece by piece from Japan, and at six hundred years old, it was the oldest edifice in California.

Oldest known, Wesley corrected himself, thinking of a few other structures, not all made by human hands.

If he hadn't been so distracted, Wesley might have appreciated the sight of the wooden castle a little more. The "mountain palace" was perched more than two hundred feet above Hollywood Boulevard.

"I've never eaten here, but I understand the food is wonderful," Wesley said evenly.

"Oh. This was a social club when we used to come here," Kat said. "The 400 Club. Oh, P. J., do you remember those brunches with Lillian Gish and Bebe Daniels?"

He smirked. "The ones where everyone would get fresh with you and you'd get fresher back?"

"A girl's got to stay in shape somehow. Flirting is a fine art."

Wesley used his ID once more and told the maitre d' he was meeting an important client and needed to rely on the man's discretion. He was shown inside immediately. The moment they were inside, Wesley was engulfed by the tempting aromas of sumptuous feasts from all over the CalAsian restaurant. The spicy tang of exotic herbs and spices mixed with the rich smells of beef, chicken, and seafood being prepared in the kitchen.

"Couldn't you just go for a little bite?" Kat asked, nibbling on Wesley's ear.

The sudden craving for takeout, among other things, rocketed into his thoughts, but Wesley pushed such distracting desires out of his head. He had to deal with these wayward spirits then decide what to do about the invitation he'd received.

"Oh, we used to love coming here," Kat said, her arm around Wesley's. P. J. strutted happily as they drifted through the main dining area, draining drinks before astounded eyes, removing hats and plopping them on the heads of surprised socialites a dozen feet away, and committing half a dozen other supernatural pranks. Wesley would have commented if he thought it would do any good, but he restrained himself. He had a plan for dealing with these two, and as difficult as they were making it, he would stick to it.

Looking out from behind the restaurant, the view of Los Angeles was nothing short of spectacular. The Yamashiro sported acres of lush, beautifully landscaped gardens, waterfalls, and koi ponds, as well as a fourteenth-century pagoda. Because they were slightly above the smog that covered Los Angeles, the air smelled unusually crisp and clean. *Like at home in England.* Wesley reveled in it.

"Remember when this town was nothing but glamour?" Kat said wistfully to her husband.

"And mystery, my sweet. Particularly after dark."

Brooding with the best of them, Wesley thought of the decision he still needed to make and said, "There are still mysteries aplenty."

"Naturally," Kat said seductively, pinching his backside and making him yelp. "So long as the human heart exists, that's not a bullet anyone can dodge."

The group soon arrived at a lovely old wood bridge overlooking a koi pond. Wesley heard the wood creak as he walked onto the bridge, but there was no sound when the ghosts followed him onto the wooden structure. The easily excitable orange fish scattered as the ghosts peered down at them.

"Skittish little devils, aren't they?" P. J. observed.

"Perhaps the spirits moved them," Wesley said with a shrug.

Kat looked up at Wesley in amazement. "Oh, you yummy little dish. You made your first pun!"

The easily excitable female ghost allowed her hands to wander again.

Clearing his throat, Wesley gestured grandly at the pond. "There's a secret history to this place, one I think might interest you two."

Kat clapped her hands together. "Do tell!"

"About five years ago, a djinn was defeated here. As a result, a strange magick has risen up. To quote from a classic, 'Fairy tales can come true. It can happen to you.'"

"How romantic!" P. J. exclaimed.

Kat could barely contain herself. "How does it work? You must tell us!"

"I'll do better than that, I'll show you exactly how a wish might be granted." He nodded at the frigid water. "Jump in."

"It's like a wishing well!" Kat said, leaping before she looked, her husband bounding after her. They splashed about, further frightening the fish. Fortunately, the pond was secluded enough that their mischief did not draw attention from anyone inside the restaurant.

"What now?" Kat called.

Wesley smiled thinly. "Ah, yes, you see, the wish is

granted to the one standing *on* the bridge, and my wish is that you both remain where you are for, say . . . an hour?"

P. J.'s shimmer flared crimson once more. He squinted in concentration and began to levitate from the water, then stopped with a jerky motion, as if someone had grabbed him by the loafers and was holding him in place. The story about the djinn had been made up. In truth, he had set traps like this all over Los Angeles, traps that would only respond to him, and he had done so in case he ever got into a situation he couldn't handle otherwise. It was an idea he had gotten from reading books—adventure novels in which a single hero trapped in a remote locale took out countless adversaries by digging deep holes and covering them up, or placing trip wires with nets in clearings. This was simply the magickal equivalent.

"You can't leave us like this!" Kat cried. "How are we to have any fun?"

"Never trust a ghost," Wesley said, turning and heading off down the bridge. "Or someone who's been burned by one."

He only made it a few yards before he heard a frantic rustling of paper. "Dear Wesley, I know it's been an age since we've communicated, but I love you and miss you and wish this business with you and your father didn't have to come between us. . . ."

Wesley tensed and patted his pockets quickly.

"Hah!" P. J. called, shaking out the copy of the *Hollywood Reporter* he'd been waving about earlier. "It's funny the things you learn as an actor. Kat had to play a pickpocket once. She was a highly convincing one, I'd say."

"And look what else I found, two plane tickets, one to England, the other back to Los Angeles," Kat said. "Fortunately for you I cast an ectoplasmic aura around your precious letter and these nice little tickets. Wouldn't want them getting soaked and ruined."

Wesley held out his hand. "Give those back."

"Let us *out*," P. J. spat indignantly.

"Fine," Wesley growled. "Keep them. Those tickets can be replaced and I know what the letter says."

Kat pouted. Wesley never thought he could be so affected by any woman's expression and wondered if Kat was using some kind of supernatural influence. Then her lower lip trembled, and she said, "We're not out to hurt anyone. We just wanted to have some fun!"

P. J. nodded. "Yeah, and so far as that letter . . . why are you letting it get you down? Our families disowned us so thoroughly we don't even see them on the other side."

Wesley shook his head. "You don't understand. I'd love to go home for the holidays. There are old friends I haven't seen since I was a child, places I only visit in my dreams, my mother, other members of my family, so many people I'd like to spend time with again." He shuddered. "I don't know why I'm telling you this."

"Because you're lonely," Kat said. "Like us."

Wesley gripped the rail tightly. "My father . . . he's difficult."

Swimming around in a lazy circle, Kat said, "The

world's only complicated if you let it be. Talk to him."

Wesley looked away, glancing up at the stars. It was a freezing night like this—although this night was only freezing because of the proximity of the ghosts, who created "cold spots" wherever they went—when he told his father that he wanted to be a Watcher. The decision had been a simple one for Wes, one that had felt so "right." At last, he had found his place in the world.

He'd honestly believed his father would be proud of him, that the man would commend him for devoting himself to helping others. Instead, his father laughed and said three things that would always stay with him: Dreams are for fools, hope is the enemy, and heroes are nothing but pathetic attention-seekers.

Wesley turned to the glittering lights of Los Angeles, a town of dreams that so often turned out to be nightmares. *But is it really so different here than anywhere else? Or is the phenomenon just easier to see?*

So easy, perhaps, that he saw darkness where there really wasn't any?

A rustling came from the pond. P. J. was flipping through the *Hollywood Reporter* with boyish enthusiasm. Kat was next to him, her jaw dropping.

"Look here! They're doing a remake of our most famous film, *The Cat's Pajamas*! And just when we thought we'd been forgotten."

"Our pictures, our names . . . this is delightful!"

"We should have won an Oscar for that film," P. J. said ruefully. Then he brightened up. "But this is even better!"

"Indeed," Wesley said, running his hands through his hair.

"Oh, Wesley, you just have to let us out," Kat said. "We can't miss this!"

P. J. rallied to the cause. "Come on, old boy. We're good for you!"

Wesley thought of the way his father had tried to deny his dream—and found he simply didn't have the heart to refuse the spirits. "Understand something: If either of you misbehaves, I can just wish you back here, anywhere, anytime. And what I didn't tell you is that the magick only works for vanquishers of great evil so don't get any ideas when you get up here."

The story he had given about the pond's magick only being available to vanquishers of great evil was one he had made up, and his threat was a simple bluff. Nevertheless, he sensed the ghosts believed him. He murmured the words to revoke his spell and free the spirits from the pond, feeling the slight tingling in his fingers, and the tremor of power that raced from the top of his skull to the tips of his toes as his connection to the pond was severed.

"All right . . . you're free."

The spirits burst from the waters, renewed and shimmering with a beautiful blue-white light. Wesley half expected the ghosts to settle beside him on the bridge and shake themselves off like hounds who'd run into a river, but they came up James Bond dry.

P. J. threw his arm around Wesley as they walked back. "So far as that dodgy dad of yours is concerned, to heck with him, that's my advice! The man's in another country. And even if he wasn't—why let him make up your mind for you?"

Soon they were passing through the restaurant once more. Kat leaned into him. "You took command of that situation very well. Do you see the way people are looking at you? They're saying to themselves, there's a man with a purpose, with some spine. A determined kind of guy who can lick any problem!"

They are rather, now, aren't they? Wesley thought, taking in the looks he was attracting. Then he chided himself, realizing the ghosts were, more likely than not, simply sharing a bit of their seductive spotlight to keep on his good side.

The magazine listed where location shooting would begin, and so Wesley drove the ghosts to the Hollywood Athletic Club, another of their old haunts. The picture was a big-budget affair and security was tight, but Wesley knew enough names to drop from his days with Virginia—and had enough cash and spare enchantments on hand—to gain access. Soon he was inside with the spirits, staring out at a wide expanse that had been transformed into the great banquet hall of a bygone era. He still felt chilly, despite the hot lights, yet no one else the ghosts got close to reacted in the slightest to the cold they projected. Was he the only one to feel the chill in the presence of the spirits? If so, it would be as if they had singled him out, or he had some unique connection to them—but why?

Dozens, perhaps as many as a hundred extras were

on hand, all dressed in vintage clothing from the thirties, all holding drinks or little trays with food. The hall was noisy, filled with the echoes of extras chitchatting, production people shouting orders, and crew members moving heavy equipment into position. An elegantly styled marble balcony looked down on the set from three stories up, and a spiderweb of lights and electrical rigging had been spun across the ceiling, along with a crystal chandelier that appeared to be bigger than Wesley's entire apartment. The lights bathed the hall in soft amber, with warm streaks of crimson and delicate icy blues adding highlights to the hair, hats, and chiseled cheekbones of the assembled actors.

The effect was dazzling. It was like stepping back into another time. In fact, this place was so warm, so cheerful, that he was now hardly even feeling the coolness that followed him when the ghosts were near.

A copy of the *Hollywood Reporter* was draped over a tall folding chair with some actor's name stenciled on the back. Wesley picked it up and quickly scanned the piece about this production and winced in surprise.

The article from the *Hollywood Reporter* was nothing like the way P. J. and Kat had represented it. Yes, a new version of their film was being done, but their names weren't mentioned, the title was being changed, and the frothy comedy was being turned into a blood and guts horror film!

He spun to face the deceitful spirits—but they were nowhere to be found. That's why he had stopped feeling the cold: P. J. and Kat had slipped away!

"Never trust a ghost," Wesley said angrily.

He scanned the set, noting the technicians racing around to prepare a shot, several key actors being eased into various positions by scruffy-looking men and women in jeans, T-shirts, and baseball caps, and megaphones rising into the air like trumpets sounding the call for the Last Days.

He couldn't spot P. J. or Kat. Even their bright shimmers weren't giving them away.

"What are you up to?" Wesley said aloud. According to the trade paper, their simple tale of playful ghosts giving some well-deserving people their comeuppance had been transformed into a kind of *Die Hard* of the Dead. Wesley remembered their rough treatment of the poor actress at Mann's who had only mildly wounded the vanity of the spirits, and soon found himself picturing a dozen different deadly outcomes to the night's shooting: Fake knives replaced with real ones, making murderers of unsuspecting actors; a falling chandelier crushing a group of Hollywood's elite who had "developed" this mothballed property; a special-effects explosion setting off a blaze that would take the lives of everyone in the place when every door refused to open . . .

He glanced about. How could he stop the shooting without looking like a madman? If he made a fuss, he'd be escorted off by Teamsters and perhaps spend the night in jail. In the meantime, the ghosts might still have plenty of time to do their ghastly business.

From the corner of his eye, he saw a flare of light

from the balcony. A couple of figures looked down with something in their hands.

Oh, no . . . the ghosts were going to drop something on the actors from above!

"What the . . . wait!" Wesley hollered, his words drowned out by the noise of the production. He spotted a darkened stairway and made a dash for it.

Racing up the steps, Wesley reached for his mystically charged dagger and was reassured by its presence. Then he was on the long, dark corridor that wrapped around the great hall, hushed voices coming to him as the crowd below settled in preparation for a shot.

"I don't like this," a woman said, "Lloyd's of London won't like this. . . ."

"Hurry up and hook me," a low, strong male voice said. "I always do my own stunts, and this way, we'll get honest reactions, we'll have a true element of surprise."

Wesley swerved around the corner and stared at the figures he had seen earlier looking up at him in surprise. The man and woman were definitely *not* P. J. and Kat, though the man, a strapping movie star, had been made up to look like a spirit—albeit a malevolent, blood-splattered one.

"Can we help you?" the woman asked. She was blond, built like a gymnast, and her T-shirt read SAMANTHA'S STUNTS.

"If you're a reporter . . ." the man said in a patented gravely threatening tone that Wesley and Gunn had emulated from countless adventure flicks and shoot-'em-ups. He looked at the hook peeking out from the back of the actor's dinner jacket and realized they were about to do some elaborate wire stunt.

Wesley whipped out his ID and explained, as best he could, that a pair of mad fans of the original picture were loose on the set, that sabotage was likely, that whatever he had planned wasn't safe.

The actor didn't blink. He stared at Wesley, shaking his head. "You people will do anything for an exclusive, won't you. And that ID. Like that's even a real—"

Wesley decked him. The actor crumpled, flopping onto his back.

"I'm sorry," Wesley said. "But that was for your own good."

The stuntwoman threw her hands in the air. "I'm getting Security!"

"Good! Do that!"

She stormed off and Wesley heard voices from below.

"Someone took our costumes and wigs," a male extra complained.

A woman chimed in. "And our makeup."

"It's fine," the director said. "We have enough people for the shot. Quiet on the set people. And—"

Wesley couldn't allow action to be called. He leaned over the railing to call out to the production people, and gasped as a hand closed on his ankle.

"No *interviews*!" the actor growled.

Tipping forward, Wesley lost his balance and went

over the edge, his arms flailing. The entire set opened up like the sky on judgment day, gasps of horror and surprise ripped from the crowd as lights spun his way, and cameras were aimed right at him as he plunged. His right hand suddenly caught the cable that was supposed to have been attached to the actor's harness. But the line didn't hold; instead it gave only mild resistance and took him flying down in a wide arc over the crowd.

With a growl of surprise, Wesley felt the line slide from his fingers, and he was turning, twisting, and plummeting toward a table where a dozen steel candelabra stuck up at him like stakes.

"Here, now, old boy, can't leave you alone for a minute!" a familiar voice said in Wesley's ear, and suddenly he was cold again, but alight with a fiery white shimmering glow, and a force was dragging on his coat, steering him toward a pair of open double doors. The crowd blurred beneath him as he sailed over and away from the set. The floor rushed up at him, and he tumbled, rolled, and smashed into a pair of chairs.

Chilly phantom hands were on him, hauling him to his feet. "What . . . what's . . ."

"No time," Kat said, taking one arm while P. J. took the other. Together, they spirited Wesley away.

In no time at all, they were back in the convertible, Wesley nursing a nasty bruise on his end—and a wretched sense of embarrassment. Kat and P. J. had indeed changed clothes, slipping on outfits that would be seen over their ectoplasmically charged forms. Wigs and makeup had done the rest, rendering them visible to anyone else. Now cracks were showing in their disguises, and their shimmering light was almost blinding. They didn't have much longer before they'd be called back to the other side. The hour was nearly up.

"You just wanted to be in the movie!" Wesley realized. "I thought—"

"You thought the worst," Kat said. "But that's all right. We forgive you."

"Oh, I know I said never trust a ghost, dear boy, but I didn't mean *us,*" P. J. said merrily.

Kat laughed. "We're not the typical. Never have been."

P. J. drove them back to the hotel. "We only fibbed to you because we were worried you'd leap to all sorts of conclusions if we told you what that story really said."

"I punched out one of the biggest stars in Hollywood," Wesley groaned.

"One of the biggest somethings," Kat replied. "What an unpleasant little man. *Did* you notice how short he was in real life? Nothing like on the billboards."

"And they have my face on camera!"

"I think we may have done a little something to their cameras," P. J. said. "Ghostly energies can be unpredictable, and all that. And if that actor fellow is anything like the types we used to rub shoulders with, he won't want the bad publicity. No sir, this incident won't cause any problems for you, I guarantee it."

Wesley rubbed his tired eyes. "You two *saved* me . . .

and I cost you a chance to be seen on film again."

Kat snuggled him. "There's always the future, dear boy."

Shaking his head, Wesley said, "I have to do something for you. What year was it your film came out?"

They told him—and all the pieces came together for Wesley. "You didn't win an Oscar that year, did you?"

"Weren't even nominated," Kat said regretfully.

Wesley thought of the award he'd seen in the pawn shop. There was a corporeal anchor holding the spirits to the material world—and that meant they could be set free!

"I understand now," Wesley said quickly. "I see how to help you. It's that award, the one you were denied. That's what's keeping you here, and I know where it is, that must be why—"

"Don't be daft, old fella," P. J. said. "What do either of us need with trinkets and prizes when we've got the swellest gift anyone could ask for?"

"He means each other," Kat said. "Forever and always, always and forever."

P. J. grinned. "Say it like you mean it, sister."

"But—only I can see you, only I feel the cold when you're about. There must be a reason. Helping people is what I do."

"What about when you need help?" Kat asked.

Wesley wasn't sure what to say.

Kat nodded toward the envelope in Wesley's pocket.

"There's joy and pain in life," Kat said warmly. "We have to choose which one we remember."

"And what we remember shapes what we do," P. J. added.

Wesley was going to ask exactly what they meant when a siren pierced the night. Red-and-blue flashing lights lit up the night.

"Coppers," P. J. said, accelerating a bit. "I was wondering if we'd get a visit from them."

"Let me drive," Wesley said. "The sight of this car speeding along with no one driving . . . no, wait. The wigs, the clothes, they *can* see you, and you weren't speeding, so why—"

"It may have something to do with a dispute over ownership of the car," P. J. said sheepishly.

Wesley's hand went to his aching skull. "The car's *stolen*?"

"Well, you must have noticed that everyone can see it and only you can see us," Kat said. "We're certainly not about to use our ectoplasm frivolously. That bit with the bottle in the alley was one thing; do you know how much we'd have to put out to make everyone see the car?"

P. J. shrugged. "Yes, and you would know something about putting out."

"P. J.!"

"I just mean you're so generous, dear."

"Yes, I'm sure that's what you meant." Kat turned in her seat, glancing back at the police car. "We'll handle this, Wesley. You just get home and do the right thing."

"The thing that's right for you," P. J. said firmly.

"What—what are you going to do?" Wesley asked, not sure he really wanted to know.

"We'll provide a distraction, that's all," P. J. said. "Keep those fellas from following you so you can leave the car somewhere and get back home. I'd suggest a quick wipe down for fingerprints."

Kat furrowed her brow and a glittering silver energy raced over the car. "Done."

"These officers are just doing their jobs," Wesley said. "We should pull over and explain—"

"We won't be around," P. J. said, his inner light reaching its zenith.

"Don't worry, dearheart," Kat said with a bright, happy laugh. "We've done this for sixty years and we'll do it for sixty more. And no one's ever, ever gotten hurt!"

"She's not just whistling Dixie," P. J. said, taking his hands off the wheel. "Heck, old son, if we didn't do some good during our hour of life, we wouldn't be given the chance to return to the party each time. Them's the rules!"

Wesley slid over and through the ghosts, grabbing the wheel before the car could run up the sidewalk. "You mean—I could see you and feel the cold because I was chosen by some higher power, I was meant to receive a bit of wisdom and guidance and—"

"I think it was just 'cause you're a cutie," Kat said, blowing him a kiss and leaping into the air. P. J. winked and followed. The wraiths linked hands and caused a storm of strange energies to seize the street, blowing back trees, warping steel signs, forcing streetlights to bend low and burst their bulbs before the windshield of the oncoming police car, which screeched to a stop as Wesley continued on, zooming down a side road. He found a spot several blocks from the hotel where he left the car, then walked back to the hotel, this time anxious to find every pool of light, shunning the shadows, embracing the sounds, the shouts, the car horns and laughter, the fragrance of light, the essence and mystery of the night.

No one was in the lobby of the hotel, but the lights were on, warm and inviting.

Tonight he had taken his first step on the long road to understanding that some things—like the delirious behavior of the ghosts who snatched him from the street and his father's disapproval—might indeed never change, but how he chose to react to such things was entirely up to him.

Wesley made his decision. He called from his office, turning on every light.

"Mother? Yes, it's Wesley. About those tickets you sent me. As much as I would love to see my old stomping ground again, I thought it would be more fun by far if I could show you the sights here in Los Angeles . . . That's right, I'll trade in the tickets and get you booked on a flight here."

After a few more minutes on the phone, Wesley gently replaced the receiver. He smelled a heavenly scent and turned to see Cordelia bounding happily into the office with several Christmas-wrapped gift boxes in her hands. She stopped at the sight of him.

"Someone's in a better mood," Cordy said.

Wesley smiled. "Just consider me the cat's pajamas."

10 P.M.

MODEL BEHAVIOR

by Emily Oz

"Here's a thought," Cordelia offered, breezing back into the lobby. "Let's talk about me for a minute." She flashed a megawatt grin at her now-gathered coworkers, who were in various stages of general, downtime-esque research. Other than Wesley, who managed a distracted grunt, no one was biting.

"Hello? Me? Get on board, people—not only have I landed a maybe-contract with Bryan Whittiger—of the Whittiger Agency—but have I not achieved a perfect balance of fashion-forward meets hire-me-smart?" She twirled eagerly, undaunted by their lack of enthusiasm.

"I love your outfit," Fred concurred, smiling demurely over the edge of a book that weighed twice what she did. "Perfect for the party."

Picking a non-existent clump of lint off her black leather pants, Cordelia afforded herself another moment of self-congratulatory agreement. Getting the phone call from Whittiger's receptionist and being told that he'd heard of *her* and wanted to see her portfolio was impressive enough. Once he'd seen her photos, he had met with her personally to discuss taking her on. As a Whittiger model, she'd be represented by the hottest international agency around, and with any luck, given first crack at the choicest assignments available. Hands down, this was the biggest break she'd been given since she arrived in L.A. *Phase One of unprecedented fame and fortune—check*, she thought gleefully.

"Party?" Angel asked absently. He pushed aside a troublesome stack of bills to regard Cordelia with renewed curiosity. "Tonight?"

"Duh, listen much? The wine and cheese, meet-and-greet party for all of Whittiger's new models."

"It's at the beach house, and all of the clients are there, and the models get to say hello," Fred explained a touch wistfully. It all sounded very glamorous to her. *Of course, these days, tacos are still pretty glamorous to me.* One of the benefits of having recently been rescued from an alternate dimension was a renewed appreciation for the simpler aspects of L.A. living—including cheap Tex-Mex.

"Well, sure, if 'say hello' is some code for gettin' down," Gunn interjected.

"It's totally PG-13," Cordelia argued, crossing her arms defensively.

"All I'm sayin' is, Whittiger is pretty smart to be having all of his top clients over to that swank pad. He gets the models to fawn all over the businessmen, the businessmen book his agency, the models get famous—everyone's a winner." *Which must be nice,* he thought wistfully. *I wouldn't mind rubbing elbows with gorgeous women rather than scabby demons.* He allowed himself to peek at Fred, who was still skimming her tome. She and Cordelia were both totally gorgeous, each in her own way. *So it's not as if I don't know from beautiful people,* he conceded.

"Hi, I'm Cordelia Chase. Not big with the fawning," Cordy reminded him, glaring. She fished a lipstick and compact out of her handbag and touched up quickly.

Snapping the mirror shut, Cordelia suddenly narrowed her eyes and rather slowly crossed the room to where he was standing, stopping just short of his personal space. "In fact, I'm usually the fawn*ee,*" she countered pointedly. She half-smiled. "Maybe you can see why?"

"Uh, sure," Gunn said uncertainly, taking a few steps backward and glancing at Fred.

Fred shrugged back at Gunn. *What do I know from physical boundaries? I was living in a cave for four years.* "I'm sure you'll get plenty of attention tonight, Cordy. You look great. Take me with you the next time you go shopping. I could use your expert advice. Do you want something to eat?"

She rose abruptly and made her way toward the kitchen before Cordelia had a chance to answer. The sight of the slinky brunette . . . *slinking* . . . all over Gunn was inexplicably irritating. *Cordelia is* not *hitting on Charles, for Pete's sake.*

And even if she is—what in the heck do I care? We're all friends here. . . .

"I'm sorry, did you say that Whittiger has a beach house?" Wesley asked, at last turning his attentions toward the group.

"Yuh-huh! Three stories, wraparound deck, interior solarium, sauna . . ." Cordelia trailed off with a sigh. "Assuming everything goes well tonight, I'm primed for the best three months of my life." Needless to say, when she'd left Sunnydale for Los Angeles she hadn't anticipated taking up with a demon-busting detective agency, and though her values had begun to shift since she'd been battling evil, well . . . *who's to say I can't do both?*

"Three *months*?" Angel asked. He found it hard to imagine a day without the outspoken brunette.

Cordelia sighed again, this time with exasperation. "I open my mouth, sound comes out, and yet . . . Yes, Whittiger keeps a beach house for his models. Once they're signed they live there for a three-month orientation period. It's a chance for the girls to bond with one another and learn the trade. A personal trainer, dietician, and one or two veteran models live on the premises and get us into shape."

"What does Dennis think?" Wesley asked. Phantom Dennis had grown accustomed to sharing an apartment with Cordelia and was bound to be lonely without her.

"I'm sure he'll live—or, I guess, carry on with the not-living—without me for three months."

"What about your work here?" Angel wanted to know. He sounded concerned. Cordelia's premonitions—and her dedication to the cause and the crew—were equally vital to the Investigation's operations.

"That's why cell phones were invented," Cordy pointed out. "The Powers That Be won't care that I've relocated—visions will keep on as per usual—and I can still drop by the office every day. *Most* days," she amended hastily.

"Angel, you know I'm committed to the vision-girl gig, but I've got to get a life, too. And since romance for clairvoyant monster-busters is slim pickings, it's career or bust. Here it is practically New Year's Eve, and I'm pretty much alone—heck, we all are—"

"Do let's point that out as often as possible," Wesley interrupted, a tad peevish.

"—but I've got this. This is it! And it's great news! I really thought you'd be happy for me."

For a moment it looked as though Angel's nonsupport threatened to spoil her euphoria. Not wanting to crush her spirits, Angel was quick to clarify his position. "It's not that I'm not excited for you, I'm just worried," he explained. "You're compromising a lot, to uproot yourself for this guy. Is there any guarantee that you're going to get work?"

Frustrated, Cordy grabbed a fashion magazine from the oversized tote bag she'd been carrying. She thrust it under Angel's nose triumphantly. "Natascha Vaknin, age

18. Measurements 31, 22, 36. Height, 5'11". Whittiger model."

"You're gonna be living with *this* hottie?" Gunn asked incredulously, snatching the magazine away. *I am* so *in the wrong line of work. . . .*

"The photo's airbrushed," Fred pointed out in an uncharacteristically grouchy tone, crossing swiftly back into the room with a box of doughnuts tucked under her arm. She planted herself in a seat and began to munch fervently.

"She's very attractive," Angel conceded reluctantly. "In a . . . leggy sort of way. I mean, if you like that kind of thing."

"Um, right, that blond, high-cheekboned, exotic kind of thing. The girl belongs in magazines. And I belong there, too," Cordelia purred, sidling up to Angel. "Isn't it obvious? Some people," she paused, allowing her eyes to skate down the length of his body and back up again, "just have that special something." She found herself stroking him, pushing at the front of his hair. *Has he done something different with it today?* "You know, you could probably be a male model, if you wanted. What if I put in a good word for you?" Satisfied that his hair was behaving, she snaked an arm around his waist and gazed up at him questioningly.

Shaking his head, Angel disentangled himself from her uncharacteristically flirtatious embrace. "Cordelia, are you feeling okay?"

"I'm feeling just fine," she replied, stepping toward him again. "And so are you." She winked.

Fred coughed loudly. "Donut—wrong pipe," she explained, pounding at her chest.

Wesley leaped from his seat to offer Fred a sip of water. Cordelia's behavior was making him feel irrationally tense, as well. *Clearly, she's making Fred uncomfortable,* he reasoned. "Don't you need to get going if you're to be at the party on time?"

"Too true." She took another quick peek in the compact. Snapping the mirror shut she fixed her gaze at Wesley and puckered. "What do you think?"

"Perfect," he answered nervously, careful not to meet her oddly captivating gaze. He felt as if the temperature in the room had just risen by twenty degrees, inexplicably. "Do take care not to smudge before you've said hello to Whittiger," he advised.

But she was already out the door.

When Cordelia stepped into the open, sunken living room of Whittiger's beach house (the room consisted of practically the entire first floor), she was surprised to find it devoid of any guests other than models. She had arrived exactly on time—fashionably late was for people with stable careers—only to be met by an extreme lack of clients to greet. It was a bit disappointing. What with the fighting evil and all, this was likely to be the only non-work-related holiday party she attended. It would have been nice to meet even the boringest of Y chromosomes in the room, for schmoozing or even plain old conversation. *Figures,* she thought glumly.

Nursing a half-full glass of white wine, she wove

through the room, taking in the décor. Whittiger certainly had good taste. The room and as much of the house as she'd seen was done in minimalist chic, and she admired sleek chrome side tables, a slim, titanium Christmas tree trimmed in steel blue tinsel, and a long, polished mirror that adorned the far wall. She *loved* her reflection bouncing against the stark white background. She paused for a moment to tame a stray strand of her bobbed hair.

Natascha Vaknin—*the* Natascha—flitted past and Cordelia reached out to the gamine model, hoping to introduce herself. She'd heard that Natascha had three weeks left to go in the house and Cordy planned to use those three weeks to her utmost advantage. *Mentor, meet mentee. I'm all about strategy.*

"Natascha, hi! We haven't met yet. My name's Cordelia Chase. I'm a huge fan of yours," she offered. Realizing she was babbling, she extended a hand and awaited a perfunctory handshake.

Natascha merely gazed forward blankly, blinking saucer eyes at Cordelia. She pricked the corners of her mouth up in an entirely insincere smile. "Yes, hello. You will work here, no?" She drifted off without waiting for an answer.

"Okay, unfriendly much? What was that about?" Cordelia wondered aloud. She turned to a dazzling redhead who was also preening in front of the mirror. "Is she always that chatty?"

The redhead swirled slowly to regard Cordelia. "Ah, hello. I must go now." She, too, floated off in the direction Natascha had gone.

Is this a language barrier thing? The thought of spending three months shacked up with women who could barely choke out a 'good morning' was starting to sound less and less appealing. *Fame. Fame and fortune. And maybe even hottie male models,* she reminded herself. But before her resolve could deteriorate completely, she heard a commotion toward the front foyer.

She turned to see Whittiger himself descending the open slats of the staircase. He wore a deep charcoal suit and a shirt and tie in the same shade of gray-blue. Cordelia had assessed him as attractive on their first meeting—as anyone with eyes in their head would have—but tonight she was almost magnetically drawn to his eyes. *Must be the shirt,* she decided. Though Cordelia was certainly not impervious to the appeal of wealth, power, and healthy good looks, her reaction to his presence seemed to her to be extreme.

It *didn't,* however, seem to be uncommon.

Most of the models were undulating toward him, cooing as they slid across the floor gracefully, tossing perfect, shiny manes across slim, bare shoulders. There was a mechanical quality to their sexy strut, as if they were being drawn forward almost against their will.

And Cordelia found that she was, too.

"Okay, so . . . I know I've been living in a cave for the past few years," Fred began tentatively, finally pushing aside the near-empty box of doughnuts, "but does anyone else think that Cordelia was acting a little strangely just now?"

"Definitely," all three men responded in unison.

"Is it possible she was merely excited about the party, and the prospect of this new job opportunity?" Wesley suggested.

"Nuh-uh. Did you see that thing she did, where she undressed Angel with her eyes?" Gunn pointed out. "Now that's just not natural." The entire exchange had creeped him out in a big way.

"Okay, wait a minute—," Angel protested, clearly uncomfortable with the turn that the conversation was taking. "She may have been a little . . . *friendly* . . . but I don't know that she was *undressing* any—unnatural?"

"C'mon man. This is *Cordelia.* I don't care how lonely she's been lately or when she last went on a date. Girl's not hitting on any of us. I don't think she's even attracted to any of us. She just doesn't think of us that way."

"Well—," Wesley started. He thought back to the awkward kiss he and Cordelia had shared back at Sunnydale High and decided it was best not to mention that debacle. *But still—one would assume that she had been, at least on some level, attracted. . . .*

"Same as *we* don't think of *her* that way," Gunn added, definitively.

"Well . . ." Angel trailed off. *Well, what?* he asked himself. *No, not gonna go there,* he decided. "Yes. Something's up."

"I mean, she's cute and all, but we've got . . . you know . . . a job to do," Gunn finished lamely. "Can't be gettin' involved with each other."

"I have to agree with Charles," Fred said, blushing furiously. "There've never been any signs to indicate interest before now. And it's true, office romances are . . . complicated."

"Exactly!" Wesley and Gunn agreed simultaneously. Angel noted that they both glanced at Fred and quickly glanced off in opposite directions.

"*Unnatural,* though—I mean, don't you think that's a little harsh?" Angel continued defensively. "Women have flirted with me. Some very attractive women have flirted with me in my day."

"I'm sure," Fred said, nodding, still with the blushing. "But not Cordelia."

"Listen—she said it herself. Her social life has taken a hit since her days ruling Sunnydale High. We're all on demon watch twenty-four/seven. We know what it's like to have no time for romance—"

"Some of us got souls to worry about," Gunn added.

". . . it stands to reason she might turn her attentions to the familiar. Meaning, us," Angel finished loudly. He gazed ahead reflectively. "I happen to think that's *perfectly* natural."

"I think you hit a nerve," Fred whispered to Gunn, who nodded, smirking. She looked over at Angel. "So you're saying you think she *was* hitting on you?"

"No!

"But she *could* have been," he finished somewhat lamely.

Ignoring Angel, Wesley noticed something on the counter. "Cordelia's compact. I hope she wasn't planning on using it later." He scooped it up and tossed it from palm to palm. "It's quite heavy."

"A gift from Whittiger. He gives them to all the girls. It's engraved with the agency's logo," Fred explained. Cordelia had showed off it to her earlier that week, on the day of her first meeting with Whittiger.

"Yes, well, regardless of how uncomfortable Cordelia's behavior was making us, I think we need to consider the idea that something is . . ." Wesley peered more closely at the etchings that bordered the small metal mirror. "Hmm . . ."

"'Hmm' what? I don't wanna be hearing no 'hmm,'" Gunn said. He'd been sitting next to Fred at the computer, surfing the Whittiger Web site. Research was rarely less painful than the experience of watching Fred scroll past the roster of newly signed models, but at the first sound of Wesley's musings, the parade of hotties was all but forgotten. *Anything that starts in "hmm" usually ends in "gross," "monster," or "dead." Which is not exactly in the holiday spirit.*

"No, I suppose not. Speaking of familiar—this logo—I don't believe it is a logo. I recognize it."

"Recognize it, copyright-infringement, or recognize it, bust-out-the-books-there's-a-demon-on-the loose?" *'Cause, with the 'gross,' 'monster,' and 'dead' . . . Cordy's going to be so disappointed.*

Wesley sighed. "The latter, I'm afraid."

Mortification, thy name is Cordelia.

The would-be ingenue could barely believe her own behavior. Since Whittiger had descended the staircase she had joined the throng of Stepford models in their adulation. Something about the scene didn't feel right—she didn't *want* to seduce him—he was her boss, or would be soon, after all—but she couldn't seem to stop herself. And neither could any of the other girls.

"Please to let me hang your jacket, Mr. Whittiger," Katia, a willowy brunette, was saying. Cordelia turned to her.

"Excuse me," she whispered, "but do you think it's odd that we're all so desperate to cater to this man? And where is his coat-gathering help? People who aren't invited guests, after all? Don't you think something's going on here?"

Katia stared at Cordelia. "I must go and hang jacket," she explained, as if to a two-year-old.

Cordelia grabbed her by the arm. "Wait. Listen to me. I know from what I'm saying. Something about this scene feels a little"—she paused and flashed a bright, sunny grin at Whittiger—"I *love* that tie"—and tugged again at Katia—"brainwashy."

Katia giggled and languidly burrowed back into the throng.

You've barely been here an hour. How brainwashed can you be? Get to the bathroom and call Angel, she commanded herself. She steadied herself as Whittiger drew closer. *Mmm . . . I can smell his cologne.* "Mr. Whittiger. So *wonderful* to see you again. May I get you a drink?"

"Of course, Cordelia."

Wine plus glass, Cordelia reminded herself, bracing herself against the counter. *That's all I need.*

"Are you actually fixing him a *drink*?!"

Cordelia gasped and leaped at least two feet into the air. "Angel!" She looked around. "And Gunn and Wesley and Fred, and there's something not kosher about my new job prospect. What's going on here?" She wriggled closer to Angel. "How'd you get in here?" She paused. "I knew you'd save me."

"All I had to do was ring the bell. One of the girls invited me in," he explained in a rush. "They were actually pretty eager to bring me inside. Friendly women." Redirecting his thoughts, he continued, "The compact. Does Whittiger give one to all of the girls?"

"Uh-huh. He's so generous . . . and kind . . . and sexy . . ." She pinched herself. "Again I say, gross. Stop me before I flirt again."

"We believe the mirrors are enchanted. Wes cross-checked the engraving and it's consistent with runic symbols used to initiate women into a cult of succubi."

"It looks like Whittiger is the human identity of the demon Gilgor," Wesley explained, obviously struggling not to be distracted by the models, "believed possibly to be a descendant of Lilith and an overseer of the succubi of the underworld."

"I'm a succubus? Mucho *ew.* But it does explain a lot." She hooked a finger into Angel's back pocket. "I should have known you'd figure it out." She pushed him away. "Ugh, behold the humiliation."

"So I get why all of the foreign imports are playing at empty-headed, but why I am the only girl here who senses something of the funk?"

"It's likely that the demon part of you renders you less pervious," Wesley explained.

"No perv, not me. An enchanted succubus, maybe, but not a perv. So you think he was using us to seduce his clients—and feed his ego—and keep his agency on top?"

Fred nodded. "Yeah. We're sorry."

"We know how much you wanted this," Angel added.

She threw her arms around him and smacked her lips against his cheek loudly. "So how do we stop him?"

"Wes has a theory," Angel explained, unwrapping himself—however slowly—from her grip. "Wes?"

In the doorway, Wesley was gazing into the eyes of a Scandinavian swimsuit model. "Why, yes, I could certainly use a drink," he was saying as she linked an arm possessively through his. "That would be lovely."

"Wes!"

Wesley snapped his head up. "Right, then . . . ah . . . There should be a source here, perhaps a large mirror?"

Cordy nodded. "In the living room. It makes my legs look way long." She struck a Jessica Rabbit pose as demonstration, then pointed. "Back there."

"I'm gonna get with the smashing," Gunn offered, indicating the sledgehammer he brandished. He kicked aside the large duffle in which he'd transported it. "Shouldn't be too hard. . . ." he trailed off as he noticed the chorus line of lingerie models fluffing their hair along the mirrored wall. A perky redhead caught his gaze in the mirror and winked at him.

"Ah, ah, my dear—you cannot come between a model and her mirror," Natascha chided him playfully, sidling up next to him and tapping a manicured index finger on his nose. "But you can come nearer to me, if you like."

"It's a thought," Gunn mused cheerfully.

"Oh, please," Fred groaned, "Charles, give me the sledgehammer." Careful to avert her eyes from the glass, she made her way to the mirror.

Cordelia and Angel were following close behind when Whittiger suddenly appeared. "Cordelia. Whatever happened to my drink?"

"You know, Whittiger, it's been an enchanting evening, but I think I'm going to, uh, get you that cocktail and be on my way."

He grabbed her by the wrist. "I can't let you do that."

She pressed against him sensually. *Sex appeal, don't fail me now.* "Of course you can. I think you can let me do exactly what I want to do."

He pushed her off of him. "Come now. If you know about the magick, then you must know that as the person who enchanted the mirror, I am not susceptible to your seduction. Your feminine wiles won't work on me."

"But something tells me this will."

Thwack! Without warning, Angel plunged a pointed tip into the demon's back. With a roar, Whittiger's visage gave way to the horrid countenance of Gilgor. His eyes flashed red and his skin became gunmetal gray and scaly, before his entire being melted into an oozing, bubbling puddle on the floor.

"Silver tipped. Gets 'em every time," Angel explained, twirling the stake in his hand like a baton.

"Clean up, aisle one," Cordy said, stepping daintily aside before the sludge could run onto her kitten heels.

A lanky model of the heroin-chic aesthetic wrapped her arms around Angel from behind. "My hero, no?" She breathed into his ear. Despite himself, Angel shuddered.

Fred snorted. "Really. A little self-respect, ladies," she grumbled. She grunted and brought the sledgehammer up, hard, slamming it into the mirror with adrenaline-fueled fury. In a blinding flash of light, the glass shattered, showering the room in disco hues and dusting the floor in the closest approximation of snow the coast had seen in decades.

Simultaneously, the models shivered.

"And may I say again, '*bleah,*'" Cordelia exclaimed, rubbing her hands over her bare arms. "The sex puppet wants to go home and shower. It's good to have me back again."

"Right," Fred agreed, dropping the sledgehammer in exhaustion. "Besides, what guy really wants a mindless love-slave, anyway? . . . *Anyway,*" she cleared her throat in the direction of Wesley.

He dropped the Scandinavian's hand guiltily. "Well, now that she's no longer enchanted, it's safe to say her interest is genuine. Right, Inge?"

She beamed, exposing every last gleaming, capped tooth. "I fix you drink now, no?"

"*No,*" Cordy answered firmly. "Not meaning to break up what is obviously the most sexually charged evening you've seen in a while, Wes, enchanted or no, these women are clearly not playing with a full deck. Let's face it, modeling, not so much a job for the big-brained. More like big . . . smiled."

"If they're so empty-headed, they've probably never known true happiness. . . . ," Angel mused.

"Focus," Cordy commanded, rounding up her crew. "What have we learned?"

"*Some* models have beauty but not brains," Fred suggested carefully. "Which is why it's great, Cordelia, that you'll always have Angel Investigations to keep you grounded."

"And what else?"

"Mirrors—why bother?" Angel suggested, holding open the front door.

"Now you're just talking crazy," Cordelia protested.

"I got it. Sex is bad," Gunn said.

"That we all knew," Angel agreed.

"Romance is dead," Wesley said dully, casting a forlorn glance at Inge as she giggled at something another model was saying. She seemed to be over him.

Angel threw a completely platonic arm across Cordelia's shoulder. "But we've got your back."

She ruffled his hair affectionately. "*That's* good news." Her hands dropped mischievously behind *his* back.

"Ow!"

"*Kidding.*"

11 P.M.

HAVE GUNN, WILL TRAVEL

by Nancy Holder

It was late, and the hotel was hopping.

Hey, that is one good-lookin' man, Gunn thought. *Kinda hairy, though.* The man was nappy, but Gunn had to admit, it worked for him. *Maybe someday I'll grow my own hair back.*

He didn't make a habit of finding other guys attractive, but there was something about the tall, dark, and handsome stranger that made him look twice. The light was dim in the lobby so Gunn couldn't completely make him out. But he was curious, and even more intrigued by the large numbers of guys milling around Handsome Guy, some of them with earphones and a lot of them with weaponry. Something happened to threaten this guy, it was going to be raining bullets.

Wouldn't be the first time, in this old hotel.

Wesley and Angel were talking intently with the man

and his security team, so Gunn decided to see if Fred and Cordy knew what was going down.

He crossed from the lobby to Wesley's office, only to find Cordelia and Fred primly seated on the edges of their chairs, knees locked together, ankles pressed against each other so hard they were probably leaving bruises. Their posture was total military school and their pinkies saluted the ceiling as they perched dainty teacups in pastel decorator colors on their laps.

"Hey," he said, figuring they were doing some kind of trendy new chick-yoga or something, "I am not of the flexible Y-chromosome persuasion, but I gotta say, there is one good-looking man in the lobby. And I ain't talking about Duster Boy."

The girls traded looks. Then Cordelia turned her attention back to Gunn and said in a flat monotone, "Oh, great master, would you care for one lump or two?"

"No, no, you must *bow*," came a veddy propah English-style voice behind Gunn.

Gunn turned. A man was sitting in the corner of the office on a rollaround chair. He was extremely dark-complected and his hair was slicked down. He wore a suit that probably cost more than there was in East Los Angeles, even counting all the illegal gang activity that went down over there. There was an earpiece dangling from his left lobe, and Gunn knew the bulge of a .457 in a jacket when he saw one.

Gunn watched as Fred grimaced, fighting with the tea as it threatened to slosh over the rim, and awkwardly dipped her head over her cup.

"Bowing as in face to the floor," the man said impatiently.

Clapping his hands, he stepped around Gunn with nary a "'scuse me, brother," minced over to Fred and Cordelia, and took their teacups away. They both whined and he said, "Now, now, ladies, you may have your tea back after you've shown proper obeisance. On your knees."

Fred looked to Cordelia for guidance. Cordelia put on her best don't-mess-with-me-face and said, "Uh-uh, no way."

"Protocol demands it," the man said.

"We need the job," Fred murmured. "Please, Cordelia."

Cordelia rolled her eyes and gave Gunn a don't-even-ask look as both women moved to obey.

Huh, will grovel for tea. Those have to be some good leaves . . .

Then Cordelia stopped and said, "Wait, this is not the prince and . . ."

"And you must pretend that he is the prince," the man informed her with thinly disguised impatience.

"Cordy, please. Just do it." That was Angel, from the doorway. "We agreed to do it their way."

"All right, all right," she grumped. She glanced at Fred and muttered, "Geronimo."

Both the women lowered themselves to the floor on their hands and knees, then dipped forward to touch their foreheads to the floor. Gunn had to admit it was not a hideous sight. Fighting demons kept the women of Angel Investigations in fine shape.

"Now." The man turned to Gunn as he handed both the teacups to Angel, who held them awkwardly. "You are the imposter, correct?"

Before Gunn could say, "Say what?" Angel cut in.

"He is."

"Very good." The man scrutinized Gunn, walking around him in a little circle, glancing up, down, clucking his teeth. He smelled like roses and limes. Beyond them, in the lobby, the good-lookin' guy and Wesley were still talking to the man's people. Then two of them started upstairs.

The man said to Angel, "He'll need a wig."

From their slave girl positions on the floor, Cordelia and Fred tittered. Gunn raised one corner of his mouth and narrowed his eyes and said, "Okay, I think it's time for me to hear the punchline."

"Oh? He doesn't know?" Fancy Suit Guy asked Angel, who shook his head.

"Nor has he agreed to do it," Angel added, still juggling the teacups, which looked like tiny doll cups in his large hands. "It's up to him."

"Ah." The man placed his fingertips together and put them under his chin. "Mr. . . . Gunn, is it?"

"Yeah," Gunn said.

The man elegantly cleared his throat. "I represent His Royal Highness Prince Govinda, of the nation of Bodisahtva. He has been invited to a Christmas party given by the French ambassador."

"That's great," Gunn said with only a slight edge. "He's a lucky Royal Highness."

"He is the Crown Prince of Bodisahtva," the man continued, pointing out to the lobby. "His father is ailing, and he stands to come to the throne very soon."

Gunn took that in. He glanced through the doorway at Prince Govinda. With a better opportunity to study him, Gunn noted that his suit was even more awesome than this guy's, and his loafers were wafer-thin. *Dude,* was that a Rolex on his wrist?

The lesser suit added, "As you may imagine, the heir to a throne is a vulnerable man. Other ambitious princes wish to get rid of him, so that they may become sultan."

"Speaking of wishes," Cordelia said, "I wish to get up now."

"I wish it, too," Fred murmured.

"Ah. In our country, you would be whipped for speaking like that," the man said jovially. "America, land of freedom. Please, ladies, rise."

Grumbling, both girls creaked up and sat back down on the sofa.

"Tea?" Angel asked eagerly, handing each girl back her cup.

"Bonus?" Cordelia rejoined, through clenched teeth.

"Here's the situation," Angel said to Gunn. "You probably noticed that you could be this guy's reflection in a mirror."

"Oh." Gunn was surprised. He hadn't actually caught that, in the dim light. *That explains the attraction.* He was very relieved about that.

Angel continued, "There's a plot to assassinate him at the party. They want you to impersonate him and take his place."

"At the hors d'oeuvres table, not the morgue," Gunn said archly.

"Correct." The prince's lackey smiled with very large white teeth. "Although it will be very dangerous, of course."

Cool.

"We will dress you as the prince, and your protocol advisor will meet you at the party. He will help coach you. He will tell you at all times with whom you are conversing. There will be kings, sultans, and many beautiful women," the lackey added, with a slimy smile. "The party is being held in a very luxurious, very private home. It could be a very pleasant evening."

"Please say yes, Gunn," Cordelia begged. "Fred and I were given these amazing dresses to wear." Fred nodded vigorously. Then Cordelia smiled with her own big white teeth at the lackey. "And to keep?"

"If the prince allows it." The man smiled at them. "He is a very generous man."

Those were musical notes to the ears of Miss Cordelia Chase, if Gunn knew his materialistic stick-figure, stand-up Barbie-doll.

"Why am I taking Cordelia and Fred into a dangerous situation?" Gunn asked Angel.

"The prince requires concubines," the man explained.

Gunn shook his head. "Well, I don't require dead friends."

Cordelia muttered, "But we still want to keep our dresses."

Gunn looked at Angel, who had crossed his arms and was leaning against the doorjamb, taking it all in. "Who's behind the plot to kill the prince?"

"Ambitious demons," Angel replied. "That's why they came to us, plus resemblance. One of their front men saw you at Caritas and Lorne told them about us."

The man dipped his head. "There is enmity between the families. Something to do with an ancient oil lamp, I believe, and who has legal claim to it. The lamp comes with the throne, you see." His face became a study in pissed off. "These *jinn* have traveled all the way from the Emerald Mountains of Kaf to kill the prince."

"At a party given by the French ambassador," Gunn said slowly, still trying to get the picture.

The lackey shrugged. "Well, you know the French." He frowned at Gunn. "You *do* speak French?"

Gunn hesitated, because of course he didn't speak French. He spoke some Spanish and bits of various Asian languages, most of which was unprintable, but French was not a language he had picked up fighting vampires and demons in Los Angeles.

The vampire said nothing, but Gunn knew his homeboy's eyebrow language, and Angel was bummed. No French, no gig.

We must be gonna get a whole lot of dead presidents for this job, Gunn figured. *And baby, do we need 'em.*

As usual, Angel Investigations was stone broke, and he had a whole lot of friends who had "conveniently" decided to start celebrating Kwanzaa on top of Christmas. In other words, a long list of people dunning him for gifts. And he hadn't even figured out what he was going to get Angel; he was stuck between a gag gift—a T-shirt from the Cedars-Sinai Hospital blood bank—and the easy way out—something black to wear.

"He speaks French," Cordelia chimed in, "if I get to keep my dress. And Fred gets hers, too. Because of the French." She looked at Angel.

Gunn got it: Cordelia spoke French. So she would have to go.

But Fred stays here.

"Ah." The man lifted a brow in appreciation and glanced at Angel. "A haggler. You would do well in Bodisahtva, *chère mademoiselle.*" He crossed to Cordelia and raised her hand to his lips. "I apologize, Miss Chase. I did not realize it was to you I should look for the terms to Mr. Gunn's employment."

Gunn couldn't tell if the man was being sarcastic or what.

"He can speak French," Cordelia said through gritted teeth. "He took it in high school, remember? And he has been to Paris several times."

He looked over at Angel, who shrugged as if to say, "Your call."

There was a huge amount of commotion in the lobby. Gunn turned to watch as the prince swept from the circular couch toward the office. His show runner—the guy in the office with Gunn—swallowed hard and gave Gunn a look.

"If you speak French," he blurted, "I will double the price we have already agreed upon with Mr. Angel."

Man, he's shaking, Gunn thought, glancing at the dude's hands. *He's scared to death of what's going to go down if he has to tell the prince that I haven't signed up for this gig.*

"I speak French," he said.

"Thank you, thank you," the man said in a rush. Then he collapsed onto the floor, forehead down, butt up, as the prince hovered on the threshold.

"Well?" Royal Guy said imperiously. He lifted his nose just like an honest to goodness snob and examined Gunn from head to toe. "Yes. The likeness is remarkable. Do you not think so, Mr. Mbong?"

"Indeed, Your Royal Highness," said the guy on the floor—Mr. Mbong. His voice was muffled on account of forehead crushed into linoleum. "And he is a demon hunter."

"Who speaks French," Cordelia sang out.

The prince stared open-mouthed at her. Gunn thought, *Uh-oh. A mere female has spoken in the presence of the His Royal High-on-himself-ness.*

"Um, that is, he speaks French, *Your Majesty,*" Cordelia added contritely. Then she flashed that trademark knock-'em-dead Cordy smile and asked silkily, "You want me to kneel?"

The prince was entranced. For a second all he did was stare at Cordelia, and then he walked across the room and took her teacup from her, handing it to Angel without looking at it, and lifted her to a standing position as if she were the most fragile, daintiest flower in all of Bodisahtva.

"How delightful of you to so inform us," he said to her. "And no, fair American lady, you do not need to kneel . . . at the moment." His tone was as smooth as the dulcet tones of Ricky Martin. He put Gunn in the mind of his first-grade teacher, Mrs. Delgado, who used to call Gunn her "big, big, big helper." Then give him some bogus job like dumping her wastebasket.

The prince turned to his lackey, who was still cowering on the floor and said, "Mr. Mbong, you have done well." He snapped his fingers at Gunn. "You shall be prepared for the Christmas party."

Prepared? What am I, a turkey?

Gunn slid a glance toward Angel, who looked blankly back, then to the prince, then to Mr. Mbong. No help there. That guy was not moving a muscle until his Royal Self told him to.

"You will wear my clothes, of course."

"And a wig, I was thinking, Your Royal Highness," Mr. Mbong ventured.

"I think not. He'll wear a turban instead." The prince smiled as he looked at Gunn appraisingly, obviously liking what he saw. *Which is non-royal me.* "Now I shall fulfill my royal duty with no possibility of harm to my royal person. It is Providence that brought you to me." He touched his chest, then his lips, then his forehead, and sent the thought toward heaven.

"That, and one of our business cards," Cordelia murmured. "Courtesy of Lorne."

Apparently the prince didn't hear her. With a curt nod to Mr. Mbong, he swept back out of the room, and after a suitable amount of time in which one could have, oh, cleaned the hotel from top to bottom, Mr. Mbong raised his head, heaved a sigh of relief, and got up off the floor.

As if to apologize for his leader-to-be, he said, "The Lion of Bodisahtva is very young. In fact, he is only twenty-two." Then he turned and faced them all, sweeping a courtly bow. "I will see to Mr. Gunn's wardrobe. If I may see you in approximately five minutes, Mr. Gunn?"

Gunn nodded, said, "Sure," and the man practically ran out of the office.

Gunn gave Cordelia a look. "I swear, girl, someday that mouth of yours is gonna get you beheaded or something."

"Hey, I was a princess," she reminded him. "Royal people understand each other."

"Ohhh." Fred paled and touched her neck. She cast an unwitting glance at Angel, who was still holding Cordelia's teacup.

Bad memories, Gunn figured. *After all, Angel nearly did cut Fred's head off, back on Pylea.*

He said, "Tell me, Angel, is this gig really worth it? Cuz maybe Cordelia was royalty, but I sure ain't. I mean, I got game and I can fake my way through anything. But this sounds damn lame."

"It sounds fun!" Cordelia protested. She jostled Fred in the ribs, and tea went flying over Fred's jeans. "Right?"

"Lots of fun," Fred agreed. "Fancy clothes, demons, a nice Christmas party. I haven't been to a Christmas party in over five years!" She frowned. "Christmas, not big in Pylea. No Christmas caroling, that's for sure."

"It's okay, Fred," Gunn said gently. "That stuff's all over. And you're not going."

Angel nodded. "Gotta agree there, Fred. There's no need. I'm sending you in a cab over to Caritas."

She looked dashed . . . and then rather relieved.

Gunn glanced back through the doorway. "Okay, then, I'm seeing the high side. A great suit, good food, and money to give us all nice, fat Christmas bonuses." He grinned at Angel.

At that point Wesley walked up and beckoned to Gunn. "They're ready to dress you," he said.

"Why ain't you going, English?" Gunn asked.

"I will be driving the limo," Wesley told him. "And Angel's assignment is to guard the prince back here, in the hotel."

"But I'm the prince," Gunn pointed out. Angel should be hangin' with me."

"The prince doesn't see it that way," Wesley said. "He has insisted that Angel remain with him."

Then Mr. Mbong came back, saying, "Please, sir," to Gunn, who smiled crookedly.

Okay, some weirdness, but I'm going to be wearing the finest suit in Los Angeles, he thought, *to a very uptown party. This night is shakin' out to be pretty good after all.*

• • •

Angel had to turn his head when Gunn reappeared, attired in the prince's "evening ensemble."

He was wearing a purple velvet *dashiki* that was encrusted with gold and silver embroidery and what looked to be chunks of kryptonite, but was some other glowing green gemstone since vampires and demons were real, but Superman was not. *Weird world.* His shoes were golden sandals curled at the tips like Christmas-elf shoes. Around each ankle he wore gold bangles hung with tiny jeweled bells, and he had more gold around his neck and his wrists than that amazing holdover from the innocent youth of the Me Generation, Mr. T.

But the crowning blow was the two-or-three-foot-tall golden headdress that extended straight up like a huge spray-painted hot dog bun, coated with huge gems and topped with a feather. Gunn looked like a bizarre cross between Eryka Badhu, Marge Simpson, and some guy in a Dr. Seuss book.

Moving slowly beneath his towering disco inferno of golden threads, Gunn managed to get through the door. His presentation to the prince for inspection took place in the suite next to Fred's room, and not a single member of Angel Investigations wanted to miss it. At his grand entrance, Cordelia, bundled in an oversize burnoose, had to struggle not to burst into giggles, and even Wesley's stiff upper lip quivered when the prince turned to Mr. Mbong and said, "An excellent job. There is no telling him apart from me now."

"Indeed, Highness. Do you not agree, Prince Govinda?" Mr. Mbong gaily teased Gunn.

Gunn thought about a few answers, and replied, "Oh, I'm not half the looker His Highness is."

"You are just a me wanna-be, are you not?" the prince asked. He looked around the room for everyone to be impressed by his wit.

"Oh, yeah," Gunn said dryly.

"Rest assured, you will appear to the public to be every inch the charismatic monarch that I am," the prince assured him, "or rather, that I soon will be, once my esteemed and most beloved father dies." He stared hard at Gunn and the others. "That is, if you do your jobs properly. It would be a huge loss to the nation if 'I' were assassinated."

Lotta syllables in that word "assassinated," but the first syllable applies, Gunn thought.

Then the prince said to Cordelia, "Unveil yourself, please."

Cordelia unzipped her burnoose and let it tumble to the floor. She was dressed in a golden body-hugging strapless gown. A slit raced from the floor to the center of her right thigh. The slit and hem were dotted with what at first looked like embroidered threads, but on closer inspection were chips of precious stones . . . hundreds of them. Her strappy evening shoes were also decorated with dozens and dozens of gems.

"Whoa," Gunn said.

She grinned at Angel, struck a pose, and said, "Well?"

"Very pretty." He looked uncomfortable, and she was hurt.

"Oh, Cordelia, you're beautiful!" Fred enthused. "Oh, I wish . . ." She sighed. "Caritas."

The prince smiled gently at Fred. "Your ensemble was to have been in silver. I make a gift of it to you."

"Oh gee, thanks!" Fred burbled. She smiled at Cordelia, who smiled back at her.

Then one of the prince's men said to Wesley, "If you please, I'll take you back to the limo. You may complete your inspection and then you will drive Mr. Gunn and his beauty to the party."

"As you wish," Wesley said, doing the salaam thing, touching his chest. He left the room.

"His beauty," Cordelia said under her breath.

"Yes," the prince said. "It is a tradition in my country for the prince to collect as many beauties as possible."

"Like trading cards," Cordelia grumbled.

"Exactly." He smiled at her happily. "You are my first American beauty."

After about fifteen minutes, Wesley returned. He was dressed in a black tuxedo and he wore a burgundy-colored fez. His hair was disheveled. The man who accompanied him was not the man he left with. This one was taller, and there was a stripe of green goo on the man's very nice suit.

When the real prince saw the man, he looked disgusted. He smacked him across the cheek and shouted, "How dare you come into my presence with blood on yourself!"

"Demon blood," Cordelia translated for Fred, who covered her mouth with her hand.

"There was an altercation in the limo," Wesley said, sounding angry. "We caught one of the Kaf mountain *jinn* attempted to rig the limo to blow up. Your other man—I believe his name was Wali—caught the *jinn* in the act and was killed trying to stop him."

"He's dead?" Fred asked nervously.

"His soul shall be received into Paradise, may the One be praised," the prince said, with a dismissive wave of his hand. "Now, off with you. 'I' don't want to be late!" He grinned at Gunn. "Don't drink too much champagne."

Gunn looked discomfited. His beauty was also not happy.

Cordelia muttered, "Christmas bonus," and the two swept out of the room.

The limo ride was uneventful, chalking one up for Wesley and the two dozen wards he had installed in the limo. He had also swept the limo for bugs of the spy kind, and found six of them.

But now they were out of the stretch, and Wesley had driven it away to park with the other drivers. Mr. Mbong, Gunn, and Cordy were surrounded by bodyguards, some of whom had ridden in the limo and others who had taken a separate vehicle. Cordy was on Gunn's left arm as they were greeted by a man in an Armani tux wearing a pair of very stylish Ralph Lauren glasses.

"Good evening, Your Royal Highness," said the man in the tux. Then he launched into a barrage of French.

"He's the Ambassador. Say, '*oui*,'" she whispered.

"*Oui*," Gunn blurted, and the French ambassador chuckled.

Then the man bowed, allowing Gunn's squadron of muscle to walk between them, encapsulating Gunn and Cordy in a protective bubble, and the group swept into a grand, three-story house with more wrought-iron balconies and arched windows than Cordelia had ever seen. It was beautiful.

One of the men touched an earpiece and said something in the prince's native tongue.

Mr. Mbong whispered, "It is safe to go in."

Then why are we here? Cordy thought silently.

Angel had seen Fred safely off in the cab. Now it was time to get to work.

Given the number of visitors Angel Investigations had at the hotel these days, Wesley had decided to furnish a number of extra suites for situations such as the one Angel now found himself in. He was seated beside the real prince, who had pushed the leather recliner in which he sat back so that he was almost prone. He was drinking scotch, neat.

The spoiled, arrogant young man had demanded to be entertained. Angel had suggested chess, which had been rejected, and then bridge, also rejected, and then the prince had asked him what DVDs he had. It turned out he was a Bruce Willis fan, and *Die Hard* it was.

As the two settled in with microwave popcorn, a series of loud explosions rocked the hotel.

"I am being attacked!" the prince shouted, jerking so hard that the recliner fell backward and he tumbled out of it. "I order you to save me!"

Angel shouted, "Stay down!" He ran to the windows and checked them. He grabbed the prince, who shouted back, "Unhand me, infidel!" Then he must have thought the better of it, for he added, "Take me somewhere safe, immediately!"

Angel herded him into his own suite, yelled, "Stay here!" and dashed into the hallway.

By the time he reached the stairs, the lobby was filled with smoke and dead Bodisahtvan security guards. Green-skinned demons with pointy ears and green topknots rode chopped Harleys and wheelied over the carnage, hooting and shouting. They were wielding axes and knives, and one of them threw his ax into the chandelier, sending crystal beads flying in all directions like an exploding sun.

Now they were slathering and thundering all over the lobby, until one of them held up a Louis Vuitton traveling bag and ripped it open with his teeth. He dug inside and triumphantly held up a Middle Eastern brass oil lamp that had been polished to a high gloss and was studded with jewels.

"The lamp!" Prince Govinda gasped behind Angel. "Those are Kaf mountain demons!"

Angel glared at him. "I told you to stay! What lamp?"

One of the demons shouted something and they gunned their engines, then roared back into the night through the front door and the windows they had smashed to enter. Their choppers screamed like banshees as they rode away.

"It is the Lamp of the Genie," the prince said to Angel as they watched the retreating demons. He left the sentence unfinished. "We must get it back!"

"Why'd you leave it downstairs in a duffel bag?" Angel demanded.

"No one was to know I had it. My father . . . it is the source of our power," he confessed. "It is what keeps us on the throne."

"You took it," Angel said flatly. "Without telling him."

The prince raised himself up to his full height. "How dare you question my actions! I am the Crown Prince of Bodisahtva! You are nothing but a low-class American bodyguard." He raised a shaking hand. "Now go and retrieve my possession or . . ."

Angel waited.

He added, "If they release the genie, Los Angeles will become a wasteland. That is why the owner is so feared, and wields so much power. We could turn the region into a desert with one rub of that lamp."

Okay, incentive, Angel thought.

"Fine," he said, and grabbed Prince Govinda around the arm. "Let's go."

"*What?*"

"I have to get it back. I can't leave you here alone. And all your men are dead."

Prince Govinda raised himself to his full height. Which, since he was as tall as Gunn, was considerable. "I have more men! They are at that party! Summon them at once!"

"Tell you what," Angel said. "You summon them from the convertible. We're leaving now."

He dragged the protesting prince down the stairs.

"Okay, wasn't someone supposed to meet me here and tell me who's who in this crowd and all like that?" Gunn demanded of Mr. Mbong as he and Cordelia were escorted on a red carpet into the exquisitely appointed house.

"Your protocol advisor has been detained, alas," the man announced, "but here, Highness, is one very familiar and dear to you." He looked at Gunn as if to say, *Get it?*

With a flourish, the man gestured to a tall, chocolate-skinned woman in a short red camisole and sheer black harem pants. She sashayed toward them as if her hips were made of ball bearings.

Danger, danger, Will Robinson, Cordelia thought.

The woman did the forehead-on-the-floor thing until Gunn said, "Rise."

"You Majestee," she cooed. Very French.

"Oui," Gunn replied.

"Akhmed, alas, 'e ees sick. 'E 'as a mad cow disease." She got up from her cleavage-displaying position on the floor and slithered up to standing position, all the better for Gunn's eyes to pop out as she stood up very straight. "Ah will serve in his place tonight as your protocol aide."

"Not liking this," Cordelia muttered through her teeth.

"Send your concubine away," the woman suggested, making pouty-face at Gunn by pushing out her lower lip. She smiled at Cordelia. "There is plenty to eat. You look 'ungry."

Angry, or hungry? Either way, back on Pylea I could be a very mad cow princess and I could get what I wanted. And I am not going to let some escapee from Rugrats in Paris *maneuver me away from Gunn.*

"She's good here," Gunn told the Frenchwoman.

Harem pants launched into rapid-fire French.

When she came to the end of whatever she was saying, Cordelia cleared her throat softly.

"Oui," Gunn said hopefully.

"C'est bon!" the woman chirruped. She clapped her hands and said to Gunn, *"S'il vous plaît."*

Gunn followed as she guided them to a long table laden with shellfish—lobster, crab legs, shrimp the size of Cordelia's fist. Cordy's mouth watered. The woman picked up a plate and began filling it, pausing at each dish to inquire of His Royal Highness if he cared for any . . . or so it appeared to Cordelia. Whom no one was feeding and everyone was ignoring.

Then a man in white robes and a fez appeared next to the table, laying a scimitar on a silver platter and smiling brilliantly at Gunn as if for his approval.

On the pointy end of the weapon, there was an eyeball.

The guests applauded politely, with a few "ooh's" and "aah's" thrown in . . . and a few slightly green faces that probably mirrored Cordelia's.

"Au jus?" the woman inquired.

"I'm going to be sick," Cordelia whispered.

Mr. Mbong murmured to Gunn, "Prince Govinda is very fond of goat eyeball."

"Ah." Gunn couldn't stop staring at the eyeball.

"Hey," Cordelia said, "On Pylea, I was gonna have to comshuck."

"Well, I'm afraid I'm gonna have to upchuck." He eyed the eyeball. "Comshuck guy turned out to be a totally good-looking guy you wanted to comshuck. No good can come of this eyeball."

"Ah," said a voice. Gunn, Cordelia, and Mr. Mbong turned to see the French ambassador looking at Gunn looking at the eyeball.

"He's happy for you," Cordelia whispered. "That you get an eyeball to eat."

Gunn fidgeted with his many bangle bracelets. "Can't I be too full?"

"Then it would have to be something big, like a whale eyeball . . . ew," Cordelia muttered.

"They're awfully excited about this," Gunn said slowly. Then he turned to Mr. Mbong and whispered, "How come the prince doesn't have a food taster?"

The man looked abashed as he whispered back, "Alas, he did. It was the man who was murdered earlier this evening."

Nice of you to mention that.

Also, very convenient.

"Well, I ain't eatin' nothing that hasn't been tested," Gunn said.

Mr. Mbong's eyebrows raised and lowered several times. "But you will cause an international incident if you do not eat this delicacy. It has been specially prepared for you."

Gunn crossed his arms. The French ambassador drew back, astonished. "How many usually come in a serving?" Gunn asked. "I mean, is it like sushi, where you get a certain number of eyeballs?"

"Oh, Majestee, you are so cautious," said the hussy in the harem pants.

Cordelia whispered to Gunn, "Make her eat it."

"My beauty, I give the honor of the first eyeball to you," Gunn said to the other woman, just as another servant in a white robe and fez handed him a flute of what looked to be champagne. Gunn hoisted the glass and said, "Here's looking at you."

He swigged down the champagne.

The woman was so moved by the prince's generosity that tears welled in her eyes. She said, "Oh, Majestee, ah do not deserve this honaire."

With her dainty, manicured hand, she plucked the eyeball off the end of the scimitar and popped it into her mouth. She bit down.

She keeled over.

She hit the floor.

Panic ensued as the ambassador called for his private physician, who ordered some servants to carry the stricken woman—*who looks pretty darn dead to me*—to the ambassador's quarters so he could attend to her. There was something in the way the ambassador said it, in French—a phony kind of mock-innocent lilt that screamed alarms in Cordelia's mind.

Gunn must have sensed it, too. He grabbed the scimitar off the table, brandishing it at the ambassador and yelled, "That eyeball was an evil eyeball! It was poisoned!"

Everyone in the room froze and stared at Gunn. The ambassador shouted at him in French.

"He says 'how dare you,'" Cordelia translated. "Also . . . 'attack him!'"

Then, in a swirl of morphing, dripping, melting faces, many of the party guests transformed into extremely muscular green-skinned demons with pointy ears and heads that were bald except for a topknot of green hair that cascaded down their backs. Their teeth and fingernails were sharp and scimitar-shaped, and they all rushed at Gunn, Cordy, Mr. Mbong, and the bodyguards. The ambassador hung back with the humans, who began to race from the room.

"They are the forces of Duke Narthala!" Mr. Mbong cried. "The Kaf mountain jinn!"

Then Prince Govinda's bodyguards morphed into yellow-skinned demons with huge purple mouths, and Mr. Mbong changed too.

Gunn had no time to register surprise. "How do I kill them?" he yelled, as he slammed his fist into the face of the demon who had served him the eyeball.

"The same as humans!" Mr. Mbong cried.

Cordelia picked up an ice sculpture off the table and whacked another demon. Then she grabbed a chafing dish and hurled it at the third attacker.

Gunn got down to business, body-slamming two Kaf

demons out of his way and handily decapitating a third.

The now-demonic Mr. Mbong scurried under the buffet table, tangled his legs in the white cloth, and pulled all the food onto the floor with him. Sauces and crab legs went flying . . . and several more goat's eyeballs rolled between Cordelia's feet.

"Ew, ew, ew!" Cordelia yelled, trying not to step on them.

From beneath the table, Mr. Mbong stuck out his head and announced, "I am translating from our native demonic tongue for you. The ambassador had the eyeball poisoned. He is trying to overthrow the regime!" He paused, listening, and added, "Oh, Prince Govinda, how could you?"

"How could he what?" Cordelia asked, as she kneed another oncoming demon. The assailant doubled up and fell to his knees.

"Prince Govinda stole the Lamp of the Genie from his father and brought it here," Mr. Mbong told them. "The French ambassador and Duke Narthala have stolen it in turn, from the hotel!"

"Christmas bonus!" Cordelia shouted. Then she plucked a serving knife from the mess on the floor, winced, and cut off her dress at the thighs so she would be able to fight better.

"Oh, this is capital! Capital!" Prince Govinda cried as Angel floored it.

They were going up the 10, swerving in and out of the traffic, gaining on the biker demons with each passing mile. The demons rode like, well, demons, as they edged out innocent bystanding vehicles, rode the shoulder, and caused crash after crash as they fled.

"This is a hunt!" the prince added. "I am a superb hunter. I have downed many elephants."

"They're endangered," Angel bit off. *There.* He recognized the demon who had held the lamp above his head. It was a good bet that he still had possession of it.

Angel zeroed in on him, dogging him, and the demon looked back fearfully over his shoulder.

I'm right, Angel thought. *He has it.*

"Faster! Faster!" Prince Govinda shouted, beating his hands on the dashboard.

Angel clamped his jaw shut so he wouldn't waste precious time responding to the moron . . .

. . . until the man flipped open his glove box and asked brightly, "Do you have a gun? A shotgun, perhaps?"

"Shut that. And shut up," Angel growled. He was on the verge of morphing.

"What did you say to me?"

And in that moment, it was the prince who did the morphing, into a yellow-skinned demon with purple eyes, lips, and porcine nostrils.

Angel blinked. "You . . . you're not human," he said.

"Yes, I am a demon. We are all demons in Bodisahtva. Did you not realize this?"

Angel said nothing. He had returned his attention to Lamp Guy, who was shrieking down the freeway as fast as his Harley could take him.

• • •

"We're not making any headway here," Cordelia said, just as Gunn decapitated another demon. "Oops, wrong, sorry."

With the help of Prince Govinda's bodyguards, they had somehow managed to cut a swath from the hors d'oeuvre table to somewhere near the main entrance. But Gunn was getting very tired, and Cordy was about to collapse.

Mr. Mbong was in the other room under the table, cowering in terror, which was just as well because he was so scared he had forgotten how to speak English.

Everyone was fighting, and Gunn figured the only reason they'd made it this far was because of all the magick Wesley had thrown his way.

Then there was a roaring and a grinding, and Gunn realized it was a car. From past adventures with Wesley, he prayed it was English driving the limo to their rescue. He gestured to Cordelia, shouting, "Come on!"

Tires squealed; a horn blared "shave and a haircut," and the door crashed open.

Wesley it was.

Gunn had no idea how many bodyguards they still had left—a few had fallen valiantly—but the loyal yellow demons held their ground, giving Gunn, Wesley, and Cordy a chance to get away.

Wesley squealed the hell out of there.

About that time, the limo phone rang.

Cordelia picked it up. "Angel?" she asked breathlessly.

"It is I, Govinda!" cried the voice on the other end.

"We are running the Kaf to the ground."

"You stole a lamp!" Cordelia cried.

"That is very true," Govinda told her, "but Angel and I will retrieve it shortly!"

"The French ambassador tried to poison you," Cordelia said. "With a bad eyeball."

"Ah, such treachery," the prince said. "Well, I must go. I have battles to win. The hotel is a disaster," he added breezily. "Dead bodies everywhere. Good-bye!"

He hung up. Cordelia looked at Gunn. "They're going to get the lamp," she said.

"I say we go back to the hotel," Gunn suggested. "If Angel needs us, he'll call there."

Wesley nodded. "A sound plan."

"Soundest one so far," Gunn grumbled.

Angel and Govinda chased the bikers all the way to the Santa Monica Pier, which was decorated for a California Christmas. The boardwalk rides were going strong and a quartet dressed in Victorian costumes was singing "Jingle Bells." There were lots of human beings strolling along, eating bags of popcorn and cotton candy, and having no idea what was going on until one brilliant soul cried out, "Someone's shooting a movie!"

Such was the culture of Los Angeles that everyone politely gave the demon bikers and Angel a wide berth, a few primping in case they ended up as extras in a scene. That made it a lot easier to corner the bikers, who did not seem to want to sail off the pier on their bikes and land in the Pacific Ocean. One by one, the bikes ground to a halt at the very end of the pylons, and the enemy demons looked unhappy and frightened.

"Kaf die in water," Prince Govinda told Angel. "As do my kind."

Angel pulled the car to a halt, leaped out, and shouted at the prince, "Go around to the left. We'll attack on two flanks."

"Excellent, excellent," the prince burbled. He began to sneak with theatrical stealth, lifting his knees high, then carefully placing his huge yellow feet down on the ground. Angel shook his head but said nothing.

They could have reached out and touched a number of the Kaf, who stood still and clicked their teeth like those wacky windup toys. But the Kaf who had stolen the lamp had ripped it from one of the saddlebags on his hog and was holding it high in the air.

Angel began to lose patience, and advanced.

"One step closer and I rub it!" he yelled.

"Not good, not good," Govinda called to Angel. "We had better back off."

Then, taking advantage of Angel's moment to consider that, the prince launched himself at the demon with the lamp, throwing him to the ground. The others could only look on as their leader easily tossed the prince off himself, got to his knees, glared at both the Crown Prince of Bodisahtva and at Angel, and rubbed the lamp.

Angel braced himself.

A huge burst of energy shot from the lamp, like a firestorm wind, blowing and surging through the crowds and the concession stands. The waves at the end of the pier rose and crashed, sending droplets everywhere.

Smoke billowed from the lamp—huge, roiling clouds of it, dark gray and smelling of sulfur and patchouli.

An enormous face spread across the night sky, obliterating the moon and the star field, casting a pall over the glittering pier. It was demonic, with a huge mouth pulled into a rictus, narrow slanted eyes, and its ears and nose elongated to the point of parody.

The face glared down at the demons and people on the boardwalk. The Kaf looked completely stunned. Evidently whoever had told them to steal the lamp had provided sketchy operating instructions, if any. Govinda stood with his legs planted apart and his hands on his hips. Angel just waited, bracing himself for the destruction of Los Angeles.

The immense face said something in a language Angel did not know. Its voice rang and vibrated, and Angel spared his last thought for Cordy, Gunn, Fred, and Wesley, and hoped that they would be far enough away to survive whatever this thing was about to do.

For a moment there was silence. Then the prince threw back his head and began to laugh. The Kaf were baffled.

"Oh, this is rich!" the prince cried. "My father is a wily old bastard!"

"What's going on?" Angel demanded.

The prince was wiping tears of laughter from his eyes. "He knew I would try to steal it."

"How do you know?" Angel said.

"The face." The prince raised a hand and gestured at it. "The lamp is a fake. The face is a joke. It basically said, as you would so quaintly put it, 'Tag, you're it.'"

Angel blinked at him.

Then he rushed the bikers. The one with the lamp went over the edge of the pier first. The second one followed within seconds.

By the time Angel had dispatched the fourth, the others were riding away on their motorcycles.

Angel watched them go. In a tone of contemptuous disgust, he said to the prince, "Let's go."

"No!" Govinda protested. "The night is young! Let us go after them!"

"I'm going home," Angel said.

He got into the convertible. The prince caught up with him, leaped in with a flourish, and said, "Let us go, then!"

Meanwhile, back at the hotel . . .

. . . Gunn put the finishing touches on the prince's outfit, placing the oversized, elevator-looking turban on Govinda's head.

It's like decorating a Christmas tree, he thought, as he stood back to survey the prince in all his ostentatious glory.

The prince had commanded that the survivors of his delegation clean up the hotel, which they had done with amazing speed. It seemed that both species of demon evaporated like foam when they came into contact with water. Disposing of the bodies was the easiest of the operation, which included boarding some windows and the front door, and a lot of scrubbing.

Now his father had sent in his top security forces to "extract" his son and bring him home.

"I do not want to go," the prince said for perhaps the two-dozenth time. He and all his lackeys had resumed their human shapes.

"All good things must end," ventured Fred, who had returned from Caritas.

"Ah." The prince beamed at her. "In my country, you would be a queen."

"Hello? Me, too," Cordelia grumbled. "In fact, already been a queen. Okay, a princess. But they didn't have a queen. Princess was as high as they went."

Wesley and Angel regarded the prince with less than Christmas spirit.

"You neglected to give us valuable information. You nearly cost us our lives," Wesley said. He had been dressing the prince down and the prince had taken it remarkably well. He was still giddy from his and Angel's adventure.

"However, you are still alive." The prince preened and said to Fred, "You should have seen my prowess as I overcame the enemy. They were begging for mercy."

Angel rolled his eyes but kept his silence.

"Wow," Fred said, clearly impressed. "That must have been exciting." She wrinkled her nose. "But, you know, a lot of your men, well, they died tonight."

The prince waved a hand. "They died, true, but in the service of their royal family. They surely reside this moment in Paradise."

He turned to Wesley. "I will not fail to reward you and your people," he said. He clapped his hands and one of his lackeys approached, carrying a suitcase.

"Your payment," the prince announced.

"I am uncomfortable around emotional displays of gratitude," the prince proclaimed, "so I insist that you wait until I am gone from this place to see the lavish amount I have given you."

"We thought there would be an invoice. Followed by a check," Wesley said.

"I have rewarded you far beyond your dreams."

"Good, cuz I didn't get to keep the dress," Cordelia muttered.

"You can have mine," Fred whispered earnestly to her.

Cordelia smiled gently. "That's okay, Fred. It's yours."

"And so . . ." The prince touched his chest, his lips, and his forehead. "'All good things,' lovely virgin." He beamed at Fred.

"I'm also . . . a . . . oh, forget it," Cordelia huffed.

The bodyguard laid the suitcase on the lobby counter.

"Your Majesty, your father awaits your return," one of the black-suited men sternly reminded the prince.

"Good-bye, my friends," the prince said, inclining his head the merest fraction.

Then he swept out of the establishment.

The five members of Angel Investigations waited one minute more. Gunn tapped his fingers, glanced around, and said, "Since I was the one who almost had to eat the eyeball, I'm opening the treasure chest."

"That's fair," Cordelia said.

With a bit of style, Gunn clicked the latches on the exquisite leather case. *This guy's so loaded . . . this reward is gonna be the answer to all our prayers. Christmas bonuses, Easter bonuses, Fourth of July bonuses . . .*

He opened the lid.

Oh. My. God.

"What is it?" Fred asked, bubbling with excitement. "Jewels? Gold? Lots and lots of cash?"

Gunn held it up.

It was one single hundred-dollar bill.

Angel muttered, "I'm gonna kill him."

"Stand in line," Cordelia grumbled.

"At least we're all still alive," Fred pointed out. "And we're always broke, so it's not like we haven't come out ahead on this one."

"Thank you, Ebenezer Scrooge after he's had the dream," Cordelia said miserably.

Gunn handed the bill to Wesley and said, "And God bless us every one."

And then the hotel clock chimed midnight.

12 A.M.

GENEROUS PRESENCE

by Yvonne Navarro

"Is this Angel Investigations?"

Cordelia looked up from where she'd been straightening things behind the counter. A grumpy-looking delivery man was squinting at the lobby and its assortment of chairs, couches, and lamps. Youngish and dressed in the standard industrial blue, he looked anything but happy to be here.

"Yes. May I help you?"

He frowned at her. "Looks like a hotel to me."

A corner of her mouth twitched in irritation, but so much had already happened today that she just wasn't up to word-warring with a stranger. "It's almost Christmas. Would I lie to you?"

He shrugged and slid a clipboard toward her, then pulled a pen from the pocket of his shirt and dropped it on top. "Whatever. Sign here." He pointed to a space on the paper facing her.

Cordy glanced at it. "Sign for what?"

"Box in my truck. I'll go get it."

Before she could question him further, the guy spun and strode away. Her frown deepened as she watched him go, trying to read his body language. Was he in a hurry because it was the Christmas season and he just wanted to get his deliveries done so he could get to his own shopping or errands, or was there some other reason? Like maybe he didn't like whatever he was delivering, maybe it was something evil—

Stop it, Cordelia told herself. *Not everything in the world is evil. Especially this time of year.*

While waiting for the guy to come back, she tilted her head and listened. Yes, there it was—the sound of life in the hotel, muted but definitely present. Fred, Wesley, and Gunn were talking in low voices in Wesley's office, probably discussing the night's earlier escapades. Angel was around somewhere, likely changing into a fresh set of clothes, although everything he wore seemed to look the same. The hotel creaked now and then, sighing as the mild California wind moved through the cracks here and there in the foundation and the windows, resettling itself repeatedly as old buildings tended to do.

Cordelia sighed. She wished she could go on home . . . but at the same time she didn't. They had all decided to come down here every day until Christmas, and out of what? A misguided sense of duty, perhaps, and in return, today all they'd gotten was trouble since dusk. But was what waited at home any better? Her apartment was lovely, but the only company there was Dennis, and she couldn't even *see* him. She'd come home one evening last week to find her resident nosy ghost had come across the few Christmas decorations buried in her closet and hung them here and there, but she didn't have a tree or anything truly festive like that. And now here was this delivery guy, showing up on the evening of the longest day of the year. What kind of good could come out of that? It wasn't like he'd be bringing them a big crate of—

"Here you go, Miss."

—presents.

Cordy's mouth dropped open as the man heaved an obviously heavy box onto the counter. To her startled vision it looked *huge,* and she suddenly felt like a kid who'd just run down the stairs on Christmas morning to find the mother lode of toys under the tree. At two-feet square, whoever had sent it hadn't gone for the dull-as-your-grandmother's-shoes brown paper cover, and even wary as she was, Cordelia found herself unable to resist the urge to touch-test the wrapping.

Wow, she thought. *This box is wrapped in red* silk.

"Hellloooo?"

Cordy pulled her gaze from the box and realized the delivery guy was still standing there. "What?"

He shifted, looking crabbier than ever. "Hey, I know it's pretty and all that happy-sappy, but I still need a signature before I can get back to my last-minute deliveries. You think I like delivering packages on the graveyard shift at the height of the holiday season? It's one in the morning. I got a life, you know? And I hadn't really planned to just watch everyone *else* have a great holiday season."

She started to retort, then set her jaw against the words. Had the package been sent via the mail, Wesley could have picked it up on his earlier post office jaunt. But that wasn't the case, and it wouldn't do any good to rail at some stranger about all the bad that had come down on them just today, much less on a twenty-four/seven basis. "Right." She grabbed the pen and scrawled her name on the next empty line on his delivery list. As she did, her brain automatically processed a few of the names above Angel Investigations. It only took a millisecond to register the information—a couple of law firms and three shops around town that she *knew* sold dark magick stuff—which bumped her suspicions up another notch.

The man was already heading for the door when she called, "Hold it just a minute."

He turned, clearly not pleased. "What is it now, lady? You want to say 'happy holidays' before you send me on my way?"

Cordelia raised an eyebrow. "Not quite. Where did you say this package came from?"

He gave an impatient shrug. "I didn't. But if you really want to know—" He brought up the clipboard and flipped through a few pages. "Here it is," he finally said. "Wolfram and Hart. Happy already?"

He spun and this time Cordelia knew nothing in the world would keep him around another second. She tried anyway. "Wait—"

"Merry Christmas already!" he shot over his shoulder. Then he was gone, and it was just Cordelia.

And the box.

She'd been standing there looking at it for a good ten minutes when Angel walked in. Wesley, Gunn, and Fred weren't far behind. "Hey," Angel said, then his eyes widened at the sight of the package she'd pushed to the end of the counter. "Where'd that come from?"

She folded her arms as the other four gathered around to examine it. "It's nothing. Just a little season's tidings from our pals at the law firm."

Wesley scowled. "Wolfram and Hart. How generous."

Gunn put a hand on one corner and pushed experimentally. "Whatever's inside, it's heavy."

"I think the key word in that sentence is 'whatever,'" Wesley said.

"Should we open it?" Fred asked.

"No," Angel said without hesitating. "Let's let sleeping monsters lie. We'll just send it back." He looked around. "Who delivered it?"

"Driver's long gone," Cordy said. "And wasn't he just full of merriness at having to drive around in all the holiday hectic."

They all stared at the package without saying anything. It *was* beautiful, covered in red silk and tied with multicolored satin ribbons that were all very festive. There were even a few small glass ornaments wound into the center of the bow where all the ribbons came together. It was very harmless looking, very inviting.

"Look," Fred said suddenly from her spot at one side of the box. She had to stand on tiptoe to see at eye level with the top of it, and maybe that's what made her able to notice it. She pushed a finger delicately under the line of ribbons and pried at something with her fingernail. "There's a gift card tucked under the bow." She looked at each of them. "It can't hurt to open the card, can it?"

They looked at one another, but no one seemed willing to guess at it. "I don't know," Wesley said at last. "One wouldn't think so, but . . ."

"It's just a piece of paper," Gunn said in an exasperated voice. "If they're gonna try anything dirty, it'll be *in* the box."

"I think Gunn's right," Fred said. "Statistically speaking, the statement that 'good things come in small boxes' is really just a cliché that originated when—"

"Let's just open it," Angel interrupted. "Paper doesn't bite. At least not yet." Before Fred could keep going, he snatched the cream vellum envelope out of her hand and tore it open. Inside was a stiff card made of that same cream stationery; edged in gold gilt, it bore a short note in a decidedly feminine hand.

"Christmas is a time for forgiveness, for letting go of the past (at least for a little while), and for being generous. These gifts have been carefully picked for each of you to reflect a bit of what you are. Merry best to all of you at Angel Investigations."

—Lilah

• • •

"Oh, how nice!" Fred exclaimed.

"Nice?" Gunn's laugh was harsh and loud. "Nice and about as trustworthy as a bank robber around an unlocked money vault." He shook his head. "No way—we should ship this thing right back to them, preferably with a couple of sticks of dynamite attached. We all know you can't trust *anything* those people do." He caught Fred looking at him quizzically. "At least *almost* all of us know it."

"Gunn's right," Wesley said. "There's no telling what could happen if we open this box, what kind of unspeakable demon could materialize right in this room—"

"Or not." Cordelia backed up and sat on the edge of the desk. She lifted her chin and her eyes glinted defiantly. "Maybe something *will* jump out at us, and maybe something won't. But are we going to just sit here and be too afraid to open it? Like a big bunch of cowards?"

They all stared at her, then Wesley spread his hands. "Cordelia, our own safety dictates that we be extremely thoughtful indeed about the course of action we choose to take when dealing with the unknown. In our business, the very laws of probability—"

"—aren't in our favor," Fred finished for him. "Given the amount of evil in the world, and even when taking into account our place in it, in reality, it's much more likely that something bad will happen if we open it."

Cordelia glared at her. "Fred, you aren't helping."

She ducked her head. "Sorry."

"Come on, you know if there's a one-in-a-thousand chance that the mucho mondo monstrosity could pop out of that red-wrapped cardboard, we'd be that one." Gunn looked disgusted. "I say we burn the thing. Quickly."

"Really." Cordelia's chin lifted higher and her gaze zeroed in on Wesley. "So what you're saying is that the next time you find some cobweb-covered book that looks all great and evil and mysterious, you'd rather burn it than open it and see if there's anything inside that might be worth anything."

Wesley's mouth worked for a moment. "That's not at all what I meant, Cordelia. And you know it."

She stood, then began pacing back and forth, looking vaguely like a trial lawyer offering a closing argument. "I don't know any such thing. In fact, I actually agree with Fred—all our experience points to exactly that. I mean, we're talking about *Lilah* here, and when has she ever done anything that didn't turn right around and bite back? But if *everything* we checked out was bad or evil, we'd be burnt toast by now." She waved a hand around her. "Look at the way we live—if we run from the things we don't know, we'll be running from everything. And if we don't *open* this box, what kind of a message does that send to Wolfram and Hart?" She tilted her head. "The big, bad Angel Investigations team, afraid to open a *box*?"

Gunn scowled. "That's not the way it is at all—"

"Damn right," Cordelia said, and before anyone else could utter a word, she stepped forward and yanked on the tangle of flamboyant ribbons that came together at the top of the package. The oversize bow slipped apart instantly, dropping like a waterfall of color down the side of the box to land in a rainbow-hued puddle at its base. Everyone tensed—

—but nothing happened.

"Scary, huh?" Cordelia rolled her eyes.

"Actually, yeah," Fred said with a nervous laugh. "It was, kind of."

"Cordelia's right," Angel said suddenly.

Cordelia looked startled. "I am?"

"We can't let those slimeballs use scare tactics on us like this. If we do, they'll have us afraid to open our own mail."

"Angel, I don't think—," Wesley began.

But Angel's fingers were already lifting the gaily wrapped lid. "Lets show Wolfram and Hart that we can grin and make merry with the best of 'em."

And then the lid was off and lying on the counter.

For a very long moment they all simply stood there and waited, muscles tight, ready to fight, expecting anything from a horned three-headed lizard monster to a screaming, club-wielding ogre to come bursting out.

Nothing.

Without realizing it, all five of them had backed up to a theoretically safe distance. Now they crept forward, a step at a time, craning their necks to peer inside.

"Is anything . . . moving in it?" Fred asked in a tremulous voice.

"Not yet," Wesley answered.

Gunn's expression was dark. "It's only a matter of time."

Angel's next step took him to where he could look over the edge. "I don't see any—"

"Oh, *look*!" Cordelia hurried forward as the others jumped back, then watched in astonishment while she reached into the box without hesitation and began pulling out smaller gaily wrapped packages.

"Marvelous," Wesley muttered. "Now we get to go through this all over again." He eyed the pile of boxes accumulating on the counter. "And again."

It didn't take long for Cordy to spread the gifts out on the counter; then she set the bigger box aside on the floor. It was definitely a pleasing sight: five festively wrapped boxes of various shapes and sizes, each labeled with a simple tag bearing the name of its intended recipient in the same flowing hand as before—presumably Lilah's or her lackey du jour's.

"They sure are pretty," Fred finally said in a small voice.

"Yeah," Gunn agreed, but he sounded gritty, like he was speaking with his jaw clenched. "Pretty just like grandma's nightcap on the big bad wolf."

Angel looked at Cordelia, then shook his head in resignation, as though he knew there was no way these boxes weren't going to be opened. "What the hell," he said. "Let's sort 'em out."

Cordy's smile was bright with anticipation. "Finally! I was wondering when someone around here would realize we deserve a little something *good* for a change."

"I think this is a serious mistake," Wesley announced. "We don't know anything about what's in these boxes. We—"

"Maybe there's some tape," Cordy said. Her expression didn't change, but there was a tinge of ice on her words. "We could use it across your Mr. Grinch mouth."

"Fine." Wesley held up his hand. "Have at it, then. I won't say another word. But I'm certainly not going to fall into this trap by opening—"

"This one's for you." Cordy thrust something at him.

Wesley's words stuttered away as he stared down at the box he was holding, a rectangle easily fourteen inches long and nine across. It was covered in deep red velvet around which had been wrapped dozens of thin, curling gold ribbons; when he held up the box to inspect it, the ribbons trailed down longer than the box, twirling and glittering in the light like fire.

"Maybe it's a shirt," Gunn said matter-of-factly.

Angel tilted his head. "It's about the right size."

"A . . . shirt?" Wesley looked puzzled. "Why on earth would Lilah buy me a shirt? Bit heavy for that, anyway."

"Fred, this is yours." Cordelia offered the slender young woman a smaller package covered in fragile-looking sparkling white. The ribbons wrapped around it were made of the same soft and puffy fabric.

Fred took it and held it gingerly. "I guess they don't believe in wrapping paper," she said. "This is organza."

Angel shoved his hands in his pockets. "The decadence of lawyers, I suppose."

"Decadence this," Cordy said, and brought out a box for him.

The vampire looked anything but pleased, but still accepted the box that was clearly a great match to his style. He hefted it with one hand and ran his fingertips over the top with the other. "Black jacquard," he said. "Classy choice. And heavy." A plain black satin ribbon was angled across it in a double diagonal design, as if Lilah had intentionally avoided anything that might resemble a cross.

"Hey, I'm starting to feel like the odd man out," Gunn said. "I know Lilah and I aren't close, but—"

Cordy held up the next one, the oddest shape of all of them. "Not gone, and not forgotten. This one's for you."

Gunn took it tentatively, turning it over a couple of times. "I don't know whether to be happy or run like hell."

"It certainly looks interesting," Fred offered.

And indeed it did. It was just over a foot and a half long and nearly four inches deep, and while it was clearly in some kind of a box beneath a double layer of flocked, iridescent dark blue taffeta, the shape of it was skewed, bent into an elongated gentle crescent. Instead of a bow or ribbon, the upper edges of the box were trimmed in beaded fringe, reminiscent of intricate Oriental needlework.

"Well, I've never been much on appearances, but this is almost too pretty to open," Gunn said.

"And last but never least," Cordelia announced, "is mine." She held out her own gift box for inspection.

Definitely a clothing-sized box, its covering of shimmering, teal-colored organza was held in place with long, braided strands of tiny faux pearls. "This is a pretty amazing wrap-job. Honestly, I think Lilah must have stock in a high-class fabric company."

No one said anything for a long moment as each of them contemplated their personal bundle of the unknown. "Well," Fred said at last, "I suppose we should put these aside and wait for Christmas Day to open them . . ."

Cordy's eyes widened. "Wait—for what? Permission? Christmas is four days away!" She looked down at the box in her hands, then back up at her friends. "Screw *that.*"

Without waiting to see what the others would do or say, Cordelia slipped her fingers beneath the cascading string of pearlized beads and tugged. There was hardly any resistance at all—the spot where they were tied together came apart in what almost seemed like a neatly orchestrated spill. The strand draped over Cordy's palm and revealed itself to be a very nice little necklace. "Awesome," Cordy said with satisfaction. "I love it when you can wear the wrapping, too."

With Cordelia as their cue, the other four pushed aside their reservations and tore into their own packages, although with a little more reserve because of the exquisite coverings and the knowledge of who had sent them. Caution or not, it was only seconds before streamers of lovely ribbon and the blocks of high quality fabric littered the counter and floor. Every gift had an interior box that was every bit as beautiful as its wrapping—brocaded patterns, gilded swirls of gold, silver-and-red metal, imitation gemstones as accents.

"I don't know why she bothered to wrap this stuff," Gunn commented. "I wouldn't have."

"That's because you're a man," Cordelia said offhandedly. "You don't appreciate anticipation."

"No, I just want to cut right to the good stuff," Gunn retorted. "Why waste time?"

"They say that people who wait to open gifts have a higher IQ," Fred said, peering at the square box in her hands. "It says something about their ability to—" She bit off her own words, her cheeks reddening. "Wait—that sure didn't come out the way I wanted it to."

A corner of Gunn's mouth turned up. "Right." But all the hurry seemed to have gone out of his movements.

Fred looked distressed. "I'm sorry. I didn't mean to—"

"Oh my *God*!" Cordelia suddenly squealed.

They all jerked and Angel nearly dropped his still unopened box. "What? What's wrong?"

"Wrong?" Cordelia's face was luminous. "What could possibly be wrong—*look* at this!" She'd opened her box and was now pawing through layers of sparkling interior tissue paper. In another second, she pulled something free and held it up for everyone to see. "Wow!"

They stared at it for a few moments. Then Gunn cleared his throat. "Uh . . . nice sweater."

Cordelia's eyes widened; then she laughed. "Sweater? This isn't just any *sweater*—don't you have any fashion sense at all?" She pulled the top back until it spread out against her torso. "This is a *Missoni* sweater *set*—never in a million years would I be able to afford something like this."

Angel eyed it critically. "Well, it looks nice and everything, but it can't be *that* expensive."

"Try four hundred dollars plus," Cordelia shot back. "Depending on which Rodeo Drive store you happen to frequent."

Even Wesley looked impressed. "That's quite a bit of change for something that only has sleeves on one of its two pieces."

"It just looks like snakeskin to me," Gunn said. "What's so great about that?"

Cordelia smoothed out the fabric, flipping open the outer sweater to reveal the sleeveless one inside. The print on the fabric did look a bit like snakeskin, golds and browns that shifted with the folds of the material. A layered cowl neckline fell perfectly from the shoulders of the inside piece. "Oh, I just love it," Cordy murmured. "And it feels incredible, like having a piece of cloud against your skin. Lilah may be evil queen of the legal field, but she sure has great taste."

"Could be drafty," Angel quipped. When Cordy ignored him, he rolled his eyes and glanced at the others. "One down, four to go. Okay, who's next?"

They all hesitated, trying not to appear too anxious. Gunn, still smarting from Fred's unintentional remark, looked like he might *never* open his at all. The moment stretched on—

"Fine," Wesley said decisively. "I'll go next." The box inside his velvet-covered package was also red, rich and deep, and he turned it over in his hands and hesitated. "It feels . . . warm."

"That's probably just the power of suggestion," Fred said helpfully. "Red is a very intense color and the mind automatically associates it with potency and eroticism."

Wesley pressed his lips together. "I can do without adult toys, thank you very much."

"Aw, open it," Gunn said with a grin. "Might be fun."

Wesley frowned at him but finally set the box on the counter and worked the top free. As he studied what was inside, his expression melted into astonishment. "I don't believe it!"

"What?" Gunn and the others crowded around. "Is it hot?"

"You *bet* it's hot!" Wesley pulled his gift from the box and held it up. "Unbelievable!"

"It's a book," Cordelia said. "Another one of your rare ancient textbooks, I supposed. More dry than hot."

"Oh, no—not at all." Wesley placed the book on the counter gingerly, as though it might break. "This is a very rare edition of *Firestarter* by Stephen King, lettered and signed. This cover—" he pointed to it "—is *asbestos* covered in aluminum cloth. There were only twenty-six of these made in 1980." He looked completely awestruck. "This book is incredibly valuable—a collector's dream."

Cordelia squinted at it. "Can we sell it?"

"You don't sell something like this." Wesley glared at her. "Books like this one end up behind alarm-wired glass cases in contemporary museums."

"It's a wonderful gift," Fred put in. The others nodded, and she gave Gunn a sidelong glance. "How about if I go next?" Beneath the white wrapping had been a palm-size box covered in more simple white, and without waiting for an answer she carefully pried the lid free. "Oh my," she said softly. She turned the box over and yet another box, this one made of glittering crystal, slid onto her hand.

"It's beautiful," Cordelia said excitedly. "Open it—I'll bet it's jewelry."

Fred paused and chewed at her lip, but nothing bad had happened to anyone else . . . yet. She inhaled and lifted the lid.

Inside, nestled on a soft bed of white velvet, was a crystal Rubik's Cube. "It's gorgeous!"

Wesley's eyes darkened. "And just how would our acquaintances at Wolfram and Hart know that such a gift would interest Fred? I can't recall if Lilah and Fred have ever actually *met*—"

Gunn's mouth twisted. "Please. Like they haven't gotten down and dirty on assembling a Fred dossier to go with the reams of paper already in the Angel Investigations files."

"No doubt," Angel agreed. "Those people don't need a formal introduction to dig."

Gunn peered at the cube over Fred's shoulder. "How do you know when you've got the squares lined up?"

Fred lifted it to eye level so they could all see it. "There's a pattern etched into the crystal. Possibly a snowflake."

"That's certainly in keeping with the season," Cordelia said.

"Puzzles make me nervous," Wesley said. "Every time we solve one something bad happens."

"That's not actually true," Fred said. "Solving puzzles provides the answer to problematic situations, not the other way around."

"Come on, Gunn," Angel said. "Open it up."

A corner of Gunn's mouth curled, almost in distaste. "I suppose." No more hesitation, no more stalling—he yanked the top of his odd-shaped box free and looked inside.

"Okay," he said. "I take back everything bad I ever said about Lilah."

"What is it?" Wesley crowded up next to him.

Gunn lifted the object so that everyone could see. "It's a knife," he told them. "A damned *fine* one, at that."

"A *kukri*," Wesley said, examining it as Gunn turned it in his hands. "Ancient Burmese, I believe. Made of silver, and look at the embossing on the scabbard—that's genuine gold inlay." His eyebrows shot up. "I believe that's an ivory handle rimmed with real rubies."

"Ivory?" Cordelia scowled. "Don't they know it's illegal to use elephant tusks? They're endangered animals!"

"They weren't endangered when this was made," Wesley told her. "Normally *kukris* are made with yak bone as the handles, or, more commonly in the military, wood. They come in a multitude of sizes, including a huge ceremonial size that's often used to cut off the heads of water buffalo with one swipe."

"Ew," Cordy said. She'd been about to touch the knife, but now she drew her hand back. "Like we don't get enough blood with the demons—we have to add big dumb animals to it too?"

"Whatever," Gunn said, clearly impressed. "You think it's sharpened?"

"Without a doubt," Wesley said dryly. "I'd be careful if I were you. Soldiers in the Nepalese army wear them at their waists, on the left side. Most of the time they're drawn and resheathed right-handed without looking, and it's quite common for new soldiers in training to cut off their fingers." He nodded, apparently as pleased at the gift as Gunn was. "This will definitely be a fine addition to our weapons inventory."

All eyes turned expectantly to Angel. Cordelia looked at the last package on the counter. "Your turn, Angel."

He shuffled his feet a bit. "You know, I'm really not into this whole Christmas gift thing. I mean, it's the vampire existence and crosses and all—"

"Don't be a dud, Angel." Cordelia reached over and picked up the package, then thrust it at him. "Wow—that's heavy."

"Nah." Angel tried to look nonchalant. "I'm really just not into this," he repeated. "I—"

"Angel," Wesley said severely, "as I recall, it was *you* who insisted we couldn't let Wolfram and Hart frighten us. And if my memory is correct, the words 'slimeballs' and 'scare tactics' were involved." He folded his arms. "In all fairness, you offered quite the encouragement to the rest of us to open our packages. As they say, what goes around comes around. Now get on with it."

Angel's mouth worked and he looked around a little helplessly. "I . . . All right. Whatever."

Cordelia's expression turned mischievous. "I'm thinking our tall, dark, and vampire here is afraid his attempted onetime romp with Lilah might have gotten him a holiday gift on the less-than-pleasant side—a little tit for tat."

Angel cleared his throat sharply, then pressed his lips together and worked at the lid to his box without much enthusiasm. "That wasn't me, remember? It was that old guy who stole my body, and I was kind of hoping she'd just forget about that."

Gunn snorted. "First of all, I don't think Lilah cares about the details. Second, I'm thinking she's most definitely the kind to hold a grudge."

"But her note did say that this was a time for letting go of the past." Fred sounded hopeful. "So far everything's been really nice."

As the last word left her mouth, the lid came free and fell to the side. Angel stared at what was inside, then scowled. "Great."

"What is it?" Wesley and the others moved in close.

Angel sighed, pulled the object out, and held it up for everyone to see. "A mirror."

"A mirror?" Cordelia repeated. The bewilderment on her face matched the expressions of her friends. "A *mirror*?"

"I don't think repeating ourselves is going to make it any clearer." He shoved the box aside with his elbow and set down his gift.

There was a long pause; then Wesley offered, "Well, it's a very nice one, anyway." He stepped in front of Angel and picked up the mirror, hefted it to test its weight, then studied the frame. The reflective surface was an elongated oval in a highly polished frame about four inches around with rounded edges. It was dense and dark, with a grain that was almost reptilian-looking, mostly black with a strange tan pattern that held occasional subtle hints of green. There was no denying it was exceptional—it seemed to demand that they look at it, pulling their gazes back when they let it wander elsewhere.

"Looks kind of creepy to me," Gunn said. "Like it's . . . watching us or something."

"I think it's very beautiful," Fred put in.

"Yes." Wesley agreed. He was clearly impressed. "I believe this is Coromandel ebony. It's highly prized as a material for weapons because of its strength and density, although it's rare enough so that most of the masters consider it wasteful if the weapon is actually used as anything but a gift for a very respected instructor." He smiled and angled the mirror to better see the almost imperceptible grain. "Legend has it that the wood gets this burned black appearance because it first grew from a charred twig dropped on the ground by a couple who hid in a gourd during the great flood."

"Marvelous," Angel said sourly. "I'll use it every day. Remind me to send Lilah a thank-you card for her insight."

"Insight?" Fred asked.

"Yeah," Angel ground out. "Lilah's note said that each gift reflects what we are, remember?" He actually sounded bitter. "She pretty much hit it on the head with the other presents, and when I look into this thing, I see nothing. That about covers it all, doesn't it?"

Standing there, looking at their own gifts, it was obvious no one knew what to say. Suddenly Angel looked chagrined. "Hey listen, don't pay any attention to me. I told you—Christmas just really isn't my holiday of choice. I'd much rather do St. Patrick's Day and have a good glass of green beer. The whole caroling thing has nothing on a good Irish drinking song."

"Angel, you have to keep in mind the source," Wesley said. He looked pained on Angel's behalf. "On the surface, Lilah is a beautiful, articulate woman, but the truth is she's nasty and cunning, very underhanded. Pretty on the outside, but the inside's rotten, indeed."

No one else seemed able to think of anything to add, and after a few moments Fred picked up her crystal Rubik's Cube and settled on one of the lobby chairs. As if on cue, Gunn, Cordelia, and Wesley found their own spots to sit back and examine their gifts. Angel stayed at the counter, leaning forward on his elbows and staring at where the mirror lay off to the side, an ill-concealed grimace on his face.

"This isn't so difficult," Fred murmured. When Angel looked over at her, her fingers were working nimbly at the cube, turning it this way and that. Under her attention, the snowflake pattern was rapidly taking shape, and the whole thing was looking disgustingly silver and Christmasy.

A few feet away, Wesley was delicately paging through his asbestos-covered copy of *Firestarter* with an utterly enchanted expression on his face. "The man's an incredible fiction writer," he said to no one in particular. "Listen to this passage right here." Holding the book carefully, he stood and began to read from the opened page, walking back and forth as he did so, a smile of admiration on his face.

"'Fear made her heart pound and her knees weak. She dodged through the trees, moving like a black leopard through a jungle, hardly looking back at the men who tracked her. They were evil and deserved to die, and she began to chant beneath her breath as she picked her way through the moonlit forest. "Burn," she whispered to herself. "Let them all burn, but do it slowly so they can appreciate the extent of my anger. I will kill each and every one of them with fire, very slowly, and I will enjoy listening to their screams. . . ."'"

No one thought he'd been listening, but now Angel raised his head and stared at Wesley. "What was that?"

"Amazing writing, isn't it?" Wesley nodded to reinforce his statement. "I really think no one else in the world has his touch for characterization *and* plot. The man will no doubt go down in history—"

"I read that book," Angel interrupted. "Absolutely nowhere in it does the little girl—Charlie—say anything like 'I will enjoy listening to their screams.' In fact, that doesn't even sound like Stephen King's writing."

Wesley looked from Angel to the book, then back at the vampire. "What are you talking about? That's not what I said. The passage I read from—"

"Got it!" Fred exclaimed. "Oh, look—it's awesome!" Her face was shining as she held up the completed cube, which showed a vaguely snowflakelike symbol on each side. It seemed to pick up every piece of light in the room and reflect it in triplicate, much like the way candlelight enhances the sparkle of diamonds.

"Wow," Cordelia said. "You're not kidding. I don't think I've ever seen anything so beautiful. It's—"

"Full of ancient Amratian symbols," Wesley broke in.

Gunn leaned forward, trying to see the cube better. "Ancient who?"

"They were Egyptian, dating back to 4500 B.C.," Wesley told him as he came closer to examine Fred's cube. "Those aren't snowflakes at all, but symbols of some kind, and while what we *don't* know about current mysticism could fill entire libraries, imagine how little we know of what went on in the world back then, when civilization was just beginning to discover the idea of architecture and individual dwellings." He looked horrified. "Our knowledge of them comes almost exclusively from the contents of their graves, but like the Celts, they probably relied heavily on the supernatural for protection from real and imagined enemies."

"Well," Fred said, but there was a definite tremor in her voice. "It *seems* harmless enough. . . ."

"I don't think we ought to assume—" Angel began, but something like a roaring directly in front of Fred's chair drowned out the rest of what he was going to say.

Fred screamed and flung the crystal away, then scrambled over the side of her upholstered chair. The cube bounced a few feet and stopped; then a spiral of white-gold light began to form around it. The center of it spun faster and faster, and it was like they were looking straight into a blender filled with gold-flecked liquid. For a long, painful moment they were nearly mesmerized, but the spiral inexplicably subsided to barely a pinpoint of harmless light. Then someone—it wasn't clear who—screamed, *"Fire!"*

They all jerked as a long, thin column of flame sprang up at Wesley's feet. He yelped and skipped backward, still clutching the limited edition. For a moment it looked as if the fire would be sucked toward the spinning circle of light, but it jerked back and followed after Wesley, zipping along the floor at his shoes like a living lizard of heat. He leaped away, twisting this way and that around the furniture, but the fire kept following. Wesley was clearly its only target.

"Wesley, look out!" Fred said.

But her warning was too late; looking back over his shoulder instead of where he was running, Wesley ran full tilt into one of the lobby's floor lamps and went down in a tangle of metal rod, lampshade, and cord.

For a second they all froze, then the flames licked around his ankles. *"Arghghgghghghgh!"*

"His pants are on fire!" Cordelia shrieked. Everyone tried to head toward Wesley at once, but Cordy was the closest. She'd been sitting in her own spot, thoughtfully fingering the silky feel of the Missoni sweater set; now she did the first thing that came to mind—she grabbed a double handful of the fabric and tackled Wesley at foot level, wrapping the sweater around his ankles to smother the flames. She and Wesley rolled, arms and legs flailing, as the others jumped into the fray. Wesley writhed while Cordelia struggled with his ankles and then finally let him go.

"Thank God!" he gasped. "I thought I was grilled for sure!"

"Are you all right?" Angel demanded. "Burned?"

"Singed around the edges a bit, but I'll survive." Wesley looked around a little wildly. "Where did the fire come from?"

"I think it came from your 'Stephen King' book," Fred noted. "Look at it now—I don't think that asbestos cover was the real deal."

Wesley reached over, snatched up the book, and then almost dropped it. The cover was hot. It had gone black and smoking, and there was no sign of the original title on it. When he cautiously opened the cover, the pages inside were burned and flaking at the edges, and very obviously *old*—older than a copy of *Firestarter* by more than a few centuries. Wesley swallowed when he saw what was written inside. "Apparently the cover wasn't the only illusion," he said. "This isn't the text from *Firestarter* at all—more like some sort of spell book, or demonic journal."

"Well, that explains the fire," Angel said. "You saw one thing, but when you read it aloud, it came out as what was really written there. Like you said, some kind of spell."

"Cordelia," Wesley said, turning to her. "Thank you—"

"Probably the only time in my life I'll own a piece of Missoni clothing and I had to go and use it as a fire blanket," she said forlornly. She held up the sweater, but it was clearly ruined, covered with soot and charred along the entire left side. She pressed her lips together, wadded it in a ball, and tossed it at the trash can next to the counter. Then she brightened. "But hey—I've still got the inside piece. I'm going to put it on before something horrid happens to it, too."

"Do you think that's wise?" Fred asked. She looked worried. "After what happened with Wesley's book?"

"You were the one who said statistically speaking, we'd be fine," Cordelia shot back. "I'm just going to slip it on over my T-shirt and see how it fits." A quick move and a wiggle and the Missoni top went over her head and slipped into place; she tugged it down and spread her arms. She finished by adding the necklace that had formed from the box's string of mini pearls. "Well, how does it look?"

"Oh, that's great," Gunn said, but his gaze was fixed over Cordy's shoulder, not on the textured sweater she'd pulled over her slim figure.

"What's the matter?" Cordy asked, looking confused. "That's really not the reaction I was expecting—"

"It's back!" Gunn yelled. He grabbed her wrist and yanked her forward. "Get down!"

That tiny pinprick of light before the fire, so easy to forget, had blossomed again—or rather, *exploded.* Perhaps in the back of their minds, they'd thought it was just a pretty little light show, the prize for Fred's solving the puzzle cube. But that was clearly not the case. The swirling center was back, and now there was a roaring sound coming from it. A dank, hot wind was screaming through the hotel lobby, picking up papers and anything else light, and quickly gaining strength. Soon it would have enough muscle to pull larger objects—like people—into the dark blackness that had appeared at its center.

"It's a vortex!" Angel yelled. "We've got to close it!"

"How?" Cordelia clawed her way backward. "And where does it go?"

Fred was clinging to the edge of the counter, staring at the mass of whirling color with almost paralytic horror. "I think it goes to . . . another dimension." Her terrified words were almost lost in the booming of the wind. "It's come for . . . *me.*"

"Well, it can't *have* you!" Wesley shouted. He still had the burned, bogus book in one hand, holding it tightly against the pull of the vortex. "Not now, not *ever*!" He'd been gripping the edge of a couch with his other hand, and now he let go of it and leaped forward.

"Wesley, don't!" Angel grabbed for the other man and missed, but Wesley hadn't been aiming for the vortex. Instead, he went *behind* it, to where Fred had flung the cube away when the first whirlpools of light had emanated from it. He rolled and came up next to the crystal cube, and for the first time, they realized that it was definitely the source for the vortex, like a mini projection box. Without hesitating, Wesley raised the heavy book and smashed it down on top of the cube.

Bright white light instantly filled the room, nearly blinding them as it washed out everything. The roar of the vortex was replaced by something low and ominous and . . . *dying,* perhaps the closest thing to the sound of a downed elephant that any of them had ever heard.

Then there was nothing but silence.

"My, wasn't that fun," Gunn said flatly. "I just can't wait to see what's next." He'd placed the *kukri* off to the side, and now he looked at it as if it were something covered with pond scum. He looked at Fred and frowned. "Fred?"

"Oh, no," Cordelia said. She hurried over to the slender woman, who was still clutching the counter with white-knuckled fingers. Cordelia pushed Fred's hair out of her eyes. "Hey, you in there?"

"Vortex . . ." Fred's voice was nearly a whisper. "Like on Pylea. It almost sucked us in. *All* of us, and it would've been *my* fault." Fred gulped in a ragged breath, finally breaking her fixed stare. "I can't believe I didn't realize—"

"Which says it all," Angel put in. "That great light show wasn't your doing, it was Lilah's—face it, the woman is underhanded and nasty. These gifts"—he waved his hand at the past and present remains of Lilah's generosity—"were never meant to be anything but—"

"Moving!" Cordelia suddenly shrieked.

"Pardon me?" Wesley asked automatically.

"It's *moving*!" Cordelia started skipping around in front of them, her hands pulling at the Missoni top she'd donned over her T-shirt. "It's—it's *tight*!"

"Hey, she's right." Gunn tried to grab at Cordelia but she jerked out of his range, twisting in all directions as she yanked at her top. "I can *see* it!"

"You guys, I can't—" Cordelia's voice broke off; then she managed a final, single-syllable word: *"Breathe!"*

"We've got to get that off her!" Angel shouted as Cordelia collapsed into a knot on the carpet. "It's alive or something!"

They reached for her, trying to hold her down, trying to pull on the sleeveless top, trying to do *anything*. But the sweater and necklace were *changing*, re-forming into another shape that could only be described as pythonlike, swelling rapidly upward to curl around Cordelia's neck. Above the living fabric, her face was turning an alarming shade of reddish purple.

"Do something!" Fred cried. She was yanking frantically at the collar, but nothing was working—the harder they pulled, the more firmly the sweater-snake settled itself around Cordy's torso. "She'll suffocate if we don't get her some air!"

"Damn it!" On his knees next to her, Gunn jerked

himself to his feet, then snatched up the Burmese *kukri*. The edge gleamed in the lobby's light as he pushed between Angel and Wesley and slid its razor-sharp edge up the side of the undulating fabric that was now wrapped around Cordelia's neck. The fabric parted, leaving behind a thin sheen of blood that he prayed was from the sweater and not Cordy. The sweater top writhed around her and she gasped for air, her chest heaving as a little of the pressure was released. Instinctively Gunn kept cutting as Angel, Wesley, and Fred clawed at the snake-patterned material. More blood, more agonized inhalations from Cordelia, until finally she was free and the bewitched Missoni sweater lay in a half dozen twitching and ragged pieces on the floor.

Cordelia rolled herself into a ball next to what little was left of it, squeezing her knees protectively. "I should have known," she half sobbed. "A Missoni—I should have known it was way too good to be true."

"You couldn't have known," Fred said soothingly.

"Yeah," Gunn agreed. "It was just a blouse—"

"Sweater," Cordelia corrected, as she uncurled and sat up. "It was a Missoni *sweater* set."

"Whatever," Gunn said. "It was, like, cotton or something. So who could've expected it—"

"Would start crawling up your wrist!" Wesley jumped forward and grabbed Gunn by the right shoulder, then used both hands to begin shaking Gunn's arm.

"Wesley, what the hell are you doing—hey!" Gunn's eyes widened as he looked down and saw what lay below Wesley's grip. The *kukri* he'd used to cut Cordelia free of the sweater-snake had *melted,* the handle flowing and sinking itself into the flesh of his palm. Gunn pushed free of Wesley's grip and started jerking his hand up and down like he was trying to shake some particularly foul liquid off his fingers. "Whoa!"

But it was no good, and Gunn realized that no matter what he did or where he ran he wasn't going to be able to outrun *himself.* After a few seconds of scrambling around the lobby with the others trying to follow, they all simply stopped in the center. Gunn held out his right hand and they stared at it, with no clue how to stop what they were seeing. Second by second, the metal was integrating itself into Gunn's hand, creeping upward like living silver mercury. Now it was wrapped around the thumb pad; now it was stretching the rubies and carvings up and around his wrist. "What is this?" Gunn asked, horrified. He held his hand out, trying to keep it as far away from the rest of his body as possible. "Some kind of *Witchblade* nightmare?"

Angel grabbed him by the elbow. "There's got to be some way to stop this," he said desperately. "We can't let it keep going—"

"Think fast, folks. I wasn't really looking at amputation when I rolled out of bed this morning!" Gunn's gaze skipped around the lobby, searching for something, *anything,* that he could use to free himself.

"There must be something we can use to halt its progress." Wesley spun, searching as well.

Suddenly Fred crouched and scooped something off the carpet. "Here—try this!" She held something out.

Angel snatched the object from her hand. It was a piece of glass, one of the sides of the now-shattered crystal box. A piece had been broken out of the bottom, giving it a slightly angled edge, but other than that it was whole. There was no time to pause or wonder if it would work; Angel grabbed Gunn's arm and jammed the angled piece of glass into the skin just above the crawling metal. Gunn yelped as the edge of the glass bit into his arm.

There was a moment when it looked as if the metal might simply flow over the glass, and they all nearly panicked; then it swelled up and fell over onto itself, like water hitting a retaining wall or a dam. It started to flow backward and Angel followed it with the glass, scraping Gunn's arm bloody as he went. Gunn groaned between his teeth but held his ground, fighting the instinctive urge to pull his arm from Angel's grip. Down, down, down, until the mercury-like substance streamed back toward the metal tip on the handle of the *kukri*, drawn to itself and its origin. Still, a few tentacles of the stuff clung hungrily to Gunn's palm, and Angel took a chance, betting that the metal wouldn't find his own cold flesh as appetizing. Quick as a whip, he dropped the piece of crystal, grabbed the *kukri* by the back of its blade, and ripped it free of Gunn's hand.

This time, Gunn did cry out—he couldn't help it. Blood splattered Angel and he shook his head to keep his thoughts clear, then pitched the knife to the ground. It lay there, tipped with Gunn's blood and looking like nothing more than an everyday deadly weapon. Except now no one wanted to pick it up.

Finally Cordelia lashed out with her foot and kicked it off to the side. "Vicious little thing, isn't it?"

Wesley nodded as Fred ducked behind the counter and came up with a roll of paper towels for Gunn to wrap his injured hand and wrist. "Yes, indeed. We'll have to work out a way to either destroy it permanently, or store it where no one will accidentally pick it up. Quite interesting the way it tried to integrate itself with living flesh, by the way. I haven't seen anything like that since—"

"There's still Angel's gift," Fred interrupted. "Every one of us has gotten some sort of awful fallout from what Lilah gave us, so this isn't over."

All eyes turned toward the counter, where Angel's mirror still lay facedown as Angel had turned it. Ignoring his arm, Gunn took a tentative step toward it. "Great," he said. "What's next—maybe a monster jumping out of it? Seven years of bad luck if we break the damned thing?"

"Or another vortex," Fred said tremulously. "A portal to another dimension, like the cube."

Cordelia shook her head. "No, Lilah would never be so mundane as to repeat herself in the same set of gifts. It'll be something different, something worse—"

"No," Angel said softly. His friends stared at him as he walked over to the counter and lifted the mirror, then turned it upright to where they could all see the glass. "No," he repeated. "It's not going to do anything, it's not going to *show* me anything. It's . . . nothing at all." He slammed it back down, and the glass rippled but didn't break. "It's dead. Just like me."

Wesley looked from Angel to the mirror, his face white. "Angel—"

"Her note said the gifts are a reflection of each of us, right?" He laughed a little bitterly. "How much more on track could she be?"

"If the gifts reflect those who receive it, they also reflect the giver," Wesley said. "Remember what I said earlier? That woman is stone cold, pretty on the outside but corrupt on the inside—like every one of these pretty little packages she sent."

"Except this one." Angel pointed to the mirror. "It's utterly benign. It doesn't do anything but exactly what it's supposed to—reflect the person who received it. Me."

Angel turned his gaze away from the mirror, unable to look at it anymore. When it came right down to it, in a way wasn't he the same as Lilah? Everyone told him, and sometimes he even believed, that he was good, but wasn't that just on the *out*side? Inside, he was what he was—a vampire, the undead, an animated monster. It was only by the "grace" of a Gypsy curse that he carried the only thing that kept him from being truly evil, a soul. So fragile and elusive, yet without it, he was worse than Lilah, worse than most of the creatures he fought so hard to destroy. But there was more to add to the mix—as evil as she was, Lilah still had her soul, and he had never been that much of an abomination when he was alive.

"You are *so* wrong."

He lifted his head at Cordy's sharp words. She marched over to the mirror and dragged it off the counter. "Come and look, guys. You, too, Angel." Warily, Wesley, Gunn, and Fred approached her as she moved to stand at Angel's side. "Here—stand right next to me. And we'll all look in it together."

"What for?" Angel asked. He sounded almost belligerent, his usual stoicism crumbling a little in the face of the unseen wound Lilah had inflicted. "I know what I don't look like."

"Tell me what you see, Angel," Cordelia ordered. He started to pull away but a gentle hand on his elbow—Fred's—stopped him. "I mean it. Tell me what you *see.*"

He cleared his throat. "You," he finally said. "And Fred, Wesley, Gunn."

"That's right." Cordelia stared into the mirror and the eyes in her reflection were piercing. "What makes a man is not *just* the man himself, Angel. It's everything he is—his life, his *friends.* Maybe you can't see yourself in this mirror, but you can see the other parts of your life, and those parts count for a lot."

Wesley's hand fell on Angel's shoulder. "She's right, Angel. While it's true that an attractive surface can mask unpleasantness, the opposite is also true—something that looks ordinary and everyday, something you *see* every day, can provide the foundation for good in a person's existence."

Angel frowned and started to argue, then felt his objections melting away. Cordelia was right, as was Wesley—he had friends in his life, comrades who would fight at his side against the very same kind of evil that had brought these so-called "gifts" into their lives today. They would probably die for him, and he for them; a smile slowly spread across his face and he threw an arm across Cordy's shoulder and gave her a hug.

While it was true he might not be able to see his reflection in a mirror, he was meant to be in Cordelia, Fred, Wesley, and Gunn's world, as they were meant to be in his.

1 A.M.

THE ANCHORESS

by Nancy Holder

It was nearly one A.M., and the adventures appeared to be over.

"Which is interesting," Wesley commented, as he hung up his Bavarian fighting adz in the hotel weapons cabinet. "That we're finished, I mean. This is the longest night of the year, when evil holds sway over the earth. And yet, it's quiet now."

"That's not interesting, English," Gunn drawled, as he munched on a taquito. They had gotten some Mexican takeout at the lone open eatery down on La Cienega. Everyone was starving. And cautious. They had made the food run while fully armed. Now Angel had gotten some pig's blood out of the fridge and was sipping it discretely while he helped Wesley store the weapons. "That's good news."

The others wearily nodded in agreement. Fred took some crossbow bolts out of her pockets and gave them to Angel, who replaced them in their box next to a row of crossbows still hanging in the cabinet. Fred was to the crossbow born, Angel thought, rather like another young woman warrior on the side of good—the reigning Slayer, back in Sunnydale.

"Yet it's not what I would have expected," Wesley persisted. "The lack of activity," he added. "If anything, I would have expected things to really shake up about now. The hour between one and two in the morning has been called the hour of darkest magicks. It's that dark night of the soul one reads about."

"When one has time to read," Cordelia grumped, "and not spend the longest night the way *we* have. By the way, just in case any of you has forgotten, my Christmas list is hanging up in Angel's office. Also, I made a .pdf file, suitable for downloading."

Gunn snickered, and Cordelia narrowed her eyes at him. Still grinning, he raised his hands in a "don't shoot me" gesture and dabbed at the corners of his mouth with a paper napkin.

"More heart attacks occur between midnight and three A.M.," Fred offered, then shrugged and giggled in her Fredadorable way at the dismayed reaction she got from Cordelia. Gunn and Wesley both gave her smitten looks, which Cordelia caught and Fred completely missed. "Just thought I'd mention it."

"And on that happy note," Cordelia drawled, "I'm going home. Home to my pretty apartment, which is quiet, and only has one supernatural thing in it, who is my very nice and unobtrusive house ghost. Not to have a heart attack, not to have a dark soul thing, just to sleep." She sighed with contentment at the thought. "Although I guess I have a nice unobtrusive ghost because his mom had a heart attack after she walled him up. Hmm."

"It's the circle of real estate," Gunn suggested.

Angel gestured toward the stairs. "Maybe you should just stretch out here."

She cocked one eyebrow at him. "Because you think your wage slave is going to get up in a few hours to do some typing and filing? No way, Nighttime Superstrength Vampire Guy. I'm beat and I'm taking tomorrow—or rather, the rest of the day—waaaay off."

He looked mildly hurt. "You can stretch out here so you don't have to drive when you're so sleepy."

"Oh." She scratched her head and moved her shoulders. "That's so thoughtful."

"I can be Thoughtful Guy." He looked to the others. "You've seen me be Thoughtful Guy." He tried again. "Cordy, you should stay. It's too late for you to drive."

Fred nodded. "Very thoughtful." She dimpled and blushed.

Cordelia yawned. "Tempting as that is . . . and you're the only man who's tried that line on me lately . . . I think I'll go home."

"Maybe Dennis will give you a loofah," Fred said, smiling hopefully. "That would be nice."

"A bubble bath." Cordelia wiped the blood and demon goo off the machete she'd used and handed it to Gunn, who was passing beside her with an armload of other slicing objects. "Thanks, Gunn." She moved her head in a slow circle. "That sounds so . . . ohhhhh . . . ohhhh . . . *ohhhh* . . ."

Wesley cleared his throat. "Yes, I'm sure that his loofah gives you a great deal of . . . pleasure, but must you be so Herbal Essences about—"

"Ooooh," she moaned, and Angel said, "Vision!"

"She's having a vision!" Fred cried, racing to the sofa to get Cordelia a pillow for soft landing.

Cordelia spun around like a top and collapsed into Angel's arms. She was nearly convulsing, and Angel held her tightly. The others crouched around, trying to lend support, unable to help, as always. The visioning "gift" was Cordelia's burden to shoulder alone, and there was nothing anyone could do until she got through the ordeal of receiving one.

As it concluded, she slumped and went limp, and Angel eased her head onto the pillow Fred had so thoughtfully provided. Cordy pressed the fingertips of both hands against her forehead, taking a deep breath, then dropped her hands to her chest and said hoarsely, "Ow."

"That looked bad," Fred announced.

"It was." She licked her lips and touched Angel's shoulder as he bent over her. "Listen, it's that weird Stonehenge thing they set up for the Druid Days of Christmas. There's some wanna-be sorcerers or something . . . white robes . . . they're going to sacrifice a girl." She took another breath and looked up at Angel. "We have to stop them, Angel."

"Griffith Park," Wesley filled in. "They put up a dolmen ring for the Druid Festival. Tonight's the winter solstice. It makes perfect sense that someone would want to sacrifice someone."

"They're going to do it soon," Cordelia said urgently. "Really, really soon."

"During the dark night of the soul, just like you said." Fred grimaced sadly at the others. "No rest for the weary, huh?"

"Or the wicked," Angel said. To Cordy, he added, "You stay here."

"No. I'm going," she insisted, pushing herself up to a sitting position. Angel rose and carefully helped her to her feet.

"You don't need to go," Wesley pointed out. "You're exhausted, and now this . . ."

Cordelia looped her dark, bobbed hair behind her ear and shrugged. "I do need to. I'm supposed to be there." She looked at Angel. "I don't know why, but I know I should go."

He nodded. She could be stubborn in situations like these.

Wearily, but with determination, they all got their weapons back out of storage. Cordelia traded the filthy machete for a broadsword. Fred put her crossbow over her shoulder. Gunn kept his specially made hubcap ax and Wesley hefted his adz. Angel put a few stakes in his pockets, but other than that, he was his own best weapon.

Moving briskly, they retraced their steps back out of

the hotel. The engine of Angel's convertible was still ticking as it cooled down. As they began to cram into the front and back seats, Angel said, "Maybe we should buy a special Angel Investigations van."

"Can't afford it," Cordelia shot back. "Hey, maybe the sacrificial victim is rich. And will be grateful."

Wesley's face grew shadowed, and Cordelia knew he was thinking about Virginia, his old girlfriend. Not realizing that his little girl was no virgin, her father had planned to sacrifice her to the goddess Yeska. Wesley had saved her, and they had had quite a relationship. Then reality intruded—Wesley had been shot by a zombie cop—and Virginia had realized she couldn't handle it if Wesley got killed. And hey, with demon-fighting, it could happen any day.

Or night . . .

"Anybody want a taquito?" Gunn asked, raising the large bag.

"Me," everyone said . . . everyone but Angel.

Armed and chewing, they drove to Griffith Park.

Griffith Park was home to many things—the famous observatory, an exquisite view of glittering downtown Los Angeles, and a strange little place called Train Town. The rolling lawns and palm trees were recognizable in many Hollywood films. A noteworthy amount of demonic activity also took place there. Lorne, the Host of Caritas, had informed the group that in Los Angeles, demons hired location scouts, just as film and TV producers did, to search out convenient and useful places to conduct their rituals, battles, and killings, and Griffith Park was one of the most popular locations in Los Angeles to foment evil.

"My guess is that there's some kind of inharmonic convergence there," Lorne had offered. "Like a hell-mouth."

That would explain a lot, Wesley thought now, *including the strange, queasy feeling I have right now.*

Or it might be that taquito . . .

Angel parked as closely as possible to the Stonehenge re-creation. They were actually behind it; the parking for the public faced the base of the ravine in which it had been built. They had a bird's-eye view from where they stood of the large stones circling a natural amphitheater-like basin. As the Druid Festival closed at dusk for each of its five days, no provisions had been made for illuminating it for public view; now, torches on staffs flickered and billowed in the chilly December predawn night.

Wesley took point, grimly watching as six white-robed figures pranced ridiculously around papier-mâché recreations of the huge stones out on England's Salisbury Plain. They'd gotten the placement of the stones correct—there was the interior set of bluestones, and the outer lintels and sarsens he knew so well from many a field trip to the site. The props were crudely done, especially considering that they had been fashioned in a local special effects shop, at least according to yesterday's article about the Druid Festival in the *Los Angeles Times.* But the construct itself was sound. And yet, to what purpose?

Americans, Wesley thought. *Who on earth out here in Los Angeles actually knows or cares a fig about the Druids? Yanks have more Renaissance fairs and Scottish games than all of the British Isles put together. They threw us out, insisted upon defining themselves as something other than Englishmen, but when it comes down to it, they spend an awful lot of time watching British sitcoms and reading up on the exploits of the Royal Family . . . and prancing about in inaccurate getups sacrificing virgins.*

Wesley began to climb down the ravine. The others fell in behind him and did the same.

As if on cue, the six men below them began to chant in a sort of low-grade hum that quickly grated on Wesley's nerves.

"Hey," Gunn whispered to him as they crept through the manzanita and white sage underbrush, "is it my imagination, or do those guys remind you of the guards in *The Wizard of Oz*?"

"It's your imagination," Cordelia whispered behind the two of them. "And stop making so much noise, Gunn."

"Excuse me?" He looked over his shoulder, narrowing his eyes at her. "You tellin' me how to run my game? I was sneaking into vampire nests while you were still shakin' pom-poms and praying for field goals." He gave her heeled boots a glance that dripped with ridicule. "And I'm not the one lookin' like a *Charlie's Angels* wanna-be, makin' too much noise with my damn shoes."

"For your information, our team always made their field goals," she hissed.

"Rah rah," he snickered.

"Hey." Angel waved a hand at them. "Hush, you two."

"Who you tellin' to hush?" Gunn challenged, but he hushed. Cordelia did too.

It was uncharacteristic of Gunn and Cordelia to spar during a sneak attack. They'd actually moved past that point in their relationship . . . or so Wesley had assumed.

We're all very tired, Wesley thought. *The longest night of the year is proving to be just that.*

Then the Druid guys drew away from the stones and raised their arms toward the bright full moon. Their sleeves slipped down, revealing circular Celtic knot tattoos. Each man—all six of the figures were male—held a curved, jeweled knife in his right hand, the wicked-sharp blades flashing in the moonlight.

Blood dripped from the crescent-shaped weapons.

On the altar lay a girl clad in a white robe. She had long flowing hair like Fred's, and a wreath of laurel leaves was twined across her forehead. Her feet were bare. Her arms and legs were bound to the altar by wicked-looking hooks. She was gagged.

Blood trickled from each of her wrists.

"O . . . kay. I know *I'd* rather be shopping," Cordelia said anxiously.

So would that girl, Wesley filled in.

Fred murmured, "She's a little cyanotic, which means that she's already lost a lot of blood."

Then Wesley raised a hand and pointed to the left, giving Gunn the signal to move out. The tall street fighter nodded once and began to make a circle through the brush toward a towering palm tree. Wesley made a similar gesture to the right, giving Angel that direction.

Cordelia, he gestured to angle between the path they were on, and the wider half-circle Angel was making. Fred, toward Gunn.

He hefted his adz and made straight for twelve o'clock.

Or a little thereafter, he thought, as the Los Angeles Druids registered the attack and began to wildly shout.

One hour, to be precise.

He broke into a run.

And then everything began to shimmer.

Salisbury Cathedral,
the Salisbury Plain, England.
A.D. 1329

Sister Elizabeth broke into a sweat as she rolled in a delirium on the rushes of her cell. Faithful Brother Thomas knelt by her side, praying his rosary, his tonsured head bowed in fervent prayer. He had lowered the wooden window that was her only portal to the outside world and locked it tight. But as it was situated at ground level, to the right of the main facade of the cathedral, she was afforded little privacy.

Anchoresses were thought not to require privacy. In

fact, moments when they were left alone might prove to be the moment when Satan came to violate God's chosen handmaidens . . .

But I don't believe that is what has happened, in her case. No matter the evidence to the contrary.

Yet he was terrified . . . for himself and for her.

"It is he . . . the demon and his followers," she panted. "He comes at last! He is here, to steal my soul!"

"Hail Mary," he chanted in Latin, but her writhing and her suffering distracted him from his office. "My sister, be calm, be still."

"I see him, with his glowing eyes and his fangs. He is the drinker of blood. They worship him . . . there is another demon who follows him, one with green skin and crimson eyes. He is the leader's troubadour." She tugged at her wimple. "I'm burning with fever, Brother Thomas. The fires of hell itself are consuming me!"

"Hush, my child, hush," he begged her, casting an anxious glance over his shoulder. If the others should hear her . . .

"Don't you understand? He is here!" she screamed, grabbing at his sleeves.

"You . . . you are dreaming," he said firmly.

There had already been whispered accusations of witchcraft against her. She was in a precarious situation . . . as was he, her spiritual confessor and, perhaps, her only remaining friend within the cathedral walls. Perhaps it was because he was a little bit in love with her that he continued to trust in her; or maybe, as the second son of a widely traveled family with holdings in many lands, which he had visited, he was more sophisticated and worldly than many of his brother monks. Whatever the case, he did not view her strange visions as evidence that she should be burned alive for witchcraft.

Others did.

An Anchoress was said to enjoy a special, private communion with the Sacred Heart of the Lord and Savior, Jesus Christ. Her ability to see into the spiritual realms was bestowed upon her at His holy will. Such a daughter of the Church must be safeguarded and treasured like any other special gift. Accordingly, she was walled alive into the cathedral, into the sanctuary of Holy Mother Church herself, and guarded night and day. The only entry into her sanctuary lay deep within the church itself, behind the altar . . . a narrow, gated door through which only men who had taken holy orders were allowed to go. Three were chosen for this special task: Brother Thomas, Brother Mattias, and Brother Joseph.

Mattias had died soon after being given his new duty. And Sister Elizabeth had tearfully demanded that Brother Joseph be forbidden entry into her cell again, casting much suspicion upon his conduct with the lovely young girl. But since he denied any impropriety, the Abbot had declared that the only thing to do was to honor Sister Elizabeth's request. The special honor was taken from Brother Joseph . . . and thus it was that Brother Thomas became the only monk to enter Sister Elizabeth's cell, to bring her food, and to hear her confession.

Jealousy was rampant.

It was then that mutterings against her began.

The world outside was oblivious to the politics inside the cathedral. As far as the laity were concerned, the monks took care of the precious Anchoress, providing and caring for her—and some said, treating her as a prisoner.

People from all over the countryside made pilgrimages to speak to her, to ask her counsel, to learn from her about the mind and soul of God. They brought her offerings, usually in the form of food. Some worshiped her as a saint, which the Church did not permit, but did little to discourage. The pilgrims always gave alms to the Church, often quite generously.

Even before the affair of the three monks who cared for her, Elizabeth's installment as the Anchoress of Salisbury Cathedral had been fraught with problems. Brother Andreas, who had singled her out from the peasant girls of the nearby village, had been later discovered to have a secret wife and three children, and he was burned at the stake for his transgression. Then, though Elizabeth had sworn that nothing would please her more than to become the Anchoress, she had changed her mind once she had been walled into her cell. She had begged them to release her and to free her from her vow of obedience to the Church in her new vocation.

Then the visions had begun. They were torturous, frightening images of another time and place. They concerned a charismatic demon who masqueraded as an angel. Riding with his companions in a conveyance powered by magick, he battled and murdered other demons. His counselor was a dark-headed woman much like herself, who saw visions as she did.

She is the consort of a devil—am I one, too?

"They are battling priests in white robes," she told Brother Thomas, gasping as in her vision, one of the priests fell back from the others. His hand was pressed to his side; blood gushed through his splayed fingers.

And then she saw the dark-haired woman grabbing her head. She saw into the lady's mind, and what she saw was . . . herself. *She is seeing me! She is having a vision of me!*

She gripped Brother Thomas's robe. "She and the demon are at the Stone Circle!"

"Just outside our walls?" Brother Thomas asked, astonished.

"Yes, yes!"

There was a sound behind Brother Thomas, the whoosh of sandals dashing through.

Someone has been listening, he thought. *Someone has heard her ravings.*

Icy fear gripped his heart as he patted her thin fingers, which were twining into his roughly woven cassock. Her small, heart-shaped face was wrenched with terror, and he feared for Elizabeth . . . and for himself.

The battle had been going very well. Once engaged by Wesley and company, the Druids had given up the fight and were falling back. They'd all agreed that minimal damage was the most preferred outcome; these were human beings, and they had a code about killing folks.

As the Druids beat feet, Gunn had a clear chance to hack through the bonds of the girl on the altar, hoist her over his shoulder fireman style, and move back toward the ravine.

Then one of the Druids charged him, his curved knife raised. He was chanting in Druidese, and behind him all the fake stones of Stonehenge began to jitter and glow.

Whoa, real magick, Gunn had thought. *I think we underestimated these guys. They aren't wanna-be's. They're already are's.*

Gunn was about to kick the knife out of the man's hand, but then there was a loud pop and some sort of swirling vortex thing surrounding his attacker. Startled, Gunn had stumbled backward over a rock.

Next thing he knew, Cordelia let out a bloodcurdling shriek and fell to her knees, grabbing her head and screaming.

Vision, Gunn thought, glancing at her. Carefully he laid the girl he was carrying on the ground and started toward Cordy.

Then everything blurred, shifted, and glowed; his surroundings were crazy with bright lights and strange, whooshing noises, and the next thing he knew . . .

Once again, we are not in Kansas anymore.

Nor were they in Griffith Park. He lay about two feet away from Cordelia, who was whimpering softly, on a vast, windswept plain. Moonlight gleamed down on them. *Lucky thing, or Angel would be toast.* In the distance, shapes rose against a stony sky . . . very familiar shapes.

It's Stonehenge, Gunn realized. He glanced around, saw Wesley and Fred slowly sitting up. Then, a bit further on, Angel was silhouetted in his long coat, staring at the circle of stones. He wheeled around, saw Cordelia, and ran to her side. Gunn met him there.

"I'm okay, I'm okay," she murmured, although she was so obviously not. "Oh, man, that *hurt.* I . . ." She looked past Angel to take in the view. "Where *are* we? What . . . what happened?"

"There they are!" a voice cried.

Angel got to his feet and stood protectively in front of Cordelia as Gunn turned to see what was up.

Guys in helmets and armor had massed in a line behind them. As Gunn watched, stunned, about a dozen more clomped up on horseback. Their horses were enormous, and laden with armor just like their riders, as well as long drapey things that looked like horse nightgowns. They carried sharp-looking spears, lances, and swords.

Cavalry around here don't go in for light artillery, he thought.

Then a man dressed in nothing but a very itchy-looking brown robe and a pair of sandals sauntered up on a donkey. He said to the most decked-out of the warriors, "It is as she confessed to me and Brother Thomas. Our Anchoress has summoned her witchly cohorts here from the pits of Hell."

Cordelia frowned up at them. "Excuse me?"

"Silence!" Donkey Guy thundered.

She swallowed hard, then looked at Angel and said under her breath, "Okay, what's going on? I can understand them, and they're definitely not from around here, so I'm wondering, hey, magick, or universal translators like on *Star Trek*?" Scowling, she added, "We're not on Pylea again, are we? Because, you know, not loving that place. Well, loving the later version, when they started worshiping me, you know. It was kind of like high school. . . ."

"Cordelia, please stop chattering," Wesley ordered her in a loud voice, as he rose. "We need to focus, all of us. Especially on the men with the very thick and heavy slicing weapons."

He regarded their visitors calmly and raised his chin. "We come from another place, true," he called. "But we are not from Hell, nor are we witchly cohorts, and we mean you no harm."

There was a moment when no one spoke. Then Donkey Guy said simply, "Seize them."

The men in helmets slid off their horses, each landing with a heavy *thud* on the ground. They reminded Cordelia of the "spacemen" from *ET*, grim and faceless and determined. Despite their bulky body armor, Gunn detected severe pecs and 'ceps. Their weapons were to die for—literally.

As they strode toward the gang, Wesley said, "Gunn, Angel, stand down."

"Hey, man, we can take 'em," Gunn protested. "I'm not just gonna stand here and . . ." He looked down at his hands—no ax. "And say 'uh oh' like a guy in a badly written TV episode. Yo, our weapons are not part of this group hysteria."

"My crossbow's back in Los Angeles," Fred mourned.

"Even more reason to try to use reason," Wesley pointed out.

"Wesley's right," Angel said firmly. "We don't know how many of them there are. Plus we don't know where we are and these guys might be our only clues."

"If we are back in Pylea, I'm resigning," Cordelia grumbled. "I'm totally giving up on the good-guy biz. If we start running into Pylea people like some bad remake of *Wizard of Oz*. You know . . . like Groo . . . oooh, maybe we'll find Groo." She brightened and called to the intruders, "Okay, guys, chain me up." She smiled at Gunn. "First the mistreatment, then I'll have a vision, they'll crown me queen, and we'll all go home."

"Wherever that might be," Gunn replied.

"Hey, we've gotten back from wacky otherworldly places before," she reminded him.

"I think you should ask The Powers That Be about frequent flyer miles," Fred observed, then chuckled sadly and said to herself, "Joke."

"Here they come," Angel said, gazing at the phalanx of armored men and horses as they clomped a few more feet toward them. "We go quietly, as long as nobody on our side gets hurt."

"Agreed," Wesley said.

Gunn sighed. "Copy that."

Cordy sighed. "I wonder what's going to happen to that girl back in L.A. The one we didn't manage to save."

"Um, she was losing an awful lot of blood," Fred said.

"We're no good to her dead," Wesley reminded them.

The five of them slowly stood, showing their hands—no weapons—and Fred started to lose her self-control. The wind whipped her hair and whistled over the blasted earth as the heavy metal footgear of the horsemen thundered with each step they took. Against the pitch sky, they advanced menacingly on their quarry, so loaded up with protective layers that they looked like walking versions of Gunn's war wagon, with spiky collars and elbow slicers and what appeared to be oversized switchblades pointing out of their shoes.

Then they drew closer, and Fred was trying very hard not to freak out. Everything about them was . . . relentless. She could easily see one of the horsemen spearing them all like a giant shish kebob and not thinking another thing about it. These guys had not gone to empathy school.

They were less than a foot away now, and everything about them loomed deadly. Horse sweat and man sweat mingled with just a hint of the crystal musk notes of Cordelia's brand new Mat perfume. Fred had already bought her the matching body lotion for Christmas.

She sent a thought balloon skyward: *Hello, Fred to The Powers That Be. I'm thinking that a nice Christmas bonus for Cordelia is in order, okay?*

Two of the soldiers or guards or knights or whatever they were approached Cordy. The metal of their armor was rusty in places, and was that caked blood on the right one's gauntlet? They clamped some chains around her wrists and dragged her toward the monk.

The religious man pulled a cross out of his sleeve and stuck it in her face. Though Cordy snickered and tried to look like, *Puh-lese, you've got to be kidding,* both Fred and she glanced over at Angel. A cross in his face and he would probably vamp. And if he vamped, there was no telling what these people might do.

Then thunder rumbled overhead, and the leader of the soldiers said, "A storm is coming. Brother Joseph, you can finish their examinations later. In the harbor of the dungeon."

Cordelia grumbled, "'Dungeon' and 'harbor' don't belong in the same sentence."

"Except that they're both nouns," Fred offered, trying not to scream as two of the warriors grabbed her wrists and chained her as well. Gunn, Wesley, and Angel were each given the same treatment, and everyone was herded over to the man on the donkey. He did the cross thing to each one of them, but Angel was far enough away not to react to the symbolic object.

"Stay the course," Wesley reminded them as they were pushed between two of the warhorses and the monk gestured at the group to begin walking. "Be patient."

• • •

Patience . . . a virtue I was never good with, Gunn thought drearily.

Each of the Angel Investigations team had been thrown into separate cells of the dungeon of what looked to be an enormous church. It was cold. Gunn's floor was bare stone, wet and mossy, and there was no ventilation.

No one came to check on him, feed him, or give him water. That was cool; when he was working the streets of his hood, he could be a hard-ass too. Sad fact was, putting the fear of God into your enemy paid off.

Then he heard shuffling in the hallway and someone saying, "Be careful of her. She's a witch."

"Cordelia?" he said aloud, then figured that was pretty stupid, because he didn't want to put her name and "witch" in the same sentence around a bunch of religious fanatics.

Then he heard bitter weeping, and a man's voice that bellowed over it.

"This is your last chance to confess, Elizabeth. Do it now, in my presence, and we will only burn the demon and his followers."

"Thomas . . ." moaned the person who was crying. It was a woman, maybe just a girl. Gunn got his dander up. He knew about witch trials and forced confessions, how they were all fixed ahead of time. That girl didn't stand a chance no matter what she said. "Talk to Brother Thomas."

Same thing goes for us.

"He has abandoned you. He has stolen away in this dark night of the soul to leave you to answer for your crimes. When we find him, we will deal with him." There was a beat. "Now, confess!"

"I am an Anchoress," she pleaded. "I see what God shows me."

"The devil has beguiled you. You have abused your office to poison the souls of those who sought your aid."

She replied, "You're doing this to me because . . . because when you came to me, I refused you . . ."

There was the resounding crack of a sharp slap and a low sob of pain. Gunn clenched his fists.

I ever get out of here, whoever's doing that is gonna pay . . .

"Don't lie in an effort to save yourself." The man's voice was harsh. There was another slap.

"Brother Joseph," said another man. "Perhaps we should restrain ourselves. She is our Anchoress. . . ."

"*Was.* She has summoned these evil strangers into our midst. I heard her myself. And Brother Thomas helped her. He brought her the blood of a young virgin as a sacrifice to seal her unholy bond with the demon."

"She has not yet been proven guilty," the other voice said reasonably.

"That is not so, alas," said a third male voice. "I have just come from the cell of their leader. He is indeed a demon. I saw him change before my very eyes into a fiend of Hell. His eyes glowed with hellish fire and teeth became fangs. It was hideous to behold."

Angel? Gunn thought. *They finally tried that cross-in-the-face with him, I guess.*

"Christ Jesus preserve us," said Brother Joseph. The other two men muttered something that was probably Latin.

"What do you have to say about that, child?" asked the newcomer sternly. "How did he become your master? Did he come in the dark of night, when you should have been at prayers? Did he visit you in the guise of a handsome young man, who seduced you?"

"How could anyone visit me?" she cried shrilly. "I'm watched night and day!"

"By Brother Thomas," Brother Joseph said cruelly. "And he has shown his true colors."

"I'm doomed," she wept. "You are going to burn me alive."

"You, the demon, and those he holds in thrall," Brother Joseph confirmed.

No mistaking the glee in that man's voice, Gunn thought, enraged. *No mistaking the pleasure I'm gonna take in tearing him apart with my bare hands. . . .*

The three monks opened the door to Cordelia's prison cell and glared at her. The tallest, ugliest of the three—*not that we are talking beauty contestants here to start with*—kicked at the filthy straw she had burrowed into for warmth and said, "Rise, witch. You'll be warm enough very soon. Before this hour is up, we will take you and your friends to the burning place."

"I'm guessing it's not the same as the laughing place," Cordelia said under her breath.

"One of your company is sick with fever," he added. "God is punishing him in this life by showing him what it will be like for him in the next. And for you."

Her eyes widened. "Who? Who's sick? Is it Fred?"

"He is not the blackamoor, if that is to whom you refer. The other man."

"Wesley?" she asked shrilly. "Can I see him?"

The monk sneered. "So that you can cure him with Satan's power? I think not."

"You guys are so twisted," she said drearily.

"Would you care to make a confession of your diabolical nature? He whom you serve has revealed himself to us."

"Serve . . ." She hesitated. She'd seen movies about the Salem witch trials. She knew they were really good at lying about what they had and hadn't seen in order to get their victims to confess. "When you say serve, are you talking about serving people something to eat? Like rye bread? Because you see, some colonists of my country ate bad rye bread back in Salem. And wow, they thought a bunch of other colonists were witches. But, *wrong*, they were just innocent—"

"*Silence*," the man said, and he struck her a blow across the face that snapped back her head. "You will speak when spoken to."

"But I was spoken to," she protested. "You asked me a question!"

The monk took a step back. He gazed at her with the weirdest look on his face and said, "In so many ways, you are her sister."

Then worse than the slap, he trailed his fingertips down the side of her face.

Cordelia shuddered with fear and revulsion.

They came for Wesley as he burned of fever. Something was very wrong with him; he was dreadfully ill, so plagued with disease that he lay unmoving on the freezing stone floor although a rat trundled by very close to his face. But his captors showed him no mercy on that account; indeed, they seemed to feel that it was his fault that he was sick.

"You will not escape the flames by seeking pity," said the tall ugly one. "You will not escape at all."

If I wasn't so sick, I could play this game, Wesley thought, frustrated. *I read nearly every medieval manuscript on demonology and witchcraft during my internship at Watchers' Headquarters in London. But I can't think straight. With the high fever I have, it's a wonder I can think at all.*

"Get up," the monk said contemptuously. "We will prepare you now for burning."

"There are no questions for me," Wesley ventured. "No chance for me to confess, and to recant."

"We have all the proof we require."

"But Brother Joseph . . ." one of the other monks protested. He was young and still had a few of his teeth left. His pale face was chapped from the wind and he looked very frightened. "That is not how we are to do it."

"These are wild times, Brother Michael," Brother Joseph said. "Think of it—of the three monks assigned to care for her, she insisted that I be released from my duty. She killed Brother Mattias with her witchcraft, and then she beguiled Brother Thomas into helping her with her black magick."

"That is so," the nameless monk agreed. "I have often wondered of the things said about her. And about him, as well . . ."

"I witnessed their spellcastings myself. There is my word, which stands as proof. And then, there was the transformation of the devil, right before our eyes."

Angel changed, Wesley thought. *Then we're really for it.*

Brother Michael nodded and crossed himself. "You're right, Brother Joseph," he murmured uneasily. "I only wish . . . I wish that something could be done to spare them from the flames." He added very quietly, "It is such a terrible death."

"When the imps of Satan are involved, there can be no mercy," Brother Joseph intoned.

"Amen," the other two monks intoned.

The door to Fred's cell opened. Three hooded monks faced her, one holding a cross. All she could see of the three of them were their mouths, turned down in very dour frowns.

"Um, hi," she said, forcing down all the terror and panic that had welled up inside her ever since they'd been transported here. Her eyes were welling with tears.

Wordlessly, the one with the cross gestured for her

to rise. The youngest of the three monks held out a folded piece of white cloth. Uncertainly she took it.

The cross-holding monk said, "You will wear this garment to the burning place."

Fred had been in the process of unfolding the cloth. It was a very baggy dress. She said, "Sorry," and began to hand it back. "I don't think it's my size."

"Put it on," the monk said, "or we will do it for you."

Angel stood at the front of the cart, the right side of his face blistered, his hands bound, the sign of the cross burned into his forehead. Beside him stood a young girl in a white nun's habit, and she had been badly tortured. She had sunk to her knees, and she was weeping uncontrollably.

"She's an Anchoress," Angel explained to the others. "They wall her up alive, make her give advice to supplicants and prophecy. Most of them went mad."

"Being walled up," Cordelia muttered. "That'd do it."

"Some people theorize that Joan of Arc was an Anchoress," Angel continued.

"And she died at the stake," Cordelia recalled, shuddering.

Under cover of darkness, they were taking them to the burning place. Very few onlookers witnessed their procession, though they were surrounded by the armored knights and many men on donkeys or walking, carrying torches. There were probably about fifty, all told.

Cordelia, Gunn, and Fred stood behind Angel and the girl. Wesley had been thrown into the back of the cart, and he was moaning with fever.

Everyone in the tumbrel, including Angel, wore execution garments of pristine white.

Cordelia muttered, "The hell of it is, that girl back in L.A. is probably dead."

"Maybe we were meant to save this one," Gunn ventured.

"If you figure out how, let me know," Cordelia shot back.

Wesley moaned, and Angel glanced anxiously over his shoulder. He tried to tell himself that this was the inevitable outcome of their being transported here; that his change had not sealed their fates. But he couldn't help the guilt he felt; they'd sprinkled holy water on him, then branded his forehead with a silver cross, and he couldn't help his transformation. Of course in this time and place, he was considered a demon.

Then again, he was considered a demon in his own time and place, too.

It was the dead of night. Everything had happened so fast. He saw politics at play, swirling around Brother Joseph, who definitely had a grudge against the Anchoress. What little Angel had been able to understand was that she had been having visions of Cordelia, the others, and him, and sharing them only with one trusted monk. And this guy, this Brother Joseph, had been jealous of that.

Also, I think he tried something . . . and she wouldn't go for it.

"I'm sorry," he murmured to her.

"Speak not to me, Satan," she hissed, through swollen, bruised lips. "I abjure thee!"

He sighed, very sorry, and said to the others, "There's always a way out, unless we're dead."

And then the cart crested a rise, and the rings of Stonehenge appeared. Dozens of torches illuminated the ancient stones, and six tall poles, each of which was seated atop an enormous pyre of wood.

"Thinking dead would be a nice way out about now," Cordelia grumbled.

Me, too, Angel thought.

And then Cordelia cried out and fell to her knees, caught up in the agony of another vision.

At the same time, the little nun in white began to writhe as well.

Words came jumbled, and the two women spoke them in unison:

"O spiritus Neyilon et Achalas, accipte sacrificum vt Nichil contra me et contra clayem istam . . . I invoke the key of Pluto to open all locks . . . *valeat sera vbi ista clauis poneteur . . ."*

There was more; Cordelia rattled it off as best she could. Images came fast and furious, in the jump-cut style to which she had grown accustomed.

Stonehenge . . . Los Angeles . . . the girl . . . a Druid guy . . . chanting . . .

She saw the guy with the knife very clearly; he was surrounded by a shimmering magickal glow. The girl lay on the altar, and her chest was rising and falling very shallowly.

She's still alive . . .

Druid Guy was stomping around shouting, "*We* were supposed to go through the portal! Not *them*! Joseph is gonna pay for this!"

Then another image blasted into her mind: It was Brother Joseph standing before a portal, talking to the guys in L.A., beckoning them . . .

And then Angel was holding her. And Gunn was cradling the Anchoress. Now they were crouching below the field of vision of their guards, and no one stopped to investigate. Maybe they figured the women were swooning in fear.

Cordy said to Angel, "Angel, the Druids in L.A. . . . they were trying to come here, to this time."

Farther down on the cart, Wesley was repeating the words she had spoken as if committing them to memory.

"We never had time to wonder why the Druids were performing a ritual. It was to come here."

She blinked at him. "But we got sent here instead of them." She nodded as she put the pieces together. "And one of them back there was trying to come through just now, by reciting the spell again." Catching her breath, she realized something else: "The portal stays open only as long as that girl is alive. When she dies, it's closed."

The young nun stared at Cordelia. "Portals—you are speaking of the entrance to Hell!"

Cordelia gave the girl a long look. "You saw it, too."

"No, no," the Anchoress moaned. "I saw nothing."

"Listen," Cordelia said firmly. "We're going to die unless you and I work together. Brother Joseph is mixed up in this."

The girl took a deep breath. Her hands shook. "If you mean to beguile me . . ."

"No." Cordelia gave her a gentle smile. "I just want to save you."

The nun looked up at Angel. "But he . . ."

"He's a good guy."

Angel nodded. "I am."

"Come on. We don't have much time," Cordelia prodded.

The other girl nodded, lowering her head as she gazed at her tortured hands. "I saw that, too," she said. "What you saw. There are men from another place who wished to come here, but I . . . I summoned you instead . . ." She looked stricken.

"I don't think you summoned anyone," Angel told her. "I think it was someone else."

Angel turned his head and looked at the man on the donkey who was leading the procession. He was the tall ugly monk who had been so quick to condemn them all for witchcraft.

"Brother Joseph," the Anchoress breathed. "He *knows.*"

Cordelia nodded. "I saw him in my vision too. He set this whole thing up, probably back when he was taking care of you. I think you were having visions before you realized it."

"He was helping them cross over here."

"Maybe he was going to come to our time," Angel suggested. "Open the portal for them, go back through."

"With black magick," the girl murmured, crossing herself.

"He wanted you silenced, so you couldn't tell anyone," Angel told the girl.

"No. He wanted to sacrifice me," the Anchoress said slowly staring off into space. "That is the rest of the vision. There must be a sacrifice on either end, once they travel through the portals. That girl in the place where you dwell, and I, here."

"Looks like he may get what he wants," Gunn bit off.

They had reached the mystical stone circle of Stonehenge.

Perhaps three dozen monks were waiting for Brother Joseph and the cartful of witches at the pyres of Stonehenge. The wood had been slathered with pitch, to make it hot. The burnings would be quick . . . save for Elizabeth's. Brother Joseph had promised that the little Anchoress would die more slowly.

So that she will last long enough to make the transfer, Angel realized, as he allowed himself to be tied to his stake. Now that he could see Brother Joseph up-close and personal, the grim determination on the monk's face was obvious.

One by one, the others were led to their stakes, their arms tied behind their backs. Even Wesley, who was already half dead with fever, was forced to stand.

Their white garments flapped in the wind; the torches flickered and blazed. Angel could smell that the wood was green; it would not burn quickly even with the pitch. Cordelia, Gunn, Wesley, and Fred were in for hellish deaths . . . but the Anchoress would take forever to die. She would practically be roasted alive.

Once they were bound to their stakes, the prisoners received the sentence of Holy Mother Church directly from the lips of Brother Joseph, who stood in front of the massed warriors and monks, his cross raised high. He looked insane with triumph.

"For the crime of witchcraft, I abjure thee! May your souls burn in Hell with your lord and master, Satan!" he shouted.

He made the sign of the cross over them, and six monks came forward to touch their torches to the cords of wood.

Cordelia stared wild-eyed down at them.

"Chant . . . ," Wesley managed to rasp.

"Oh, my God!" she shouted, as the fire took hold of the bottom layers of wood. She went blank.

"Chant!" Wesley invoked the words: *"O spiritus Neyilon et Achalas, accipte sacrificum vt Nichil contra me et contra clayem istam* . . . I invoke the key of Pluto to open all locks . . . *valeat sera vbi ista clauis poneteur* . . ."

Cordelia took up the chant.

The fires licked at the pyre, at all of their pyres.

The Anchoress joined Cordelia in reciting the spell.

Then Brother Joseph must have heard them above the roar of the flames. He began to shout, "No! Stop! They are calling to Satan!"

Then Fred and Gunn added their voices.

Brother Joseph grabbed the torch of a nearby, startled monk and hurled it at Elizabeth. It arced, then landed in the center of the stack of wood.

Angel joined in the chant last.

The air around Stonehenge shimmered with an ethereal green glow. The bluestones and lintels and sarsens glittered and crackled with magick. As the monks shouted and began to scatter, a vortex formed at the center of the circle, and the Druid leader from Los Angeles tumbled into their midst.

"It's here," Cordelia cried. "The portal's here!"

"And it's open," Wesley managed. "Look."

Beyond the shimmer, Angel could see parts of the recreation of Stonehenge in Griffith Park.

"Hey!" the Druid guy shouted. "I made it. You can go through now!" He came toward the monk, who backed away from him and waved his arms as if to warn him off. Then he froze and pointed to Angel and company. "Those guys tried to stop me!"

"Hush, you fool!" Joseph shouted.

"What's wrong?" the Druid guy demanded. He looked around. "What's going on?"

"Brother Joseph?" queried the monk whose torch he had taken. "Are you in league with these fiends?"

"What? No!" Joseph cried. He pointed at the Druid guy. "I know him not! Seize him!"

The monks obeyed; in the ensuing confusion, Angel easily broke the chains and ropes that held him. Then he leaped to Cordelia's pyre and quickly freed her. There was no way to get her down the bier other than to throw her down bodily, which he did.

"Run to the portal!" he ordered her.

"Not till everyone's safe!" she shouted back.

She picked up a piece of burning wood and used it as a weapon, keeping the monks at bay.

But then the heavy artillery moved in—the knights in their armor, with swords drawn and maces twirling above their heads.

"Hurry!" Cordelia called frantically to Angel.

Angel freed Gunn next, who took the chance to leap to Fred's pyre. After Gunn untied Fred, the two of them jumped to the ground. Angel moved on to Wesley, and carried him slung on his back as he reached the ground.

Only the Anchoress was left tied to a stake, and Angel looked up at her just before he prepared to hurtle himself up her pyre—to burn in the attempt, if he had to . . .

At that moment, the Druid guy and Brother Joseph took up another chant . . .

The vortex shifted direction; the shimmering became a glowing green strobelight . . .

Angel, Cordelia, Wesley, Gunn, and Fred were sucked into the magickal portal. There was a mind-churning moment and then . . .

. . . they landed on the ground in Griffith Park.

"No!" Angel yelled angrily, while Cordelia shouted, "Somebody call nine-one-one!"

The sacrificial victim lay on the altar, still bleeding. The amount of blood from her wrist cuts, which had pooled on the grass below her, was astonishing.

Wesley staggered and fell to his knees. Gunn pulled out a cell phone and punched in the number.

"Damn! Gettin' the fast busy sound," Gunn shouted. "I'm not gettin' through."

"Try again," Fred urged.

"Angel, we have to go back," Cordelia said to him. "We have to save that girl. She's going to burn to death."

He nodded. "We can try the chant again."

"No luck," Gunn announced.

"You and Fred take her and Wesley to the nearest hospital," Angel told him.

"She's going into cardiac arrest!" Fred said. "Gunn, do you know CPR?"

Cordelia took a breath and gazed into Angel's eyes. "If we get it open and go back, and then she dies . . ."

"We're stuck there," he said. "I can go alone."

She smiled grimly. "Like hell you can."

Gunn carried the girl to Angel's convertible, and Fred helped Wesley walk. *A good sign that he can walk.*

Angel began the chant, and Cordelia caught up. The shimmering returned, and Angel took her hand. She smiled up at him and said, "Here goes nothing."

They were thrown back to the fourteenth century once more.

And this time, a man stood behind Elizabeth's stake,

trying to untie her while at the same time fighting to keep his long monk's robe from catching fire. An armored warrior was scrambling up after him, and the Anchoress was screaming. The flames had the hem of her execution robe.

Angel grabbed the sword of the nearest knight and threw it to Cordelia, who took on the nearest monk. Angel wrested a spear away from another warrior and fought his way through the frenzy of monks and fighters. Every face he blurred past spoke of terror and confusion. Then one of them fell back from him, and Angel realized that he had vamped.

He took advantage of their fear to make a path for himself, trying not to kill any of them. A quick glance in Cordelia's direction reassured him that she was managing to hold her own.

Then Brother Joseph planted himself in Angel's way. In his hand he held a cross.

Before Angel could dart around him, another monk flanked him. Then another, and another, until there was a solid wall of monks holding crosses.

"Help me!" shouted the monk who was trying to help Elizabeth.

"Angel, we've got to get to her!" Cordelia cried.

"She must suffer for her sins," Brother Joseph cried in ringing tones. "Only then will God spare us the evil that has come among us!"

Then Angel saw the Druid guy off to one side, gagged and held by two warriors. He raced over, yanking him away with ease—no crosses—and dragged him back to stand beside Cordelia.

He pulled off the man's gag.

"Tell them what's going on!" Angel demanded.

"He set it up!" the Druid guy said fearfully. "Oh, man! He had this chick who could see things. And then he did all these spells and he found us and it was, like, we were going to switch in the portal and . . ." He looked anxiously at Angel. "I don't want to do this. I want to go home."

Brother Joseph looked pale. "I have no idea what you're talking about."

"You liar," Cordelia hissed.

Then she launched herself at Brother Joseph. She still had the sword Angel had thrown to her, and thanks to Angel's training, she knew how to use it. While she parried and lunged, Angel thrust the Druid guy at the monk and made it to Elizabeth's pyre.

The fire burned; the heat alone hurt more than he remembered; it seared him to the bone, but he fought on. Scrabbling, stumbling, every part of him in agony, he inched his way to the young girl and the man who was trying to keep her garment from going up in flames, although his own monk's robe was burning up his back.

Angel batted him out first, then yanked at Elizabeth's chains and ropes, pulling them apart. The metal was white hot in places. Then he pushed them both off the pyre. The logs tumbled everywhere, igniting the robes of the monks closest to it, and creating a firewall between the escapees and the bad guys.

The three had landed in a heap on the other side of

the flaming logs. Then Angel saw a second pair of sandaled feet and looked up into the face of another monk. It was the young one who had accompanied Brother Joseph, the one who had looked so frightened and uncomfortable.

As the knights and monks began to circle around the fire, the young monk tightly held the reins of Brother Joseph's donkey, his face distorted with fear.

"Take her away, Brother Thomas!" he said quickly. "Bernadette runs fast, for a donkey."

The other monk inclined his head. "God bless you, Brother," he said. "You will be made to suffer for this kindness, if Brother Joseph prevails."

"God will prevail," the young monk said, with a brief smile. He glanced over his shoulder as the monks and warriors spotted them and began to rush toward them. "Hurry."

Quickly Brother Thomas turned to Elizabeth. He put his hands around her waist and lifted her onto the donkey. "Such was the flight of Our Lord's Mother into Egypt," he said to her. He turned to Angel. "I don't know who you are, demon . . ."

"Angel," Elizabeth said.

Then Brother Thomas got onto the donkey with the Anchoress, and the donkey started up at a decent clip.

Then a few of their adversaries came forward to do battle with Angel. But he could see that their hearts weren't in it; they were terrified about what had happened. The devil was winning this hand, and they didn't want to lose.

Gradually they lost the rhythm of the battle, giving Angel a chance to beat a fast retreat into the sarsen circle. They seemed even more afraid of Stonehenge than of him, he realized with some satisfaction.

Then Cordelia darted out from behind the largest of the stones. She still had her sword, and it was covered with blood.

Of the Druid guy there was no sign.

He said, "How'd you get out of there?"

She shook her head. "I honestly don't know, Angel. A miracle?"

They chanted.

"Wait!" Angel heard him shout. "Wait for me!"

But it was too late.

The portal disgorged them back in Los Angeles.

Cordelia's weapon fell to the ground.

Her cell phone connected them to Gunn, who said, "We're at the hospital. She . . . she didn't make it."

"Oh, my God," Cordelia breathed. To Angel she said, "She died." Then she blurted, "That means the portal's closed. That guy is stuck back there." She set her jaw. "Good."

She listened for another moment, then reported, "They gave Wesley something and he's already feeling better. They think it was some kind of contaminated water or something. He said there was some water in his cell and he drank it."

Angel nodded grimly.

"We'll meet back at the hotel," she told Gunn. "We'll grab a cab."

"Copy that."

Cordelia disconnected. They looked at each other.

She sank into his arms and began to cry.

He held her.

"It's over," he said.

"The darkest hour of magicks?" she asked.

He waited a beat and then he said, "That, too." He nodded at the blood-soaked stones and grass. "We need to put some distance between us and this place before we call a cab."

"I'm so tired," she said.

He picked her up in his arms and began to walk. After a few moments, Cordelia drowsed against his shoulder.

The longest night of the year, a night of bonfires and magicks, was nearly over, too.

2 A.M.

BUMMED OUT

by Doranna Durgin

Brrrr. Cordelia pulled her borrowed coat tightly around herself—and then thought better of it. Borrowed, much used, seen-better-days . . . okay really *nasty* coat.

Angel leaned closer to her, dressed similarly in a torn wool shirt jacket and dingy red watch cap, his fingers breaking out of every seam of his knit gloves. "Think of it as an acting job, Cordelia."

"For which I should win some sort of award," Cordy said in instant rejoinder, unable to suppress a nose-wrinkling wince. Here they were in the smog-dark night hanging around skid row, watching the streets around the Union Rescue Mission while trying to avoid the notice of the cops from the LAPD Central Division one block away. Only days before Christmas—and were they at the Hyperion Hotel drinking the eggnog left over from earlier that night?

No. Were they admiring her spoils from the holiday shopping coup of the day? No. They were dressed as homeless people, skulking around on this cold, cold night. *Who says it doesn't get cold in Los Angeles?* It had to be below fifty out. No one here looked warm enough—well, except for Angel, who was pretty much a one-temperature-fits-all kind of guy.

Cordelia resisted another urge to burrow more deeply inside the filthy coat—thank goodness she had on her own warm sweater underneath—and blocked the sight of her surroundings with tightly closed eyes, comforting herself with the quick recitation of beauty tips. *Shiny hair: Mash an avocado with one tablespoon of olive oil and a teaspoon of baking powder. Mix, apply, soak, rinse.*

"Look alive, Cordy," Angel said with another nudge.

She opened her eyes to give him a queenly frown. "I could say the same to you."

"Touch-*y*," he said, recoiling a little more than necessary, that startled puppy-dog look in his eyes. She hated that. At least when he went all broody, she knew it was usually safe to ignore him.

"Touchy?" she repeated, and struck a thoughtful expression. "What can we do this holiday party night besides some casual time travel? Oh, I know—put Cordelia in smelly rags and send her out in the cold to wait for bad things to happen." She gestured at Fifth Street, the small gated park behind them, and the looming mission a block away—at the clusters of genuinely homeless people, some wearing tinsel in a feeble nod to the season, some curled up in a misery that knew no season. "You expected me to be a in *good* mood? Whose bright idea was this, anyway?"

She hadn't ever really known. Thinking back on it, she only knew it hadn't been *hers*. Thinking back on it . . .

Cordelia Chase sashayed into the classiness of the Hyperion Hotel lobby.

Okay, *aging* classiness.

Okay, once *some*one had somehow *thought* this place was classy, but Cordy herself couldn't see it. On the other hand, she was here now, and that gave the place a certain amount of class right there, didn't it? Especially since she had just scored at a once-in-a-lifetime holiday sale at the makeup counter of Bloomingdale's and even now carried the bag high, a trophy waiting to be noticed.

Odd. They'd all been here when she left . . .

Her shopping trophy lowered slowly to her side. "Guys?" she said. "Hello?"

No guys. And no Fred, either.

"I get more reaction than this from Phantom Dennis," Cordy told the lobby, and matter-of-factly deposited the bag behind what had once been the check-in counter. As she shrugged off her festively red sweater-jacket, she finally heard a raised voice from the Hyperion's inner courtyard. An unfamiliar raised voice. She slid the sweater back up over her shoulders and pushed through the courtyard doors.

The gang was here, all right, gathered beside the worn fountain in the late afternoon light. Fred, still a bit spooked; Gunn, looking pretty much like he could handle anything, as usual; Wesley, looking very serious, as usual; and Angel, looking distracted and pretty much on the edge of a good brood. As usual.

The clients . . . now *they* weren't usual. Angel Investigations had helped soccer moms, demons, and just about everything in between. But they'd never had clients like these, who looked to be the union reps for the L.A. homeless. And not just the homeless, but the *really* homeless. Not *I'm living out of my car for a few months* but *my home is the streets and I left my sanity somewhere else on the way to getting here* homeless. Union Rescue Mission regulars.

Not so long ago, she wasn't so far from being among them. Broke, living in a dingy little apartment . . . Angel's arrival had changed all that.

"Cordelia," Wesley said, in that half admonishing, half questioning way he had.

"In or out, that's what my mother always used to say," Cordy said inanely, letting the door close behind her and inwardly wincing at her own too-chipper voice.

Wesley said, "Yes . . . well, right." Not helping at all, and she made a face at him for it. He stood by the fountain with his arms crossed and his hands tucked under them, wearing his attentive face. The others stood loosely grouped beside him, except for one man who sat at the fountain. He looked long-term tired, and his green-yellow bruises were clearly from a beating. At first glance Cordy judged him to be fifty; at second she realized he wasn't much older than Angel. Or than the age at which Angel was pretty much stuck. He held a much-battered Angel Investigations business card between thumb and forefinger, flexing it slightly in a nervous gesture.

"You're just in time," Gunn said. Angel didn't say anything, just did that slight lift of an eyebrow that more or less meant *and here we all are.* "These gentlemen—"

"And lady," prompted the shortest of the figures in a cracked voice, hidden beneath about twenty layers of clothing and two watch caps. Also wary and bruised.

"And lady," Wes said without missing a beat.

Gunn didn't miss a beat either. *"Clients,"* he said. "These *clients* have a pretty serious problem."

Cordy thought that was understating the case considerably, but she put her own attentive face on even as her thoughts drifted back to Christmas shopping and the nice sweater she'd seen that she thought would suit Angel. *Gray enough to fit his image, not* too *expensive because let's face it, he does tend to show up with rents and tears and bullet holes in his clothes more often than the average person—*

"—so we're going to join them near San Julian Park tonight," Wes said in a *that's that* voice, which let her know she'd missed a lot. "Blend in, so to speak. I'm almost certain we've got mimic demons at work, and we need to flush them out."

"Excuse me?" Cordelia blurted. She searched her

memory of the past few moments and came up with a vague notion of atypical incidents among the homeless, most of whom usually watched out for each other. Startling clashes of violence and temper, and most recently, a killing. They feared something among them—

She tried to erase her totally-taken-by-surprise face, but too late. They'd all turned to look at her—even the clients, who until now had simply been nodding at Wes's Cliff's Notes version of their story. Angel nudged Gunn with a subtle elbow and nodded at Cordy. "Shopping," he said, as if that explained it all.

"It's the holidays. I'm only doing my duty," Cordy said, inserting what she thought was just the right amount of haughtiness. "Um, can I, uh"—she nodded at the lobby doors—"talk to you guys?"

They just looked at her. Widening her eyes for emphasis, she repeated the gesture. "Now?" she added.

With a defeated obedience she knew to be perfectly false, they trooped into the lobby. She lowered her voice to a stage whisper even though the small gathering by the fountain didn't seem interested in eavesdropping. "Did I have a vision about helping these guys and someone forgot to tell me? Because, you know . . . the visions? If there was a real problem, don't you think I'd know about it?"

"It's the longest night of the year," Angel said. "Maybe the Powers That Be are saving you." He gave her a deadpan look. "For the really good stuff."

"Yeah, like that ever stopped them before," she shot back with much sarcasm. "What about those missing carolers? Weren't we going to look into that tonight?

Maybe sing a few seasonally appropriate songs while we're at it?"

"This is helping the helpless," Gunn said. Behind him, Fred sat on one of the circular lobby couches, curling up in that way she had of being very small and barely noticeable. "Isn't that what we do?"

"Well, *yeah*," she admitted. "But, we won't be around to help the helpless very long if we don't have a way to pay the holiday bills!"

Angel gave her a startled look. "What holiday bills?" he asked, apparently going unheard by the others.

Wes all but spoke over him, his voice dangerously close to patronizing. "Cordelia," he started.

"Cordelia nothing," she said. "You know I'm right. We have *got* to get some paying customers." She winced a little inside; she knew better. But she was also the one handling the bills right now, and the very thought put more panic than thought into her words. "*Look* at them!" She gestured expansively and then snatched her arm back, realizing it would be just as revealing as words to the members of the small group outside, some of whom were now trying to peer through the glass doors. And then she sighed because she did look at them, and she knew they needed help. Faltering a little, she finished making her point anyway. "They're *bums.* Do you really think they came here expecting to pay us for our time?"

Gunn frowned at her, looking much taller than she'd prefer he did unless he was agreeing with her at the time. "I'm not so sure that's P.C., Cordy."

"Whatever, then. Homeless. Indigent. Housing-challenged."

"Mumpers," Angel said, inserting his words perfectly into the fleeting instant of silence between them all—and begetting more silence.

"Mumpers," Cordelia said flatly.

Angel looked at them all as if surprised to see he was suddenly the center of attention. "Mumpers. Beggars." He got that faraway look on his face, the mixture of memory and regret and, sometimes, guilt. "They'd come out on solstice night, pretending to be upper class, telling stories about the hard luck they'd fallen on. Begging. I can remember my mother . . ." There his voice trailed off, and he shook his head. "Anyway. They were always out on the one night when everyone else knew to stay at home."

"Where it was safe," Wesley said, and gave him a pointed look. "I imagine memories of your childhood aren't your most recent memories of mumpers, are they?"

Angel returned Wesley's look with one of his own, an even expression. "No," he said. "They aren't."

"Ah, so that's it," Cordelia said. "You fanged a couple of mummers—"

"Mumpers," he said.

"—and now you want to make up for it by helping these people?"

"No," Angel said, and shook his head quietly. "I want to help them because it's the right thing to do."

"It's the right thing, Cordy," Gunn agreed, though he was not often one to jump in on Angel's side.

"I know." Cordelia sighed expansively. "Maybe I'll get a retro-vision or something. Now just what is it we're going to do?"

It had seemed almost reasonable at the time. But at the time, Cordelia hadn't thought about the cold or the stiff, stained clothing or the awkwardness of knowing the skid row residents would be able to take one look at her and know she didn't belong here.

She only hoped the mimic demons couldn't do the same.

And the mimic demons! What was that about? Demons who mimicked their prey, hanging around, sucking all the good vibes out of people like dopers getting a high, and leaving only the anger and hate and meanness, with predictable results. Arguments and fights and finally killings. As if the homeless community didn't have enough problems already!

"Facial," she muttered comfortingly to herself, leaning back against the tall wrought-iron bars surrounding San Julian Park. They couldn't even go inside the mission where it was warm—the place had security guards, access cards, and plenty of watchful eyes along with its rows and rows of bunks and the Mommy and Me room. The mimic demons kept their trouble outside where it was harder to spot just who was doing what to who. Not only that, they were so good at it that Wesley hadn't been able to provide even a vague description of their natural form.

Wesley came up beside her, trading places with

Angel; Angel took his turn at slow patrolling, walking the street while trying to look staggery but looking as usual as though he were a black cat gliding through the night. Cordelia closed her eyes again. "Four tablespoons of plain yogurt, two tablespoons of grated orange peel. Mix and massage into skin . . ."

"Or you could simply suspend a ball of wax between your eyes," Wesley said.

"Oh, *please,*" she said. "What kind of beauty tip is that?"

"An ancient Mayan one," he said, sounding cheerful to be pontificating even though his nose and ears were red with cold and the scarf he had wrapped around his neck looked genuinely crusty. "They considered it a great beauty to be subtly cross-eyed."

She merely gave him a look and changed the subject. "I still don't get how we're supposed to spot these mimic demons. I mean, since they're so good at mimicking and all."

"We probably won't spot them," Wes said in a matter-of-fact way. Then, as Cordelia frowned at him, he added, "That is, we won't spot them by how they *look,* but by what they do. Or don't do. Once trouble breaks out, we look for the ones who aren't involved."

"Ah," said Cordelia. She fussed at the over-long sleeve of her coat, found something icky, and rubbed the sleeve against an iron bar of the park fence. "You mean they'll stand off to the side looking blissfully buzzed?"

"Exactly."

"I can't wait," she muttered. She pushed off from the fence and said, "I'm too cold to just stand here. I'm going to walk with Angel for a while."

"You do that," Wesley told her. "I'm sure he'll appreciate the company." She gave him a skeptical look, not sure if he was being clueless or sarcastic. As usual, he seemed immune. "See if you can spot Gunn while you're at it."

She'd seen Gunn not five minutes earlier, swathed in totally uncool clothes, so she wasn't worried. She merely waved an acknowledgment at Wesley as she headed down the cracked sidewalk.

She easily caught up to Angel. He'd stopped at the corner and was just standing there, his head slightly cocked, looking ever so much like a vampire about to pounce.

"That's not helpless," she told him, "that's hulking."

He didn't answer right away. Ah. Brooding, then. Then his expression turned puzzled and he said, "What?" as if she'd been speaking a foreign language.

"We're supposed to be helpless," she said, shoving her knit hat back from where it had fallen over her forehead. Not her own knit hat because would she ever own such a thing? But Wesley's, because she drew the line when it came to what she put on her hair. "You don't look helpless. You look hulking and strong and . . . possibly hungry?"

He gave her a startled look.

"Okay, then, not hungry. But hunting."

"Maybe hunting," he allowed, and his expression grew closed again, his face full of shadowed angles in the streetlights.

"Oh, I get it," Cordelia said. She crouched by the corner of the building, trying to look less like herself and more like a homeless person seeking a quiet spot to be cold. "Thinking about the mumpers again?"

Angel crouched beside her, close enough to share warmth—if he'd had any to share. He didn't answer; he didn't look at her. Even the dingy red watch cap didn't tone down the casual intensity of his presence.

She nodded in understanding. "Got a lot of them, did you?"

He looked right at her, catching her eye in a penetrating gaze, as if saying *this is what you want?* "It was the longest night of the year, Cordelia. Everyone else was inside. Year after year, they'd make their rounds, dressing their parts, out walking the muddy roads. They knew the risks, but—"

"But they were hungry. Or cold."

"Or sometimes it was just what they did best," he said quietly, but his voice held no judgment. At least, not for the mumpers. "Mostly they didn't even have someone to miss them."

"*You* seem to miss them," she observed.

"Not exactly." He shifted uncomfortably, and she knew it wasn't because he was tired of crouching there. "I . . . regret them."

She couldn't help a short laugh. She'd never had much sympathy for the evil of Angelus, not after all the trouble he'd caused them. Not even when he who had been Angelus now had his soul back and had also paid for what had been done. "And you think helping these people is going to make up for those others?"

He looked at his past through shadowed eyes. "They dressed for the role," he said. "The men put on the aprons and stories of respectable tradesmen fallen ill. The women played widows or faithful wives whose husbands were ill unto death. As if they'd have better luck if they pretended to be like the people they were begging from." Oh, he was far away, all right. She didn't think he was remembering the mumpers' role-playing or their luck. She thought he remembered their necks. But then he suddenly turned to look at her, back in the present, his voice completely normal. "I suppose for some of them the stories were even true."

Cordelia quit thinking about Angel and thought of herself again, of her own family's fall from grace. Of how fast it had happened, and how easily. How *true.* She said nothing. She thought instead about those things she often depended on to make her life seem right again. *A black tea bag soaked in cold water and placed on each eye for ten minutes will reduce puffy eyes.*

She felt better immediately.

Angel, too, was quiet for a moment. Then he said, "There's no *making up* for those others, Cordy. You know that."

"Yeah," she said. "I do. It's just every once in a while it seems worth saying."

They fell silent as Cordy considered the warm

mission lobby, and by extension the towering edifice of the San Pedro entrance and the huge cross impressed right into the front of the building. She didn't think she had much chance of talking Angel into relocating their little sting operation. She considered withdrawing her arms inside the oversize coat altogether, where they could luxuriate in the warmth of her thick sweater without feeling . . . crawly, and just happened to glance down toward Main Street in time to see a lurching figure heading right at them. She said, "Angel . . ."

He said, "I see him," and stood up. Good thing, too, because Lurching Man was definitely heading straight for them, and everything but the darkness fled before the stench he brought with him.

"Okay," Cordelia said under her breath. "Someone was bound to be drunk."

"Tha's *my* spot," Lurching Man pronounced thickly.

"Okay," Cordy said again, brightly this time. "We were just keeping it warm for you. Weren't we, Angel?"

"Something like that," Angel said, helping her up, and Cordelia was glad to see that in spite of his general broodiness, he wasn't looking for trouble.

She gave her wrist a quick glance—although her watch was wisely absent—and gave a wild guess at the time. "Oh, look, almost two-thirty. Time to go!"

"*My* spot!" said Lurching Man, and true to established form, lurched right into Cordy.

"Hey!" she yelped. And "Ew!" and "Get off!" as they performed a strange tussling dance-fight in which Lurching Man's greatest weapon seemed to be his breath.

"This could have gone better," Angel muttered. He neatly spun the man, barely tapped him on the chin, and then lowered him gently to the ground to lean against the building.

"Ew!" Cordy said, brushing her arms off until she realized that the coat could hardly have been any worse than before. She glared down at Lurching Man, peripherally aware of someone else's approach. "I guess you've got your spot, all right." Then she glanced at Angel, uncertain. "Do you suppose the mimic demons . . . ?"

He gave his head a short shake. "Just drunk, I'd say."

She didn't think he sounded entirely sure.

The figure approaching them stopped under the nearest streetlight so they could see it was one of the men who'd brought them here, the young one with the bruises—one of the first victims of the changing mood on the street. Now his sweatshirt hood was up and tied tightly closed, covering what had been totally skanky hair, and he kept his hands jammed in the pockets of what Cordy had first taken to be a vest but now saw was the sleeveless remains of a regular coat. "Thanks," he said, looking sadly at the man on the ground. "He was doing so well until these last few days. I don't know which hit him harder—the holidays or these mimic demons you say are the problem around here."

"You sound like you don't believe us," Cordy said, more than a tad defensively. Here they were risking their butts and wearing bad clothes—

But the man gave a short laugh. "Naw," he said. "It's

just that there's so many demons around here, it's hard to keep track." He nodded at Lurching Man, who'd started gently snoring. "His is drink." When he looked back at Angel he said, "You've gotta do something. Half of us are just barely holding on as it is."

"We *are* doing something," Angel said, but not without understanding. He nudged Lurching Man's leg out of the way so no one would step on him in the darkness, and they started a slow walk back toward the park.

Cordelia put herself on the other side of Angel from their new companion. She said, "What's your demon?"

"*Cordelia,*" Angel said, sounding exasperated.

"Don't tell me you're not wondering," Cordelia said, tossing back hair she'd momentarily forgotten was trapped under the knit hat.

"It's no secret," the man said. "Gotta gambling problem. Can't lick it. Most of us have problems we can't lick. Some of us are still trying; some of us aren't. But we don't have any hope to spare, and these . . . creatures . . . are taking it."

Cordelia thought of day after day sitting inside her grungy pocket-size apartment, waiting for the phone to ring. Always just enough success with the smallest of bit parts to keep her hoping. But even now she could feel all those times that she'd pondered giving up. Felt them strongly. The homeless man gave her a perceptive look in the pool of light from the street lamp they passed and for that moment she felt more like it was a spotlight, illuminating all her innermost feelings. She kept her face desperately casual, but the remembered despair swelled into something so strong that she suddenly could barely walk, barely put one foot in front of the other . . .

"Cordelia?" Angel said, frowning at her. "What—?"

A more familiar feeling struck her. Her legs went all rubbery; she felt her eyes roll back, and the world disappeared. In its place came a tumult of flashing images and shooting pain—*men fighting, blood everywhere, a pile of bodies with their arms and legs flung about like so many pick-up sticks, a strobing series of movement behind foliage-bars-foliage, the towering cross on the front of the mission—*

"—not fair!" she cried, finding herself in Angel's arms, leaning back against him while he supported her entire weight. "We're *here,* so lay off already!" The vision fled, leaving her momentarily blind to anything but the fierce pain in her head. But it faded quickly. Astonishingly quickly. She blinked and took a cautious look at the bête noire world of garish streetlights and concrete and the metal bars of the park just half a block away. "Oh," she said, finding her feet again. "That's not so bad. Why is that not so bad?"

Angel waited until he was sure she had her balance and then carefully stepped back. "The Powers That Be are giving you a break."

Their companion looked at them both askance. "What are you talking about? What was that? Does she have fits or something?"

"Only when someone expects me to make the coffee," she told him. To Angel she said, "I saw bodies.

Lots of them. They all looked"—she glanced at the man—"well, like him. Like *us.* It was right here. I think that's why it wasn't so bad. The vision, I mean. What I saw was bad enough. In the park . . . but aren't those park gates locked?"

"Every night," said the man. Nameless Man. He jammed his hands in the pocket of his hack-job vest and scowled for no apparent reason.

"Well, there's someone in there. Some *thing.*" She gave the park a narrow-eyed stare and then looked at Angel. "Just how up-close and personal do these mimic demons have to be to do their thing? I mean, wouldn't it be safest for them to hole up in the one place no one else can get to?"

"They clear that place out before they lock it up," said Nameless Man. He still stared at her, as if he could be all casual about the presence of the supernatural until he saw it himself. In *her.*

On the other hand, she supposed it was pretty dramatic to see a vision smacking her around. Always nice to know she could still command attention—even if the thought brought her no actual comfort, and instead seemed to recall the despair she'd felt at her general lack of success in that area. If there was one thing an actress needed to be able to do . . . She scowled, dragging her thoughts back to where they'd started. Responding to Nameless Man, who she suddenly wanted to slap. She clenched her hands into fists at her side. "*Mimic* demons," she said, glancing at Angel to see that he was one thought ahead of her, his complete attention on the park, his demeanor no more broody than usual. She could fight it, she realized. As long as she kept telling herself they weren't *really* her feelings, she *would* fight it. Too bad the general homeless population had no idea what lay behing the troubles—only those few who had come to the hotel. She sighed and turned back to Angel. "Wes didn't have much to say about them. Do we know these things can't mimic"—*foliage-bars-foliage*—"bushes? Or a nice fence post? And did you happen to notice how these past moments have so thoroughly lost their uplifting charm?"

"Yes," said Nameless Man through gritted teeth.

Angel said nothing, but his already long strides grew longer and Cordelia found herself skipping to keep up, which for some reason annoyed her tremendously. She was on the verge of reaching out to grab his arm, in spite of the folly of such a thing, when a tremendous ruckus broke out just past the park gates. People materialized as if from nowhere—homeless, not-homeless, Cordelia had no idea—converging on the same spot as though drawn by the initial, single shout of protest from—

Wesley? Was that *Wesley*, desperately trying to crawl out from under the heap of humanity?

Angel made it there in a heartbeat—albeit not his own—and began flinging people away from the pile. They made a seething crazy quilt of colors, and the craziest thing about it was the way they flung themselves right back into the mess. Beside Cordelia, Nameless Man gave a wordless growl and launched himself at the fray—except Cordelia grabbed him and spun him around, not with her strength, but by using his own momentum against him.

Uh-oh. Mistake. For his eye held a crazed gleam in the unnatural streetlamp light. His fist drew back, and Cordelia suddenly realized that for all the demons she'd bashed, all the vamps she'd dusted, she didn't want to face this human. She gave a shriek of protest and steeled herself to land the pointed kick she had ready, but something plucked Nameless Man away and tossed him up against the park fence.

"Gunn!" she said in relief. And then, "Where have you been!"

"You think this is the only little disagreement breaking out on the street?" Gunn grunted, blocking another man as he staggered back at them and then shoving him away from the seething pile—even as two more flung themselves into the fight.

Despair flared within her. "We can't keep up with *this!*" she said, even as she tripped another would-be combatant charging to the scene. "And Wesley's in there!" Despair switched to renewed annoyance, and in that moment she just *knew* that Wesley had done or said something stupid, something blithely offensive. She wanted to hurl herself on the top of the pile and fight her way through to pummel him herself. . . .

She gave an abrupt shake of her head. "Whoa," she said. "That really sucked. We've got to put a stop to this."

"No argument from me," Gunn said. "I'm beginning

to feel a little too itchy for comfort, and I don't mean in that personal way."

Angel staggered back from the growing melee, blood trickling from a dozen little injuries. He said to Gunn, "A little help here?"

Gunn gave a short shake of his head. "Losing battle, Angel. No way we're gonna break them all up."

"We've got to find the mimics," Cordelia said rather desperately, unable to see any sign of Wesley, although several of the combatants had collapsed, too injured to stand and yet still fighting. "I saw bodies . . ." She jabbed a pointing finger at the park. "*There.* My vision—"

Angel didn't wait to hear any more. He yanked the still-dazed Nameless Man aside from the gate and kicked at it, not once, but twice. Just as Cordelia winced at his failure, he went all fang-face in ire and really bashed it a good one. The gate lock gave way; the gate crashed open with a force it was never built to endure and then swung crookedly, the top hinge broken. Cordelia glanced at Gunn, and together they rushed into the block-size area. Then they stopped short, almost immediately defeated by shadows and nooks and crannies . . . and demons that could mimic anything close to their own size.

But Angel didn't hesitate. He grabbed up the wooden bench nearest the entrance and smashed it to the ground, tossing one of the planks to Gunn and another to Cordelia. She was so startled she fumbled it, glancing anxiously at the growing number of injured people just outside the park . . . and at the endless supply of people replacing them. If Wesley was smart he was curled up into a little ball at the bottom of it all.

He *was* smart, sometimes. She just hoped this was one of those times. But she doubted it. She doubted she could do anything to help this mess, this horrible, horrible mess.

Stop it, Cordelia Chase. No mimic demon was going to mess with *her* happy vibes!

Angel's face was back to normal, his expression back to grim. "We'll never find them by eye," he said. "Just start hitting things. Everything—the trees, the benches, the pavilion pillars—"

Gunn nodded, hefting his plank. "I like it," he said. "It's a good plan." He raised his voice, aiming it toward the center of the small park. "And I really *feel like hitting things.*"

"What in this picture doesn't belong?" Angel said, menace in his voice. He smashed the plank against a second bench, and then against the base of a street lamp within the park. "Oops, city property. Belongs. How about—"

"This," said Gunn with satisfaction, eyeing a bush outside the small bank of wintering plantings across the cement walkway from the small pavilion. He took a couple of practice swings with the plank, shouting over his shoulder to be heard above the noise of the fight. "Dibs!"

And Cordelia, who'd simply been standing there with her plank in her hands, watching Angel's bench-bashing and blinking at the explosive power behind each blow, happened to glance at the park entrance and discovered they'd finally drawn the attention of the brawling street denizens, and not in a good way. She threw herself against the gate to close it.

It wouldn't, naturally. Not all the way—just enough to give her hope. But there was nothing left to latch it, and now that it was closed, the people outside it sounded suddenly all the more determined to come in. They shouted a jumble of demands and threats at her.

"Guys," she said, her voice just a tad higher than normal. She jammed her plank against the gate to create a makeshift latch and then put her back to it, digging her nonexistent worn-sneaker heels against the walkway. "Five-inch spikes," she moaned as someone punched her shoulder; someone else plucked the hat off her head. "That's what I need right now. A little traction—"

But the rubber soles of the sneakers gripped just fine. If only the old canvas hadn't started to rip . . .

"Angel!" she called desperately. Behind her the crowd shoved and shouted and—ew, was that *spit*?

"Demon-hunting," he said by way of an answer, and she looked over just in time to see the bush between Angel and Gunn unfold itself into a squat lumpy demon.

"Mr. Potato Head?" she said in astonishment, gasping as she lost a few inches of ground. "We've been hunting Mr. Potato Head?"

"Mr. Mashed Potato Head," Gunn growled. The potato-shaped demon squeaked in dismay.

"Crinkled-sliced chips," Angel suggested, eliciting another squeak. He leaned over to meet the creature's marbled gray eyes, looming close over an otherwise seemingly featureless face. "Leave these people alone, and you get to live. Any questions?"

Behind Cordy, the gate shuddered. "I don't think you're getting through—but *they* are! *Do* something!" Her sneakers scrabbled against the walkway, losing another inch in the seams. Another minute and she'd come out of them entirely, and then the little park would be swarming with frenzied crazy people, the potato would get away, and they'd be right back where they started—assuming they didn't get too broken in the process.

Her feet slipped. The frenzied crazy people battered her gate with noise and their bodies. And Cordelia's eyes opened very wide as two artistically placed garden boulders beside Gunn shimmered and bulged and suddenly became squat lumpy demons. *Huge* squat lumpy demons.

Gunn gave them a surprised look, and then looked back at the smaller one. "This must be Baby Bear, then."

"You heard me," Angel said to them. "You're not welcome here. Point of fact, you're not welcome anywhere. But especially not here. Not anywhere on my turf."

"Or mine," Gunn said. "And that just about covers the West Coast, wouldn't you say?"

But Mama and Papa Potato Head didn't squeak in dismay. They didn't quail before Angel. Their protruding eyes narrowed and their bulgy surfaces shifted and their mouths—

—their *mouths*—

Gaping wide mouths were hinged at the back of their heads and filled with rows and rows of sharklike teeth.

"Flip-top heads," Gunn said in disbelief. "Wesley never said a thing about flip-top heads!"

Annoyance crossed Angel's features. "Be that way," he said to the posturing demon—and swung. Cordelia heard the *crack* of his bench plank—

No. She heard the *crack* of her own board finally giving way before the assault on the gate. Now she was the one who squeaked, suddenly envisioning herself caught behind the gate as it slammed open and back against the fence. "What is your problem?" she muttered to the mob, a meaningless mumble of protest . . .

Except maybe it wasn't all that meaningless. What excuse did they have now? Angel and Gunn had the demons fully engaged—a quick glance confirmed as much, revealing Gunn's desperate dodge away from what had turned into an amazingly fast dumpy little demon and its gaping maw—and still the people threw themselves at the gate, mindless and heedless of the damage they took. Even as Cordelia felt the darkness of the demon-driven negativity lift from her own heart—the demons were too busy fighting to siphon off everyone's happies—the crowd pressed on, too far gone to stop now. Here, in the middle of a cold holiday night when they should be indoors spreading what comfort and joy they could take, they spread chaos instead, locked into that which the mimic demons had started. Even as Wes disappeared beneath them, and Angel and Gunn fought for them, they came on.

Cordelia flipped around to face them—a terrifying sight, inches from the distorted faces of those in front.

She opened her mouth to bellow at them, to snap some sense into them—

And suddenly realized it would just feed their all-too-human frenzy. That they'd had enough of anger and hardship and cruelty piled on their already cruel lives. That they needed what the mimic demons had already taken from them, all the kindness and understanding and the things this season was supposed to bring out in everyone, no matter their faith.

But her mouth was still open. Still ready to bellow. So bellow she did, squeezing her eyes shut. "Si-ilent night!" Then a deep breath, and even louder, "Ho-oly night!"

In the background, she could hear Angel's grunt of effort, Gunn's shout of warning.

"All is calm!" Cordelia bellowed, hitting one or two of the actual notes to the Christmas carol this time. "All is—"

She suddenly realized her voice rang—or shrieked, depending on your point of view—into silence.

She opened her eyes.

The people on the other side of the gate stared at her aghast.

"What?" she said. "It got your attention, didn't it?" But as much as they reacted to her, they reacted to the scene behind her, which they'd finally noticed. She cast a quick glance over her shoulder just in time to see the last mimic demon, the biggest one, lunge at Angel with its mouth open wide. Angel met it with a powerful kick right on the snout, forcing the flip-top head back even further—and widely enough that he was able to jam the remains of his bench plank past the sharky teeth and into the demon's mouth, propping it open.

The demon made a gurgling noise and backed away, its stubby Potato Head arms waving in a futile effort to reach and remove the plank. It bit down hard—

And forced the wood right up through the roof of its mouth. As Angel and Gunn backed away, staggering a little in the aftermath of the fight, the demon stiffened, tottered slightly in place, and fell to its side with a meaty thud.

The people looked like they might want to cheer, but as if they also weren't quite sure it was the right thing to do.

"There," Cordelia said to them, glad they'd moved away from the gate a few steps. "It's over. No more fighting!"

They looked at Cordelia, looked at the demons, and looked especially at Angel—no doubt they'd seen him pull some typically inhuman move during the fighting. "Go on," she said, making a shooing motion at them. "You made so much noise, the cops'll probably be here any moment. They're only a block away, after all."

That did it. Within moments they'd eased into the darkness, most of them heading for the mission and its warm coffee and warm beds. Cordelia saw her hat on someone's head and patted futilely at her own head. Terminal hat hair. She sighed heavily and said out loud to no one in particular, "To diminish freckles, rub them with a freshly cut eggplant every day."

"Or . . . ," said Wesley's not-too-steady voice, "you can always acquire . . . a nosebridge . . . to create that sleek, straight profile the Mayans found so attractive . . . between those slightly crossed eyes."

"Wesley! You're all right!" She reached between the bars of the fence to help him stand.

"I seem to be," he said, not sounding entirely certain. His glasses hung askew over one ear, and he made a token effort to brush himself off. "The first layer of those who so gleefully piled atop me seems to have protected me from the rest of them. Really, I have no idea what got them started—"

Cordelia nodded at the demons. "Standing right in front of the demons as they sucked all the good out of people?" she suggested.

"So that's what they look like!" Wesley straightened his glasses just long enough to get a glimpse of the mimic demons—one of whom Gunn suspiciously nudged with his foot as if he thought the demon was mimicking being a dead mimic demon—and then the glasses fell apart in his hand.

"Sorry about that." Nameless Man came up behind Wesley, reaching past him to remove what remained of Cordelia's improvised gate latch and tossing the bits of wood carefully to the side with the look of someone who'd marked a thing of value. *Firewood,* Cordelia realized. "You can see why we needed help."

Gunn gave the demon a final little kick. "Maybe some of your people can clear these things out before anyone comes around asking questions."

"Already got someone on it," the man said. He hesitated. "You know we can't pay you."

"We already covered that," Angel said, lifting the heavy gate so it could open without scraping along the cement walkway. "I told you, we're being paid."

The man tipped his head in a highly skeptical look. Without even knowing she was going to say it, Cordelia added, "No, really. It's true." And then she guessed it was. Angel had his reasons for taking this job; she'd discovered she had some of her own.

They checked each other over for grievous wounds and found none, made sure Wesley was steady on his feet, and—taking Cordelia's advice about vacating the area before anyone official showed up—headed for the San Julian entrance of the men's dorm area. There they took off their borrowed outer clothes, preparing for a chilly walk back to Angel's GTO and the jackets they'd stowed there. Cordelia apologized for the torn sneakers as she pulled them off and slipped her feet into the flats she'd had stuffed in her sweater's big side pockets. And then, hesitating, she took off the sweater itself, giving its warm knit sleeves a last pat as she put it in the pile with the other returned belongings.

They took the long way around the Union Rescue Mission, avoiding the park and any attention it might have garnered. As they walked the quiet street back to Angel's car, he glanced at her and said, "Did that help?"

"Yeah," she said, thinking again of how good it had been to find him when she'd felt so alone, and so desperate she couldn't even admit it to herself. *Not then, anyway.* "A little." She looked back at him. "You?"

He gave her the smallest of smiles. "Yeah," he said. "A little."

3 A.M.

ICICLE MEMORIES

by Yvonne Navarro

"Man," Gunn said. "I *never* want to go through another night like this one. I'm exhausted."

Wesley, slumped on one of the chairs across from him in the lobby, gave a small nod. "I'll certainly second that. I can't remember when we've had such a plethora of difficulties in one evening."

Gunn smirked. "Plethora?"

Wesley looked at him in surprise. "It means—"

"I know what it means," Gunn retorted. "I'm just waiting for you to break out the college duds and podium."

"Humor him," Cordelia said. "He likes big words."

Gunn's eyebrow raised. "I'd hoped wandering around cold on the streets would numb the part of his brain that makes him talk."

"Very funny." Wesley scowled. "I hardly think that criticizing me for my vocabulary is appropriate. Surely you can find something else on which to focus."

Gunn grinned. "Want me to make you a list?"

"For a couple of guys griping about being tired, you sure seem to have energy to rag on each other." Angel was standing next to Cordy by the lobby's counter. "Or is this your version of staying in the holiday spirit?"

"Everyone's cranky," Cordelia said with a sigh. She leaned forward on her elbows, resting her hands on her chin. "It's only an hour or so to dawn—I vote we pack it in for the night and head home. Fred's smart—she already went upstairs to bed."

"I'm not sleepy," Angel said.

"Well, bully for you," Gunn told him. "Us mere mortals are running out of gas here. We—"

"Hey!" Cordelia suddenly stood up straight. "Who spilled water over there by the couch and didn't clean it up?" She leaned down behind the counter and pulled out her trusty roll of paper towels, then slapped it angrily against her palm. "Since when do I look like a maid? How rude is that?"

"Water?" Angel turned in the direction she was now heading. "Wait—we cleaned up everything from the party, didn't we?"

"Apparently not." Wesley got up and joined them as Cordelia tore off a wad of paper towels and tossed it on top of the small puddle, then pushed it around with the toe of her shoe to soak up the moisture. He peered overhead. "I hope we don't have a leak somewhere."

"What could be leaking?" Angel asked, following Wesley's gaze. "Center of the room, no access to the outside walls from here—"

"Darn it, there's another one!" Cordelia exclaimed. "To the right of the counter."

Now Gunn got up and joined the two men. "Man, ceiling leaks are the worst, especially in a building like this. They can start at a crack in the brickwork outside, then travel along a beam and not show up until three or four stories later. You got a leak, it could be coming from the freaking fifth floor. Repairmen call it tuck-pointing hell."

"Marvelous," Angel said with a sour expression. "That's just what we wanted to hear."

"Just keeping you informed," Gunn said. "Knowledge is power."

"Rah rah," Angel muttered. He stared hard at the ceiling. "But I still don't see where it's leaking."

"Okay," Cordelia said. Now she sounded totally peeved. "Three times is *not* the charm. Where the *heck* is this water coming from?" This time she bent down and swiped at it with a pull from the quickly diminishing paper towel roll. Her hand hit the liquid, then pulled back. "And it's *freezing*!"

"That doesn't make any sense." Wesley went over and crouched beside her, then touched a finger to the puddle she was trying to mop up. "It's probably a good fifty degrees outside, and the water wouldn't be much colder."

"Hey, guys?" Fred's voice filtered down from the railing overhead. "Is it just me, or is it getting colder in here?" She came down the stairs, and they could see she was wearing flannel pajamas under a heavy terry cloth robe. Still, she was rubbing her arms, trying to generate some warmth. "Okay, it's a little better down here, but it's not exactly a southern California night. More like . . . I don't know. South Dakota?"

Gunn reached out to pat her shoulder, then almost recoiled. "She isn't kidding—even her clothes feel cold!"

"Are you sure the heating vent is open in your room?" Wesley asked. "Sometimes—"

"Of course it's open. I already checked."

The look Fred shot him was gentle but chastising, and Wesley looked appropriately embarrassed. "Of course you did."

"Well, the furnace fan is working but that's not enough," Angel said from across the room. He was bending in front of one of the vents with his hand in front of it. "I can feel the circulation, but the air isn't very warm."

"Let me see," Cordelia said, and hurried over to join him. "You've got that whole vampire thing going—you don't feel tired, you can see at night, you might not even notice if the temperature's falling." She waved her hand in front of the vent, then shuddered. "Jeez, who turned on the air conditioner?"

Wesley pressed his lips together. "Looks like I'll have to go down and check the furnace. Maybe the pilot light went out."

Cordelia's eyes widened. "Great—now we could get blown up?"

"No," Fred told her. "While the fan might still function, there will be an automatic safety shut off to the gas valve."

"Yeah, well." Cordelia didn't sound convinced. "Just don't go down there and flick any lighters."

"I'll take a flashlight. And I'll turn it on *before* I get down there," Wesley promised.

"I'll go with you," Gunn offered. "The way things have been going tonight, I don't think anyone should go in a basement or a closet, or even a pantry, without backup."

Wesley nodded. "Good deal. Let's go."

"Take a coat," Fred called after them. "If you think it's getting cold up here, just imagine what it'll be like down there." She looked pained. "In the dark."

"It'll only take a minute," Wesley said.

"Yeah," Gunn added. "If we're not back in ten minutes, send the big guns."

"Not funny," Cordelia said grumpily. "I think we've had enough of that today, thank you very much." But the two men were already gone, headed in the direction of the service stairwell.

"It's probably just the pilot light, like Wesley said," Angel said to break the uncomfortable pause that followed. "We shouldn't jump to conclusions."

"We shouldn't underestimate it either," Fred began, then dropped into silence at Angel's warning look and curled up in a ball on one of the chairs, huddling inside her heavy robe. Cordy said nothing as she pulled a sweater off a peg behind the counter and slipped it on, driving her hands into the pockets to protect them against the now quickly dropping temperature. Despite what Cordelia had said, even Angel could feel how chilly it was in here—something was way off-kilter with the furnace. He hoped it wasn't going to be some three- or four-thousand-dollar replacement deal. Southern California it might be, but heat was still an occasional necessity for nighttime . . . although it was *way* colder in here now than the typical West Coast evening, even for December twenty-first. "I know," he said suddenly. "I'll go start a pot of coffee to warm things up. Regular or decaf?"

"Regular," Cordelia said, a little grumpily. "If it's not real, it's not worth it."

"Right."

He was only in the kitchen for a few minutes, but they dragged past, and the temperature kept dropping. When Angel returned—he was too impatient to wait for the pot to finish brewing—he realized he could see the breath fogging in front of Fred and Cordelia and a line of frost accumulating along the edge of the front counter. "All right, how long has it been?"

"It feels like forever," Cordelia said. "But I think we're talking about six or seven minutes."

"That's long enough," Angel said decisively. "If they'd found the problem and lit the pilot light, you ought to be feeling some warmth by now. I'm going down to check on them."

"Not by yourself, you're not." Cordelia stood at the same time Fred unfurled and climbed out of her chair.

"I'm a little better equipped to take care of myself," Angel pointed out.

"Says you." Rather than stay back, Cordelia and Fred both headed for the service stairway. "Coming?"

Shaking his head, Angel followed, then lengthened his stride to move in front of them before either could open the door. When he put his hand on the knob, the metal was frigid, like touching an outside lamppost in ten degree weather—not a good sign. The blast of arctic air that washed over them when he pulled open the door was anything but welcoming, but at least the light switch on the wall worked; he could see where Wesley and Gunn had left it on. The light itself was more in the not-so-great realm: thin and faraway, a dribble of illumination from a bare bulb down at the bottom of the stairwell.

"I hate basements," Fred said. She was trying to be brave, but there was a tremble in her voice. Nevertheless, she followed Angel and Cordelia down the stairs.

While each step downward took them closer to that pathetic source of light, it also brought a noticeable drop in the temperature. It didn't bother Angel, of course, but the girls were quickly shuddering with cold. "What is this?" Cordelia complained. "Northern Alaska?"

"It sure seems that way," Angel answered. He pointed. "Look."

Fred and Cordy followed his direction, and their mouths fell open in surprise. As they stepped off the last of the stairs, their feet—Cordelia's in sneakers and

Fred's in slippers—sunk into two inches of *slush*. "What the heck?" Cordelia back-stepped and almost slipped. "How can it freeze up like this inside?"

"Without the proper conditions, it can't," Fred said. "There's a very specific threshold of moisture to temperature ratio that you have to cross, not to mention a whole bunch of other criteria." She glanced up at the high ceiling and her expression grew even more amazed. "Look—almost all the pipes are covered in icicles!"

"Where are the guys?" Cordelia asked. "I don't see them."

The three of them peered into the basement, but the only thing visible was more ice and snow—the stuff blanketed everything, from boxes and old furniture to pieces and parts of unidentifiable objects. They couldn't tell one thing from another.

"The laundry room," Angel said. "That's where the furnace is. They would have headed there. Come on."

Fred drew in a breath, shivering at the chilliness of the air. "Gunn? Wesley?" No answer.

"Okay," Cordelia said, as she picked her way across the snow-covered floor. "I was never much into the whole skiing thing, you know? There are good reasons for choosing southern California."

"I thought your decision had more to do with the whole movie career aspect," Angel said.

"That, too."

"In here," Angel said. "Gunn, Wesley—whoa!" He stopped short in the doorway, and Fred and Cordelia, both watching where they put their feet on the slippery floor rather than Angel's back, bumped full tilt into him.

"Hey," Cordy protested. "Brake lights, please!"

"What's wrong?" Fred said. She tilted to the side until she could see around Angel's shoulder. "Are they in there?"

Instead of answering, Angel took a couple of steps farther into the low-ceilinged laundry room. The women followed, then stared at what awaited them.

Wesley and Gunn were there, all right, standing as though paralyzed in the middle of the room, which itself had been transformed into a miniature winter wonderland. Snow layered everything like a thick white comforter, covering the industrial washers and dryers that lined one wall, piling up in a small mountain that came to within a foot of the front of the furnace that was still laboring in the back corner. The furnace's efforts to keep up had only melted the snow building up along the pipes and clotheslines and caused it to flow into icicles that reached all the way from ceiling to floor like stalactites.

"Wesley," Angel said harshly. "Gunn—can you hear me?" He started to move forward, then realized that he couldn't—the snow had immediately flowed into the space he'd created when he'd pushed open the door, circling behind him and around Fred and Cordelia. His feet were somehow pinned to the floor. They weren't frozen or cold, but he couldn't move them either. There was something else down here, too, back in the corner between the last of the oversize washing machines and the wide table that had been built there for laundry folding. He wasn't sure what it was, but it *was* moving, and since the four things in this place besides him that were supposed to move—Wesley, Gunn, Cordelia, and Fred—were all accounted for, this was definitely not a good thing.

The thing in the corner, bulky and ponderous, white like the rest of the room, shifted again, as though it were trying to pull itself forward and out. Angel tried to turn toward the women, but could only move his upper body; twisting as best he could, he looked back over his shoulder. "Cordy, you and Fred get back upstairs—"

But it was way, way too late, and the gazes that stared back at him were as blank and empty as the whiteness that was quickly surrounding them all . . .

Wesley thought he could still feel himself . . . more or less. He was cold, in a vague, this-is-happening-to-someone-else sort of way, and he knew he really ought to make himself move, get out of this frigid little basement room and find some heat.

But it was all a matter of making that choice.

And choices, he did have—right there in front of him. There was the option of forcing his slowly numbing limbs to work, or lingering, just for a bit longer, on the images that were playing out in his head.

In a way, he knew that none of them were true. This was obvious because he could see himself in the images, and being what he considered a reasonably intelligent man, he knew that he would never be able to see *himself* doing anything unless he was looking directly into a mirror. It was just as obvious that this wasn't the case, since he was watching a current version of himself talk and laugh with his parents—right there, only a few feet away, sat his mum and dad, smiles on their faces as they gathered in front of the yule log and his mother set out a beautiful Old English trifle, rich with Devonshire cream, almonds, strawberry jam, and more. They were in the front sitting room, and while Wesley remembered the room well from his childhood, this time it was different; the formerly dark and gloomy colors were brightly festooned with cheerful seasonal ribbons, and the traditional mince pies and Christmas crackers waited on the lovely mahogany sideboard. In the background, Wesley could even hear the muted sound of the Queen's Christmas message, a sure sign that it was afternoon and Christmas dinner—roast goose, stuffing, and potatoes—was soon to follow.

In a way, Wesley realized he was holding his breath, waiting for the inevitable. But it never came; there was none of the usual hypercriticism that his overcontrolling father could be counted on to level in Wesley's direction, none of the silent and ever-rigid disapproval that always emanated from his mother's gaze when it turned in his direction. This time there was only warmth and love and approval, all those feelings for which he had yearned the entire span of his childhood.

In the back of his mind, Wesley knew there was a more realistic present day, one where his legs and hands were achingly raw with the cold of an unnatural interior winter. But the radiance of his parents' love, never before experienced, outweighed that—literally overrode the iciness creeping through his veins and body. That feeling of cold was probably nothing more serious than the fire burning itself out in the fireplace, and a simple rekindling would take care of that, wouldn't it? What he was seeing in front of him was the kind of Christmas that *should* have been, the type of happy holiday that the other children in his life had so taken for granted but which he had been denied. Wesley had wanted this, *exactly* this, for so many years . . .

How could he turn away from it now?

From the corner of his eye, Gunn could see Wesley standing only a few feet away, could see the way the dark hair on his friend's unmoving head was slowly being dusted over with snow. At first the snowflakes had melted from Wesley's body heat, giving his hair a little bit of a wet sheen; now they were "sticking," as those who lived in colder climates liked to say of snow that gathered on the streets and didn't melt, and slowly piling up on top of each other to give Wesley a close-fitting cap of pure white.

Did his own scalp look the same way? He had no hair to insulate the snow from his body heat, so more of it would melt before it "stuck." But he couldn't feel his scalp, couldn't feel *anything*, in fact. His entire body was just . . . there, like some big piece of cheek flesh that had gotten a massive shot of Novocain from the friendly neighborhood dentist. It would have worried him, except he had other things to think about right now.

Like what he could see from the corner of his *other* eye.

His sister Alonna sat at the tiny table in the dining room of a small apartment, and Gunn could see himself sitting across from her. It was Christmas—that much was obvious by the red and silver garlands hung across the windows and the dozen or so Christmas cards she'd taped up along the sides of the dining room door—the place was too small for a tree, but Alonna wasn't going to let that stop her from being festive. They were laughing about something, probably some inane joke or crack that he'd made; in the time before her death, he had been like that, cracking jokes now and then, making smart-alecky but not cruel remarks about life in general. It was funny to see himself doing that now, because he could tell by the way Alonna looked that she was older than she had been when she'd been turned into a bloodsucker herself. There was something on the table between them . . . a photo album, pages splayed open to pictures of times past and times that never would be, they *couldn't* be because the people in them—friends and relatives—were long dead and gone.

But . . . were they really? He had to wonder, because Alonna wasn't a vampire here, no sir; that was proven by the glitteringly bright sunshine pouring through the double set of narrow windows behind the table. He could see the light painting her face with warm, butter-colored stripes, watched as dust motes danced along the rays like gold glitter. It made Alonna more beautiful than she'd ever been, and it made Gunn happier than he'd been in years. After all, Alonna alive and happy, this small, clean, cheerful apartment, the *sunshine*—this was the way things should have been, the way it all would have worked out if he'd just done a proper job of protecting her the way he'd promised. She'd be alive and laughing, just like this, and right now, and while he might be a little chilly around the edges—landlords were always skimping on the darned heat in apartment buildings—all he wanted in the world to do was watch her and not break the enchantment of this marvelous vision. . . .

"Guys," Angel said desperately, "you *have* to snap out of it or you're going to freeze to death. You can't just stand here and let it . . . do whatever it's doing to you!"

It had taken immense effort, but he'd finally been able to force himself to move. Everything was sluggish though, as if the fluids in his body had gone to slush; still, whatever dark force kept his dead body animated also kept him from fully freezing. It didn't take a rocket scientist to know that the rest of the gang would not be so lucky.

Angel gritted his teeth and made his legs work, dragging his feet forward under the weight of the snow layered over them. It felt like it took forever to cross the few feet of space and put himself in front of Wesley and

Gunn. They stood side by side, their gazes locked on something that only they could see—actually, Angel wasn't even sure they were seeing *anything*. Or if they were, were they seeing the *same* thing? There was no way to tell.

"Wesley?" Angel tried to bring up his hand and wave it in front of Wesley's eyes, but it felt weighted and slow, as though he were trying to lift a hundred-pound dumbbell through chilled molasses. "Wesley, can you hear me?" He finally got his fingers up to eye level and passed them—oh, so slowly—in front of Wesley's face. No response. "Gunn?" he asked, turning toward the other guy. "Are you in there?"

No response, not even an eye blink. Angel shuddered, but not from the cold. It was more of a sympathy movement—there was no doubt that his two friends were well on their way toward hypothermia. If he wanted to save their lives, he was going to have to find a way to get them out of here, but in his present condition, Angel didn't think he could lift an empty laundry basket, much less a full-grown man.

He turned back and looked toward the women, but they were in the same state, standing as though paralyzed, staring into oblivion. "Cordelia?" he asked hopefully. "Fred?" Neither answered, crushing his hope that they might be reachable because they hadn't been subjected to whatever this was for as long as Wesley and Gunn had. He grimaced as he studied their faces and saw traces of blue starting to form above the delicate lines of their lips.

Angel heard movement off to the side and swung toward it, his body leaden. Yes—there *was* something in the corner, something he'd almost forgotten about in his thoughts of his friends. What was it? There was only one way to find out, and he plodded forward, each leg feeling as though it weighed two hundred pounds. Four steps, then five, and another, and he was only six feet away from the whitewashed shadows when the beast rose up in front of him. . . .

There was glitter and glamour and more movie stars than Cordelia could shake a Versace handbag at. In the back of her mind, Cordelia knew she was in the laundry room—of course she was—but in the front of her mind, the place where dreams and desires are made, she wasn't even close. Instead she was in a mansion on Palos Verdes Drive, forty-plus rooms overlooking the Pacific Ocean just north of the Royal Palms Beach, thank you very much. She knew just the one, too—she'd passed it dozens of times during her years in La-La-Land, always wondering how the huge, pale pink structure looked on the inside if all those balconies and walkways led to rooms that held as much allure as the outside of the building did. Not too far down the road was the famous Portuguese Bend, where the land was literally moving constantly, because of fault line shifting; one never knew when a crack might appear in the road, and the highway had repair lines drawn across it all along the way like wide concrete scars. This was about as much unpredictable excitement as Cordelia was interested in dealing with.

Well, now she finally knew all about the inside of that lovely pink palace.

Stars and producers and directors drifted in and out of doorways, chatting with each other and with her as if it were the most natural thing in the world. And it *was*—that was the beauty of it; this was *her* mansion, *her* party, these were *her* friends. She wasn't a wannabe actress wearing a seashell bikini in a tanning lotion commercial where the focus was the hot bod on which she was expected to rub the oily glop. She was *herself* here, Cordelia Chase, winner of two Oscars for best actress and halfway through directing the first of her own movies.

She smiled and nodded at people as they passed by, accepting compliments from James Cameron and Ron Howard on her sequined Valentino gown, and exchanging pleasantries with the likes of Kevin Costner and Susan Sarandon before deftly sidestepping Russell Crowe. She was wiser than that, knew better than to get involved with a heartbreaker like him—better to keep her options open for someone single and a little lower on the naughty scale.

Besides the house and her friends and acquaintances, there were classy one-carat diamond earrings—real ones—in her ears and a diamond and ruby pendant around her neck that matched her exquisite gown; a seven-thousand-dollar bracelet encircled one wrist, and even her designer shoes—notorious things for being secret sources of aggravation—were comfortable. Oh yes, it was a fine life indeed, and she was *so* glad she'd come out here instead of heading off to college after that horrifying tax debacle back in Sunnydale. It hadn't taken long at all for several of the top producers and directors to recognize her talent, and now look at how far she'd come.

Cordelia smiled again automatically as someone touched her arm, one of the studio directors she'd been dealing with over the past week and who was trying to cultivate a better relationship with her for the future. She listened to what he was saying with only half an ear, pulling away slightly and managing—just barely—to suppress a frown at how terribly, terribly cold his fingers were. . . .

Wow, Fred thought. *Look at all the fun I missed.*

Christmas in Texas—there was truly nothing like it in the world, at least as far as she was concerned. And wasn't it great that she was suddenly being given the chance to experience all the ones she'd missed during the time she had been stranded on Pylea? There was her mom and dad, and—oh! There were her two favorite aunts, both wacky as boxes of gift nuts, but then everyone knew you kind of had to cut a little slack for family members.

Laughing and spinning—gosh, it seemed like all those years of missed holidays were somehow happening at once. There were people in here she didn't even know, but she was also just as sure that they were family members, second or third cousins or the married sister-in-law of someone's brother. Texas was big on family, just like it was big on tradition, and she had this weird sort of compound vision going on, kind of like a fly's view of the world through a number of its eyes' ommatidiums. Hers were limited to five views but of course they were all at once; she could see one view that included each of the years she'd spent on Pylea. Now she knew how they would have been spent had she not been sucked through that stupid portal.

It was so cool, like watching a progression of life frame by frame. In each one the tree in her parents' big living room changed, of course, because they *always* had a real tree, never any of this plastic or silk stuff. Sometimes it was a little bigger, sometimes a little smaller. One year it actually tilted a few degrees to the left—obviously Dad hadn't quite gotten the trunk straight in the tree holder. New ornaments were added and the tree got more and more crowded—the Burkle family had never believed in Decorating Lite. Tucked haphazardly among the soft pine needles was everything from little wooden cowboy boots to brass cacti and armadillos, from multicolored hand-blown globes to little replicas of the Texas state flag.

In her mind, Fred wandered from visual to visual. The gifts changed as much as the tree, wrappings and ribbons morphing magickally from one year to the next as the season's styles changed as quickly as the clothes. She saw with amusement that during those five years her mother had reupholstered the living room furniture not once, but twice—she always had that "Martha Stewart" flair for making a house look fancy. The thought made Fred grin; how horrified she must have been the first time she'd seen Fred's room at the hotel in Los Angeles, with its thousands of mathematical calculations scribbled haphazardly across every free wall surface.

Dinnertime, and Fred didn't know which scene to look at first. Yeah, people had their traditions, but in her house Dad was the Christmas cook, and they never knew from one year to the next what was on the menu for the big day. One year they had big beef barbeque ribs drenched in spicy homemade sauce, the next turkey stuffed with roasted chestnuts and sausage, the next an orange-glazed goose stuffed with dried fruit and plump cranberries. And don't forget the spiral-sliced ham, or the year Dad had *really* surprised them by going all Italian on them, right down to the dark chocolate ravioli with white chocolate sauce for dessert. Fred could literally *feel* how stuffed she was from overeating, how pleasantly numb she always got when she pushed away from the Christmas dinner table and retreated to the family room with the rest of the relatives, sinking gratefully onto the couch to languish in the familiar food coma.

The only thing wrong with the picture was that this time she couldn't quite find her favorite afghan to keep away the chill that always nipped at her hands and feet when she overate . . .

"Great," Angel said. "What are you supposed to be? The hell-demon equivalent of Frosty the Snowman?"

The quip sounded funny in his head, but coming out of his mouth it was all wrong, so thick and palpable with cold that the words seemed to have actual *weight* on the air.

Weight was exactly what the demon-thing in front of him had—the creature was huge and blobby and white. From where Angel stood a few feet away from the hotel's industrial-size water heater, he could see that the winter demon filled the corner across from the furnace with snow, but there wasn't anything pristine or pretty about it—instead it was kind of fuzzy and uneven, with a fur covering that was mottled white and gray like the folds of skin on a dirty polar bear that had mutated to gargantuan size. Everything moved in an unpleasant rolling motion as the creature hauled itself forward and came closer; somewhere in that mass was a face, but it, too, had that unsettling shifting thing going; first it seemed to be on the left side, then the right, then somewhere a little south of what might be the beast's head. The only reason Angel was convinced he was actually seeing a face at all was that there were two predatory, pinprick eyes, bloodred above the circular dark shadow of nose.

And, of course, the creature had a mouth. Didn't they always?

Its mouth was round and toothless. Somehow Angel found that far more frightening than if he'd been facing something with double or even triple rows of razor-edged teeth. A shark he could deal with, he'd at least know what to expect if the thing managed to take a bite out of him. But this . . . who knew what would happen, or even if anything was *supposed* to. Creatures that didn't have teeth usually fed some other way, and the fact that his friends were standing here paralyzed and probably hypothermic went a long way to support his notion that this particular beast was going for the mental menu rather than pure flesh. It probably lived off energy, and getting it was easy—it simply siphoned off its victims' body heat.

"Let me go, you overgrown snowball," he said. His teeth were grinding together in his effort to move. It took a lot of cold to freeze a vampire into immobility, but this thing might actually be able to do it; this was actually starting to scare him. "I'm dead and I don't give out heat."

Something, a parody of a voice, slid through his mind, drawing that same arctic cold through his brain cells.

Vampiiiiirrrrreeeee . . .

"That's right," Angel managed. "I'm your classic bloodsucker." He fought against the hold on his limbs but was only able to shuffle backward a couple of steps. "Dead. Kaput. No heartbeat, no—"

Alll thingsssss giiiive outtt ennnnergyyyy . . .

So he'd been right about what this was—not just heat, but an energy hunt. Okay, he could accept that, but what was the mechanism *holding* Fred, Wesley, Gunn, and Cordelia down here? Cold would be a factor, sure, but they still should have been able to move at least enough to back out of the furnace room, head back upstairs and out of the creature's holding range while they regrouped, warmed up, and came up with a better plan. Instead, they'd stepped through the door and literally *stopped*, and if they weren't exactly frozen in place, they were well on their way to it.

He had to snap them back to the present.

"Time to go," he said. "And my friends are going with me." Angel turned, still moving excruciatingly slow, like sap down the side of a tree in rapidly freezing temperatures. But speed didn't matter right now, at least not as it pertained to him—even if he had to do it one inch at a time, he'd drag the others out of here. He'd start with Wesley—

Vampiiiiirrrrreeeee . . .

The voice inside his skull was cold and silky, like decadent white chocolate ice cream. It stretched on and on and on, and Angel tried in vain to ignore it.

I haaaavvvvve sssssommmmmethinnnnngg toooo sssshooooowv yoooouuuou. . . .

Winter in Sunnydale wasn't really all that much of a winter. Angel had been in climates a lot colder than this, had spent many a night scrambling to find shelter from the local blizzard, not because it actually bothered him, but because he really wasn't into the feel of wet clothes against his skin. He also really hated the squishiness of soaked shoes. Now and then it rained in Sunnydale, but even that didn't happen often; sometimes he missed the snow and the winter and whole feel of the Christmas holiday thing. The soul inside him made him yearn for things like that, and now, tonight . . .

Angel remembered this one. Christmastime in Sunnydale not so very long ago, and he had been particularly tormented that year, suffocating in guilt from his past memories of what he had done to others, including his own family members. The images had haunted him and nearly driven him insane; he had been so maddened that he had even considered ending it, had planned to greet the sun in the morning and make the final curtain call to this miserable thing that passed for his existence. But then there'd been . . .

Buffy.

Then.

And now.

She walked next to him, saying nothing. Her small hand was tucked neatly into his much larger one, and he could feel its warmth, its *life,* pulsing against his palm. In fact, he could feel more than that—he could feel her *love,* that soul-deep emotion she harbored for him in spite of the fact that he was, when it came right down to it, a bloodsucking monster. It radiated all around her like a sort of psychic aura, as though she were a human candle and her emotions the glow from the flame. And around them was that absolutely *incredible* snowfall, the one neither of them had expected; it filled the air with white, crystalline beauty, softening the edges of a town that could sometimes cut its people down with scythelike sharpness.

"The turkey will be done by the time we get home," Buffy said. "Mom and Dawn are taking care of the salad and the vegetables, and you know Mom—she's like

Timer Lady, always big with the organizational skills. Willow and Tara are bringing dessert, and Xander says Anya's big into appetizers this week—she found some recipe for shrimp-cheese puffs that she's dying for everyone to try. Riley's bringing raisin-fruit bread from this Scandinavian bakery he found just outside of downtown, and Spike, true to form, is bringing alcoholic punch. Drusilla told me that every dinner table needs flowers, so she's bringing three dozen black-red roses." Buffy's head turned and she gave him a smile that was so dazzlingly beautiful it made Angel's heart ache. "Faith doesn't cook, of course, but she said she and Mayor Wilkins could handle picking up two containers of Cool Whip and a bag of Christmas candy. Everything's coming together perfectly." Buffy nodded to herself. "It's going to be great, Angel."

He kept walking, feeling peaceful and self-assured, shrouded in the feeling of being wanted and loved by this young woman. There was a tiny place in his mind, like a mental splinter, that told him the things Buffy had said didn't make sense; he ignored it because he *wanted* them to be so, wanted to walk into Buffy's house and see Joyce Summers choreographing a Christmas dinner extravaganza for people—and creatures—who in any other reality were mortal enemies. His undead existence had never included a true Christmas holiday and now he found that he desperately wanted just that, complete with presents and laughter and frolicking around the Christmas tree. He had thought Buffy was gone from his life, had witnessed firsthand the heartbreak she'd experienced at her mother's funeral; now he felt like all those bad experiences had happened to someone else, some other vampire named Angelus who'd grown up in a more ruthless and unloving time and followed that existence with his own history of bloodshed.

He was here now, and Buffy was here now, and they had such grand plans.

"Let's stop and go in here," Buffy said. She tugged him to the side and he followed her without thinking about it, without questioning, climbing a set of wide concrete steps. It wasn't until he heard the squeal of unoiled hinges that he realized she'd pushed open the door to a Catholic church and was leading him inside. He pulled back and she turned to look at him, her eyes clear but puzzled. "What's wrong, Angel?"

"Buffy," he said hesitantly, "you know I can't go in there. The crosses—"

She smiled at him and for a moment he lost himself in the vision—she was *so* beautiful. "Of course you can, Angel. Everything is all right. This is the way it should have been."

"Should have been?" he repeated.

She nodded. "Between you and me, between all of us."

Buffy took another step, but he still couldn't make himself follow. That mind-splinter was back, bigger this time, sinking into his brain far enough to sting. "Let's . . . not," he said. "I'd rather keep walking."

"I understand." She let the doors to the church close

behind her and together they descended the steps, careful not to slip in the clean snow that was blanketing everything. "It's just a beautiful thing, snow in Sunnydale."

He nodded. "Kind of a once-in-a-lifetime event, I think."

They kept walking, enjoying the snowfall but never really feeling the cold. Past so many of the familiar old landmarks—Angel had forgotten how much he missed this little town. Sunnydale Mall was draped in festive lights and decorations, a blinking swirl of color that was almost painful to view. On the outskirts of the main entry was a small crowd and a fire truck with its lights flashing; three or four suited-up firemen milled around with the crowd and looked at a fire hydrant from which gushed a steady stream of water. Oddly, none of the firemen seemed inclined to do anything to stop it; instead, they laughed and talked among themselves and the crowd.

As Angel and Buffy passed, Angel realized that the puddle of water from the hydrant was growing, seeping toward them on the sidewalk and washing away the snowfall's accumulation. Curious, Angel leaned over and ran his fingers through the quickly accumulating puddle of water. "Wow," he told Buffy. He held up his fingers for her to see. "It's warm."

She nodded and her expression changed, slipping into a much more thoughtful mode. "Yes," she said solemnly. "If they're not careful, it's going to melt all this snow. Maybe you should help them."

Buffy slipped her hand back into his and he shuddered, because this time, the touch of her flesh was as cold as that of a corpse on a December morning . . .

Maybe you should help them . . .

The thought reverberated in Angel's mind even as the frigid touch of Buffy's hand jolted him out of the pseudomemory. But for the feel of her ice-covered fingers, he would have been content to stay in the memory, even knowing in his subconscious just how bizarre the whole thing was. Cold wasn't something that generally bothered him—being a vampire kind of took the bite out of it—but for Buffy's touch to be like that, at a time when everything else between them was at near perfection, was wrong on too many levels to count.

And the nastiness of the here and now was almost enough to make him surrender to the urge to dive back into the false memories.

Snow had drifted nearly up to Angel's knees. It enveloped almost everything—washers and dryers, cabinets, his friends. They had to be hurting by now, maybe even frostbitten. The beast was clearly getting stronger, extending its range; Angel could turn his head just enough to see that the blanket of white had moved far beyond the doorway to the laundry room and into the other areas of the basement, driving away the darkness and replacing it with bitter cold and frozen moisture. By now the beast's custom-made winter was probably working its way up the stairs and into the main lobby, where the puddles of water that Cordelia had first complained about had been its first finger hold.

Maybe you should help them . . .

It took immense effort, but Angel swiveled his head back in the direction of the snow creature. The thing was pulsing about ten feet away, like some sort of huge white whale—inhaling and exhaling rapidly as it fed on the nearby but fast-fading sources of life energy. If it got beyond this room, what then? All of Los Angeles awaited, like a big old human buffet.

Maybe you should help them . . .

Buffy's words kept turning in Angel's mind, often enough to be aggravating. Yes, he had to help them, but how?

He scowled at it. The thing was made of snow—it couldn't be stabbed or chopped or even blown up. It could probably be melted, but even that was iffy; the furnace seemed to be fighting a losing battle over there. There wasn't any snow on the appliance or right next to it, but it had sure managed to pile up pretty close, within only five or six inches. The same thing went for the water heater—

The water heater.

Angel's gaze focused on it, then traced its outline to the top, where a half dozen water pipes went in and out of it. Half of them fed cold water in, and these were easy to spot—a thick layer of ice had formed around them and icicles had formed where the heat of the room had melted the snow at the start of all this. But the other three—they were still clear of snow and ice, the heat from the water inside helping each maintain its warmth. The pipes came straight up, then went off in three directions to feed the plumbing throughout the hotel. And one of these was right over Angel's head.

The snow beast made a noise that Angel found vaguely disgusting, like an animal belching after eating too much. That made him even angrier than he already was—it was his *friends* that this creature was "eating" and he just wasn't going to stand here and watch that happen.

With every last bit of stubbornness and strength he had, Angel willed his arm to move.

He got it up and over his head and managed to close his fingers around the hot water pipe. Heat burned against his hand, lessening the numbness—a good thing, because while he'd gotten that far, Angel didn't think he had it in him to actually *pull* downward. The warmth at least let him fold his fingers tighter, and if he couldn't exactly pull, he *could* drop.

Angel bent his knees and let the weight of his body crash to the floor.

Clutched firmly in his grip, the pipe came down with him, adding a scream of metal and a welcoming hiss of steam as the pressure broke in the hotel's water system. Hot water jetted from the jagged end of the pipe in Angel's hand, spewing in all directions. Something like a roar filled the room, a garbled version of that earlier mental kiss that had floated so easily through Angel's mind. There was nothing gentle or soothing about it now; the beast was bellowing inside his head—

STTTTOOOOPPPPPPPPP

—until Angel thought his brain was going to explode out the back of his skull. The heated water from the pipe hit the ice and the snow, and sent mist and warm fog everywhere, which made the winter demon shriek louder, and this time there wasn't anything at all recognizable about the sound—

ARRRRRRRRRGBHGHGHGHGHGHGHHGHG

The screeching cut off in mid-syllable and water—warm and welcome—splashed his face. Angel blinked, then squinted, not realizing until then that he'd had his eyes squeezed shut. He was covered in *wet* and for a brilliant, panic-filled second he had the notion it was holy water and he was going to start boiling from the outside in. Then it sunk in that he was okay, just a little washed-over, and the pipe he still clutched in his now-thawed hand was spraying the laundry room with life-giving warmth. So much warmth, in fact, that directly in front of him was a rapidly melting pile of white goo that had once been the arctic monster; Angel wasn't sure, but as he stared at it from beneath water-logged eyelashes, he thought he saw the thing's red eyes throb a final time before dulling and disappearing altogether.

He heard groaning behind him. When he turned, Angel saw his four friends finally starting to move again, forcing their limbs into action to reestablish circulation. Poor Wesley—his lips were quite blue, a startling contrast against his pale skin. The others didn't look much better, and as they helped each other stumble back upstairs,

Angel gave the flooding laundry room a final spraying with hot, hot water, hoping it would chase away the lingering cold.

The last of the night's stars were hanging over the L.A. skyline by the time they were all huddled in robes and sweatpants and sweaters, dry and recovering in the lobby.

"Man, that was a cold way to end the day," Gunn said.

"Not funny." Cordelia sent him a sharp look. "We all nearly froze to death."

Gunn raised an eyebrow. "Who said I was joking?"

"Yes," Wesley mused. "And all because the creature was able to deceive us with our own memories."

"Not really ours," Fred corrected gently. "They were fabricated."

"True," Wesley agreed. The five of them had shared their experiences, although Angel didn't know if there were pieces of the 'what might have been' that each was keeping private. "I think we each had an empty spot, or a . . . *wanting* inside us that this demon was able to latch onto and manipulate."

"Nasty thing," Fred muttered, although her gaze remained a little far away.

"It was so pretty," Cordelia said softly. "Was it what could have been, or what should have been?"

"Does it matter?" Angel asked. Once he'd washed away the last traces of the snow beast, he'd come upstairs and changed into dry clothes, recovering much faster than the others. "I think the point is what Fred said—it was *fantasy*. What we saw was all fine and dandy, but it wasn't real. We need to stay grounded in reality and appreciate what we have now."

Gunn's eyes widened. "Yeah? And that's what, exactly?"

"Each other," Fred said suddenly. Then she blushed. "I mean—"

"That's *exactly* what she means," Cordelia said firmly. "Sure, what I saw was almost everything I've ever wanted. But the almost part? That was you guys. You're my family now. The past wasn't so great for any of us." Her gaze raked them all. "If you ask me, I'm pretty happy with the here and now."

Wesley nodded. "Cordelia's correct. We have a . . . challenging existence, to say the least. But we have each other and we can make our own good memories, day by day."

Angel took in Wesley's words, then grinned. From where he sat, he was the only one who could see a glimpse of the outside world through one of the curtains that hadn't quite closed. None of the others had noticed. "That's right on the mark," he said cheerfully, and the rest of them looked at him in surprise. He rose and strode toward the window, motioning for them to follow. "Let's start now," he told them, "with a memory of our snow demon's last hurrah for the City of Angels."

He pulled the curtain carefully aside, and they all gasped at the scene outside.

Snow.

Not much, not nearly enough to bring back the fear

of what they'd encountered in the laundry room. Still, there it was, like glistening silver in the early morning air.

"Yeah," Angel said as they crowded around the window with him. The scene outside reminded him of that snowfall in Sunnydale with Buffy, the *real* one rather than the false scenario with which the winter beast had tried to conquer him. He found himself giving Cordelia and Wesley a hug, and they, in turn, clung tight to Gunn and Fred. "Sometimes the best times are in the present. It's time to make our own future memories and leave the bad ones behind."

And like his wisdom, the snow outside was already melting into nothing but memories.

4 A.M.

YOKE OF THE SOUL

by Doranna Durgin

On this Winter holiday, let us stop and recall
That this season is holy to one and to all.

In truth, Angel was glad to be alone. Of all the nights, this Solstice night generally dragged out long and weary, in a season Angel already found to be wearying. Hanukkah, Kwanza, Christmas, Ramadan, even good old Yule . . . vampires not welcome, soul not withstanding.

Sometimes it was a good thing simply to get away from it all and enjoy the silence. No tinned carols on loudspeakers, no cards, no blue and white or red and green. Just the dark of deepest night and nothing bringing out the memories of his own early holidays . . . when he'd *had* holidays. Before he'd turned from his father's son into the scoundrel Darla had embraced.

Funny how he couldn't stop thinking about those memories anyway. About the spices and scents that had filled their household, the visitors, the laughter . . . the *belonging.*

He closed his eyes, took what would have been a deep breath had his lungs actually been functioning. *You're here to work. To* save *people.*

And to do that he had to find them.

Angel opened his eyes to the darkened garment district. Warehouses, warehouses, and more warehouses, each assigned to a general area much like a department store interior. "Accessories," Cordelia had said, emerging from a vision looking a little more than dazed, offering their first real clue to an ongoing case. And then, "No, women's wear. No . . ."

"Gotta narrow it down a little, Cordy," Gunn had said, at the time thinking he'd be part of this little expedition. Two more carolers were missing. There was trickle-down word of others, gone missing on their way to and from late night parties. And now Cordelia's vision made it plain that whatever peril they'd encountered, tonight was the last chance to save the singers.

She gave him an exasperated look. "You think I don't know that? I'm just about running on empty here, Gunn." She released a huge post-vision sigh, lifting her hands so they could pull her to her feet. Automatic procedure after so many visions. Rock 'em sock 'em visions, she sometimes said, especially when she ended up on the floor. The floor of the Hyperion Hotel, this time. They lifted her, steadied her, and gave her a chance to push her hair back from her face. She said, "Just head down Los Angeles Street and don't go south of Pico. I'm almost certain this is about the missing carolers." She gave Angel a particularly dark look. "And we're running out of time."

And so here he was. Looking down the length of Los Angeles Street, weighing whether to head right for accessories or left into the blocks set aside for women's wear, pretending the memories hadn't gotten to him. That hunting missing carolers on a Solstice night took the place of joining in the singing himself.

"I don't get it," Fred said, holding out her paper cup for a refill of leftover eggnog. Paper plates held convenience store cookies. Limp if sparkly decorations hung over the computer monitor, the lobby desk, and the stairway, along with snowflakes cut out of construction paper. Hastily applied holiday cheer in a hotel that was finally warm. Wesley had given the effort a wall-eyed but wisely silent reaction, and Gunn hadn't appeared to notice. And Fred . . .

Lost in thought. Not getting something.

"Nothing unusual about that," Cordelia responded, popping the spout on the eggnog carton and obliging with the refill. "What exactly don't you get this time?"

"Angel."

Cordelia gave a little laugh. "None of us gets Angel. At least, not usually. Wouldn't worry about that one."

Fred gave her eggnog a thoughtful stare. "But he

seems so sad. And he just wanted to go out on his own."

"He's a loner," Cordelia said. "That's what loners do."

"I don't think he *wants* to be a loner," Fred said into the eggnog. She cradled it with two hands, as though it might escape . . . or it needed comforting. With Fred it was hard to tell.

Since Cordelia wasn't sure if Fred was still in the conversation or if she'd started one on her own, she didn't say anything. But Gunn, with his big manly mug of eggnog—no puny little Dixie cups for him—said, "Hey, look at us. Hanging around an abandoned hotel lobby in the middle of the night, Christmas only a few days away, and a rip-roaring private office party in progress. Who would want to miss this?"

Cordelia shot him a scowl. "I did what I could. My credit cards are maxed out as it is, and it doesn't look like the *office* is going to be paying me back for this one, does it?"

"At least we had carolers," Wesley said, dutifully injecting cheer.

"Yeah, *client* carolers," Gunn said.

"Yes, well . . . there is that." Wes gave his Dixie cup a wistful look. "Not that I'm ordinarily one to go for the drink, but it does seem like we might have at least *lightly* spiked the eggnog."

"Uh-huh," Cordelia said. "And then you'll cover my back the next time we go out tonight? There *will* be a next time, you know. I mean, look at our Solstice track record."

"I just wonder," Fred said, briefly lifting her gaze to glance at them. "If he ought to be out there alone, I mean."

"He's just taking a look around." Gunn remained singularly nonchalant. Not worried. A little too obviously not worried. "He's supposed to call if he finds anything—but those directions you gave him weren't all that good. No big surprise if nothing happens."

"Hey, *you* try keeping all these visions straight," Cordelia said, struggling to keep the bitter note from her voice. *Who needs spiked eggnog when you have a nice mix of headache meds making the world all surreal? More surreal than it usually is around here, anyway.*

"Never mind," Wesley said in his quite firm way. "We can use the opportunity to identify what Cordelia saw. Or try to. It would help if the carolers had been able to add to the description."

The first caroler had gone missing days before, and the group claimed to have lost several members since then. Always someone who didn't show up at the night's starting point, or never made it home afterward. They hadn't even realized it at first—they were a decent-size group, and it was natural for a couple of them to be absent at any given time. But as they'd rallied for Solstice night, the situation had become evident; they'd come to Angel Investigations to report it. And finally Cordelia's vision had given them a place to start.

Cordelia gave a hefty sigh, and suddenly realized

the others were looking at her, frowning and quirking eyebrows and doing all the things that said they were wondering if the visions had finally gotten to her. *Ew. As if. At least . . .*

Not yet.

"They could have at least sung *one* song before hitting the streets," she said peevishly, though it hadn't been what she was thinking at all.

She'd been thinking how determined the carolers were. How this was their special season, and they weren't to be deterred from celebrating it despite their worry. Determined people.

Like some other people she knew. A certain vampire among them.

Angel eased down the empty street. No sign of life, nothing to fit Cordelia's vision of people dragged limply to their doom. A sheet of paper fluttered across the asphalt like an obliging urban tumbleweed. He watched it with the frustration of knowing that someone somewhere—right *here* somewhere—was in trouble, and he hadn't yet done anything to change that.

Someone. *Somewhere.* "Don't you remember any details about the warehouse at all?" he'd asked Cordelia, trying to wring any bit of actual detail from the vision.

"What's to be specific?" she'd said to him, and gulped the water Wesley had brought, reaching for it with a trembling hand they'd all pretended not to notice. "Warehouse blahblahblah, dank basement blahblahblah, bad lighting blahblahblah . . . the usual."

"Right," he murmured to himself, easing toward Twelfth Street through shadows within shadows.

A scuff of sound caught his attention and made him hesitate. Another, and he was sure. Someone moved out between the two giant garment warehouses to his right and now walked the shadows with him. A young woman. Ahead of him . . . unaware of him. With the soft speed no human could emulate, he closed the gap—and by then he knew there were others ahead of his quarry, those whom she followed. She herself was not used to the shadows, to judge by the careless spill of her uncovered bright blond hair. And not someone used to the chase—her blood was high in her veins, her heart pumping hard. She was young, and scared.

But she didn't waver. And he thought whatever she followed with such fear and persistence must be worth following indeed.

Accessories and women's wear. Specific enough after all.

Together they moved down the street, heading straight toward St. Joseph's Church. *Surely not the church . . .*

No. The young woman hesitated, then turned the other way at the corner. By then he'd come up nearly on her heels; he'd gotten a glimpse of something ahead of her that had vaguely human proportions, but definitely wasn't human. When she hesitated at the steps down into a warehouse private entrance, he was close enough to throw his arm across the doorway to block her—and then to clamp a hand across her mouth when she reacted with a startled cry. He said, "I don't think you want to do that."

She scowled, and although she had both hands free and could have shoved him away she only gave him a pointed look until he removed his hand from her mouth on his own, remarkably composed for a teenager only just accosted in the darkness. "Don't want to do what?" she said, sounding accusing. "Make noise, or—"

"—go into that building."

She crossed her arms, a defiant gesture that would have been more convincing had it not also looked like she was hugging herself. "I think that's exactly why I'm here. Why are you here?"

He gave the slightest of shrugs. "It's my job."

She gave a little nod, shifting impatiently. "Not nearly as good as my reasons."

"If you're following what I think you're following, you don't have a reason good enough to go in there."

"That *thing* just dragged my sister *in there.* And I think it took my uncle last week." She gave him a good hearty dare of a glare, one that said *top that.*

He couldn't. He realized, then, who she was. "You're one of the carolers."

She gave him a look of a different sort. He wasn't quite sure what it meant until she said, "And you're one of the people who are supposed to be helping us."

"We *are* helping you," he said, trying not to sound defensive.

"Uh-huh," she said, entirely unconvinced; like him, she kept her voice low, though she shifted again, eyeing the open spot between Angel and the wall like a target. "That's why you barely listened to us earlier, and practically left the hotel before we did."

Something came up, he wanted to say. But didn't, because how crass would that be—the implication of *something more important than your family.*

Over time, he had finally learned that nothing was more important than your family, even if it was made-family and not born-family. Because perhaps you'd used your born-family up.

Or even killed them.

He looked at her a moment, and finally he said, "I'm here." He reached for the inside pocket of his black leather duster, his fingers closing around his cell phone. "The rest of us will be here as soon as—"

"Oh, right," she said, cutting him off. "And I'll bet you think I'm going to wait. Some *thing* just dragged my sister into this place and you think I'm going to wait while whatever happens to her—*happens.*" She pushed past him.

He hesitated, his hand still on the phone. "You *really* don't want to go in there—"

"We all waited for you this evening, and then we went out to sing," she said bitterly, tucking sleek hair behind her ear. "That's when my sister was taken. I caught a glimpse of them . . . I followed. And I'm not waiting any longer, not when she needs help. You want to come with me, then come on." And she went.

Choices. Grab her and give away their presence to every demon ear within hearing distance when she protested, or go with her, scope out the situation, and pull back long enough to call the gang.

He went.

"Not that one," Cordelia murmured, leaning her head back against the circular back of the hotel lobby's conversation seating as she nixed the illustration of Wesley's latest demon suspect. She'd switched to water when the eggnog turned heavy in her stomach, and now she took a sip of her Evian.

"Look at this one," Fred said from beside her, tracing her finger over the thick page of an old book she held balanced in her cross-legged lap. She paused at the woodcut illustration of the demon, momentarily distracted by its crater-pocked skin, but returned to the text. Wesley leaned over her shoulder, scanning quickly over the page, wincing slightly at the illustration. Then his eyes fell upon the text.

"This *is* a good one," he said, appropriating the book after a slight pause that passed for asking permission. He held it out before Cordelia, who straightened to take a closer look at the creature.

Much like her sketch, it appeared almost human. There was all that hair? fuzz? fuzzy moss? where it shouldn't have been, and the skin had that bluish color and cratered texture, but the proportions were basically human. Well, human if you'd been taking steroids and working out at the gym twice a day for months. Not even Ah-nold could have measured up to the biceps depicted in the woodcut illustration. Or the—

"Wishful thinking," Wesley murmured, hastily retrieving the book.

Fred seemed oblivious. "It's them, then. Those Drannoth demons. And according to that text, we don't have much time."

After a brief but silent struggle over who would take the lead, Angel preceded the young woman down predictably dark stairs with a predictably abandoned look to them. Upon first moving back to L.A. he had wondered why there was such an underground warren of abandoned warehouse rooms and tunnels, but no longer. No one in the warehouses would admit it, but they all knew better than to venture into those lower levels. He tried to decide if the thick musty smell was normal *eau de warehouse* or peculiar to the demons living here.

"Nola," the young woman said quietly, treading close on his heels as they reached the bottom of the stairs. A high narrow hall led out before them, not looking to turn bright and cheery any time soon.

"What?"

"My sister's name. And my uncle's is Owen. You didn't ask."

He crouched over patchy concrete to eye something

that glistened in the oblique light of the single dim, wire-enclosed bulb up ahead of them. At least someone had left the lights on. "And what's yours?"

A pause. "Kath. What've you found?"

After some thoughtful consideration, he said, "An icky spot."

She crouched beside him, careful not to block the light. "Is that good?"

Gurgly laughter came from directly above them. "Not for you!"

Angel sprang aside, putting his back to the wall, finding the dim shape clinging in the high corner, ready to fight. But the dim shape made a loud hissing noise and the air turned thick with silently falling mist. Even as Angel reached for Kath to grab her hand and haul her right back up the stairs, the mist sank into his skin, stole his strength, and bore him down to the hard concrete. Kath landed beside him.

The laughter echoed bizarrely in his ears and faded with his consciousness.

"What do you mean, we don't have much time?" Gunn said, putting his mug down on the lobby's check-in counter and giving Fred a wary look, apparently unaware that eggnog licked at the corners of his mouth, stark against his dark skin.

Fred gave him a crooked little smile and pointed to her own mouth; Gunn hastily scrubbed his lips. Wesley paced through the lobby, book in hand, paying no attention to the byplay. "The Drannoth demons renew their clan not through reproduction among themselves, but by kidnapping others and putting them through a sort of . . ." he hesitated, looked at Cordelia, and chose his words with care. "I suppose you might call it a conversion process. One that occurs on Solstice night."

"According to that book, anyone's fair game," Fred said. "Except for most of the other demons. Vampires and such."

"Angel should be okay, then," Cordelia said, letting out a big breath of relief she hadn't realized she'd been holding. She glanced at her watch. Wee hours of the morning, longest night of the year. Daylight wasn't far off now . . . daylight and a very long appointment with her bed. Phantom Dennis would probably even have it turned down for her, with those nice clean sheets she'd put on only yesterday afternoon. A lifetime ago.

Fred and Wesley exchanged a glance.

"What?" Gunn demanded.

"Most of the other demons," Fred said gently. "Including vampires, usually. But—" she looked at Wesley, who came to the rescue.

"They key in on beings with souls," he said. "The craters in their skin aren't from poor adolescent hygiene, they're sensory organs. So even though Angel *is* a vampire, and would otherwise be of no interest to the Drannoth . . ."

"They'll know he has a soul," Gunn said flatly.

Cordelia jerked at the cold trickle down her chest, realized she'd forgotten to keep the Evian bottle upright, and set it beside her on the round seat, brushing futilely at herself. "Wonderful. So he's out there, and we should have heard from him, and these Drannoth demons will consider him good building material."

"You keep saying he can take care of himself," Fred offered tentatively.

"Yes, but he's used to being the exception when it comes to this sort of thing," Cordelia said. She let her head drop, resting it in her hands and trying to think beyond the sudden concern and her equally sudden irritation that Angel had insisted on going out there alone—even if she *did* know this season could be hard on him. Too many conflicting memories, too much not-quite-belonging.

She thought back to her vision, trying to dredge more information from it. Anything to cut down their search time. Some better clues than *between accessories and women's wear.*

"Cordelia?" Wesley's voice came from a distance; Fred's light-as-a-bird touch landed on her arm.

"What?" she said, lifting her head to find them all looking at her.

"You were humming," Gunn said. "An old-sounding tune. I mean like not-this-century old."

"'Bring a Torch, Jeannette, Isabella,'" said Wesley, who had pinned her with the oddest look of all. "It's a sixteenth-century French song. And I rather doubt it's any coincidence that it came to mind."

"Considering I've never even heard of it, I'd say that's a good guess." Were these visions sneaking into her head in a seriously spooky way, or what? Then again, just having visions in the first place was spooky enough. She told Wesley, "I'm not even going to ask how you know."

"I'm eclectic," Wesley said.

"You spend too much time at home alone," Cordelia countered.

Wesley said stiffly, "Just because I choose to—"

"We knew this was about the carolers," Gunn interrupted. "And we know the Drannoth convert their people before the night ends, right? I say we don't waste any more time. Let's start where Angel started."

"I don't see where we have much alternative," Wesley agreed. "We'll all go."

"All of us?" Fred asked uncertainly, voicing the thought before Cordelia could get to it on her own behalf.

"All of us." He said it with that taking-charge tone. "And now."

They went.

Angel came to awareness with a humming in his ear. He would have given his head a shake to clear it—except his head didn't move when he tried. The realization served to clear his thoughts. *The hallway, the demon, the falling mist . . .*

And the humming didn't come from his ears at all. It merely reached them, a sweet and sad voice that nonetheless offered some comfort.

It stopped. Kath said, "You're awake."

He didn't answer immediately, instead caught up in the astounding realization that he was gently but securely webbed up against a hard block wall.

"You *are*, aren't you? I thought I heard . . ." Her voice faded into uncertainty.

Angel gave her a belated reassurance. "All wrapped up and nowhere to go, but I'm awake."

"We're the only two," she said sadly. "The others . . . they're sedated or something."

"Others. . ." he repeated. He opened his eyes, found them covered with filmy webbing, and immediately tried to bring his hands up and rip it away.

"No!" Kath said. "Don't! I think this stuff reacts when you move—puts you out again or something. This is the third time I thought you were coming around, but you keep moving, and then you go away again. I've been very still and I've been awake for . . . I guess a couple of minutes. It seems longer."

He froze, waiting to see if the world would fade out again. After a moment he said, "It was pretty. The humming, I mean."

"An old Christian song," she said. "We use the melody."

Ah. Holiday stuff again. For once his state of body reflected his state of mind during the holidays. Trapped.

Something on the other side of the webbing moved, something big and bulky and . . . annoyed. "You two mind?" it said in a gurgly voice similar to the laugh from the hallway. "I'm trying to prepare myself for the replenishment. Prayers and rituals and important thoughts. It's bad enough I've got chrysalis-sitting duty . . . I don't need you interfering with my preparations."

"Chrysalis-sitting duty?" Angel said, wishing he didn't think *chrysalis* implied what he thought it probably did.

The indistinct bulk shifted. "Chrysalis," the demon said in irritation. "That would be you. Latecomers, but still plenty of time for the transformation."

Transformation. Yeah, it definitely meant what he thought it did. "Actually," Angel said, "I'm feeling a little chatty. How about you, Kath?"

She hesitated, but then responded in kind. "Really chatty," she said. "And sing-y, too. Which seems only fair, since you seem to have half our choral group here." She began to hum again.

"Ooh, singing," Angel said. He turned back to the demon, what little bit he could turn at all. "It's only fair to warn you—you probably don't want to be here if I start to sing."

"Gotta love you people," the demon said. "It's your own fault that you're here. Won't let go of Solstice . . . just keep coming out to sing. Easy pickings. Between you and the late night party-hearty contingent, we kicked butt this year." Then he gave a *tsk* of disapproval and annoyance. "Not an appropriate thought for the replenishment. You're going to ruin my holiday if you don't shut up."

"I feel your pain," Angel said. "Just let me out of here and you can feel your pain, too."

"Holiday?" Kath said. "Just what *is* this replenishment?"

The demon gestured broadly enough to be seen through the webbing; his voice turned enthusiastic. "The night of the year we take our winter harvest and replenish the clan by transforming you into—"

"Demons," Angel said flatly. "Got news for you, pal . . ."

"Yeah, yeah, so you're a vampire. We know that. You've got a soul, that's all we care about."

"I bet I can find some way to make that a mistake," Angel told him.

Kath said, "You're a vampire?" in a shocked little voice.

"With a soul," the demon said defensively. "We're really very fussy about who we transform."

Angel muttered, "That certainly makes being cocooned in here all worthwhile."

The indistinct shape hesitated, as if uncertain how to take dry sarcasm. Then he shook his head. "You're just ruining my holiday spirit," he said, and came up to Angel's confining chrysalis, giving it a mighty kick.

"Oh yeah, *that's* fair," Angel said. "Kick the vampire when he can't kick back." But the demon only watched with his arms crossed, looking satisfied even through the webbing and in the dim light. Within moments, Angel understood why, for the webbing responded to the insulting blow and the world drifted away again.

The cold night air revived Cordelia—though not quite enough for her to forget it was so far into the middle of the night that it was almost morning. She'd gotten used to working the after-dark hours, but this time of year there were just so many of them . . .

"Los Angeles and Eleventh," Wesley announced. "I believe this is where you suggested he start."

"This is it," Cordelia said, emoting all the patently false cheer she could dredge up. She offered a gloved gesture that encompassed the endless landscape of warehouses surrounding them. "He should be here. Somewhere."

Block after block of garment warehouses, and not a single one of them with a neon sign that said *Demons Be Here.* They'd have to do this the hard way.

"Time's a wastin'," Fred said, with a more earnest kind of false cheer than Cordelia had offered up.

Gunn didn't waste time with any cheer at all. He hefted a gleaming battle-ax and said, "Let's go."

Just head down Los Angeles Street, Cordelia had told Angel.

So they did.

O Holy Night, the darkened sky enfolds us.
'Tis the night we sing praise to rebirth.

Angel woke to singing. "How long?" he asked immediately.

Kath stopped singing. "Not long," she told him. "Just long enough for me to ask a few more questions of our annoyed demon baby-sitter. *Chrysalis*-sitter. He's gone off to do some deep breathing, I think. He said the others hadn't been awake nearly since they came in, they all struggled so much, and he's put out that we didn't do the same." She hummed a few measures of "The First Noel" and picked up with lyrics that didn't quite fit what Angel remembered. "All celebrate the eternal light . . ."

More than anything, she sounded like a young woman trying to pretend she wasn't terrified. But she broke off rather abruptly and said, "Within the hour, the rest of the clan will come in and soak us all with demon goo. Then the chrysalis webbing molds to our bodies and begins the transformation. By morning we're Drannoth demons."

"Demon goo?" Angel repeated. "He said that?"

"Well. Not exactly. But close enough." She was silent a long moment. Then she said rather distantly, "Even the demons know this is a special time of year. Ironic, in a way." After another thoughtful pause, she added, "He said that our souls would provide the spark for the transformation. That they'd be consumed."

Just when he thought he'd gotten Wolfram & Hart off his back for a while, here was someone *else* who wanted his soul . . .

She said, "How does a vampire *with a soul* celebrate the season?"

"I don't remember saying that I did." But he winced inside, drawn inexorably back to his memories again. Family. Laughing and feasting and family and friends, and even strangers.

"Everyone has something this time of year," she said, sounding quite sensible. "Solstice is the yoke of the year . . . it's renewal for everyone. Christmas, Hanukkah, Yule, Ramadan, Kwanza . . . surely there's room for you there somewhere."

"I think you underestimate the complications of the situation," Angel said.

"And I think you overestimate them," she said. "Look. Even the darkest part of this longest night contains the promise of lengthening days. No matter whose religion you look at, that's what it's all about—rebirth, re-examination of self. If you exist, you have reason to celebrate. If you exist, you have the right to renewal. No one can take that away from you."

He gave her a sideways look—or at least, gave the direction of her voice a sideways look. "The Drannoth are giving it a good try—and using their own renewal. Irony, eh?"

"That's not spiritual renewal," she said with some asperity. "It's just weird demon sex."

The cocoon webbing seemed to tighten around him, sticky and encompassing and totally offensive. "When you put it that way," he said, "it so makes me *not* want to be here."

She'd gone back to humming, but broke it off to say in a troubled voice, "I'm afraid to try anything. I'm afraid if this stuff puts me back to sleep again, the next time I wake up, I'll be a demon and my soul will be gone. I'm . . . I'm really afraid."

She had a point. The Drannoth would be back any time, and then they'd both be without souls. What would he be then? A double demon? A Drannoth vampire? But his next struggle could be his last. He thought about those moments he *hadn't* used to call the gang, wondered if they were still waiting for him at the hotel, wondered how long they'd wait before they realized how wrong the night had gone. "Sing," he told her. "I'll think of something."

But he didn't think he would.

They found no sign of Angel.

"This is no good," Gunn said as they met on the corner of Los Angeles and Pico, looking back over the territory they'd covered. "Are we even sure he came here? I don't even see his car."

"If he followed Cordelia's vision he did," Fred said, rubbing her mittened hands together. "Though it certainly does look deserted."

"It does," Wesley agreed. "But we've got to go back up this way to get to Gunn's truck, so we might as well be alert for signs as we go."

"Signs of what?" Fred wanted to know.

"'There be demons,'" Gunn suggested. "Or 'Do you know the way to San José?'" Hastily he added, "Not that I've even *heard* a sissy song like that—"

"We know, we know," Cordelia told him, breaking the huddle to head back up the street, entirely uneasy about the whole situation. "Only rough nasty music for you."

"Right," Gunn assured her. "Nasty music."

"Now that that's settled, shall we take another look around?" Wesley came up beside Cordelia in his best Rogue Demon Hunter mode, checking every layered shadow, peering into all the nooks and crannies. Fred and Gunn fell into step behind them, and they made slow progress back up the street. Although Cordelia wouldn't exactly have called it progress, because they weren't actually achieving—

"You're humming," Wes said abruptly. Accusingly.

"It happens," she told him. "Look, I really just want to get back to the hotel. Maybe Angel left a message there. And my feet are killing me already!" Then she took in the expression on his face, the way the other two looked at her, and realized the accusation hadn't been accusation at all, but startled realization. Cautiously, she said, "And what was I humming?"

"That song," Fred said. "The one you said you didn't know."

As one, they looked around. Standing on the street midblock between Eleventh and Twelfth streets, enclosed in a canyon with walls made of warehouses, they looked for any faint sign of recent activity.

Nothing. They turned back to Cordelia.

She waved them off. "Don't look at *me.* I've just got some kind of subliminal vision memory-thing going on. I'm not your dowsing rod. I can't even think of that tune if I try to do it on purpose." She pointed at herself. "See? No humming."

Not looking entirely convinced, Wes said, "Let's just check the doors on this block, shall we? Not the front doors. We need to find the back doors. Delivery doors. Old-looking doors."

"Back doors it is," said Gunn.

Cordelia followed them to the first building, humming random notes in an off-key way.

Just in case.

Angel tried moving slowly. Ever so slowly. Testing the limits of the webbing, and testing its response.

It didn't put him to sleep, but it didn't give way before him either. It gently stretched to accommodate him.

Kath had been silent for some moments, but eventually she said sadly, "I don't think we have much more time. I hope my sister . . . my uncle . . . my friends . . . I hope none of them ever found out what their fate was to be. They're all gentle people. They don't deserve this."

"And you do?" Angel said. "Okay, *I* probably do, but I don't *want* it."

Not that it stopped them from coming. Because coming they were, capturing his attention as his keen hearing picked up the first scuff of a footstep, then faint gurgling laughter. He said quickly to Kath, "I'm going to try something. If it doesn't work—"

"Make it work," she said, a desperate edge in her voice as she, too, heard the approaching demons.

If it doesn't work . . .

He'd be asleep in moments, never to wake up with a soul again.

Angel went fang-face. As the demons filed into the room, he released himself to the kind of violent fury he normally kept under excruciating control.

He tore through the webbing and left it in shreds behind him. It oozed a sticky substance, trying to subdue a victim it no longer held, an empty cocoon in a long row of cocoons sitting snugly side by side and stacked several deep in the big square underground room. He could see Kath's cocoon—like his own, the webbing still retained some translucency, and her bright blond hair shone through.

The assembling demons—festively attired in bright orange to offset their bluish skin and mulch-colored hair, carrying various bowls and implements and scrolls—stopped short, blocking the only exit. Beside the small and wizened leader stood a demon of just the right size and shape to be their chrysalis-sitter.

Angel smiled at him, an expression meant solely to expose his fangs. "Vampire," he said. "I found a way to make that a mistake after all. *Your* mistake."

Of course they rushed him. Not all of them, but enough to keep him busy while the others shouted at each other, clamoring to know who'd brought the mist . . . when apparently none of them had.

He understood immediately. Even as he ducked a wild blow, popped up to grab the off-balance demon and swing him first into the block wall and then back into the attacking throng, he realized they couldn't simply put him back to sleep.

But they could still kill him. Kill him and go on with their ceremony, shy by one insignificant soul. He threw a duck-pivot-kick and looked desperately for a weapon. The room held nothing but a massive, elaborately decorated table totally not to his taste, and the cocoons. Big heavy thing, squishy things. Not that he wanted to get near that webbing again . . .

"Yo! Angel!" Gunn's voice but no sign of anything but blue pocked gurgling demons, pouring into the room with one goal in mind.

Angel tossed aside a blue demon in a terrifying orange plaid, met the next one with a precision punch to the throat, grappled with a third . . . grappled with a third . . .

The third just smiled at him. The third stood unmoved, as muscle-bound as any of them and more. As Angel gave swift consideration of his alternatives, the demon quite deliberately flexed all those muscles. Even the other demons paused to watch, respectful of their comrade, starting to bare their own gruesome smiles.

"Yo! Angel!" This time, above the closely gathered and bobbing heads, metal flashed.

"Excuse me," Angel said to the demon who faced him, and thrust his hand up. Over their heads, skimming the tops of their mulchy, Spanish moss hair, a familiar battle-ax whipped through the room. Angel snatched it out of the air and watched the demon smiles fade. For a single charged moment they stared at one another, weighing the change in odds. Then the demons released a collective gurgle of a roar and surged forward.

Angel waded in.

Within moments the cocoons were stained blue with an entirely different demon goo than intended. Gunn and Wesley fought their way into the room as half the demons fought their way out, and Cordelia and Fred, their hands still protected by mittens, slashed the cocoons open—starting with the only one calling for help. Kath tumbled out to the dank floor and immediately joined in the rescue efforts.

And then the demons ran. They dropped their scrolls and vessels and left behind their dead and they ran. It took Angel a moment to realize it, hunting for the next muscle-bound enemy and finding only those they'd already vanquished. He and Wesley bumped into one another, exchanged a startled glance, and slowly straightened from their battle-ready stances. Gunn surveyed the results of the encounter, flipping his ax up and catching it in the most casual of ways. "Good thing I brought two," he said, and grinned.

"Isn't it," Angel said, handing off the borrowed weapon as he walked by, catching Gunn by surprise so he fumbled his nonchalant ax-tossing and both weapons clattered to his feet.

"Great," Gunn muttered. "Cool, really cool."

But Angel had eyes only for the cocoons and their

former occupants. They sprawled across the floor and across each other, an untidy heap of sleepers still dressed in whatever they'd been wearing when they were snatched. Carolers in coats and gloves . . . a few party-clad revelers. They all looked wrinkled and a little damp, their skin waxy. "Will they be okay?"

"It might take time for some of them to come around," Fred said, sounding authoritative as she occasionally did when she forgot to be uncertain and wary. "The longer they've been in there, the longer it'll take for the effects of these . . . these . . ." she waved in the direction of the gutted cocoons, "these *things* to wear off."

Kath looked up from where she crouched over a young woman who looked slightly older than she and remarkably similar of feature. Her sister. She stroked Nola's hair with trembling relief. "Thank you," she said. "Are you all right?"

"All right?" Angel flexed his shoulders, taking a deep and unnecessary breath simply because it felt good. He grinned at her. "More than all right. I feel like a new man."

Oh Holy Night, the stars are brightly shining.
It is the night of the Sun King's rebirth.
Long lay the world in winter's darkness pining,
Till he appeared to bring warmth to the earth.

They walked the middle of the street in the dark of the night. Behind them, reviving members of the caroling group stayed to help those who emerged more slowly from what had been a very long sleep. But Kath walked with them, at least for a little way, carrying the gratitude of her friends and offering them a serenade in her sweet clear voice.

"That's really pretty," Fred said. She plucked a strand of webbing from her arm and shook it free of her fingers. "It's been so long since I heard Christmas carols. I've even forgotten most of the words, I guess. I don't know those."

"How about 'Deck the Halls'?" Kath asked her. "That'll work for both of us."

Until then Cordelia had been content to walk along without thinking too closely about the words, but just—*finally*—enjoying the music itself. Kath's words brought her from her tired reverie to say, "*Both* of us?"

Kath grinned. "Sure. Didn't you know those were pagan songs? We were caroling Solstice, not Christmas."

Gunn said, "But 'Deck the Halls'—"

"Was ours before it was yours. But it shares nicely, don't you think?"

Unexpectedly, Angel said, "It does, doesn't it?"

"Wait," Cordelia said in abrupt trepidation. "That doesn't mean you're going to—"

Gunn said, "Whoa, whoa, I've done danger duty for the night—"

Wes said, "You're not going to—"

Fred said, "What—?"

"Sing," Angel said. And he did.

5 A.M.

THE SUN CHILD

by Christie Golden

Earlier that night . . .

The moon was a waxing crescent, no longer the Maiden's slim bow but not yet the Mother's ripe fullness. It silvered the ocean, beach, rocks, and the few hardy trees that could survive in such briny soil, and shone down benevolently upon the Coven of the Singing Stars.

They stood in a circle around an altar, hands joined, voices raised in a resonant, single-syllable chant. Upon the altar were the antlers of a stag, a knife with an intricately carved hilt, a slew of unlit golden candles in various shapes and sizes, and a cup filled with a dark red fluid.

The chant faded away. The figures clad in black released their hands. All eyes turned toward Ravenwing, the High Priestess. She was pale and tall, with hair as black as the raven's wing from whence her magickal name had come. She turned her face up to the moon-light, closing her eyes.

"Blessed Lady, Maiden, Mother, Crone, tonight we celebrate your aspect of the Mother. We salute you, Lady."

Ravenwing bent, took the cup of red liquid, and drank. Solemnly, the large ceramic goblet was passed around the circle and all drank. When the cup returned to Ravenwing, she gave it to Frey, the High Priest.

He lifted the cup and intoned, "Blessed Lord, Dying God and Dancing God, Holly King, Oak King, we welcome you on this most sacred night." He too toasted and drank, and when the cup had again made it around the circle, he poured its remaining contents on the earth. "So mote it be."

"So mote it be," the coven members replied as one.

Frey knelt and lit the candles. Warm, golden illumination joined the cool, fey light of the moon. They stood in silence, awaiting the precise moment.

It came. As one, they sang the traditional song, one they had performed every Yule, finishing up with:

Happy Birthday, dear Oak King,
Happy Birthday to You!

No one could resist grinning. Mirth bubbled in Ravenwing's voice as she said, "The circle is open, but unbroken. Merry meet, merry part, and merry meet again!"

Now that the circle had been officially closed, the air of formal ceremony dropped like an old cloak, and everyone began chatting and laughing. Ravenwing refilled the now-empty cup with more grape juice and again it was passed.

"Ta-da!" said Morganna, flourishing the special treat she had made for the "cakes and ale" portion of the evening, which Frey referred to as Snacks for Witches.

"Oh, Morganna, that's *soooo cute*!" squealed Ravenwing. Morganna had made a birthday cake with a smiley-faced sun on it.

"Nice ritual, you guys," said Dove, licking yellow frosting from her fingers. "Wish we could do something about that, though," she said, indicating the digital clock with red letters that sat next to the candles. "It kind of spoils the mood."

"Yeah," said Frey. "But there's really no other way to get the exact moment right. Watches are too hard to read."

They ate and drank for another half hour, and then Frey said, "Who wants to start drumming?"

Everybody yelped "Oh, yeah!" and hurriedly rushed to get their drums out of their tents. Everybody, that is, but Ravenwing and Morganna. The High Priestess put her hands on her hips and sighed.

"The Park Service is awfully nice to let us use this site, but they'll stop letting us have it if we trash it." She frowned, stooped, and picked up a cigarette butt. "Damn it, Ra, you need to pack this stuff out!" She waved the butt in the air in Ra's direction, though he was off hooting and hollering with the others. She wished he'd quit. *These things could kill you.*

"Nobody thinks if *I'd* like to drum up the sun," Ravenwing muttered, putting the offending butt in the trash bag along with the paper plates and cups.

"Here, why don't I take care of this?" offered Morganna. "You've told me how to put away the coven tools."

"Are you sure? You love to drum."

"Hey, it's only twelve thirty," said Morganna, pointing to the bright red numbers on the clock. "We have hours yet."

"Well, all right. Thanks, hon." Ravenwing hugged the younger woman, then scurried to fetch her own bodhran.

Morganna smiled after her. *You are such a suck-up,* she told herself. She looked at all the trash and the altar and grimaced. She set to it, humming a pagan chant to make the time pass more quickly.

She heard a rustling in the forest. "Too close, I'm over here," she called, thinking it was one of the guys trying to find a good spot to take a leak. "And remember to bury it with the trowel," she called as an afterthought.

The sound grew louder, and she heard a low growl. Morganna froze, her heart racing. There had been something said about bears . . . and mountain lions . . . and who knew what kind of weirdos liked to play in the woods after dark.

Slowly she turned around.

They were upon her before she could draw breath to scream.

Her last thought was a desperate wish that they hadn't dismissed the protective circle after all. . . .

Angel closed the door to his room and fell on the bed. It had been a long, long night. He was very grateful that it was after five and things had finally settled down. Wesley had sent them all home. "Unless, naturally, there is some pressing emergency," he'd added, pushing his glasses up the bridge of his nose with a forefinger.

"Naturally," echoed Cordelia, making the single word a monument to sarcasm.

"Never an emergency around here," said Gunn. Wesley had frowned and was about to retort when Angel interrupted with a "Great, thanks," and made for his room. He thought he'd had his eyes closed for about a minute when the door opened.

"Angel?" It was Fred's sweet, tentative voice. "Gosh, Angel, I'm so sorry to wake you, but you'd better come down."

He rolled over and glared at her with eyes that itched from lack of sleep. "Emergency."

"Oh, yeah." She nodded her head vigorously. "Really big, urgent, girl-and-baby-being-chased-by-spiky-nasty-demons kind of emergency."

Soon, soon this night would be over. He groaned, rolled out of bed, and followed Fred down to the lobby.

The client had her back to him. She was tall and slender, but curvy in all the right places. Blond wavy hair fell to the middle of her back. A long dress of midnight blue hugged her body, and yet somehow managed to be formal. Gunn and Wesley had stupid grins on their faces even as they were clearly trying to be businesslike, and Cordelia just looked pissed.

"What seems to be the trouble?" At the sound of his voice, she turned to look at him. Angel almost collapsed. Outside of an old-master painting, he'd never seen anything that gorgeous.

Her eyes were large and sapphire blue. Her face was a perfect oval with high cheekbones and the sort of mouth that made the term *rosebud* suddenly seem like not much of a cliché at all. Her arms cradled a small child, who seemed amazingly well behaved. But what made her more than beautiful, what made her exquisite, was the look of hope on her face. Whatever she wanted, Angel was going to see to it that she got it.

The moment their eyes met, though, the look of hope died. Resigned sorrow filled her face, and she shook her head sadly.

"You are not Angel," she said. Her voice was like a breeze, like a bell, like every corny phrase he'd ever heard.

"Oh, yes, yes I am," he said, aware that his voice had a desperate edge to it.

She smiled a little, sadly. "What I meant was, you are not *an* angel," she amended.

Gunn snorted. "Got that one right."

The woman gathered the baby closer in a protective gesture. "Then you cannot help me," she said, and her eyes filled with tears.

"I'm certain there's something we can do, Miss . . . ?"

She stared blankly at Wesley.

"Mrs.?" offered Gunn helpfully. Still the radiant woman looked at them, clearly not understanding.

"You got a name?" Cordelia asked bluntly.

She smiled. "You may refer to me however you would like."

"Serena," said Fred abruptly, startling them all. Everyone turned to look at her and she turned bright red. "It suits her," she insisted.

Angel had to admit that it did. "That work for you?" he asked. She smiled and again he felt all quivery in his legs. Was it really just because she was that beautiful? There was something almost overwhelming about her. . . . He took a deep breath, steeled himself against her charms, and valiantly tried to get down to business.

"I'm not an angel," he said, "but we do run a good investigative business. We specialize in things that aren't . . . that aren't of this earth." *Damn, that sounded lame.*

Serena brightened and cuddled the child closer. It still hadn't done anything but look at them with bright blue eyes, and as Angel guided Serena to a seat, he saw that the infant wasn't just young, it was clearly only a few hours old.

Wesley had apparently come to the same conclusion

and asked, "Are you well enough to have left your bed?"

"Bed?"

"Your baby," said Wesley. "It's clear you just gave birth a few hours ago."

Serena threw back her head and laughed. Angel swallowed hard. "Oh, no, he's not my child." As Wesley formed the next obvious question, she added, "But he is in trouble, and I must protect him. They want to kill him. Before sunrise. I've been running from them since midnight, when he was born."

"Who would want to kill a baby?" asked Gunn.

Serena's blue eyes were steady as she turned to look at him. "Demons," she said.

"Ah," said Wesley, nodding and looking very wise. "No doubt newborn's blood is part of a ritual."

"Ew," said Fred, recoiling and looking with pity and horror upon the child.

"Very ew," said Cordelia, "and *so* last millennium. You'd think these demons would get bored using the same ingredients all the time. No wonder they're so cranky."

"Cordelia has a point," said Wesley. "It's a grim fact that baby's blood is commonly sought after for use in dark magick. It's going to be difficult to narrow it down. Do you know what specific ritual they're planning on performing?"

Serena nodded, and pulled the baby closer to her impossibly perfect breasts. "Yes," she said. She turned to Angel. "You know about tonight," she said.

"It's a dead man's party," said Cordelia. "All night long. Believe me, we've had a taste of it. We're all going to be real happy campers when tonight's over."

"That's exactly what they don't want," said Serena. "They have found a way to make tonight last forever, and if they slay this child, it will indeed come to pass."

"They've got a way to stop time?" asked Fred.

"No," replied Serena. "A way to make sure the sun never rises again." Her voice grew thick as she spoke and she clasped the child fiercely. Tears slipped down her cheeks to trickle into the swaddling blanket. The baby looked up at her, but didn't cry.

Angel felt a chill. "Eternal darkness," he said softly, more to himself than to them. "Endless night. I can see how that would be a goal worth striving for—for some."

"But they've already failed," said Wesley, with the authority of one who knew he was right. "The sun has already risen on most of the world."

Everyone visibly relaxed except for Serena. Her gaze was disconcertingly steady and solemn as she regarded Wesley.

"Are you sure?"

They all stared, and then Cordelia ran for the computer as Angel picked up the phone.

"We're closed, come back tomorrow." As Lorne spoke, he looked at the spilled drinks, crumbs on the tables, and trash on the floor that was mute testimony to a long night of hearty partying. Business was always good on Winter Solstice, but the cleanup seemed to take until the new year.

"Lorne!" Angel's voice had a tinge of desperation to it, making Lorne all the more anxious to hang up. He was far too tired to tango with anything Angel was having trouble with.

"Angel, it's bedtime," he said. "Night-night, or day-day, as the case may be."

"I need a favor."

"No, really? Why, you've never asked anything of me before," the Host replied, turning the Sarcasm-O-Meter from Laconic Ironic to Searingly Scorn-Dripping.

"Turn on the TV," Angel continued.

"You've got one, turn it on yourself."

"Kicked in by a Skrak demon two weeks ago. Turn on the TV."

"Now this is getting ridiculous," muttered Lorne as he trudged into his bedroom and grabbed the remote. "You're starting to live vicariously through me, and that's scarier than a . . ." He stared, frozen, at the images on the screen.

"Are you watching the news? Lorne?"

"Yeah," said Lorne, barely hearing Angel repeating his name. "Heavy mojo, Angel."

"What's going on?"

Lorne tried to form the words as he watched the local L.A. anchor, his blow-dried hair askew and his eyes a bit wild, describe the "strange meteorological phenomenon" that had begun at 12:01 at the international date line.

"Is there anything about the sun not coming up?"

"Well, they're calling it a heavy layer of debris, probably caused by a passing comet, that's temporarily preventing the sun's rays from reaching Earth," said Lorne, "which doesn't explain the fact that I can see stars twinkling over the New York skyline."

He heard Wesley muttering something about it being after nine A.M. in New York. "Yes, kids, it's morning in America," said Lorne. "What do you know about this?"

"It's . . . complicated."

"I'll be right over."

Cordelia sighed in relief when the computer successfully booted up. "You know, if someone around here would cough up a few bucks to get DSL, we'd never have to turn this thing off. Wouldn't have had to call Lorne," she said archly to Angel.

"Don't even have the bucks to get a replacement TV," Angel replied. "What's going on?"

"Man, the crazies are out tonight," said Gunn, leaning over Cordelia's shoulders. "Lot of end-of-the-world cults having one big celebration."

"They may not be so crazy after all, if what Serena is telling us is true," said Angel. He turned around just in time to see the beautiful young woman sink onto the ottoman, and was by her side in an instant.

"You're shaking," he said. She turned her oval face

up to his and for the first time he saw the exhaustion in her eyes. "When was the last time you ate?"

"I don't eat," she murmured.

Angel looked at her, his eyes narrowing.

"Hey," said Cordelia, turning to glare at her. "Now that's just not healthy. Anorexia is *so* not cool."

Suddenly Serena looked frightened. "I mean I—" She closed her mouth with an audible click.

Despite an almost overwhelming desire to protect and shelter this woman, Angel felt suspicion gnawing the back of his mind. He wanted desperately to believe her story, but suppose she was one of the bad guys? There was something about her that was not quite right, that was more than human . . . or maybe less than human.

He reached and grabbed the baby before she could react. Serena uttered a soft cry that almost broke his heart, but Angel held the baby close.

"You don't eat, huh?" he asked. "Do you sleep? Or breathe? You're perfect, Serena. Too perfect. I don't think you're even human."

"Please," she cried, falling to her knees and reaching out to him imploringly. "Please keep the baby safe."

"Angel—," began Wesley.

"You guys must know something I don't," said Lorne, opening the door and running lightly down the steps. "Women never get on their knees and beg for me."

"Lorne, what is she?"

"She's a fetching little minx, that's for sure. Oh, you mean if she's a demon or something?" Gallantly Lorne reached down to Serena and eased her up. "Come on, sweetheart. Can you sing for me?"

Oddly, the words relaxed her. Her face eased into a radiant smile. "I sing all the time. At least, I did. . . ."

He smiled reassuringly at her. "Like the Phantom said to Christine, sing for me, my angel of music."

Serena closed her eyes. Of course, she had the longest lashes Angel had ever seen. Her full red lips parted and a sweet, pure sound issued forth.

No one moved. Angel felt tears welling in his eyes and wiped at them clumsily. He couldn't understand a word of the song, but it moved in his blood, along his nerves, into his heart and brain like the sweetest caress imaginable. All was well, and all would be well, and he was loved and cherished and worthy and precious. . . .

Gently, slowly, as though it hurt him to do so, Lorne extended a green finger and placed it on Serena's lips, silencing her haunting, breathtaking song.

"So, what is she?" asked Gunn, his voice oddly hoarse. "Some kind of siren?"

Lorne took a deep, steadying breath. "Oh, no, my friends. She's no demon. She's exactly the opposite."

The blood from the latest victim, a young woman whose sweet nature made her flesh succulent, ran down Kansa's jaws. A long, forked tongue crept out to catch every drop. He was not used to eating so frequently, but he found he enjoyed it. It was hard staying in this dimension, but the human flesh he and his group needed to consume every hour kept them anchored and strong.

The fact that this girl had been a witch made her even tastier. He extended a claw to pick out a chunk of flesh that had gotten caught between two fangs.

The pleasant moment of satiety was disturbed by Irina. She floated over to him, her soaked chemise clinging to her, her hair plastered to her skull, her face green with decay. He frowned. *The rusalka is such a wet blanket.* He smiled at his unintentional pun.

"Time grows short," the demon-ghost of a drowned Russian girl chided him. "We have less than four hours before we are forced back to our realm."

The pair of kappas leaped agilely over the carcass to sit on either side. Of necessity, the monkey demons of Japan had superb balance. Their power resided in the magickal fluid cradled in the indentation of their skulls. Perhaps it was because their brains were short-changed in order to make room for their magick; but Kansa found them incredibly stupid. Now they just sat and grinned at him, tongues lolling. *Idiots.* There were much smarter demons in Shinto folklore, but he had to admit, when they could focus, the kappas were powerful.

"We need to keep up our strength," Kansa said to Irina. "Eight of us have already faded back to whence we came for lack of sustenance. And yet I see some bones left," he said reprovingly, looking around at the others, a veritable United Nations of demons from every culture on the planet. "Someone's not being a good member of the Clean Plate Club."

"You think this is just a lark," Irina snarled. Of all of them, she alone could not be physically harmed by the mighty Kansa. "We have had over twenty of Earth's hours to catch a girl and a baby, and yet here we are. Perhaps someone else should lead this group."

Kansa snarled, rising to his full height of nearly twenty feet. Everyone but Irina quailed. "Do you think that this is as easy as drowning a leering peasant boy?"

"I know it's something *you* haven't been able to do," Irina retorted, her red eyes blazing.

The other demons, from the nagas to the trolls to the imps, froze in shock. No one ever, *ever* mentioned Kansa's famous failure. Kansa, too, went very still. He saw fear finally flicker in the rusalka's eyes.

"You will not speak of this," he said in a low voice of warning.

"And if I do?" Her voice was high with fear, though her words were defiant.

"We made him a human," said Kansa. "We can do the same to you." He stepped forward to where she hovered in midair. "And you will be delicious."

She cringed back and flew upward. Satisfied, Kansa grunted. He grabbed the remaining bones, crunched them down in a few bites, and nodded to himself.

The being of Good—no one could bring themselves to call her an "angel," so they'd come up with this less-knee-jerk-reaction term—gazed curiously at a ham and cheese on rye. She picked up the pickle with long, slender fingers, then glanced over at Wesley, who'd prepared the snack.

"You, uh, put it in your mouth," he said.

Cordelia snorted.

"You should tell us everything if you want us to be able to help you," said Angel. Serena paused, confused.

"If I put things in my mouth, I will not be able to speak," she pointed out.

"Ooh, such good table manners," said Fred. "Not talking with your mouth full, I mean. But I guess you would have good table manners, wouldn't you, if you were an ang—" She flushed and didn't finish the word.

"Angel's right," said Wesley, having no difficulty uttering the term when it was used to describe a vampire with a soul. "Perhaps you'd better talk to us first and eat afterwards."

Serena lowered the pickle. "Very well. Anything to save him. He must be saved."

"Or big ol' eternal darkness will descend, we got that part," said Cordelia. "But you kind of left out the 'I'm a divine being of good' part."

"I'm only a guardian," said Serena. "To protect him. He's the precious one. I suppose I might as well tell you everything, since you already know so much." She looked at them each in turn, and then said, "He's the sun."

"Whose son?"

"No, not *son,* Sun." They stared at her, still not comprehending. Serena sighed. "The sun in the sky. He's the God."

"He's God?" squeaked Cordelia, staring with new respect at the infant cradled in Fred's arms.

"I am not explaining myself well," said Serena.

"I believe I'm beginning to understand," said Wesley. "In many religions, the sun is viewed as male, and the moon as female. Of course, Amateratsu, in Japanese mythos, is the sun, and she is—"

"Wes," said Gunn.

"Oh, sorry. As I was saying, many cultures see divinity as male and female, and all things of nature fall onto one side or the other. Fire is male, water is female. The sun is male, the moon is female; day is male, night female; the sky is male, the earth is female; and so on. Hence the term 'Mother Earth.' And nearly every culture has some kind of festival of light held around the darkest time of the year, like Hanukkah and Yule. Even the birthday of Jesus Christ was determined to be around this time of year, as Christ was supposedly the light of the world."

"Pick up the pace, Wes," said Cordelia. "The night is passing." She made a face. "At least we hope it's passing."

Wesley adjusted his spectacles. "So this night is considered the birthday of the God. According to the Celtic wheel of the year, the God's growth establishes the seasons. In spring he's a youth, summer a man, in the fall he's a willing sacrifice—"

"Whoa, whoa, you lost me here," said Gunn.

"Somebody's gonna kill this little tyke around Labor Day?"

"Early August, actually," said Serena, appearing completely composed as she uttered the words. "Lammas, or Lughnasad. He is a willing sacrifice, dying as the crops are harvested to ensure bounty for the people through the long winter. He is born again at Yule, and the cycle continues." She smiled softly. "As it ever has been, and ever shall be."

The baby cooed and waved his tiny, curled hands.

"Too bad I can't get in touch with Willow," said Cordelia. "She knows all this witchy stuff."

"I do too," said Angel, surprising them. "Hey, I'm Irish. I remember dancing at Lughnasad. The old ways aren't entirely gone." He smiled fondly, remembering. "And at Beltane, dancing around the bonfire with the women who were . . ." He came back to the present, coughed, and ducked his head. "Anyway, the celebrations of the Wheel of the Year haven't been forgotten."

"Quite," said Wesley, a touch disapprovingly. "According to folklore, the God is not alone in the Wheel of the Year. He is born of the Goddess, grows to manhood, um . . . joins with his beloved, dies, enters Her womb, and is reborn. The Goddess is eternal, but the God is born, dies, and is continually reborn."

"What I don't get is that—don't mean to be disrespecting you here, Serena—this Wheel of the Year thing is pretty much symbolic, right? If the God is in the sun and in fire and in the crops and stuff, then he's not out cruising on Saturday nights, know what I mean?" said Gunn.

"You are correct, Charles," said Serena. "But the demons have found a way to make him take on human flesh."

"And if he's human," said Fred softly, "he can be killed."

"And if he is killed," said Serena solemnly, "your world will have no sun."

They stared at her in silence, waiting for her to continue. "I have been fleeing them since the first turn of midnight, heading ever westward. Since I am as mortal now as the Sun Child, I have had to use your clumsy means of transportation. I have only been able to stay ahead of them because they are forced to make a sacrifice in each time zone, within an hour after midnight." Her eyes welled with tears. "The loss of life . . . it is hard to bear, but if I stopped and helped, more would die."

She wiped her eyes and looked at Angel pleadingly. "We know of you, Angel. Though I misunderstood your name."

"The Powers That Be connection, huh?" asked Cordelia.

Serena nodded. "I do not have the strength to keep running, and this is where the land gives way to sea. I had to make a stand here. And they will come for him."

"So, what are we going to do?" asked Fred. She

clearly expected answers, and when none came forth, her small face crumpled.

"Look," said Gunn, somewhat desperately, "we've been in tight situations before. It's just a handful of demons, right Serena? And we've just got to stall them until midnight, that the deal?"

Serena shook her head. "Kansa is the leader. He has managed to liberate at least one demon for every culture as Time presses forward."

"And he's been doing it for, what, twenty hours?" said Cordelia. "You do the math." She flopped back in her chair. "Well, at least it can't get any worse."

"Kansa," mused Wesley, frowning. "Why do I know that name. . . ." He hurried to a stack of ancient texts piled carelessly on the floor next to the Yellow Pages and a pile of Snickers wrappers. "Oh, dear."

"Man, I hate it when he says that," said Gunn.

"Kansa is an ancient Indian demon-king," said Wesley. "When Lord Krishna was born—Krishna being an incarnation of Vishnu, who is—"

"The God," said Angel, looking at the infant.

"Right. When Krishna was born, Kansa tried to kill him." He kept rifling. "He was tricked and Krishna survived. Kansa sent six demons to kill Krishna, and they all failed. Legend has it that Kansa will never stop until he succeeds."

"So it's like a personal thing," said Fred.

"It's worse," said Lorne. "We've won the demon lottery, kids, but I'd rather see Ed McMahon with an oversized check than this character and his fan club. Going to be hard to keep little Sun Guy safe."

"I think I know what to do," said Angel.

They waited on the deserted beach, which was hardly more than a small spit of land surrounded on two sides by sheer, rocky cliffs and on the third side by water. When the sea was rough, this little beach would disappear altogether, swallowed by the angry ocean. Angel and his friends waited impatiently for the boat to appear.

"Let's run through this again," said Cordelia.

"It's simple. The guy that owns the boat owes me a favor," said Gunn. "The demons expected that Serena would have to make a stand here in L.A. So we get her out of L.A."

"Where's the boatman going to take her?" asked Fred.

"Don't know," said Gunn, "and the less we know the better."

"Wish he'd hurry up and get here," Cordelia complained. "This wind is starting to bite."

"Not as badly as we will," came a deep, rumbling voice.

They turned to see shadows milling on the cliff above them, scurrying down along its sides, scampering along the small stretch of beach toward them.

"Damn it!" cried Gunn. He reached for the stack of weapons they had brought just in case, but Lorne was faster. Hissing, the green-skinned Host seized Gunn and yanked his arms behind his back, trussing him up like a calf with a length of rope he'd hidden in his coat.

Wesley dived for the weapons as well, but Angel was there first, his face twisted into its vampire visage. Grabbing Wesley, he slammed him viciously against the cliffside. Wesley's eyes rolled back in his head and he went limp. Angel dropped him like a discarded toy.

Both Fred and Cordelia had managed to grab weapons. Fred aimed a crossbow at Angel, then gasped as she realized that she had neglected to put a bolt in its groove. Bravely she swung the empty weapon at the vampire, who clutched it and forced her back and down with it.

"You tricked us!" screamed Cordelia, charging at Angel with a broadsword too big for her to wield effectively. Angel easily sidestepped her clumsy blow, and Lorne grabbed her and shoved her face down into the sand. He sat on her until she ceased struggling. The betrayal had seemingly broken Fred, who huddled up next to the flailing Gunn and buried her face in her hands.

Quick as a snake, Angel turned to the one remaining person. Serena clutched the baby to her breast and stared at him. "We trusted you!" she cried.

"I'm sorry," said Angel, "I really am. But we're demons, Lorne and I. In the end, that's all we are. Give me the baby and I'll let you go."

"Never!" she shrieked, then turned and plunged into the water. Angel splashed after her, grabbing the baby with one hand and holding Serena down into the water with effortless ease. She struggled, splashed, and rose up at him with a strength he hadn't expected. He shook her off, then struck her, turning his attention back to the horde of demons leering down upon them.

Still, the baby made no sound. Clutching it, Angel called, "Which of you is Kansa? I deliver the baby only to him!"

One of the nightmare silhouettes straightened. Angel blinked as the creature rose and kept rising, until its twisted shape stood fully erect. The thing was at least twenty feet tall. He could distinguish horns and tusks and claws, but it was the eyes that captivated him: red, glowing eyes, like the embers of a dying fire.

"I am Kansa, King of Demons. Give to me what is rightfully mine, and you will be spared."

"Mighty generous of you, but I think I'll take my finder's fee first." Angel lifted the child to his mouth. Deftly, using a single razor-sharp canine, he sliced a thin line along the baby's soft, small neck. Blood hit his tongue, and it was so sweet, so pure, that his knees almost buckled. It was all he could do not to bury his fangs in the infant's throat and drain him dry.

The single jolt of pain, though, did what he wanted it to do. This infant, the sun incarnate, had never known pain in his entire brief life as a human baby. The cut made his small chest heave, then the little God began to cry in terror and pain, wailing, as all hurt children do, for his mother.

His mother heard.

At once the earth beneath Angel began to tremble.

Wind came out of nowhere and lashed the waves to dangerous heights. The demons above him cried out in alarm. Kansa bellowed a challenge, but it was drowned out by the shriek of the wind. Angel had been afraid they'd awaken something that might destroy them as easily as it destroyed the child's true enemies, but that was a risk he'd had to take. He only hoped he'd gambled wisely.

"Let's go!" he cried, holding the screaming baby close and sprinting along the slim stretch of beach toward safety. Wesley sprang up from his semblance of unconsciousness and extended a hand to haul an alert Fred to her feet. Lorne helped Cordelia up and assisted Gunn in untangling the not-very-tightly-tied cord that had been casually roped around his wrist. Angel looked around, fear rising in him. "Where's Serena? Serena!"

She was gone.

"Come on!" Cordelia shoved him hard. They splashed through water and wet sand away from the angry ocean. It was not a moment too soon. An enormous wave rose from the churning sea and to Angel, who looked back at that instant, it looked like a human hand. A woman's hand, with slim, tapered fingers.

The tidal wave crashed down upon the cliff, sweeping dozens of demons into its dark depths. Heads and flailing limbs emerged, in all shapes and sizes. The cries of fear were almost—almost—enough to rouse pity. Again the earth shuddered and Angel fell, taking the impact with his shoulder and preventing the baby from being injured.

The infant still screamed lustily. Lying on the vibrating earth, Angel saw the cliff beneath which he and his friends had been standing a moment ago crumble and slide into the ocean. Again the waves came, and when they receded there was not a single figure to be seen.

"Angel!" screamed Cordelia. The waves were rising again, and this time, the deadly ocean force was directed against them.

No! thought Angel. *I'm holding the baby . . . we saved Him! Serena . . . where is Serena?* Frantically he clutched the baby close and shut his eyes.

"Blessed Lady, stay thy wrath!" The voice belonged to Serena, but it was stronger and louder than any human voice could possibly be. Angel felt light beating against his closed lids and when he opened them, he thought he must be hallucinating.

Serena was glowing. And *flying*. She hovered in the air above the angry ocean, white wings beating steadily, arms reached out in an imploring gesture.

"These are friends to You and Yours. They saved Your Son, Great Lady. They called You to help them save Your Son."

Angel sat up on the wet sand and held the little God out at arm's length. The baby's sobs had ceased and he stared at the ocean with fascination. He began to kick excitedly and coo.

Slowly, the waves subsided. The earth again grew stable. Angel closed, then opened his eyes in relief. He got to his feet as Serena floated toward him, landing silently on dainty feet in the sand before him.

"Serena, I'm glad you're okay. I thought for a minute I had . . ." She smiled ethereally, and he went cold inside. "I did, didn't I? I drowned you. I thought you knew the plan—that you understood, you were pretending. I'm so sorry."

She smiled. Light poured from her, a soft, blue, clean light that didn't hurt Angel's eyes at all. "I did what I had to do," she said, "just as you did. I was incapable of standing by and watching Him be harmed, even a little, even by one who was trying to protect Him. Do not be distressed, Angel. As you see, what I really am is unharmed. I have merely returned to my true form. Death and life are not quite what you think. Are you not dead, vampire? Yet you seem to live. You yourself are a paradox."

Angel was not comforted. "I was supposed to help you . . . and I—I killed—"

"What I am cannot be truly killed. Surely you see that now. But at that moment, His life was vulnerable. And it is He whom your actions have saved."

She extended her arms, and reluctantly Angel gave the now happily gurgling baby to her. He felt a deep ache in his chest; why, he didn't know.

Serena looked up at him with deep compassion. Gently she reached to brush his face with her fingers. Angel made a soft sound; only once before, with another beautiful, fair-haired woman, had he felt such a loving touch. She rose on tiptoe and gently kissed his cheek. Her scent was of jasmine and honeysuckle, of sunlight and laughter and joy, if such things had a fragrance.

A single feather, small and downy, fluttered from her wings. She knelt and picked it up, pressing it into Angel's hands. "It will not last," she said, "but for a time, this is His gift. To say thank you."

She was moving away from him now, distant and unreachable as a star. Effortlessly her wings began to beat and she rose, her face turned toward the east, and she lifted the child who wriggled with joy in her grasp.

"Serena!" Angel cried suddenly, his skin prickling with swift, certain, ancient knowledge. "This Sun Child, this . . . He's been born as a human baby before, hasn't He?"

Serena turned her calm gaze to him, and did not reply. But she smiled, softly, secretly, and Angel had his answer.

"Call the sun, bright Child!" Serena cried. "Be as You were meant to be!"

The baby god ceased to squirm and grew quiet. With a grace and composure that should have been impossible in a newborn, he spread his small arms. The darkness began to lessen. As one, Angel and his friends turned toward the east. With unnatural swiftness, the sun began to emerge over the horizon. No creeping dawn this; this sunrise came at a charge, a gallop, covering a world with light that had been so unhappily denied.

It was only when the sun was fully upon them that Angel realized that he was in no pain. His friends looked at him, shocked, and in mute explanation he extended a hand that cupped a single, small, downy feather. Already it seemed to him that its luster was fading. The God's blessing—the gift of sunlight—was only temporary. But it was precious. Angel turned his face up to the celestial light and felt its heat caress him.

"'Out of the shadows of night the world rolls into light; it is daybreak everywhere,'" quoted Wesley, softly.

"Longfellow," Fred said, nodding as she recognized the quote.

Serena was gone. She and the infant divinity had returned to the place they belonged. It was time Angel and his friends did the same.

"Let's go home," said Angel, his voice thick with an odd combination of pain and joy commingled.

The longest night was over.

ABOUT THE CONTRIBUTORS

"The House Where Death Stood Still" is PIERCE ASKEGREN's (it's Swedish!) first *Angel* story, but he hopes it's not his last. As a warm-up, however, he has cowritten or written an alarming amount of material, much of it having to do with comic books. This includes five novels based on Marvel Comics characters: three Spider-Man books cowritten with famous comics guys Danny Fingeroth and Eric Fein, one about the Avengers (guest-starring the Thunderbolts), and one about the Fantastic Four (his favorites). He's written three short stories for anthologies based on Marvel properties and cowritten a fourth with comics artist John Garcia. For a change of pace, he cranked out short stories for *The Chick Is in the Mail,* in Esther Friesner's popular anthology series from Baen Books, and for Jean Rabe's *Historical Hauntings,* from DAW. Most of this is since 1995, but way back when, shortly after the earth cooled but before the dinosaurs roamed, he wrote comics scripts for the long-gone Warren Publishing Company (*Creepy, Vampirella*). The year 2003 should see the publication of his science fiction novel, *Villanueva,* the first of three from Ace Books. Pierce lives in Northern Virginia, where he writes business proposals and such. If everything goes as planned, by the time you read this, you should be able to visit him at www.askegren.com.

JEFF MARIOTTE is the author of several Angel novels, including *Haunted* and *Stranger to the Sun*, as well as, with Nancy Holder, the Buffy/Angel crossover trilogy Unseen and the Angel novel *Endangered Species*. He's published several other books and more comic books than he has time to count, including the multiple award-nominated horror/Western series Desperadoes. With his wife, Maryelizabeth Hart, and partner, Terry Gilman, he co-owns Mysterious Galaxy, a bookstore specializing in science fiction, fantasy, mystery, and horror. He lives in San Diego, California, with his family and pets, in a home filled with books, music, toys, and other examples of American pop culture. More about him can be gleaned from www.jeffmariotte.com.

CHRISTOPHER GOLDEN is the award-winning, *Los*

Angeles Times best-selling author of such novels as *The Ferryman, Strangewood, The Gathering Dark,* and *Of Saints and Shadows*, and the Prowlers and Body of Evidence series of teen thrillers, several of which have been listed among the Best Books for Young Readers by the American Library Association and the New York Public Library.

Golden has also written or cowritten many books and comic books related to the TV series *Buffy the Vampire Slayer* and *Angel,* as well as the script for the Buffy video game for Microsoft Xbox, which he cowrote with frequent collaborator Tom Sniegoski. His other comic book work includes stories featuring such characters as Batman, Wolverine, Spider-Man, The Crow, and Hellboy, among many others.

As a pop culture journalist, he was the editor of the Bram Stoker Award–winning book of criticism, *CUT!: Horror Writers on Horror Film,* and coauthor of both *Buffy the Vampire Slayer: The Watcher's Guide* and *The Stephen King Universe.*

Golden was born and raised in Massachusetts, where he still lives with his family. He graduated from Tufts University. There are more than six million copies of his books in print. At present he is at work on *The Boys Are Back in Town,* a new novel for Bantam Books. Please visit him at www.christophergolden.com.

SCOTT CIENCIN is a *New York Times* best-selling author of more than fifty books from Random House, Simon & Schuster, and many more. He has written

Buffy the Vampire Slayer: Sweet Sixteen and cowritten *Angel: Vengeance* with Dan Jolley. He has worked on the Jurassic Park, Star Wars, and Dinotopia franchises, written for Marvel and DC Comics, and is the author of the critically acclaimed Vampire Odyssey and Dinoverse series. He lives in Ft. Myers, Florida, with his beloved wife, Denise.

DENISE CIENCIN has a Masters degree in community counseling and has worked with at-risk teenagers, displaced homemakers, the developmentally disabled, and many other populations in crisis. She was listed in *Who's Who in America*'s 2001 edition. She has also written in the field of neurology and neurosurgery and worked with her husband on the majority of his fiction output, providing research, co-plotting, and much more. "It Could Happen to You" is her first credited work.

EMILY OZ is an editor of children's books living and working in New York City. She loves Angel—but she misses Doyle.

Los Angeles Times best-selling author NANCY HOLDER has written many Buffy and Angel projects for Simon & Schuster, including *Endangered Species* (with Jeff Mariotte); *The Book of Fours*; the first two volumes of the Buffy *Watcher's Guide* (with Christopher Golden, Jeff Mariotte, and Maryelizabeth Hart); and *Angel: The Casefiles* (with Jeff Mariotte and Maryelizabeth Hart.)

With Debbie Viguié, she has a new series entitled Witch. *Witch: Wicked* was released in October 2002. She lives in San Diego with her daughter, Belle.

YVONNE NAVARRO spent her youth making up stuff in her head and drawing pictures to go along with the stories. When she grew up she started writing more and more, and now she's had seventy-some stories and over a dozen books published, and she's even managed to get a few cool awards (most recently the Bram Stoker award for *Buffy the Vampire Slayer: The Willow Files, Vol. 2*). In her spare time she studies martial arts, and she recently got married. As if having the ceremony in historic Mount Moriah Cemetery wasn't different enough, the town had to be evacuated in the middle of the reception due to a forest fire. She and her new hubby are in the process of running off to Arizona. Yvonne maintains a big old Web site at www.yvonnenavarro.com with all kinds of fun stuff on it. She's also the owner of Dusty Stacks Bookstore (www.dustystacks.com). Come visit!

After obtaining a degree in wildlife illustration and environmental education, DORANNA DURGIN spent a number of years deep in the Appalachian Mountains, riding the trails and writing science fiction and fantasy books. She's moved on to living in the mountains of northern Arizona, where she still writes—*Changespell Legacy* is the latest—and rides, focusing on classical dressage with a Lipizzan who thinks too much. Meanwhile, there's a mountain looming outside her office window, a pack of dogs running around the house, and a laptop sitting on her desk—and that's just the way she likes it. Next best is channeling Angel and Cordelia (with much gratitude to Ellen Cannon Reed and Lady Bridget for the use of their Solstice Carol stanzas in "Yoke of the Soul"). Please visit her at www.doranna.net.

CHRISTIE GOLDEN is the author of twenty novels and fourteen short stories in the fields of fantasy, horror, and science fiction. She won the Colorado Author's League Top Hand Award in 1999 for her historical fantasy *A.D. 999,* written under the pen name of Jadrien Bell. She feels quite comfortable writing about a vampire with a soul, as she launched her career in 1991 with *Vampire of the Mists,* in which she created the tormented elven vampire Jander Sunstar. Readers of *Tales of the Slayer* may remember her contribution, "The White Doe." Golden currently lives in Denver, Colorado, and continues not to be related to another writer of *Buffy* fiction, Christopher Golden. Readers are invited to visit her Web site at www.christiegolden.com.

Buffy
the vampire slayer™

. . . A GIRL BORN

WITHOUT THE FEAR GENE

FEARLESS™

A SERIES BY

FRANCINE PASCAL

PUBLISHED BY SIMON & SCHUSTER

3029-01